PRAISE FOR *HOW FIRES END*

"Beautiful, mesmerizing, consoling, and under immaculate control, Marco Rafalà's *How Fires End* is a powerful novel about the religion we create for ourselves as we face that which perhaps even God has not imagined for humanity."
—Alexander Chee, author of *Edinburgh*, *The Queen of the Night*, and *How to Write an Autobiographical Novel*

"Marco Rafalà ignites all kinds of fires in this brightly burning novel fueled by old vendettas and unresolved resentments. A tremendous, well-crafted debut."
—Idra Novey, award-winning author of *Those Who Knew* and *Ways to Disappear*

"*How Fires End* is a raised fist of a novel, one filled with men's brutal tenderness and tender brutality. It is both a subtle and powerful indictment of the silences between generations and a poignant testament to the bond between sons and fathers of all kinds. A blazing debut by an important new Italian American voice."
—Christopher Castellani, author of *Leading Men*

"*How Fires End* explores the complicated bind of family, attempting to answer the age-old question of where family history ends and the self begins. This is a beautiful meditation on time, memory, and consequences."
—Kaitlyn Greenidge, author of *We Love You, Charlie Freeman*

"What happens when the fires we nurture with hate die? *How Fires End* is a breathtaking multigenerational story of fathers and sons who yearn for warmth amid the ashes of their own secrets and lies. Generous, bold, epic, Marco Rafalà's novel is a triumph."
—Brando Skyhorse, award-winning author of *The Madonnas of Echo Park* and *Take This Man: A Memoir*

"*How Fires End* struck me at my core. Part mourning, part witness, this is a story that yearns to make peace with the endless, brutal wounds of war. It will haunt me with an unanswerable question: How do we heal from the pain of the unspoken when a family's secrets are carried—across seas and generations—out of love and protection?"

—Natalia Sylvester, author of *Chasing the Sun* and *Everyone Knows You Go Home*

"*How Fires End* commences with such authority and grace that it hardly seems the work of a debut novelist. There is a great weight in the tenderness and simplicity of the voice of the narrators. It has gravitas without any sacrifice of beauty."

—Victoria Redel, author of *Before Everything* and *LA Times* Best Book of the Year *Loverboy*

"This is a wondrous novel that burns with secret histories, arcing across space and time, voiced by characters who speak their separate truths with resilience and dignity. A gorgeous debut."

—M. Dressler, author of *The Deadwood Beetle* and *The Last to See Me*

"What happens when faith blinds us to our own humanity? *How Fires End* is part war story and aftermath, part mythology, a lamentation shot through with melancholy and pathos. Rafalà writes of the mothers and fathers and sons and daughters of Melilli, Sicily, with such care and tenderness that to read it was like listening to the breathing out and collapse of an accordion—history folding over onto itself, sighing out a mournful story on notes of stone and stars. We yearn with David, grieve with Salvatore, shoulder the yoke of history with Vincenzo, console and heal with Nella as each tells a story of wars waged, battles lost, and secrets kept."

—Susan Bernhard, author of *Winter Loon*

"This multilayered, astonishing novel takes you into the heart of a dark family legacy and twists you up with emotion on every page. *How Fires End* is beautifully written and startling in its revelations. I can't stop thinking about this heartbreaking book."

—Crystal King, author of *Feast of Sorrow* and *The Chef's Secret*

"Marco Rafalà's *How Fires End* is a devastating and gorgeously conceived novel of tragedy and redemption spanning generations and continents. The past is never the past for the Vassallo family; it stalks and curses their lives, first in Sicily and then decades later in America. Heartbreaking and beautifully wrought, Rafalà's haunting debut is a must-read exploration of the perils of personal and political histories and how we try to overcome them."

—Hannah Lillith Assadi, author of *Sonora*

"A rich and unforgettable novel about heritage and loss, about our futures and our roots. *How Fires End* is intense and absorbing—a virtuoso performance by Marco Rafalà."

—Kristopher Jansma, author of *The Unchangeable Spots of Leopards* and *Why We Came to the City*

"A haunting debut novel that shows us how the dark secrets of the old country can never be repressed. This is a poignant and powerful immigrants' tale of reckoning, tragedy, and the search for redemption in a Sicilian family that learns it can never shed the claws of its past, even in this new American life."

—Cheryl Lu-Lien Tan, author of *Sarong Party Girls*

"Marco Rafalà speaks to the Sicilian American experience as no other since his fellow of the New School, Mario Puzo. He writes with care, wisdom, and compassion. Sharing in his novel is sharing in the better part of living."

—John Reed, author of *A Still Small Voice* and *Free Boat: Collected Lies and Love Poems*

HOW
FIRES
END

HOW FIRES END

A NOVEL

MARCO RAFALÀ

Little
a

Published by Little A, New York

www.apub.com

Amazon, the Amazon logo, and Little A are trademarks of Amazon.com, Inc., or its affiliates.

ISBN-13: 9781542042970 (hardcover)
ISBN-10: 1542042976 (hardcover)
ISBN-13: 9781542042994 (paperback)
ISBN-10: 1542042992 (paperback)

Cover design by Faceout Studio, Derek Thornton

Cover illustrated by Tran Nguyen

Printed in the United States of America

First edition

*For the people of Melilli, Sicily, and for my father,
the best of them.
For my mother, who made sure I always had books
in my life.
And for Ziu Sal—your absence haunts us still.*

NELLA

PROLOGUE

"I had three brothers," she began, "but now—" Nella took a deep breath, held it in, let it out slow. "Now I am the last Vassallo. After me, there will be no more. But our families, yours and mine, they were there in the beginning with the statue."

She paused to sip her hot cocoa. The boy watched her, hungry for more. He didn't move, not even to brush the curls of unkempt dark hair from his eyes. Her face wrinkled into a smile and she set the cup down, still holding it with both hands. She continued, not stopping until the cup had long grown cold.

"My father told my brothers and me the story of how the statue of Saint Sebastian came to the village of Melilli, the village we once called home. Like so many stories, this one started with danger. A ship was caught in a furious storm and ran aground in Megara Bay. The hull cracked open on the rocks, and the waves pushed our saint ashore. All the sailors survived. They thanked their cargo for their lives, but none of these men could lift the statue to carry it off. Word spread, first among the shepherds, then to the local villages and cities, until news reached the bishop of Syracuse. In three days, he came with clergy and a crew of men to claim the saint. Again the saint was too heavy to lift. From all over the province, people gathered on the beach, waiting their turn to try to break the spell and lift the statue. Some of the men built a fire. Some of the women cooked. At night they prayed, and in the day their prayers failed them.

"When the procession from Melilli arrived, our priest claimed the statue, saying, 'Since the making of the world, Saint Sebastian has been painted here on the grotto wall in our village, here before even Sebastian himself was born. This is Melilli, the martyr Sebastian, tied to a tree and porcupined with Roman arrows.' Then our men raised the statue on a wooden pallet and placed the poles upon their shoulders, and a great cheer went up among them as all the clergy prayed and made the sign of the cross. 'E chiamamulu paisanu,' they shouted. 'Prima Diu e Sammastianu.' He is one of our own. First God, and then Saint Sebastian. Another cheer seized the men, and they carried the saint home, our ancestors, a Vassallo and a Morello, among the bearers.

"Our families held hands and sang together bringing their patron saint home to Melilli. In the piazza, on the ridge overlooking the bay, their knees buckled. The men cried out. A force had suddenly burdened them with a weight they could no longer carry. The priest kissed the wooden crucifix around his neck and said, 'No man can shoulder the might of God.' So they left the statue there and built a church around it. This was May 1414.

"As children, my brothers and I loved that story. As children, we believed—as everyone believed in those days—that Saint Sebastian would protect the people of Melilli forever. When earthquakes destroyed much of our village, it was by his glory our families lived to marvel—the statue unharmed among the ruins. Etna erupted. We prayed to him, and our homes were spared. He saw us through all the wars and years of unrest and revolt in our history.

"'Saint Sebastian always keeps us safe. He will always keep us safe.' My father said these words as we hid in the cave, the war raging just outside. Gunfire cracked the air. Bombs whistled as they fell from the sky. Beneath our feet the ground trembled. The cave shook like it might come down on top of us any minute. In the back, our mother prayed her rosary before the ancient painting of the saint on the cave wall. She wanted me, her only daughter, by her side. But I wanted to work with my father and brothers. We hulled a bushel basket of almonds, the only food left to eat. All around us, Germans and Allies fought. Such noise as you would never imagine possible."

DAVID

1

My father and I sat on metal folding chairs at a card table in our kitchen, peeling the blackened and blistered skin from roasted bell peppers. Ashen flakes stuck to our fingers. It was a Friday evening in March 1986, in Middletown, Connecticut. The sunset hung framed in the bay windows over the sink, and the kitchen took on an orange glow. My father worked the pepper in his hands as a sculptor works sandpaper on stone, smoothing the coarse surface. I tried to ease off the burnt skin the way he did, but the red pepper was slimy in my clumsy hands. I ripped the flesh open, making a mess of juice and seeds on the table, like always.

"Easy," my father said. He wiped his fingers clean with a damp towel on his lap.

"I'm trying," I said.

"Beh, you try. You try but you no learn." He took the pepper from me and finished peeling it. His fingers moved with a slow and delicate purpose, a memory kept in the muscles of his wrists and palms. He was still angry with me for what happened—for my lie—and what it made him remember.

The lie I'd told my father wasn't about whether I made confession at Saint Sebastian Church. It wasn't about how I'd gotten a fat lip at Woodrow Wilson Middle School—I always lied about how I got those.

It wasn't even about the fibs I told the priest when I did finally confess. No, this was a real lie with real consequences. I told my father I was going to the library Friday after school. But that wasn't where I went. This was how I ended up in yet another fight with Tony Morello—a fight my father finally witnessed. A fight that changed everything.

Tony Morello was big for a thirteen-year-old, already a mountain. He lived in a house under the Arrigoni Bridge, and his father beat him. All the kids at school suspected, but no one talked about it. The adults, too. They kept quiet because it wasn't their business. But Tony was my business and I was his—for the longest time, he was my nemesis, and I didn't know why. If my life had been a fairy tale, then Tony Morello would have been the troll.

He wandered out from under his bridge onto a derelict side street two blocks from the library—between me and where I was supposed to be. Underdressed for winter in his zipped-up wannabe "Thriller" jacket, he lurked in the red-brick shadows of an old carriage factory. He'd written his name in the dirt of the one unbroken window, a dog peeing to mark his territory.

I pulled buzzing headphones down around my neck. There was no escaping him, no winning against him. Not even sunlight would have helped me turn this troll into stone. Mouthing off made it easier to stomach. "Just learned how to spell your name?"

Tony shoved me down and we tumbled through a dirty snowbank. His breath reeked of corn chips. He sat on my back, pushed my face into dirty snow, black with soot. When my father came barreling at us from around the corner, he moved like a gnarled old tree uprooted from the soil by gale and gravity. He moved fast, a man who knew the speed of danger.

"Get off my son!" he bellowed as he pulled Tony off me.

A truck horn sounded, low and strangled, and a red Chevy pickup with white side panels crawled to a stop in the street. Tony's father, Rocco, hunched in the driver's seat, his elbow out the window. Rocco and my father: two men out searching for lost sons. "Antonio," Rocco yelled. "Get the hell over here."

My father chased after Tony but froze in the truck's headlights when I called out for him to stop. The beams lit up the underside of his face, framed in the earflaps of his black fur trooper hat, and threw his eyes into shadow. He dented the hood with his fist.

When Tony climbed into the cab through the passenger door, Rocco shouted at him. "What did I say?" He smacked the back of Tony's head, sending his forehead into the dashboard. "You stay away from that family. They're no good." Then he leaned out the window and spat on the pavement. "Put your hands on my boy again and not even that Fascist you hide behind can protect you."

"Vaffanculo," my father cursed. He was a man used to curses. He slapped his palm against his bicep, arm raised with a fist and bent at the elbow. He stood planted in the road, forcing Rocco to drive around him. My father watched the taillights go around the corner. An oncoming car honked him to the curb. He waved the driver away, his arm the swishing tail of a donkey swatting a fly off its rump.

"What happened?" my father asked me. His Roman nose chapped red from waiting in the cold for me. "I looked for you," he said. "Where were you?" He held my chin, turned my face left and then right. He inspected the bruises the way he inspected pears at the grocery store. He made that same face, too, as he rejected the fruit, like he'd just smelled a fart.

"I hate him." My voice cracked, and I hated that even more.

"That boy, he is a scimunitu like his father. Next time you fight back." My father slapped snow from my shoulders and backside.

"I tried," I said. But I hadn't, not really. Not even close.

He touched the headphones dangling around my neck. "Where did you get this?"

I jerked away and fumbled reconnecting the headphone cord to the Walkman. "Can we just go?"

My father grabbed the Walkman and shook it in my face, and I flinched. "If you'd been at the library maybe that boy wouldn't have bothered you. See what happens when you're not where you're supposed to be?"

But he was wrong. I had been where I needed to be. I was with my new friend, Sam—the one good thing that came of that troll Tony. Monday had been Sam's first day at Woodrow Wilson, already two months into the new year. Lost on his way to homeroom, he stumbled smack into Tony's massive frame, so Tony sent Sam sailing into me— and me, into a wall of lockers. Thus, the first fat lip of that week.

I picked up Sam's blue Trapper Keeper, the flap decked out in the raccoon eyes of a Siouxsie and the Banshees sticker. When I asked him who they were, he grinned and bobbed up and down on the toes of his sneakers, high-top Converse All Stars. Black, like mine. "Are you kidding?" he asked. By Friday, Sam had invited me to his house to listen to records. I knew my father wouldn't let me go to a stranger's house, but I needed a friend, even just one. So I told my father I'd be studying at Russell Library instead.

Sam's house was only a mile from mine, but it felt light-years away. And he wasn't Sicilian or Sicilian American like everyone else I knew in this town—like me. He had the coolest hair, buzzed in the back, long and floppy in the front. His bangs were so long they touched his chin. He chewed on the strands when he was thinking hard about something. In his room, a checkerboard of album covers and posters papered the walls. I'd never seen people like these—men, women, I wasn't sure— with smeared red lipstick, heavy black eyeliner, and wild hair, each one like some dolled-up Medusa. At Sam's house, the records crackled and popped like a campfire, and I warmed in the glow of those sounds. Then he lent me his Walkman so I could take that glow with me.

When I lied to my father about going to the library, he said, "Go straight there after school and wait for me to get you." And I answered,

"Sure thing." But he grabbed my arm before I could jet, and he looked at me in that way he had, as if he could see his dead brothers in my eyes.

"Bad things happen when you don't listen to your papà," he said.

"I'll go right there from school," I said. But he only held my arm tighter, pulled it toward him until he'd pulled what he wanted to hear out of me. "And I won't leave until you pick me up. Promise."

Imagine an object so massive that not even light could escape the pull of its gravity. If light could not escape, nothing could. That was how my father loved me.

"Okay," he said, as if he could breathe again, and he released me back into his orbit.

2

At home, after the fight, I shucked off my soaking-wet clothes in my bedroom and changed into dry jeans and a black turtleneck sweater. Out the window, my father stood ankle deep in snow in the backyard. He had dragged the charcoal grill from the shed and was roasting store-bought peppers. My reflection overlaid the scene in the glass, black hair cut short and parted at the cowlick on the right—the twig offspring of that thick old oak.

Outside, I held open a brown paper lunch bag for my father to fill. The craggy lines of his face tightened in the light from the fire. His mouth sagged to a frown. He clicked the tongs in his hand, a metronome of disappointment, and turned over a pepper. The fire spat a red spark. He pulled back his hand. "See," he said, "you have to be quick so the fire doesn't bite you." He picked up a steaming and blackened pepper with his bare hand. "And you have to be strong," he said, and dropped the pepper in the bag.

In the snow behind him, deep drag lines from the grill and foot-prints alongside them tracked back to the shed. Smooth waves of snow covered his garden beds. Months of hard work and care would make those beds flush with spinach and chard, peppers and eggplant. Everything he loved grew from the hard work of his hands in that garden.

"I got a couple good hits in," I lied. "Before you showed up."

"Yeah," my father said, stretching out the sound of the word. He laughed a small laugh that made me feel small. "Okay." He squeezed my shoulder. "Go inside before you catch cold."

"What did Rocco mean by *that Fascist?*"

My father turned the peppers on the grill. He took his time with each one, a tempo set by his tongs. Click-click. Click-click. Peppers sizzled. "That word, it does not mean what you think it means."

I inched closer to the heat to keep from shivering. "So tell me."

Click-click. Click-click. The fire bit him and he shook his hand. "Mannaggia la miseria," he cursed. "See what you do?" He placed his burnt thumb in his mouth and decided what to do with me, the boy who'd lied and distracted him from his work. He hung the tongs from the grill handle and motioned for me to follow him to the tarp-covered woodpile by the old shed. I rolled the paper bag closed, set it down on the porch step, and traipsed through the snow after him. He'd made the shed himself from scraps of plywood and mismatched siding planks, roof felt and corrugated iron. Icicle teeth sharpened the edges of the rusted metal roof. A twist of black-and-copper electrical wire held the door shut.

He handed me a thin stick of kindling, and I carped, "What am I supposed to do with this?"

"You break it."

I snapped it in half.

Then he collected a bundle of thin sticks and said, "Now these."

The bundle wouldn't break. I tried again, this time against my thigh. It wouldn't even bend, no matter how I strained against it.

"Now you understand," my father said. He wiped his hands on the thick canvas of his work pants.

"Can you do it?" I asked him.

My father pulled my knit hat down over my ears. "No one can," he said. "But some men, they like to fight anyway, and men like that are crazy. Better you stay away from them."

"Is that what you would do?"

"Never mind what I do." He returned to the grill, his face lit and unlit by the cloven fire, moving in and out of darkness and light, as if he belonged to both. "What I do?" he said to the crackling flames. It was a question that clung to the air the way the smell of charcoal and smoke and sweet grilled peppers clung to my father's clothes.

Later, when we moved inside, he posed the question again. We were in the kitchen, peeling roasted peppers, and I had made a mess of mine. When he finished salvaging my botched pepper, he held it up for me to see. "What I do?" he asked. "I take care of my family." Then he dropped the skinned pepper in a clear glass bowl of sliced raw garlic and olive oil. "How old are you now?" he asked me.

"I'm thirteen."

"Dio mio," he said. "Almost a man you are. A few more years yet." With his towel, he cleaned the juice and seeds from the table. "I was younger than you and already a man," he said, "when the war came."

His calloused hands trembled. He worked the last of the peppers. His eyes locked on something in the distance, something I could never quite see. "Get me the wine," he said.

I brought a bottle of his murky red up from the basement, pulled on the white T-shirt fabric that held the cork in place. He stopped me from pouring him a glass.

"Let it breathe," he said. "It needs to breathe before you drink it." He nodded at the empty foldaway chair. His look pulled me back down into its flimsy vinyl padding. "We prayed," he said. "In caves, we prayed the bombs would not find us. Even as the mountain shook like one of Mount Etna's earthquakes, we prayed, and when the fighting stopped—" He cocked his head to one side and tsked. "They destroyed everything."

He opened a can of sardines at the counter. Then he cut two slices from a loaf of crusty sesame seed bread and dropped them into the toaster. "It was August," he said, moving into the story I knew well, the one he always circled back to even now, forty-three years later. So I did what I always did. I listened and I tried to see them, who they would have been, who we all would have been if my uncles hadn't died.

"August," he said again, this time in Sicilian. "A hot day, the day my brothers wandered away from the celebration in the piazza. I had to find them. My papà wanted me to find them. And you know where I find them? Those stupid boys." He frowned, thinking about the answer. When he spoke again, he spoke in English, his voice almost a whisper. "They were in the almond orchard playing with an artillery shell. I yelled at them to stop, I did."

When he talked about his brothers, there was a lesson in the story, unspoken—and he told me that lesson all the time. If I wasn't careful, if I didn't listen to his every word, if I didn't watch out, I could end up dead like them. A fear like that could crush you.

My father poured wine into a mason jar. He sat back down, leaned over his food, elbows on the table. He stuffed a forkful of peppers into his mouth, and bit into a slice of dark toast topped with sardines. "Those stupid twins," he said. He wagged a finger at me. "I told you to stay at the library until I came for you."

I sunk into my seat and forked green and red peppers from the bowl. "I'm sorry," I said.

The kitchen grew quiet except for the clank of utensils against dishes and teeth. My father raised his head from his food. He pursed his lips. His brow furrowed. He drank his wine, and then raised the jar to the light for me to see the rusty hues. "Just a sip," he said. "Go on. Try."

When I tried his homemade wine, I scrunched up my face. "It tastes like vinegar," I said.

He snorted like a horse. "A few more years yet," he said.

My father never talked about my mother the way he talked about his brothers. She died when I was five years old and he never mentioned her at all, so I didn't either. One day she was there, and then she wasn't. And all her belongings, all the pictures of her and of us together, they disappeared, too, as if my father wanted me to forget her. It was like she never stopped disappearing. But I still had my mother's glow-in-the-dark stars on my bedroom ceiling—the stickers she and I had put there together. The stars she had taught me how to read.

Tell me the story again, I'd say. *The one about Pisces,* and I'd point at the green constellation. *What are they?* she'd ask me, and I'd yell out, *Fish! How many fish?* she'd say. Two fish tied by their tails, a mother and her son transformed. They swam free from the monster, Typhon.

Typhon sought revenge against the gods for the deaths of his serpent-footed brothers. He stood as high as the stars, a sickle-winged colossus, roaring with the heads of a hundred wild beasts. He rained down a barrage of mountains and fire on the gods, and the gods trembled before his wrath. They changed into animals, retreating in a thunderclap of mighty hooves. The world shuddered. Waves cut the horizon with glassy teeth, an ocean gnawing at the sky, frothing at the mouth in the pitch of Typhon's storm. All seemed lost until Minerva goaded Jupiter into fighting back. But even the king of the gods could not destroy Typhon. So Jupiter buried the monster under Mount Etna, where he still spews fire and ash into the air. In this way, a volcano was born.

Sometimes my father was Typhon, fueled by an inconsolable rage for what had happened to his brothers, trapped under a mountain of rock but still burning and angry at everyone, even me. Sometimes Tony was Typhon, a stupid beast bent on mindless destruction, always able to spot the weakness in me. But now I understood that Typhon was something else, too—a secret, long-simmering hatred between Rocco Morello and my father. And my lie had banged on that secret, like an unexploded shell between them. It had freed a monster not even the gods could tame.

3

That Saturday, my father put in a half day at the factory where he worked as a machinist grinding parts for submarines and military aircraft. When he got home, he went into the basement without a word. He spritzed his long trays of white button mushrooms. Then he replaced his wine barrel's leaky wooden spigot and sealed it with a rag. In an hour, he shrugged back into his flannel-lined blue jacket and walked me to Saint Sebastian Church. Sicilian immigrants from Melilli had built it in 1931, modeled after the church they'd left behind—the Basilica of Saint Sebastian. Most Sicilian families in Middletown, even Tony's family, came from Melilli. Some, only a few, came from neighboring villages. There were even some Italians from the south sprinkled in like crushed black pepper on a salad. But most of the Sicilian families here came from Melilli. Except mine. Mine came from Syracuse.

Still, my father would tell me the story of the church as if he'd built it with his own bare hands. "You know who built that?" he asked me as we stood on the corner of Washington and Pearl across from Saint Sebastian, waiting for the traffic lights to change.

"I know," I said.

My father smacked the back of my head and said, "Yeah. You know? You know because I tell you."

The granite church towered over the street, rising from a blanket of snow. It was the only building on the south side of the block, apart from the white clapboard rectory. The afternoon light lit up the swooping lines of the facade. And at its curved peak, the stone relief of Saint Sebastian glowed.

"People from all over came to Melilli to see the statue," my father said. "It's not too far from where your zia and I grew up. We went every year for the feast."

"Aren't you forgetting my zius?"

"Zii," he corrected me. "I never forget them. Don't you believe for a second I forget them."

The traffic lights dangling from wires overhead clicked to red. The cars racing up and down Washington Street came to a stop at the four-way intersection. My father placed his hand on my shoulder and guided me across the street. He was the captain steering his ship through treacherous waters. But he couldn't see all the jagged rocks beneath the surface here. American teenagers weren't on his nautical charts.

Catechism students who had completed their confessions waited on the wide sidewalk in front of the church for their parents to pick them up and take them home. On the left, Brother Calogero watched the boys. On the right, Sister Rosalia presided over the girls in their tight jeans and puffy winter coats. They huddled in groups, their heads bent toward each other, tossing their hair and sneaking glances at the boys.

My father tugged my earlobe. "What are you looking at? Girls?"

"No, nothing," I said, swatting his hand away.

"Better be nothing," my father said. "Or you get this where you sit down." And he made a slapping motion with his hand. If he could hear me rolling my eyes in their sockets, what sound would he hear?

"Okay, behave," he said. "Come to Vincenzo's when you're done." My father only went to church for my sacraments of initiation and for the Mass on Christmas and Easter Sunday, and he never went with me. Religion was for the young and for women, he told me, to learn right from wrong. As he walked away, he called out, "Be careful crossing the street."

Cringing with embarrassment was like a dog whistle. It made a nails-on-chalkboard kind of sound that only a bully could hear. Right on cue, at the top of the church steps, the heavy wooden center door creaked open, and out stepped Tony with a black eye to match my swollen lip, but his bruise hadn't come from my fist. I shuffled up the stairs. As we passed one another, Tony shoved me to the side with his shoulder.

"Watch where you're going," he said, straightening his red leather zipper jacket.

"I'm sorry," I said, and I wanted to swallow back those words as soon as they came out.

~

Inside, arched columns marched the length of the church, dividing long central wooden pews from stubby side ones. The stained-glass windows and high frescoed ceiling dwarfed the other Catechism students awaiting their turn for confession. I slunk past them and slipped into the front pew. Three stories above the statue of Christ flanked by Mary and Joseph, the plaster walls flaked like dry skin on an old man's face. At the feet of the statues, flames played inside red tubes that shielded votive candles.

Chris Cardella, the lanky track star of Woodrow Wilson Middle School, plunked down next to me. "Heard you got your ass handed to you last night," he whispered. His navy-blue-and-white windbreaker crinkled as he leaned forward, inspecting my face—swollen lip, the skin around the swelling bruised purple, and crusted pink scrapes above my left eye.

"Whatever." I scooted to the far end of the pew and hopped the aisle to the side pew in front of the altar of Saint Sebastian. Two marble columns framed an oil painting taller than me. In the painting, the saint was bound to a tree, a splash of green leaves sprouting from the twisted branches of its twisted trunk. Arrows pierced his arms and chest. That's what he got for standing up to his enemies, for refusing to back down. Who knows, maybe he could've found another way out, if only he'd looked.

Brother Calogero hadn't come inside yet. I slipped out the side door. The last of the Catechism students gathered on the marble stairs, their voices like the cawing of a flock of starlings.

≈

The wide street-facing window of Vincenzo's café was fogged on the inside. Men sat at checkerboard tables. Cigarette smoke swirled above their heads. They shouted over each other in Sicilian, using hand gestures like punctuation. Vincenzo moved among the patrons with espresso and beer and pastries. His tall, angular frame hobbled by a bad leg. At the bar, my father sat alone, broad shoulders and thick arms hunched over the white Formica counter.

"Ciao, David," Vincenzo called above the clatter of the café. "Come stai?"

"Okay. I guess," I said with my face turned down to hide the bruises Tony gave me.

Vincenzo lifted my chin up. "There's no shame in losing a fight," he said. "I lost plenty in my time." His heavy-lidded eyes narrowed at the purple swelling and scabbed-over scratches. "Any fight you walk away from is a good fight."

My father swiveled to face me, a green Peroni bottle in his hand. "You done?"

In Catechism class, Brother Calogero had told us that lies were like vinegar—they left behind a smell, and the only way to cleanse ourselves was to pour out our hearts like water before the face of the Lord. Lies were only venial sins, though, at least the small ones. Still, when I answered yes, I looked down at my boots, at the snow around the soles, and at my wet footprints behind me.

"Iamuninni, David," my father said. "Let's go." He threw his head back and poured the last of the beer down his throat. Then he slapped the empty bottle down on the counter and reached for his wallet in his back pocket.

"Can I stay and help out?"

My father paid for the beer because he always paid, no matter how many times Vincenzo protested, and Vincenzo always protested. My father waved the objections aside and asked Vincenzo if he would mind walking me home, and Vincenzo told him that he wouldn't mind, and then he patted a nonexistent paunch and said that he could use the exercise. So my father left an extra five on the counter, tapping it with two fingers. "For whatever he wants," he said.

Vincenzo limped behind the counter to the brass and wood cash register that he'd bought at a garage sale years ago. He cranked the side hand crank to open the drawer—the only part of the machine that worked. He kept it because he liked the way it looked on the counter, old and dignified beside the framed cloth map of Sicily on the wall.

"You got your confirmation suit yet?" he asked.

"Tomorrow," I said. I took a pear-shaped bottle of Orangina from the refrigerated case. "Zia Nella's taking me."

He nodded as a way to say, *Good,* while filling a plate with almond cookies. "She'll find you something nice," he said. He led me to a window booth. The noise of the café fell away, as if we were the only ones there. "Double breasted, peaked lapel, pinstripes. The works." He pinched his thumb and index finger together and drew a straight line in the air. *Perfetto.* "You'll look sharp." He set the plate down, straddled the aisle seat, and stuck his left leg out. Then he fished two silver dollars from his pocket and slid them across the table at me. "Here, in case I forget. For when you bus the tables later."

I turned one of the coins over in my hands, thumbing the cracked Liberty Bell and the moon on the reverse side. "You never talk about the war," I said. "Why? My father only talks about the caves and how the twins died. And Zia Nella, she won't say anything at all. Like none of it ever happened."

Vincenzo scratched one of his long wiry sideburns. His gray hair, receding at the temples, was thinner than my father's hair. The fifteen years he had on my father also showed in the creases of his neck and the liver spots on the backs of his hands. He leaned into the cushioned seat back and shut his eyes. His black bushy eyebrows twitched. He winced from the pain in his leg as he rubbed it. "Did I ever tell you how I met your father in the hills outside Syracuse?" He spoke with eyes closed as if he could see a View-Master reel from the day he caught my father with his pants down around his ankles behind a row of prickly pears.

"Ew," I said. "You saw him take a crap?"

"Watch your mouth." Vincenzo sat at attention. "It was a bad time." He frowned and the lines of his face grew deep and long. I could see the weight those years held for him.

"Your father led me up a goat path to the cave in the mountain where his family was hiding. Your nonnu invited me inside and shared some food with me, maybe a little wine, I don't remember. I met your uncles then. They were so young, Emanuele and Leonello. So young." And the way Vincenzo said their names sounded lyrical like a song he'd learned long ago, one he couldn't get out of his head. "If I had stayed," he said. "Who knows? Maybe they'd still be alive. Your father forgets he was just a boy. There was nothing he could've done. Me?" He tapped his chest. "If I had stayed . . ." His eyebrows twitched again, and he swept the possibility away with the flat of his hand the way my father would do. "The Allies were invading. I could not stay."

"But the Allies were the good guys," I said.

"The good guys," Vincenzo said. "They won the war. Of course they were the good guys. You must understand, David, all the men in my unit were dead. I was alone. I'd heard what the Americans did at Biscari to the Italians who surrendered there. Seventy-one unarmed men." Vincenzo made a pistol of his hand. "What do you think they would've done with me? I had to leave."

4

Outside the cramped dressing room at Sandy's Tailor Shop on Main Street after Sunday Mass, Zia Nella tapped her foot to Madonna on the portable radio. In the back of the long and narrow shop, she stood beside two rickety racks of communion suits and dresses, chattering with the seamstress about my inseam, neck size, and sleeve length. "He's so skinny," she said. "It's hard to find clothes that fit." She was short and stout with a floral skirt that hid thick ankles, and a long-sleeved cotton blouse with an olive woolen shawl draped around her shoulders and over her upper arms. Even on the hottest summer day, my zia never wore anything but a long-sleeved top or shawl.

"Turn around," Santina said. The seamstress took my wrist with a bony, brown-spotted hand and lifted my arm. She smelled of dust and stale perfume. The black pinstriped suit jacket tightened in the shoulder. "No good," she said. Her cheeks sagged down from her eyes and her jowls wobbled. "We go back to the bigger size and take it in." She hung a navy-blue suit in the dressing room.

On the brick wall behind my zia hung two pinstriped suits—black and double breasted—tagged with the names Tony Morello and Chris Cardella.

"But I want pinstripes," I said.

"Always with the pinstripes," Santina said. "This is what I can make work for your size." She shut the curtain.

I drowned in the navy suit. My shrunken head lolled between fat padded shoulders. The cuffs came down over my knuckles. I mussed my black hair so it stuck up at odd angles—electrostatic snakes on the head of a baby Medusa. "I'm not coming out," I said. "I look ridiculous."

The seamstress tut-tutted and pulled open the curtain to a Whitney Houston song in the background. Santina knelt in front of me, took out her tape measure, and pinned me like a pincushion.

"You are a handsome boy," Zia Nella said. She licked her fingers and patted down my hair.

I jerked my head away from her touch. "Why do I have to do this anyway?"

"Stay still," Santina said. "Before I stick you."

I stared over the top of her gray head at the long wall of shirts and jackets and pants waiting for their owners to pick them up, and past a sewing table cluttered with bright spools of thread to the storefront window where Sam pressed his face against the dirty glass and waved. This was what it must have been like for the *Venera* probes on Venus with only minutes before the molten heat burned them up or the intense pressure crushed them. I wanted to disappear.

The bell over the door chimed as it opened wide enough for Sam's mother, Mrs. Morris, to poke her head through. The yellowed shade covering the windowed door flapped. "Are you open?" she asked. Framed in a towheaded bob, her face floated there, all dimples and blue eyes.

Around the pins in the corner of her mouth, Santina said, "Closed. Come back tomorrow."

Sam squeezed by his mother and into the shop. His face soured as if he could taste the pop song on the radio. He leaned against the counter and tilted his head like a bird, quizzical. "What happened to your face?"

His blond bangs fell over his left eye and he blew at them. They came back down, splayed over his face. He looped them around his ear.

"I can come back another time," Mrs. Morris said. She took Sam's arm and steered him out the door.

It had been a long time since I had a real friend, since Charlie moved away to Baltimore with his boxes and boxes of Dungeons & Dragons books. In his game, I'd been an unnamed paladin—a holy, chivalrous knight more interested in unpuzzling his arcane origins than killing monsters and looting dungeons. All we'd ever talked about was the game, and when Charlie left, even the game went with him.

I wanted to tell Sam what happened when I left his house Friday night—my fight with Tony, all of it. I wanted to tell Sam about Vincenzo, the Fascist my father hid behind, how I knew that was a bad thing and how I didn't care because Tony's father feared him.

I wanted to tell Sam all these things, but we never spoke about family matters with someone who wasn't family. The one time I'd asked why we considered Vincenzo family, my father said: *Beh, Vincenzo. Vincenzo is different.* But he never told me why.

"Who is this boy and what's wrong with his hair?" Zia Nella asked me in Sicilian. She sounded just like my father, and in their language I answered her, "A boy from school."

"Oh," my zia said. "Amicu." She beckoned Sam and his mother to stay. Santina made a fuss in Sicilian, but my zia shushed her and ushered them back inside.

"That's very kind of you," Mrs. Morris said. "Thank you."

Zia Nella took the ticket from Mrs. Morris and searched the racks. "How come I don't see you in church?"

"We're Protestant."

"David's mother was Protestant. She converted, of course."

Sam mouthed *Tony* as a way to ask me if I had him to thank for my face.

I nodded yes. In school tomorrow, I would tell him that much.

27

Mrs. Morris paid for her green dress, thanked my zia again and Santina for fixing the hemline. Sam waved as they left. The door closed behind them. He glanced back at the shop window over his shoulder. The sun pulled their shadows into long, thin figures that strayed outside faded white crosswalk lines.

～

At home, my father called me down to the basement. I helped him feed the wood-burning stove. He asked how I liked my suit, and I told him I hated it, how the one I wanted was too small, and he said, "When I was your age, I never had a nice suit." And I asked him what he wore to his confirmation, and he said, "I never got confirmed," and when I asked why, he said, "No more questions, David. Work." That was always his answer when he didn't like the question, and I knew better than to defy him, at least when he was right there in front of me.

I kept little acts of defiance, little moments of almost freedom, where he could not see them. They'd always been small—staying up past my bedtime reading fantasy and science-fiction novels under the covers with a flashlight, sitting on the back-porch roof while my father slept, cutting corners on my chores, like sweeping dust under the bookshelf in the hallway instead of into the dustpan. At least they'd always been small until the day I'd gone to Sam's. But despite getting caught, it was worth it. For the length of the albums Sam had played for me, I'd finally felt light, free from the weight of my father's gravity.

Together, my father and I checked his stores of braided onions for soft spots and sorted through his sealed mason jars of seeds collected and dried from last year's harvest, each labeled with the name of a plant from his garden.

Soon the smell of Zia Nella's pan-fried sausages cooked in their own grease led us to the kitchen upstairs. Dishes covered in aluminum foil sat on the card table, with plates, glasses, and utensils all in their proper places. I peeled back the foil and snuck a piece of meat with my fingers.

"Bestia," Zia Nella said. "Wash your hands."

From the bathroom, I heard my father and zia argue in Sicilian. When they spoke Sicilian, their voices were loud and fast, and it always sounded like they were angry, but I knew the difference.

"Your son doesn't want to get confirmed. Who put this idea in his head?"

"Enough, Nella." I imagined my father making that motion with his hand as he said her name, the one that managed to thrust you aside without ever touching you. "I work every day, long hours on my feet," he said. "The noise of those machines, even when I go to bed, I hear them grinding in my head. Enough, Nella. You are like the machines in my head, you never stop."

When the back door slammed shut, I stepped into the kitchen.

"Come," my zia said. "Sit. Eat." She removed the foil from the pasta dish and the pan of fried peppers with sausages, onions, and potatoes. She spooned heaping servings of each onto my plate. "Your father," she said, and she pointed the greasy metal spoon at the back door. "When he remembers he is hungry, he will eat." Then she shrugged into her coat and stood in the front hall at the door. She held the knob, looked over her shoulder at me, and said, "Always your father makes trouble. He doesn't think right, but you . . . I see so much of the twins in you. You are a good boy."

"It's not his fault," I said. "How they died."

She took in a deep breath. The way she clenched her jaw and shook her head reminded me of him. "No," she said, letting the air out. "That was never his fault."

5

In seventh-period science class, we talked about gravity, how it was gravity that shaped the planets into spheres. It pulled them toward the sun even as they fought against that pull. This tug-of-war forced them into orbits called ellipses and trapped them there forever.

The teacher, Mr. Clark, drew a picture on the blackboard—the fat white dot of the sun surrounded by four circles labeled Mercury, Venus, Earth, and Mars. He left out the asteroid belt and the outer planets, the four gas giants, and the last terrestrial world, the smallest and coldest, the icy world Pluto.

Sam sat in the row beside me, a moon in my orbit. Our gravity made us always show the same face to each other. His sneakers, like mine, crossed at the ankles and tucked under his chair. He sucked spaghetti strands of hair into his mouth and held his spiral-bound notebook up for me to read. He had written there on the page: *What did Saturn say to Neptune?*

When I shrugged, he set the notebook down, scribbled out the answer, and held it up again: *Uranus smells bad.*

I snorted, stifling my laughter.

Mr. Clark called on me. He perched on the corner of his desk with one foot planted on the gray-and-white checkerboard floor. "When was the *Giotto* space probe launched on its mission to study Halley's Comet?"

"July 1985," I said.

"And what fresco inspired the name of this probe?"

I knew these answers by heart from the extra-credit reading. "The probe was named after the Italian Renaissance painter Giotto di Bondone, because he saw Halley's Comet in 1301 and interpreted it as the Star of Bethlehem in his fresco *Adoration of the Magi*."

Mr. Clark returned to the blackboard and added the long arc of the comet's orbit to the inner solar system. "We know the comet is outbound from the sun," he said. "We know that in April it will be thirty-nine million miles away from us."

The period bell rang and we shot up out of our seats, but the teacher waved us back down into them. "Think about that for a minute," he said. "Thirty-nine million miles. That's really far away, isn't it? And yet, maybe one of you will see it in the sky." He grabbed an eraser and told us to finish chapter four in our textbooks by tomorrow if we hadn't already finished it, and then he released us.

I headed for the door with Sam. Mr. Clark asked me to stay behind, and Sam told me he had to jet because his mom was picking him up.

"I heard you got into a fight," Mr. Clark said. His eraser cut through the chalk drawing. "Everything okay?"

"Nothing I can't handle." White lines of orbits blurred into dusty smears.

"You're an excellent student, David." Mr. Clark turned from the board, the eraser cutting only air now. "I hope you know your mind is worth more than your fists."

It didn't matter what my mind or fists were worth, I was one lone stick waiting to be broken.

~

Tony punched my locker. I had just come down the stairs and turned the corner and was making my way to the end of the crowded hall when I spotted him. I sidestepped into the doorway of an empty classroom and peeked around the end of the long row of lockers.

"Fuck," Tony swore, shaking his hand at the wrist. All the other students gave him a wide berth except Chris, who strode up and whistled as he rapped the new dent in my door.

Tony rubbed his knuckles. "Fucking hurt."

"Well, it is steel," Chris said.

"No kidding, Mr. Obvious." Tony swaggered like a prizefighter walking to the ring. Chris followed. They were heading my way.

I ducked into the empty classroom and waited, back pressed against the wall. Seconds passed: one, two, three, four. Out in the hall, their chuckles turned to laughter at something Tony said, something about me. I heard him say my name. My ears pounded—it was like sitting inside a bass drum while a drummer kept the beat. Five, six, seven, eight. Were those seconds, or minutes? Their voices faded. Silence fell, save for the ticking of the clock like the clicking of my father's tongs. Tick-tick. Tick-tick. His disapproval found me everywhere. I'd hidden instead of fighting back.

A janitor pushed his mop bucket into the classroom on screeching wheels. I darted to my locker and opened it. A slip of yellow notepad paper fluttered out, seesawing in the air as it fell to my feet. That mountainous troll had scrawled the note, *Your dead, Marconi,* in large childish letters. My mind was worth more than my fists. Yeah, right. All the grammarians in the world couldn't protect me from Tony. I shoved the note into my pocket, grabbed my backpack, and walked home. I was glad for once that I'd missed the bus, missed Tony and Chris and the spitballs they'd send soaring my way from their back-row seats.

At dinner, my father asked if that boy gave me any more trouble, and I told him no. Later, when he walked me to Catechism class, he asked me again, and this time he told me not to lie. "I didn't even see him today," I said, and my father weighed these words for their truth in that frown he always made when he was thinking about what to say next. When I covered my fib by blurting out how scientists named a space probe after a famous Italian painter, my father swept my deflection away with a sweep of his hand, saying everything comes from Italy, even the name of this country, even a part of me, his son. U miricanu, he called me, the Sicilian word for American.

~

Saint Sebastian Church held Catechism class each Monday night at six o'clock in the linoleum-tiled basement. The overhead fluorescent lights buzzed and flickered and drained the room of color. Tony and Chris sat in my usual spot in the first row of long bingo tables. I took the seat farthest from them and from the warmth of the space heater beside Brother Calogero's feet. He droned on for an hour about the importance of the sacraments, and when the hour ended, he unplugged the space heater. Like a school bell, that was my signal.

I was first out the door, first up the stairs in a sprint, two steps at a time, and first to push through the main doors of the vestibule. Dim streetlights hummed, casting a dirty-yellow glow from their fat bulbs. In the sickly light, my father paced, hands shoved hard in his jacket pockets, nose red from the cold as if he'd been out there the whole time. Maybe he had. Maybe he'd hovered outside, waiting to protect a son from ghosts only he saw.

The sounds of the other Catechism students echoed behind me. Their footsteps and chatter and laughter herded me down to the sidewalk. My father hooked me with his arm to stop me from bolting past him.

"Let's go," I said.

"Aspetta." He tightened his arm around me and searched the faces of the children streaming out of the church. When he saw Tony, he made sure that Tony saw him, too. I don't know how my father did it. He didn't move. He didn't speak. He just stared until Tony pulled away from Chris midconversation and met my father's eyes and mine beside him. Tony wavered there. The last of the students parted around him. He was alone, a weed sprouting from a crack in the marble steps, and my father cut him down without raising a hand. Shoulders hunched in red leather, Tony grew smaller as I grew taller. And then, cowed under, that little shit slunk home.

"Now we go," my father said. As we walked, he told me about his father's almond orchard in Sicily, how some nights he slept under the almond trees when he was a boy. "They made the best fruit," he said. "When they bloomed, all the land looked like it was in the clouds." He scratched the scruff on his jaw. "One night," he said, "I walked with your nonnu by the cemetery on our way home from the orchard. The shadows of the stones moved as we went by, and there was a light in the window of a . . . mausoleo . . . Come si chiama . . . the little house in the cemetery?"

"Mausoleum," I said.

"Mausoleum. Mausoleo. Almost the same word," he said. "See how everything comes from Italia?" Then my father cleared his throat and said, "Maybe I was your age, I don't remember. It was far back." And he waved his hand in the air to show how far back in time he meant. "Anyway," he said, "there was a light in the window, and I shouted to your nonnu, *Look! Someone's inside. What do they need a light in there for?*" Then my father laughed, a watery-eyed, big-bellied laugh, and said, "You know what your nonnu says to me? *Turiddu,* he says, that's what he called me, *Turiddu, look with your eyes. This light, it is nothing but the moon.*"

He stopped and parted my hair at the cowlick with his fingers and brushed the bangs from my forehead. "My papà," he said, "he tried to teach me something. Now I teach you. Capisci?" He pointed at my eyes and said, "Look with your eyes, not with this." Then he placed his palm over my heart. "You understand?"

6

A week of heavy rain washed the dirty snow away. And Tony, too. It was a brief respite—one that wouldn't last. It never did.

Late Saturday night, while my father's snores rattled through the house, I climbed out my window onto the back-porch roof to wrap myself in a blanket of stars and blue-black sky. But instead of a starry blanket, there was only a lumpy sheet of clouds, not even a hint of starlight, just the haze from a silver-gray wisp of moon. I read Tony's stupid note again. I should've thrown it away, but I couldn't.

A pebble hit the shingles and clattered down the rain gutter. In the yard below, Sam's blond bangs flopped over his face like a waning moon. Beside him stood a girl who could have stepped out of one of the posters on his bedroom wall. She dressed head to toe in black, with an eight-inch jet-black Mohawk jutting from the top of her head like a dorsal fin. She leaned into him, whispered in his ear. His white teeth flashed in a smile. He craned his neck back up at me, lifted his hands in a question: *Are you coming or staying?*

I raised a finger, mouthed, *One minute.* Then I scampered back inside. The window squeaked like a terrified mouse when I inched it down. I froze, but my father's snores still rumbled from his room. I'd never snuck out before, and if I got caught, he might never let me leave the house alone again. I could hear him grilling me in my head already, the same questions he peppered me with on those rare occasions he allowed me out in the world without an escort. *Where are you going? What are you doing? Why? Is this for school? What time will you be done?* He never let me go over to anyone's house, and he never let me have anyone over to our house, because they weren't family.

But he also lied, bigger lies than I ever thought to tell. That day in the street with Tony's father, Rocco, he'd pounded the truck hood like a man who thought he could cow old hatreds into submission with his fists the way he'd cowed Tony with only a look. He was never alone, though. Even facing down Rocco's truck, he had Vincenzo's strength with him. Vincenzo was his bundle. I didn't want to be cowed, and I didn't want to be the lone stick that gets broken.

And there was Sam, outside with a girl and an invitation—a siren song calling me to shipwreck. Four paces to the closet and the hardwood floor squeaked. I froze again. The heartbeat of the house at night, the cadence of my father sleeping, did not stop. I grabbed dirty clothes from the closet floor and arranged them in the shape of a boy on the bed, like I'd seen on so many television shows. Sneakers in one hand and my denim jacket in the other, I tiptoed into the hall.

My father had left his door open as usual. Even in sleep he couldn't let me alone. Slants of streetlight shone through his torn window shade. And I did what he had told me to do. I looked with my eyes, not with my heart. The stalks of his hair, thinning and gray, always kept neatly combed back from his widow's peak, grew wild atop his head. In the light, those wild stalks were thinner and grayer. He looked, for the first time, old to me, feeble. He was afraid for me, his son, afraid of all the things that could go wrong in the world. But I wanted to see who I could be without that weight, without his crushing fear, for one night at least. I crept downstairs at an elephant's pace and slipped out the back door.

Sam tossed me a black Bauhaus T-shirt. "Want to go to a party?" he asked.

I laced up my high-tops and pulled the shirt on over my army-green long-sleeved tee. "Lead the way."

"I told you he'd be cool," Sam said to the girl. Up close she was pretty. Not magazine pretty, but interesting with her crooked nose and powder-white skin, black lipstick and black winged eyeliner.

"I'm Jamie," she said.

"David. But I guess Sam already told you." I toed the grass with my sneaker. "So, where to?"

~

Wesleyan University students swarmed in and around Butterfield dorms like winking fireflies on a warm summer night. They huddled in small circles or wandered from clique to clique until they found a home. Couples drifted in and out of each other's airspace, and disappeared into one of three dormitories that snaked around a central courtyard. Flyers covered a kiosk, hand-scrawled and printed announcements about shows and rides, math tutoring and music lessons. The charged thrum of the party tingled in my feet through the soles of my sneakers, a shock like a circuit being completed.

Jamie's sister, Sarah, stood in a huddle of people by a door that had been propped open with a garbage bin. They drank from red plastic cups and passed a joint. She looked like an older version of Jamie without the ghost-white makeup and Mohawk. Pink waves of hair spilled over the shoulders of her black motorcycle jacket. Her fingers were stacked with silver rings and turquoise stones. She peeled away from the others, her green peasant skirt swaying around the ankles of her combat boots.

"You brought an entourage," she said.

"You going to offer us a drink?" Jamie asked.

"You're on your own there, kiddo." She squinted at her Swatch. "If you hurry, you can still catch the band. Go to the laundry room in Butt B and follow the noise. Oh, and don't make me regret inviting you."

Jamie rolled her eyes. "Just make sure there isn't a boy in your room when I get in."

In the laundry room, screeching guitars and wild feedback echoed around us. Washing machines and dryers, exposed pipes running the length of the ceiling, even the air vibrated from the thunderous punch of drums and bass. Graffiti-covered concrete walls stretched out ahead of us—a labyrinth of dimly lit corridors deep under the earth.

"These tunnels connect to all the Butterfield dorms," Sam yelled in my ear. "There's supposed to be a door down here that leads to the main network under the whole campus."

My old D&D games were coming alive. We were a company of adventurers in search of secrets long forgotten in a maze of shifting walls and hidden treasures. We passed metal doors, some locked and some with broken locks—rooms with bare bulbs casting long shadows across discarded telephones and furniture, and rooms taken over as art studios. There was a kiln and pottery wheel in one room, and easels stood in another with canvases of every size stacked against the walls. Students lived here. They slept on mattresses on the floor. They left their clothes heaped in corners and books strewn about.

Sam and Jamie ran ahead of me into an alcove where clusters of people drank and smoked and made out under flickering fluorescent lights. All around them, red and blue faces scowled from where they were painted on the concrete walls. Political rants and propositions for sex scribbled on every inch of free space called out for attention.

I wove through the crowd, caught in Sam and Jamie's wake. The alcove opened into a large room. Inside, the band played. Their amplifiers were so loud, the sound rattled my chest. My body tensed. A mass of people jumped up and down in place, headbanging and bouncing off one another like balls in a pinball machine. Sam and Jamie threw themselves into the throng and disappeared. The air felt thick and sticky. It smelled like damp socks and cigarettes. Sweat beaded on my upper lip. I wiped it away with my sleeve, then shouldered out of my denim jacket. I let the songs—each one louder and faster than the last—shred me into pieces.

Jamie bounded out of the mosh pit. "Tie it around your waist," she shouted over the thrashing music. And she mimed tying jacket arms around her waist.

The band finished their set. My ears rang. Sam stumbled toward us. "That was awesome," he said. The room thinned out as people delved deeper into the tunnels or headed back to the surface. For the first time, I could see the musicians who were set up on the floor at the far end of the space. They all sported Mohawks except for the drummer. He sat on his stool while the singer stood behind him and shaved the sides of his head down to stubble.

"Now you're an official member," the singer said.

The drummer felt the flat blond line of hair. "Wicked," he said, and then he set to work, breaking down his drum kit.

"Bauhaus," the singer said. He waved the clippers at me. It was a question, or a dare. Or maybe it was an answer, a way to finally breathe—a way to not be afraid. I felt free in these tunnels. I wanted to carry that feeling with me, no matter the price. And there would be a price.

I sat down on the drummer's stool in that cave of a room at the heart of the maze. Electric clippers buzzed around my ears. And when I spoke, I didn't recognize my own voice. "What are you guys called?"

"I'm Hunter. That's Flint and River, and over there is—"

They all had the names of something wild. "No, I mean your group. What do you guys call yourselves?"

"Katabasis," he said. "But when we play Eclectic House, we'll be Genetic Disorder."

Sam and Jamie watched me like I was the most fascinating television program they'd ever seen. Clumps of black hair tumbled past my shoulders and fell into patterns with the drummer's towhead strands like the colored inkblots of a Rorschach test. Those weak pieces of me the night had pruned away.

"Rad," Jamie said.

Sam wagged his head in agreement. "Totally."

The bare sides of my scalp felt prickly and soft at the same time. There was no mirror, but I could read my reflection in the look on Sam's face. I tugged at my thick mane. "Gladiator-helmet head," I said. "Think I'll grow it long into a real plume."

Hunter coiled the microphone cable around his arm and tossed it into a milk crate. "Righteous band name," he said. "Gladiator Helmet Head."

"PSafe is topside," a shout echoed from the tunnels. Around us, people sprang to life, jack-in-the-boxes with their buttons pushed.

"Public Safety," Hunter said. "You kids should jet. That way." He thumbed at a tunnel behind him. "You'll end up in Butt C."

Sam and Jamie followed me through the tunnels. We sprinted around drunken students and vomit puddles, past flashes of almost-familiar graffiti and open doorways, until we spilled up a metal staircase and into the fluorescent-lit first floor of Butterfield C.

On the beige couch of the student lounge, a couple pawed at each other, oblivious to the chaos just outside the big windows and open glass doors. The party had swelled since we first arrived. It spilled beyond the dormitories and courtyard to Lawn Avenue. A drunken brawl had broken out near the kiosk. Students lingered in the swinging beams of PSafe flashlights. The rough voices of campus security apprehending the brawlers carried over the noise of the crowd.

In the hallway behind us, a shirtless resident pushed open his door and glared at us. "Fucking townies," he said. "What are you, fifteen? Don't let them find you." He nodded at the PSafe officers who had just entered the building down the end of the hall.

"Shit," Sam said. "Jamie, where's your sister? We can hang in her room until this blows over."

"No way," she said. "I'm not supposed to show my face for another two hours."

A second guy came to the door, hair tousled, shirt unbuttoned, and cheeks flushed. "Ignore them," he said. Then he sauntered into the bathroom across the way.

"Act like we belong," I said. I pulled my shoulders back, brushed my fingers over my gladiator plume. No one would chase or jump me, not tonight. Not ever again. I strolled down the narrow corridor, away from where the officers entered. "Let's go."

"This is nuts," Sam said with a wild grin.

We snaked through the dorm and found an exit opposite the courtyard. Large corner windows that had once been lit and full of people emptied and went dark. Streams of students stumbled away from Butterfield and the strobe lights of PSafe vehicles.

Cutting through a thicket of bare trees, I shrugged back into my jacket. We hopped a wood fence and walked through several backyards to get to a street clear of PSafe officers. We hoofed it past the science building and university library to Foss Hill, where we lay on our backs and stole glimpses of starlight between low-hung clouds. Sam launched into a retelling of the whole evening. When he got to the part where Hunter shaved my head, Sam turned to me and said, "Dude, I can't believe you did that."

The story grew and shifted as we each took turns embellishing it until the night sounded more like a Ray Harryhausen adventure movie than a college party we'd crashed. In our version of events, we were heroes pitted against giant, stop-motion-animation monsters: PSafe swooped down on us like pterodactyls in *One Million Years B.C.* and sprang up out of the earth like skeleton warriors from *Jason and the Argonauts*.

We all agreed, tonight was the best night ever.

7

At home, I slept until my father's shouts from the bottom of the stairs woke me. "Your zia is here," he said. "Did you eat?" I rolled over and pulled the covers up over my head. "David, you got church in a few minutes." The stairs creaked under his heavy footsteps. His long, drawn-out "ooh" signaled a warning. He was losing his patience. He lifted my window shade and flung open the curtain. "What's the matter? You sick?"

"What time is it?" I sat up in bed, squinting against the morning light. The clock on my nightstand read seven forty-five.

My father's forehead bunched into rows of wrinkled skin, speed bumps for his fast-climbing unibrow. That caterpillar on his face wanted no part of what was coming next. His eyes bulged like two hard-boiled eggs bursting from their shells. A string of Sicilian curses erupted from my father's mouth so fast I couldn't follow them. His hands moved even faster, churning air into a storm as he spoke.

In the doorway, Zia Nella's bright-blue dress was like a patch of clear sky in a thunderstorm. She gasped and crossed herself.

My father turned his fury on her. "This was that friend, wasn't it? Miricani!" There was an insult in the way he pronounced the Sicilian word for Americans. It sounded almost like merda di cane—dog shit.

"Where were you when your son did this to himself?" Zia Nella said. Then the two of them argued in Sicilian about who was at fault for what I'd done to my hair and what they were going to do with me now that there wasn't time for breakfast. They talked about me as if I weren't there, listening to every word. They couldn't let me out in public like this. There were no barbers open. There must be something wrong with me. I was sick in the head. That American boy was a bad influence. Maybe it was drugs. My father should go to church more often. He should go with me. We should go together, as a family. Maybe it was too much television. Who knew what they were teaching us in school.

In their world, I had no volition of my own. My actions were a product of some outside force, plotting the ruin of good Sicilian boys.

"I'm not on drugs," I said. They both stopped and looked at me. "I didn't learn it in school. I didn't watch it on TV. What do you care what my hair looks like? It's mine, not yours. I like it. It's cool."

"Sta zittu," my father said. Shut up. He dragged me by my arm out of bed. I pulled against his grip, but he was bigger and stronger than me, and it was useless to resist. I knew this from the times I'd disobeyed him before. Still, the impulse to flee was powerful in that frantic moment when caught. My feet shuffled forward across the carpet in the hall to the cool tiles of the bathroom. With his free hand, he plugged in the electric clippers and set to work. Clumps of black hair tumbled into the white porcelain bowl. There was no fighting him on this. But my hair would grow back. And if I wanted to, I'd cut it into a Mohawk again.

～

All through Palm Sunday Mass my stomach rumbled. My back itched from stray hairs. After the service, Zia Nella and I each took one of the small crosses made from the blessed and incensed palm leaves. She fidgeted with the cross in her hands as she spoke with the priest in the church vestibule. They were talking about me. Tony and Chris walked by with their families. In the shadows of their fathers, they snickered and wondered aloud if I had head lice. I felt the stubble on my shaved head, the uneven line where the Mohawk had been, patches of my plume. I was a caged gladiator, waiting for the contest to begin.

On the way home, large two-family houses with pitted and worn aluminum siding cast long shadows over us. Bare maple trees lined the cracked sidewalk, their roots pushing up whole blocks of the pavement. Zia Nella chose each step carefully. Her mouth twitched. The small, delicate movements of her gloved hands were like a conductor leading an orchestra through the softest passage in a piece of music as whole sections of the symphony tapered off and the bow of a lone violin swept the melody down. In her mind, she was still talking to the priest.

"What did you tell my father about Sam?" I asked.

She folded her hands in front of her, fingers interlaced. "Only that he was a nice boy for a Protestant, and your friend." She couldn't keep her hands still for long. They arced around her face with the grace of a ballerina as she spoke. "It's nice to see you have friends. But the hair, you had such beautiful hair, like the twins—" She stroked the ends of her own long black hair, shot through with gray. "Well, it will grow back."

"Sam had nothing to do with the Mohawk. It was my idea."

"But someone put this idea in your head, no?" She tapped my temple with a finger, the conductor's baton demanding attention. "What would make you want to do that to yourself?"

We stopped at a four-way intersection. At my feet, black carpenter ants swarmed a wounded beetle. The beetle scrabbled at the pavement, but with only two good legs, all it could hope for was to complete a tiny circle before the ants dragged it into the brown grass.

～

My father had left me dry toast and a plate of fried eggs covered in aluminum foil on the kitchen table. He was on a ladder in the back-yard, clearing out the gutters. In the low-slung basement, I fed the wood-burning stove with a split of firewood from the woodpile. The cellar smelled smoky and sweet—a mixture of warm stone, damp earth, and fermenting grapes. I pulled Tony's note from my jeans pocket and smoothed the crumpled paper flat on a thick slab of granite on the workbench under the stairs. *Your dead, Marconi.* With my chewed-up ballpoint pen, I corrected Tony's grammar: *You're dead.*

The ceiling boards creaked as my father came inside the house.

"What are you doing down there?" he called out from the cellar door.

"Nothing," I said and shoved the note back into my pocket.

He clomped down the narrow stairs. "I need a bottle of wine for Vincenzo," he said.

My father's wood basket wine press and hand-cranked crusher marked the entrance to the storage room he'd built with cinder blocks. The room was cool and dark. He pulled the chain and the bare bulb overhead flickered on. In the far corner, two oak barrels of aging wine with wooden barrel spigots lay on their sides on a pine-board rack. A chest freezer stocked full of vegetables from his garden sat under cobwebbed shelves of bottled wine. There was a bottle stored there for me—a fat jug of brick-red wine—sealed with rag and cork and marked with my name in black permanent marker on a strip of masking tape.

"I made that the year you were born," he said. "Your bottle is in that difficult stage." He looked me over like I was one of his dusty bottles on the shelf and he was trying to decide if I was worth opening. "Pretty soon," he said. And he seesawed his hand from left to right. "A few months, maybe another year, we can open it and see what kind of wine we get."

But he already knew what kind he'd get. More vinegar than wine, something that was only good for cooking where you wouldn't taste the sour. I grabbed a bottle for Vincenzo and followed my father back up to the kitchen. On the hollow wooden staircase, I ran my free hand along the basement wall's large jagged stones. Bits of our foundation's cracked masonry crumbled through my fingers in a fine dust.

~

The next day in school, I met Sam at his locker before homeroom. A candy-blue streak shot through his flop of blond hair.

"Cool color," I said. Then I palmed the stubble on my scalp. "Can't exactly hide a Mohawk."

"Dude," he said. "That shaved head is righteous."

Locker doors clanked and slammed shut. A river of students shouted over each other's heads. They crashed around us—two scoured boulders in the rapids, pitted and worn but immovable.

Later, as the seventh-period warning bell rang, I slipped the note into Tony's locker.

8

Mr. Clark turned from the blackboard as I walked into class late. He reminded me about our homework, and I got up and added my assignment to the pile on his desk—my answers to a series of questions at the end of the chapter we'd just read. The chapter was about the early formation of the Earth and the moon and how the moon had been formed from a cataclysmic event—a giant asteroid had struck the still-molten Earth and broken off a piece of the planet itself. And that piece became the moon, trapped in Earth's gravity, a part of the Earth that could never return home but could never escape either.

"David," Mr. Clark said. "How can scientists determine the age of the moon?"

"Radiometric dating."

"That's correct," he said, and then he chided me for my lateness and the class for not correctly answering the question. A boy sitting in the back row wondered aloud why I had to make them all look bad.

It wasn't the first time someone had said something like that about me. But I was a different boy, one who finally had the courage to give it back. "Why do you have to make it so easy?" I said.

The class broke out into a collective *ooohhh*.

Mr. Clark frowned a wrinkled brow at me, like he was puzzling out what had happened to his best student, where that quiet boy had gone. "That's enough," he said. "So, who besides David can tell us what radiometric dating is? Hint, it has nothing to do with your Saturday night plans."

~

In the hall, Tony and Chris plowed through the crowd and shouldered Sam and me into our lockers.

"Watch out, fairies," Tony said.

Chris walked backward and smirked at us. "Found a boyfriend, Marconi?"

"Step off," I said.

Tony made an about-face. "Or what?"

I slammed my locker shut and took a step forward, brandishing a textbook.

"They're not worth detention." Sam tugged at my sleeve.

"Yeah, I didn't think so," Tony said.

Sam pulled me into the river of students flowing by. Behind me, Tony opened his locker.

~

In the back row of the bus, Tony sat red faced. Beside him Chris shot spitballs at me through a straw. He taunted me, calling me Kojak, and boasted that my melon was perfect for target practice. I crumpled notebook paper in my fist, turned around, and threw it at Chris. "Quit it," I said.

Chris ducked, raising an arm to shield his face.

Tony caught the paper ball. "Leave him alone," he said. "Little bitch is mine."

"Face front or you're off," the bus driver shouted at me. He eyeballed me in the overhead mirror.

I slouched down low and started peeling at a tear in the green vinyl seat cover, picking out the bile-yellow foam padding. The crumpled paper whipped over the top of the seat back and into my lap, and the driver did nothing. The page crinkled as I smoothed it over the seat to see the hastily drawn circle with two *X*'s for eyes and a frowning line for a mouth.

At my stop, Tony followed me off the bus—two stops before his own, his footsteps ghosting mine. Run-down two-family houses and old maple trees cast long shadows across the cracked and pebbled pavement. I walked faster. So did Tony. He stepped on the back of my sneaker, and my heel slipped out of the shoe.

"You're supposed to leave me alone," I said. I knelt and tugged the folded canvas back over my heel. Tony's shadow enveloped me but he kept his distance. "That's what your father told you, right? Because he's afraid of my father."

"You think you're so fucking smart," Tony said. "You think you fucking know everything, don't you?"

I flipped Tony the bird over my shoulder as I walked away.

"Do that to my face," he said. He pulled on my shoulder and spun me around, and I swung at his fat head, but he grabbed my fist and twisted my arm behind my back. "My father's not afraid of some little bastard he chased out of Melilli."

It was a strange thing for him to say, the weakest taunt he'd ever come up with. And one that was so wrong. "You don't know what you're talking about," I said. "He's not even from there, doofus." I stomped on the toe of his pristine white Reeboks.

Tony swore and his grip loosened, but only for a second before he forced me down to the strip of brown lawn between the sidewalk and the curb. With a knee to my back, he crushed the breath out of me. My cheek ground into the dead grass. He yanked my hand up to my shoulder blade, and I cried out—so fast I cried out. I hadn't even landed a punch. "You know nothing," he said. He pulled harder. I flailed beneath him like a fish flopping around in the bottom of a fisherman's bucket, desperate to return to the salty sea. He was so heavy. I couldn't breathe. And I couldn't stop the tears. But it wasn't the pain that made me cry, though my arm burned like my muscles were on fire. No, it was because I was that twig boy again and Tony had just snapped me in half.

"My father isn't afraid of anyone," Tony said.

"Okay," I blubbered. "Okay. I'm sorry."

"We're not afraid of anyone." He gave my arm one last twist and then let me go.

9

In my bedroom, I crawled under the covers and refused to get out of bed for dinner. My father sat on the mattress edge and felt my forehead with his thick palm and said, "No fever." He let air out of his nostrils. A huffing, fire-breathing dragon. "Where does it hurt?"

I rolled away from him. "Let me sleep."

"Did you get into another fight?"

"No," I said. "Now leave me alone."

He touched my shoulder lightly but then pulled away. He sighed. "Get some sleep."

I yanked the covers up over my head and slept until noon the next day. The house smelled of simmering chicken broth with garlic and parsley. My zia bustled in the kitchen. The stars on my ceiling had stopped glowing hours ago, and I could no longer see my mother and myself in those ordinary stickers. This was how flat the night sky would be when all the stars were dead stars, furnaces extinguished. A book with all the words erased. The stories those stars told, lost. If only the story of what just happened could be so easily stamped out.

Mr. Clark was right. My fists weren't worth much after all. I sat up in bed, held my knees to my chest, and rested my cheek on my knees. My arm and shoulder still ached, an echo of Tony just under my skin, still holding me down.

~

At the card table in the kitchen, Zia Nella placed a bowl of her minestrone in front of me. Then she felt my forehead, kissed the top of my shaved head, and sat down beside me. She hunched over her own bowl, slurped the oily broth and noodles. "Eat," she said.

When we were done, we moved into the living room. I spun the television dial. Soap operas flickered into talk shows and turned into blue static with dark horizontal lines dancing up the screen. On PBS I found Carl Sagan's *Cosmos*, all thirteen episodes back to back. I sank into the couch, my head on my zia's shoulder. She watched with me. Sagan talked about how supernovas seed the universe with the materials for life. My zia wanted to know how he could know that. "It's impossible to know for sure," she said.

And I said, "It's a neat idea to be made of stars. Don't you think?" I wanted that furnace inside me—a piece of a star's fusion reactor.

She tsked. "Be careful with ideas. You get an idea stuck in your head, and goodbye, world." She rubbed her palms together the way my father did when he told me how people like us, people born donkeys, had to work hard their whole lives—and here was where he rubbed his palms together—until one day, that's it. Fini. No more life.

10

Before my zia left, I asked her if she and my father were from Melilli, and she said, "Where did you hear that?" And I told her I'd heard it from Tony. Then she pulled her hair back with a rubber band and tugged it tight against her scalp. "Come," she said.

My father kept his bedroom walls bare, and the floor swept clean. His bed, neatly made, stood centered under the window. Zia Nella pulled out a full laundry basket from the closet to get at a cardboard box in the back. Inside, a mildewed shoebox peppered with dust was nestled among stacks of glue-bound bulletins commemorating the annual Feast of Saint Sebastian. The church printed them each May for the weekend of the festival. My father had saved every bulletin going back to 1952.

He never took me to the festival. It was always too noisy for him or too crowded, or he was too tired to go. My zia and ziu took me on Sundays to watch the statue of Saint Sebastian paraded around the block, but Vincenzo took me on the rides. He'd sit with me on the Ferris wheel Friday evenings when the feast officially opened. He'd ask me about school. He'd give me tickets for all the rides and games and food I wanted. We'd stay up late together Sunday nights for a last spin on the Ferris wheel before the closing of the festival, the one night out of the school year my father let me stay up past ten o'clock. I imagined my father going to the festival without me, maybe late opening night or early before the crowds arrived, to pick up a bulletin each year. Or maybe my zia brought one back for him, a silent pact that she would brave the crowds and he would stay home, alone with the vegetables in his garden.

We used to go together, all of us, when my mother was alive.

Zia Nella took the top bulletin off the stack, the one from last year's feast, and flipped to the memorials in the back. She sent my mother's picture in every year. *In Loving Memory of Eileen Marconi.* "She was so beautiful," my zia said. She touched the small, grainy headshot. This was the only photo of my mother that we had—the one my zia had saved. In the black-and-white picture, my mother's hair looked gray, the fiery red cooled to ash. *You are missed. Salvatore & David Marconi. Antonella & Frank Lombardo.*

She put back the bulletin and took out the shoebox. She blew dust from its dented lid. Written there in faintly drawn pen strokes were my father's name and an address for an apartment on Ferry Street in downtown's North End. The return address was in Melilli, Sicily, from someone named Fiorilla.

"The war was bad," Zia Nella said. "Bad for everyone, but for some, it never ended." She held the shoebox in her lap and set the lid aside. A tarnished silver cross teetered atop a messy pile of old black-and-white photographs. She held the cross in her open palm. "After the twins died, our parents, they got sick." She made a fist around the cross and held it to her heart. "In here, they were sick in here, you understand?" And she tapped her fist against her chest. "They couldn't take care of us, and your father, he thought this was all his fault. Me? I blame the day the war came to Melilli for everything, even your mother's death. The curse of the war took her, too." She raised the cross to her lips and kissed it.

My father's craggy face was easy to read—he called it his labirinto, a labyrinth of deep lines born of long-held sorrows that grew deeper and longer all the years of his life—but my zia, inside, she was a beach of stones in every size and shape and color you could imagine. You could spend a lifetime combing those shores and never find the one rock that held the secret of what my zia was really thinking. Sometimes you got lucky, though, and the right stone washed up at your feet.

"Melilli," she said, weighing the word on her tongue. "That was our life before. We left all that behind when we came here. These pictures are all we have left. They are our secret. You understand?"

She showed me portraits of people I'd never seen before, standing in stiff positions against smooth sepia backdrops. Careful not to damage the frail edges, she held one out for me to see. She smiled at the peasant man in the photograph holding a basket of almonds. "This is my nonnu," she said. "Here he is with my nonna." She pointed at a photo of a seated elderly couple with mouths turned down in frowns, faces crumpled and sagging under the weight of old age. Then my zia moved past a dapper young man in a dark suit, his flat cap at a jaunty angle, to a family snapshot taken during the Saint Sebastian festival.

In it were two young boys—twins—and a little girl who held her mother's hand, and two grinning older boys, seven, maybe eight, years old. The taller boy, the spitting image of Tony Morello, had his arm around the other, my father. They stood on a crowded lot. Behind them, four men carried the statue of their saint on a wooden pallet hefted on their shoulders.

On the back of the photograph someone had written *Melilli, 1941* and the names: *Leonello, Emanuele, Antonella, Giuseppina, Salvatore,* and *Rocco.*

Melilli. 1941. My father and Rocco Morello, their story—and mine, too—went all the way back to that time and place. Tony was right.

11

For the first time in my life, I wanted to talk with Tony Morello. Really talk, not just hurl insults. In the halls at school, I watched him from a distance. The smaller boys—and we were all smaller than Tony—parted around him wherever he went. They exchanged nervous, shifting glances that only resolved when they spotted me. I had a perpetual target on my back, and they knew it. Chris increased the size of Tony's mass even more. Tony walked taller and roared louder in the company of Chris Cardella. That two-headed troll lumbered less, swaggered more. His insults, peppered with minchia and other vulgar Sicilian expressions, cut deeper and echoed off the linoleum-tiled floor and locker-lined walls. But alone Tony was different. Alone he shrunk, just a little, and glowered in silence.

Thursday afternoon, after the second warning bell between fifth and sixth periods, Tony stood at his locker, one hand gripping the top of the door while he made a show of rummaging through textbooks and spiral notebooks and loose sheets of paper. The halls emptied. Tony shut the door and spun the combination dial. He tugged the latch, then turned away. At the closed stairwell doors, he stared through the long, narrow window, as if contemplating making a run for it down the concrete steps and outside.

That was the first time I noticed, but when I thought back on it I recognized the small way he carried himself in the world when he thought no one was watching. If there would ever be a moment when I could talk with Tony, this was that moment. All I had to do was step out from the boys' bathroom doorway and say something, anything, and the questions about our fathers and who they were to each other would follow. But when I played out that scenario in my head, it always ended badly for me. Who was I kidding?

The clack of a teacher's heels sounded from around the corner, and Tony hustled my way. I slipped into the bathroom and hid in a locked stall, feet pulled up on the toilet seat, until the period bell rang.

~

If my father wanted to tell me what my zia showed me, he would have told me long ago. He would have sat me down in the kitchen, the shoebox on the card table between us. His fingers tracing the wrinkles on the concave lid, drawing lines in the dust. The wrinkles in his forehead deepening like old cart ruts in the dirt from a donkey-drawn cart. The wooden cart carved and painted with scenes from his past, bright colors faded under hot sun. The whining bray of the donkey showing me the pictures he'd pulled behind him all his life, and what each one did to him.

~

That Friday was Good Friday and the start of Easter break. My father took the day off work and dragged me early in the morning to Loreto's Garden Nursery for newly sprouted tomato plants. We turned off a two-lane road on the outskirts of town, into a gravel parking lot. "Closed" signs banged against the padlocked doors of two wood-framed greenhouses made of silvered wood and corrugated plastic. Those signs weren't meant for us. Vincenzo had called ahead.

Loreto, the owner, lived in a rusted trailer behind the greenhouses, on the other side of a narrow, fenced-in garden. My father stood at the chain-link gate and shouted to him. Loreto ambled out from the tree line near the trailer, zipping up his fly. Beneath his bushy mustache, a lit cigarette dangled from the corner of his mouth. He waved. "Salvatore," he said. A fat ring of keys jangled from his belt loop. He sounded like Christmas. "That your boy? They grow so fast."

"Like a weed," my father said. "Pretty soon he'll be taller than me." But he closed his fist and raised his pinkie as a way to say I didn't have enough meat on my bones.

Loreto opened the gate for us. "I have some nice tomatoes this year," he said. "Come, see for yourself."

My father pushed himself forward, clomping down a cobbled path between flower beds of yellow and pink daffodils. The path curved around a bathtub shrine of the Virgin Mary. Loreto paused by the upended bathtub, half buried with its inside painted blue, and ushered us into one of his greenhouses.

"You smell that?" my father said to me. The air was warm and moist, rich with mulch and fertilizer. "Things are growing."

He stopped to sniff potted soil and little plants—an animal searching for signs of weakness or strength—nodding his head and frowning, which was my father's way of saying: *Pretty good, not too bad, this one.* In this way, he chose his little Romas.

At home we set them in the back hall by the row of sunlit windows where my father had hung the palm-leaf cross from a nail. He never took me to church, but he always wanted me in his garden. He knelt there among the rows of his plants and cared for them. I'd never seen him pray before, scooted forward on the pew with knees on the padded kneeler. Stooped low in his garden, he was that peasant boy again, the boy who had long ago transformed himself into a donkey.

As the weather warmed, he would make me help him move the pots onto the porch and haul them back in before night, letting them stay out longer each day.

"They need to be hardened," he told me, "before transplanting them outside after the last frost."

～

Easter Sunday, my father went to Midnight Mass with Vincenzo. It was something they always did together. Vincenzo went for the candlelight. He liked the way it softened the stones. My father never talked about the Mass. He showered and shaved and combed his hair back from his widow's peak—once charcoal black, now lightened by so many strands of gray. He put on the same suit he wore to my mother's funeral and without a word stepped into the night.

He came home long after I fell asleep but was up with the dawn and working in his garden for hours before I even dragged myself out of bed and into my new three-piece suit. My confirmation was still two months away but my zia wanted me to wear the suit for Easter. I had grown out of my old black church clothes, and she said it was for the best because they made me look like an undertaker.

That morning she took me to Mass with Ziu Frank. We sat in the last pew, the red velvet curtain of the confessional behind us. We knelt when we were supposed to kneel and stood when we were supposed to stand. In the front-row pew, Tony and Chris—pious little angels in their pinstriped suits—sat and knelt and stood with their parents. The priest read from the Epistle of Paul to the Colossians. Paul urged the Colossians to shake off the worldly, to think about what was above, not what was on Earth. Rocco nodded his head in agreement. He made his son sit up straight, bade him pay attention. The epistle was an exhortation to shed the old self for a new self, renewed. The priest ended the reading at the part that said if any man had a quarrel with another man, even as Christ forgave him, so must he also forgive.

~

After the service, I removed my clip-on tie and unbuttoned my shirt collar and my two-button, single-breasted navy-blue jacket, and we went to my house for lunch. Vincenzo and my father waited at the card table in the kitchen, playing Scopa—they only knew Italian card games. They listened to music on the local Italian program on the radio, an empty bottle of wine holding the light between them.

Vincenzo threw down his brightly colored cards as we filed in through the back door. He stood up, favoring his bad leg. "There he is. There's our boy. Let me get a good look at you." He admired me in my new suit. "The secret to the two-button jacket," he said, "is to leave the bottom one open." He buttoned the top button of my jacket, stepped back and smiled. "You'll break a lot of girls' hearts."

"No," my zia said as she set the table. "He will mend them. He will go to school to be a doctor."

On the radio, a bleating accordion wailed, and an earnest man's voice lamented his dead donkey. My father clapped and stomped his sandaled feet. He brayed like the man in the song brayed, aping the lost animal that had pulled his cart. To the man, and my father, even the voice of his beloved donkey was beautiful music.

Vincenzo winked at me, then picked up the empty bottle of wine and danced with it for a dance partner. He swayed around the room, and his limp became more pronounced the more he danced, until his knee gave out. My father helped him to a chair, and Zia Nella held a handful of ice in a washcloth over his knee. Vincenzo sucked in air through gritted teeth. There were beads of sweat on his forehead.

"Stop making a fuss," Vincenzo said. He shooed Zia Nella and my father away. "I'm fine." But they doted on him as if they were his children.

They might as well have been. The war made them orphans. He came back for them, protected them, brought them to America—to their new selves.

"Look, the man is fine," Ziu Frank said, his mouth full of sliced capocollo from the antipasto plate.

"Does it hurt all the time?" I asked Vincenzo about his knee.

He shrugged with raised bushy eyebrows and an exaggerated frown. He took a handkerchief from his pants pocket and wiped his face. His eyes lit up at some thought that came to him before he spoke. "Sometimes, I can tell when it's going to rain."

"It's always going to rain, the way you talk," Zia Nella said. At the stove, she cracked the oven door open to check the lasagna. The way her skirt billowed reminded me of Gretel from the fairy tale, leaning into the fire to test its heat at the witch's prodding. "How many men does it take to burn lasagna?" she said. She took the baking dish from the oven and set it down on the stovetop. Then she breaded chicken cutlets and fried them golden brown and reheated the loaf of potato and sausage scacciata she'd made fresh that morning.

When lunch was ready, we sat around the card table, talking loudly and eating. Zia Nella and my father admonished Vincenzo to take it easy—he wasn't a young man anymore. Vincenzo boasted that he could still take on three men with one hand tied behind his back.

"Still?" Ziu Frank said. "That's not how I remember it." The tone in his voice was playful, familiar.

"Your memory isn't what it used to be," Vincenzo said. "Neither is your waistline."

Ziu Frank patted his quivering belly. It bulged out over the belt on his suit pants. "I eat well," he said. "It's true. But there's nothing wrong with my memory. There were two men and—"

Zia Nella silenced my ziu with a hand on his arm.

"There were three," my father said. He stabbed his fork into his lasagna. The tines scraping the plate sounded like fingernails on a chalkboard. "And you didn't take them on. I did."

"That's enough," Zia Nella said. There was a warning in her eyes—a fierceness I'd never seen before.

The men eyed one another in the serious quiet that followed. No one dared speak until my father raised his wineglass and said, "Buona Pasqua." Their glasses clinked and they echoed my father's words, "Happy Easter." And just like that, they shoved the past back into the dusty shoebox in the closet. But of all of them, my father should've known better. Each fall he preserved seeds from his best plants, drying and protecting them from the winter, until he could plant them again in the spring. The past wasn't something you just shoved away—it grew roots.

For dessert, we had a box of pastries stuffed with ricotta and honey and covered with candied fruits. Zia Nella cut slices of her braided Easter bread ring. Each slice of the golden bread held a dyed-blue hard-boiled egg. Standing at the stove, my father made espresso. He asked if we'd heard the joke about the newlywed couple who could not afford a honeymoon.

"David," Zia Nella said, "cover your ears." She held her hands up over her ears.

But I'd heard this one before. It was my father's favorite dirty joke.

"They spend their wedding night at the bride's mother's house," he said in Sicilian. "The husband, he takes off his shirt, and the bride, she runs upstairs. 'Mamma, Mamma,' she cries, 'he has hair all over his chest.' And the mother tells the daughter, 'That's okay, go downstairs and do what comes natural.'"

My father poured espresso into little white cups. "So she goes back downstairs," he said, passing the cups to the adults around the table. "She sees her husband take off his pants and runs to her mother crying that he has hair all over his legs, and the mother says, 'That's okay, that's okay, go downstairs and do what comes natural.' Then the husband takes off his socks, and the bride, she sees he has only two toes on one of his feet. She runs to her mother and says, 'Mamma, Mamma, he's got a foot and a half.' 'You stay here,' the mother says, 'I'll go downstairs.'"

The men erupted with laughter. Zia Nella slapped her brother's shoulder while she covered her mouth with a napkin to hide her giggle. They pulled apart pastries with sticky hands, cracked and peeled their blue eggs. They shouted over one another, laughing and licking powdered sugar from their fingers. Sunlight shone through the bay windows and threw their shadows on the wall—small shadows cast by their smaller, younger selves. The selves they left behind when they came here, carrying the ghosts of the people they could have been.

12

The week of Easter break, my peach fuzz got thicker and darker as the hair grew back in a swirl around the cowlick in the front. The familiar boy in the mirror again—a lost fish, struggling against the fisherman's hook, fooled by the flickering lure. Sam spent the week at his father's house in Stony Creek. The one time we talked on the phone, we talked about Halley's Comet, made plans to see it together.

I spent that time as I always did, alone in my room reading paperback novels that I'd bought in the science-fiction section of the used bookstore downtown, or in the high-ceilinged silence of the Russell Library, at a table in the old wing—an Episcopal church built from dark stone with stained-glass-topped windows and exposed serpentine ductwork overhead. The drop ceiling hid stone-ribbed, vaulted arches, the rib bones of an ancient dragon sheltering me in its nest among rows of books, the dragon's hoard, each printed work like captured light from long-dead stars. Tony never came in here—trolls didn't have much use for books.

~

My first Monday back in school, there was a new note in my locker. A stick figure in a hangman's noose. In the halls between classes, as locker doors clanked and slammed shut, and a river of students shouted over each other's heads, Tony crashed around me—a scoured boulder in his white-water rapids, now pitted and worn down to the size of a pebble. He made short, sudden lunges like he was going to hit me but then jerked his arm back. I cringed away from him. The smug expression on that troll's face said, *Made you flinch.* When I was alone at my locker, he snuck up behind me and pushed the back of my knee with his foot and laughed as I lost my balance and crumpled to the floor like a puppet whose strings had been cut.

Erosion changed the landscape. It wore down even the largest mountain. Small consolation. I started hauling all my textbooks with me in my backpack so I wouldn't have to go to my locker between classes, and if I saw Tony in the hall, I'd go the other way, the long way around. I'd sprint down near-empty halls with the warning bell signaling one minute before the next period, sliding into my seat just as the tardy bell rang. The threat of detention—for running in the halls or being late three times—was easily outweighed by Tony Morello grinding me down.

I used his note as a bookmark in the book I was reading on loan from the library, a hardback copy of *The Martian Chronicles*. I read and reread every chapter—at home, in study hall when I should've been studying, on the bus while Tony and Chris taunted me—and never grew tired of its Rocket Summer, its Silent Towns, its Million-Year Picnic. In the last chapter, the last story, a family fled to Mars, their home on Earth burning to a cinder behind them in one long, terrible war. That was the story I reread more than any other, until the words sunk in, like starlight finally reaching Earth. On Mars, the father burned the documents of their old lives in a campfire, and together the family looked at their reflections in the canal and saw their new Martian selves.

≈

Friday, April 11, Halley's Comet made its closest approach to Earth. Mr. Clark called it an apparition when he talked about our slim chances of seeing it because we were too far north. After school, I returned *The Martian Chronicles* to the library and ran straight home. My father walked along his garden path between rows of peas with a red plastic bucket. He dipped his hand into the bucket and splashed water around the soil of each little shoot, brushing the leaves with his damp hand.

"Can I go over to Sam's house to watch for Halley's Comet tonight?" I said. I stood in the driveway at the end of the row of potted tomato seedlings.

He stooped to pull a weed, careful to get at its root, and tossed it beyond the edge of his garden. "What's the matter?" he said. "You can't look at the sky in your own yard? You need your friend now to tell you how to look at stars?" He spread the soil around with his fingers, patting it down, where the weed had been.

"It's a comet, Dad. It won't come back for another seventy-six years."

"Life is here, David." He scooped a handful of dirt and held it out to me. "Not up there. Here, there is soil, good soil under your feet, and trees for shade right here in your own backyard." The dirt crumbled through his fingers and he wiped his palms clean. "You can do nothing about the sky."

"It's for school, for science class."

"Bah, scola." He took his hose, coiled on the lawn, and set the nozzle to a fine mist. He held it at an angle toward the sky to let the water fall as if it were rain on the long raised beds. "When you are born a donkey—" His fuzzy caterpillar unibrow crawled up his forehead, crinkled with worry or doubt. He shook his head and scrutinized me as if my face held the answer to the unspoken question—*How could you be mine?* "Wake up, David. I wait for that day when you wake up. Life is this," he said with his hand balled into a raised fist. "The sky won't help you."

He released the nozzle and motioned for me to shut off the water. Then my father coiled the hose around his arm and placed it on the hanger he'd made from scrap lumber. We moved the tomato seedlings inside and set them in the back hall on the wooden shelves, stained with dark circles from the potted plants.

My father took the brittle palm-leaf cross down from the wall above the seedlings, the cross I had brought home from Palm Sunday Mass. He fingered the ragged, crisp edges. "I catch you lying about where you're supposed to be or—" He rubbed my buzz cut.

"I won't. I promise."

"Where does this boy live?"

"Five minutes from here, near the university."

"Go," he said with a sweep of his arm. "Go, David. What do you think you find up there?"

Then he went outside to bury the brittle palm leaf in his garden, as he did every year, believing it blessed his crops.

~

In the basement, I pulled Tony's note from my pocket. I didn't want my father to see it. I didn't want him to think I couldn't handle it on my own. At the wood-burning stove, I lit a match and held the crinkled note above the yellow tooth of fire. The edge of the paper blackened and then blazed. I passed my hand through the flame. It didn't hurt, but it left a line of soot on my palm, where the heat had been. I dropped the note into the empty stove. It curled and flaked away into nothing.

13

Outside Sam's house, his silhouette and that of his mother seated at the dinner table flitted across the shade drawn over the large front window, its red shutters folded back like accordion bellows against the brick. Sam's shadow threw its arms out wide. The profile of his mother's head leaned back as if in laughter. If my mother and my long-ago uncles hadn't died, maybe my house would be like that, too—warm all the time.

I stuffed my hands in the pockets of my black sweatshirt and left, picking flowers out of people's front yards—early red tulips and yellow daffodils and pink azaleas. My mother used to slip into Indian Hill Cemetery late at night for stargazing, before she met my father. When she got sick, she made him promise to bury her at Indian Hill so she could be under the stars with the old brownstone chapel tucked away on the hillside and the gnarled trunks of thick old trees.

Thumping beats boomed from the staggered rows of a squat, brown university housing complex. Scraggly-haired students in leather jackets and studded denim huddled in the courtyard, red plastic cups and cigarettes in hand. They leaned into each other with ease—pale faces and steaming mouths. A girl with a shaved head in a black trench coat and stomping black boots whirled in a corner, adrift on the party's wild eddies. Sam's bedroom posters come to life. I slipped by them, invisible, down to Vine Street and the cemetery.

I climbed over the short stone wall and took the road that wound around the hill, past the chapel with the sheltered front entrance and the bell tower that shot up into the night sky. The rows of headstones and monuments, the faded ones and the new ones, they all looked alike at night. Shadows sprouting out of the earth.

A crimson maple with twisted trunk and branches leaned like a head of fire over my mother's grave on the grassy slope, her name carved in flat blue-gray granite. "Hi, Mom," I said. "I got a Mohawk. It's gone now. Dad didn't like it, but you would've thought it was cool. You would've convinced him to let me keep it." I toed the earth with my sneaker. "Well, maybe not, considering you wouldn't have liked how I got it." I arranged the flowers in a circle around her name—a floral wreath for a crown. I traced her letters with a finger, and a cool breeze rustled through the trees. Pulling the hood of my sweatshirt up over my head, I hunched my shoulders against the chill and sat with her the way I did when I was little, when I made my way here to her grave on my own and waited for my father to hold his hand out for me. I had never wanted to leave. I had dug my heels in, pulled against his grip, and kicked a thin layer of dirt into the air.

~

Up the winding road to the top of the hill, the peak stood without any gravestones, a smooth green dome rising above town. Some of the older kids at school said this hill was where the Mattabesett Indians were killed and buried by colonial settlers, and that's why there weren't any stones—no markers—because this hilltop was a mass grave.

I sat cross-legged and looked at the shapes of the headstones around the base of the hill in the dark and at the wall in the distance, and beyond, at the streets and houses with their cold little lights. From here,

Middletown—and everyone in it—felt small and strange like it was in another solar system entirely. I spread out on my back, searching the sky for Halley's Comet. The earth beneath me was hard and cool, and I wondered if it was the bones of the dead I was feeling.

The night was calm but for creaking branches and the low songs of crickets, a ceiling of sound between me and the stars. Right away, I spotted the Big and Little Dippers—the bears, Ursa Major and Ursa Minor. And my mother's voice—an echo out of time and space—cooed like a bird nudging its young out of the nest so it could learn how to fly. *Follow the arc of the Big Dipper handle. Follow it the way I showed you to the kite-shaped constellation, Boötes, the herdsman.*

He drove his plow and kept the heavens turning in a procession of stars.

Yes, went the dimples of her big smile.

My mother bought the glow-in-the-dark stars for my bedroom ceiling right before I started kindergarten. She told me we could put the stars anywhere I wanted, but I begged her to make them real. She stood on my mattress arranging them in patterns only her fingers knew. Then she turned off the lights and pulled the curtains closed. We lay side by side on my bed, my mother smelling like warm cocoa and a dash of cinnamon.

When I asked her what they meant, she showed me how to trace the shapes the stars formed. *See,* she said, *the two lines make a* V, and I said, *I don't see it,* and she pointed again and I shouted, *I see it!* Then she kissed my forehead and said, *That's the cord tying the fish together by their tails.* But I couldn't make out the fish, so she took my hand in her hand—her fingertips soft like mine—and together we traced the air. *Here,* she said, *follow the cord out to there and there. That's our sign, David. So if you're ever scared at night, you can look up and think of me and know you'll never be alone.*

But it was spring now, and Pisces wouldn't be out until the autumn. And even though this was the real sky, not the fake one my mother made for me, the one that never changed, I looked for the constellation anyway. Mr. Clark had said that looking into the night sky was like seeing into the past. Dead beauty engraved in the sky. Someday, a long, long time from now as the stars continued to move, the constellations would break apart, and all the old stories they told would be lost. One day, there would be no more Pisces in the sky. No more mother saving her son from a monster. But that day was so far in the future that it felt like those two fish would be together for an eternity. I'd been alone longer than the time I got to spend with my mother.

A thin brushstroke of light appeared parallel to the horizon, right where Pisces would be come October. According to Mr. Clark's handout, that was Halley's Comet. It had to be. The tail pointed away from the sun, swept outward by the heat. Debris from the surface layers stripped off. Out there, in space, the comet had passed the sun and now hurtled away toward the outer solar system. The pull of the sun pulling the comet back, stripping it down smaller and smaller with each orbit, disintegrating in its final trajectory into shooting stars burning up in our atmosphere. Streaks of color in the star-dappled night and then gone.

~

Later, after I'd gone home, I sat on the shingled roof of the back porch, legs bent up to my chest and arms around my knees. A quarter of the way up the cloudless sky hung the bright sliver of a waxing crescent moon. My father shuffled up the steep cement stairs to the backyard. He cursed when he shut the basement bulkhead door. It was old and heavy and the wood was rotting. He muttered about pulling the door off, replacing it with steel, how much that would cost. His shadow, thrown on the lawn by the outdoor light he'd left on for me, grew. It swept out, tall and thin, to the edge of his garden, then receded little by little into the surrounding darkness.

"David," he called out.

The porch steps creaked, and the metal chair's plastic seat cushion let out a long wheeze under the burden of his weight. "David," he called out again.

"Yeah."

"Go inside before you fall and break your neck."

I crawled back through the window and sat in the sill. The stars looked like the pin-sized holes on the tin grate in the confessional, and I turned away from them.

My father called for me a third time, drawing out the vowels in my name.

"Yeah."

"Scimunitu," he said. "Shut the window and go to bed."

I swung my legs around, dropped onto the hardwood floor, turned and brought the screen down hard. It locked into place with a click. Sitting there, elbows and chin resting on the sill, I stared through the dirty screen window. At the edge of the light, pea poles shot up into the night. The little shoots twining around the wood, just starting to climb.

My father went inside and turned off the porch light. He stepped back onto the porch, letting the door close behind him. "I see better this way," he said. He sat back down. The metal chair creaked, and the cushion farted. His deep, booming voice had grown quiet and thin.

In the kitchen, I spied on him from the bay windows. He took a photograph of my mother from his flannel-shirt pocket. She wore a black skirt and a white blouse with sparkles that caught the light. He touched the corners of the picture, ran his fingers over the surface as if to catch a stray hair and return it to its place. Then he turned to me in the window. His tired, bloodshot eyes invited me to join him.

Outside, I sat down beside him, one knee bent and pressed to my chest. Dirt caked the sewn rim of his work boots. The memory of her moved through the deep lines of his face. He showed me the photograph. "Do you remember her?" he said.

"Yeah."

"She was always buying white blouses, that woman, your mother. Our closet was full of them. So many I had to give away." He slipped the photo back into his shirt pocket, and then stood up from the creaking chair. He held the porch railing, looked out into the night, and asked me if I'd seen my comet, and I told him that I hadn't. I wanted to keep that moment for myself. "Maybe next time," he said. Then I asked my father if he saw his brothers, if his brothers ever came back to him, and he said, "They're gone. They can't come back."

But they did. They returned to him all the time. My mother, too. They were his stars, the ones that made up his constellation, and it was like Mr. Clark had said, it was looking into the past, the light was still there even though the star had died, and they were all pulling against one another, pulling my father in different directions, pulling me. All of us.

~

The next Monday at school, Sam asked me why I hadn't met him at his house to watch for the comet. I told him that my father wouldn't let me go and that I was sorry.

"It's okay," he said. "I couldn't see it. But we'll get another chance when we're like eighty."

"Eighty-nine," I said.

"Sounds like a plan." Sam clapped his arm around my shoulder, as if we were already old men, sitting in the yard waiting for Halley's Comet to come back around one more time.

14

When I was five years old, I cried at my mother's wake, wondering what I'd done that made her get sick and go away. What about my father? What if he got sick and went away, too? What would happen to me? I leaned into his strong arm. I wanted him to hug me, to take me in his arms and tell me it would be okay and that my mother was coming back and we would all be together again someday. But instead, his rough hand took hold of me. His thumb went all the way around the other side of my bicep and brushed the tips of his fingers. "Sit up," he whispered. So I sat up straight and wiped the tears from my face with my shirtsleeve. Maybe my father cried somewhere in private, the wounded part of him that he'd never show me.

My father shook hands with people offering their condolences, and he thanked them. His voice never cracked. Perfumed women kissed my cheek, and men who smelled of ashtrays and hard cheese patted me on the shoulder before walking back to the rows of chairs out front. They took their seats facing the closed casket. Vincenzo knelt down and hugged me. I threw my arms around his neck and wouldn't let go until Zia Nella pried my hands apart and kissed them and set me back in my chair.

Men in the funeral home parking lot smoked cigarettes beneath black umbrellas and muttered: *His brothers died, and now his wife. It is the curse. The curse has followed them.*

That night I stared at the green stars on my bedroom ceiling, trying to find something left of my mother that I could return to. The two fish tied together by the long cord of gravity, the Heavenly Knot. Venus and her son, Cupid. She had been born from the foam of the sea. The sea could save them both from the flames of the fire-monster Typhon. I climbed out of bed and went downstairs and out onto the back porch. I sat by my father's feet, holding my legs bent up to my chest. I pulled on the lace of his shoe and held it tight. He mussed my hair and let me stay out with him for a little while, like I was one of his tomato seedlings left out to harden before the last frost.

15

Monday nights in Catechism class, at bingo tables in the church basement, we learned the Apostles' Creed by heart. We recited the creed together and then wrote it out from memory in little blue books. Brother Calogero collected our books and checked them to see if we missed or changed a word. We repeated this exercise until the whole class could write and recite the creed from memory without error.

Sometimes Brother Calogero interrupted us with questions as the class read aloud in unison. He sat at his gray metal desk. His kind, untroubled face bowed down to his hands locked together, eyes closed. "What do you think that means?" he would ask us. When he posed this question about the fifth and sixth articles—*He descended into hell. On the third day he rose again. He ascended into heaven and is seated at the right hand of the Father*—Tony parroted a line the brother had often repeated, that the Lord had to suffer for the sins of man in both his body and his soul. Someone added that Christ went into hell to free the just who had died before him, and a smile pierced Brother Calogero's rosy cheeks, and he said, "This is also true."

We were supposed to find comfort in the idea that suffering begot salvation.

But my bruises from Tony's shoulder-checking me into pencil-yellow cinder block walls or gunmetal banisters at school didn't save me. His notes, slipped through my locker vents, meant to intimidate and shame me, dared me to send them back like a teacher would, all marked up. I took his notes home and shoved them in an old shoebox under my bed. My father had his box of secrets. Now I had mine.

In late April, Sam's mother bought him a used acoustic guitar and a series of half-hour lessons from a guitarist at River's Music on Main Street. When he completed his Monday-night lessons, he'd wait for me at Vincenzo's café, and I'd walk over from the church as soon as my Catechism class let out. The Monday night before the Saint Sebastian festival weekend, less than three weeks before confirmation, Sam and I sat in the corner booth. The evening rush of customers had slowed to one harried mother wrangling two young children to sit quietly with their picture books while she puzzled over the paper's crossword and drank a cup of coffee. Sam took his guitar out of its gig bag and showed me what he had learned—campfire chords, he called them. He clutched the neck near the headstock, strummed, and said, "This is a G. And if you move your fingers like this—" His wrist tensed. He barred the bottom two strings on the first fret with his index finger and stretched his middle and third fingers to notes on the second and third frets. "You get an F." He played the chord. It thunked like stiff cardboard. "That's a hard one," he said.

The woman glanced up at us over the rim of her large-framed glasses. The top of her pen pressed against her pursed lips.

"Hey, boys," Vincenzo said. He stood behind the counter with a rag in his hand. "Why don't you do that upstairs?" He gave me the key for the door at the top of the stairs behind the stockroom.

The door to his studio apartment opened into a small galley kitchen. An old metal cooking pot and a crusty cast-iron skillet hung from S-hooks on a rod above the stove. The faucet dripped into the porcelain sink, stained brown where the water plopped. I overtightened the faucet handle and the drip slowed. Sam set his guitar down on the plaid couch flanked by a pair of unmatched wooden chairs. He craned his neck at the bare off-white walls that hadn't been painted in years. Opposite the couch, hand-built raw-wood shelving ran the length of the wall under three street-facing windows. The wood bowed from the weight of double-stacked books in Italian and English—the only indication that anyone lived here.

"Where does he sleep?" Sam lifted a cushion and peered at the pull-out bed tucked inside. He leaned over the backrest and fished out a worn canvas pack from behind the sofa. He sat cross-legged on the floor with the pack in his lap. "Holy shit," he said. He drew a long, thin-bladed knife, blued with age, from a leather and brass scabbard. "A bayonet!" He inspected the pitted wood and steel handle, read aloud the word—*Terni*—stamped on the blade, and tested the weight of the weapon in his hand. "Wicked."

"We shouldn't go through Vincenzo's stuff," I said.

"But this is so cool." Sam set the bayonet down on the floor, took out a cloth-wrapped bundle, and unfolded it. He picked up each item and set them down again—dented aluminum cups, a tin opener, and a three-pronged fork—until he held the canteen. It bore the faded markings of the Italian Royal Army—REI, Regio Esercito Italiano. Then he saw the enameled lapel badge with a fasces in the center of the national colors of Italy and the letters *PNF*. "Who is this guy?"

I grabbed the pack from Sam. "No one," I said. "He was just a soldier. That's all." I nested the cups, wrapped them up with the other items, and put them back, moving a rusty first-aid kit box and a large manila envelope thick with documents to make space. An old, crinkled map poked out of the torn side seam of a small canvas map case. Stenciled on the front flap were the initials *US*. I eased the map out. The three-pointed island of Sicily unfurled like an accordion in my hands. Smudged notes filled the margins in German and penciled arrow lines crisscrossed the printed grid. A braillelike texture dotted the surface.

I turned the map over. Handwritten names in black cursive ink strokes were crammed onto the back, an illegible list but for the last two: *Emanuele Vassallo, Leonello Vassallo.* My uncles, but with a last name different from mine.

"Vassallo." I tested the sound of that family name on the air. It left my lips a thin and hollow noise, a misplayed campfire chord. Whatever history it carried, it wasn't mine. My father had made sure of that.

I held the map faceup again. A black-ink swirl encircled the village of Melilli. An ash halo around an old, dying star. I pressed my smaller thumb against a larger bloodstained thumbprint that covered one of the Aeolian Islands—a volcanic archipelago dotting the sea off the northern tip of Sicily—and words spilled out of me like prisoners in a prison break: The story of the twins and how my father tried to save them. How he faced down Rocco Morello in the street. The box of festival bulletins in his closet, the photos from Melilli, the one of him and Rocco together there as children.

Sam sat back on his haunches, his knees under him. What I must have looked like to him in that moment with all the inmates gone. I imagined this silence was what it must be like just before you die. You touch on something strange and big, get a catch in your throat, and the words never come.

"My family is so boring compared to yours," Sam said. "You think he was in the Mafia?" Sam jutted out his chin, pinched his hands together in the air, and in a bad Marlon Brando impression from *The Godfather,* he said: "Your father, he came to me seeking justice for the death of his brothers."

"I'm serious," I said. But I was laughing, too. "Why would they change their names?"

16

Who were the Vassallos? And what did it mean to not know I was one?

When I was younger, my father liked to say that I was always with my face in a book. Even at the card table in the kitchen, I flattened paperbacks out with one arm so I could read while eating. He told me not to, but I did it anyway, until one day he got sick of it. He grabbed my book, lost my place, and set it on the counter. "After dinner," he said. But I retrieved the book and marched back to the table. He laughed at my defiance and told me that I was either brave or stupid, and then he bent me over his knee and spanked me and asked me which one it was. When he released me, I ran to my bedroom in tears and slammed the door. I never read at the kitchen table again. My father had his answer.

I was an alien to him. That was what he said when he said the words: *You are always with your face in a book.* And it made me think of Mr. Spock on *Star Trek*, how he suppressed his human half. The half he inherited from his mother. My mother was American.

Who were the Vassallos?

At the library, I flipped through a book on the Second World War, pages and pages of black-and-white photographs of soldiers dead in the dirt and soldiers with their rifles hugging the dirt, bombed-out homes and a barefoot boy in tattered clothes. He stood in a pile of rubble, held his filthy face with filthy hands. That boy—he could've been my father captured on film moments after the explosion that pulled his brothers, in pieces, away from him. His life before, the one he and my zia left behind when they came here. He got as far away from Sicily as he could, crossed an ocean, and learned a new language. But inside, his thoughts were still Sicilian, bound by a basaltic life. Inside, he smoldered.

My father liked to talk about all the great men of history—all Italians, of course. Galileo Galilei. Guglielmo Marconi, no relation, the true inventor of radio. Amerigo Vespucci, a navigator so great that two continents bore his name. But my father never spoke of the Vassallos.

~

On the third Friday in May, opening night of the Saint Sebastian festival, Vincenzo and I were first in line for the Ferris wheel. The wheel cut a towering profile against the rectory, lit by ground-level spotlights. The hub flashed a beam of light that swept around the spokes like a pulsar.

Vincenzo patted the operator's arm while slipping him a pack of cigarettes in a firm handshake. He never bought tickets for rides or food at the festival. He never needed them. He bartered and traded favors. For three days, he was a king walking among his subjects.

The Ferris wheel carried us high above the red-tiled roof of the church and came to a stop at the apex of a revolution. Our gondola swayed back and forth. I squinted against the breeze. Below us, neat rows of houses with little yards sprawled eastward into a zone of commercial brick buildings and parking lots, long rows of old tenements fronting Main Street and ending in the North End at the Arrigoni Bridge. Dark against a pink-and-purple sky, the bridge's two steel arches spanned the Connecticut River into Portland. A ribbon of asphalt—the Route 9 corridor—separated downtown from the waterfront's Harbor Park boardwalk at the elbow of the river.

Who were the Vassallos? That unanswered question was a black hole my family spiraled around. Without knowing that hole had ever existed, I'd lived my life feeling as if something was missing—an amputee and his phantom limb. The ache of nothingness.

"How's school?" Vincenzo asked me.

"How come you never had any kids of your own?"

Vincenzo scratched one of his long wiry sideburns and looked down at his café. "There was a woman in Rome," he said. "Maria." He whistled and shook his hand, swaying a limp wrist. "She was something else. We could have—" His shoulders slumped with the memory. He circled his own unanswered question. "Beh, that's life," he said. He mussed my hair. "Don't worry. You'll meet a nice girl someday."

"But what happened?"

"Beh, what happened. I was too young, too caught up in what I'd lost to see what I'd found. I was no good for her." He fixed his sights on the bridge in the distance. "Sometimes love, it's not enough. For some, it's too much." He tapped his temple with an index finger. "It makes them crazy."

My father and my zia severed themselves from their surname, but they could not stop circling their lost brothers. What did Vincenzo lose that made him cut this woman from his life yet still invite her memory to haunt him?

"Everything okay? That Morello boy, Tony, he still giving you trouble?"

Vincenzo asked the question with such kindness, and I could see in the way he pressed me to him that he only wanted to help. So I sank into Vincenzo's arm and told him what I could not tell my father.

"Notes?" Vincenzo raised his black bushy eyebrows. "What kind of notes? He threatening you?"

"Promise me you won't tell anyone. It'll only make things worse."

"Family is everything, David. A wolf pack, stronger than steel. No outsider can break the pack that stays together. Let me tell you something. When I was your age, there was this boy in school, a real troublemaker, wouldn't leave me alone. Bigger than me. Maybe a year or two older. People like that, people like Tony, you have to make them respect you."

"How?"

Vincenzo made a fist. "With this." He held his knuckles to the tip of my nose. "These people, they go to school their whole lives and still they learn nothing. You understand? Tony bothers you again, you punch him in the nose. He still doesn't learn, you hit him and you keep hitting him until he stays down. You show him what it means to go up against us, show him that you are fierce like the wolf. You do that—" He mimed washing his hands. "Problem solved."

I tilted my head back over the rim of the seat. We were wolves. Our gondola jerked and swayed. The dizzying feeling of falling into the sky lessened as we were brought low to the ground by our slow, creaking orbit around a neon star sputtering with life.

17

In an hour, Sam met me at the café. Loud Italian music from the festival's PA system spilled out into the evening and echoed off the walls of nearby buildings. We opened the umbrellas over the sidewalk tables and wiped the tabletops clean. Inside, Vincenzo turned on the espresso machines and heated the little cups with the steam nozzles. He opened a bag of coffee from the freezer and poured the beans into the grinder.

A short, fat man walked in—an Italian, overweight version of Steve McQueen with wool trousers, a blue turtleneck, and a tweed blazer with a matching flat cap. He held a metal cashbox tucked under his arm.

Vincenzo filled the filter cup with ground coffee, tamped it down, and motioned with his head for the man to go into the stockroom. When the man returned, he had Marlboro cartons sticking out of his blazer's side flap pockets. He stepped out of the propped-open door and tipped his hat to us, then crossed the street into the festival crowd.

"David," Vincenzo called from the counter. "Help me with something. Your friend, too."

Café supplies lined the metal shelves of the stockroom—espresso machine cleaners and accessories, glass bottles of sparkling water and cans of soda, coffee filters and stacked cases of beer. Marlboro cigarette cartons in uneven stacks two rows deep took up shelf space above the beer.

Vincenzo didn't smoke. He sold the cigarettes for favors or extra pocket money, "a little business on the side," he liked to call it while pushing the tip of his nose sideways with his index finger. He reached behind the cartons where the other man had stashed the cashbox filled with tickets for the festival, and gave me half a roll for all the rides, games, and food we wanted.

I tore the tickets from the perforated ticket roll and divided the spoils between Sam and me. "You can't tell anyone," I said, stuffing my denim-jacket pockets. He zipped his lips with an imaginary zipper. Then we brought out bottles of sparkling water and cans of soda and stocked the refrigerated case.

"Okay, boys," Vincenzo said. "Go have fun. But be careful, eh? I mean it." He pointed his first two fingers at his eyes, then out at the festival and said, "I got eyes out there. You understand? Don't make trouble unless trouble makes you."

∿

A galaxy of green and red lights hummed above our heads. A canopy of stars pulled down to Earth and strung on a wire from concession stands to game booths to all the rides. Bumper cars bounced against one another, their drivers laughing and turning steering wheels wide. The galleon whirred to life. It swayed back and forth in wider arcs, sweeping higher with each swing. Children with cotton candy and candied apples squealed and chased each other. They darted and wove through the maze of teenagers and adults.

At the pizza fritta stand, Fulvia stood with one hand on her hip and a metal serving spoon in the other. She owned the flower shop on Pease Avenue and always wore her silver hair in a long braid. I pulled out a clump of tickets from my pocket and counted out enough for two orders topped with tomato sauce and grated Parmesan.

She spooned sauce over the fried dough, sprinkled on the cheese, and handed us our food on two paper plates. "You got a guardian angel in Vincenzo," she said. "Be good to him."

I turned around and my paper plate flipped up against the white T-shirt under Tony Morello's red leather zipper jacket. The fried dough snailed down the front of his shirt in a trail of tomato sauce and then flopped on the pavement. Our sneakers were splattered red.

What happened next, happened fast: Tony grabbed my collar and pulled back his free arm, hand balled into a trembling fist. Fulvia darted around the table, shaking a clean spoon and cursing in Sicilian. And Chris Cardella inched back from the fray, a frightened dog about to bolt. "Come on," he said. "We're supposed to stay away from him."

"Moonwalk on out of here, Michael Jackson," Sam said.

"I can fight my own battles," I said.

Fulvia caught hold of a clump of Tony's curly hair and pulled him off me. She pushed the troll down over the table, his pimpled face pressed sideways on a stack of paper plates, and thwacked his backside with the metal spoon. She was thick, strong for a woman her age. "You want me"—she paddled him while spitting each word—"to tell your father?" Two more blows, each one harder than the last, two exclamation points for Tony's ass. He winced, his face tightening with each strike, but he did not cry. Fulvia had pulled the pin from a hand grenade, and she was about to release the handle.

"No," he said. His violence tempered for the moment. "Don't tell him."

When she let go of Tony, she patted his cheek and said, "Smart boy. Now clean that up." Then she stepped back behind the table and fixed me another pizza fritta.

Tony scooped the fried dough off the pavement and tossed it into a trash bin. "I'll get you for this, Marconi," he whispered.

"Let's go," Chris said. He tugged on Tony's jacket sleeve. "Your dad will do more than spank you with a spoon if he finds out."

"Shut up." Tony jerked his arm free. "You shut the hell up." His slow-burning fuse turned on Sam next. "And you." He poked him in the chest. "No one told me to stay away from you."

Sam swatted Tony's finger away like it was a mosquito.

A snaggletoothed sneer curled Tony's lip. He knew that Fulvia watched him now, that she had been drafted into Vincenzo's army of snitches who looked out for me. *I got eyes out there.* Tony tossed up his hands in mock dismissal and said, "See you around, ladies." *You can't hide behind that Fascist forever.* Then he marched a slow, crooked retreat through the crowd with Chris tagging along after him.

⌀

Fulvia hadn't done me any favors. She'd only made things worse, and now I would end up paying for her well-intentioned mistake. On the church steps, Sam and I ate from our greasy paper plates. He wiped his mouth with the back of his hand and asked me if I was okay. I shrugged. No one could help me escape from Tony's malice. I had to meet it head-on. I had to be faster, meaner, and more brutal, the way Vincenzo had told me to be. Only then would Tony leave me alone.

Sam leaned forward with his elbows on his knees and said, "Don't worry. We're a team. I'll always have your back."

"Like family," I said. And Sam spit into his hand, held it out to me, and said, "Brothers." "Brothers," I echoed and spit into my own hand, and we shook on it.

⌀

In the church vestibule, Brother Calogero opened boxes with a utility knife. He pulled out bulletins and stacked them in neat piles on a table set up in the corner. When he saw me, he smiled and motioned his head toward the stack. "Take one," he said.

Back outside on the steps, I sat down next to Sam. "The bulletins I told you about in my father's closet," I said. A photograph of the statue of Saint Sebastian filled the first page. The statue wore a large red sash and a skirt of dollar bills that draped to the floor. On the next page, the story of the life of the saint and his martyrdom spooled out in a riddle of misspelled words and punctuation errors. Sebastian served the Roman Empire as captain of the Praetorian Guard and, in secret, cured the sick with prayers. He consoled imprisoned Christians until betrayed and sentenced to death. But the arrows failed to kill him. Refusing to flee Rome, he confronted the emperor, and the emperor had him bludgeoned to death. Over a thousand years later, a statue of the saint washed ashore in Sicily. Peasants from Melilli carried it to their village when no one else could lift it. They called him their soldier-saint—and he had been, a soldier in life and in death.

"I don't get it," Sam said. "What's the big deal about that?"

"That is everything," Rocco boomed. A cigarette dangled from his mouth, ash falling at each word. He leaned against the stone railing in his black pinstriped suit and a button-down white shirt, open at the collar, showing curly, gray chest hair and a red horn pendant that was long and twisted like the horn of an antelope.

I let the bulletin fall shut and set it on the steps beside me. "You and my father were friends once."

"Friends," he said. He ground his cigarette butt into the heel of his dress shoe and flicked the butt onto the sidewalk. "Your family and mine, we carried the statue home, we built the church. Long years our families lived and worked side by side by the grace of God and our soldier-saint. But your father—we weren't enough for him. He turned his back on us."

Rocco's mouth fixed into a thin, taut line. His eyes narrowed at yellow-flowering weeds swaying from a crack in the concrete. "Friends," he said again. "We were like brothers. Before he broke my heart, before—" He held up his hands and stared at them like he didn't recognize the swollen hairy knuckles, the bony swan-neck fingers, and the three crooked fingers of his left hand ending at the upper joints.

The leathery skin of his face twitched with a memory. He waved his deformed hands in the air like he was erasing something between us. "Stay away from him," he said to Sam. "Stay away from his family. The saint has cursed them all." Then he kissed his pendant and hurried up the sidewalk to the rectory.

"What do you think happened to his fingers?" Sam asked.

I stuffed my hand into my jeans pocket and felt the note Tony left for me today in my locker. "I don't know," I said, "but I bet he deserved it." I balled the slip of paper in my fist and said, "Let's find Tony."

18

We made a plan. Sam would wait in a vacant corner of the lot, behind the empty stage truck where bands played in the earlier hours of the festival. I would be the bait.

I wandered through the concession tent and around the game booths, past the swing ride and the Tilt-A-Whirl, until I found Tony and Chris riding wooden horses on the carousel.

"That ride's for girls!" I shouted over the music from the calliope.

Tony climbed down from his bobbing white stallion. It felt good to see that boy jump when I called. He zigzagged between the rows of horses, grabbing hold of barley-twist poles like a monkey swinging from tree to tree. But Chris would not follow. He remained, steadfast, on his black horse even as Tony went back for him and tried pulling him down off the saddle. Chris gripped the pole tighter and cocked his head away from his friend's invective.

The operator, an old man with a thick gray mustache and cigarette-stained teeth, cut the ride short. "Scemu," he said. The carousel slowed. He chastised Tony to wait until it came to a full stop—and to not bother getting back on for the rest of the festival. But Tony stepped off the still-moving platform, straightened his jacket, and lumbered through the young children with sticky, cotton-candied fingers forming a line with their parents.

Seconds passed, but to me those seconds felt like hours. The Vassallo name echoed in my mind—the name my father had left behind. The invisible name I had not known I carried. It muted the whirring machinery and blaring music and shrieking children. I exploded into a run for the stage truck. Tony gave chase. His thundering hooves dampened when Sam swept down from the starless shadows like a cleansing storm, a dark fist that landed the first blow. I grabbed a fistful of Tony's curly hair and pulled his head back. His arms flailed—the monkey lost his balance and toppled backward, and I punched him in his side as he went down. He hit the asphalt hard. His eyes widened, and he covered his face with his arms. All this time, Tony Morello should have feared me.

I kicked him, and Sam joined in, kicking him again with more force. We fought like wolves. We snarled and growled. "Son of a bitch," I yelled. "You son of a bitch." We were the children of the sickle-winged colossus, and no one, not even the gods, could stand against us. I straddled Tony, my knees pinning his arms. I became the mountain and the fire thrown by Typhon. I stuffed Tony's note into his mouth. "Eat it," I said, forcing his jaw shut.

Tony spit out the note and bucked me off him. We staggered to our feet. He stood frozen in place as if petrified by Medusa's glare. My hands shook. The pulsing rhythm of my heart beating in my ears goaded me on. My fist hurled at him like one of Typhon's boulders. Sam swung at him, too, but Tony's tree-trunk arm blocked the blow. He struck Sam's face with a left hook. Sam stumbled back. One step. Then two. Tony lunged at me, arms swinging wide like a windmill. But my fist landed first—the weight of a thousand days of bullying breaking his nose. Blood flowed over his mouth and down his chin, mixing with the tomato-sauce stain on his T-shirt. He cradled his nose and howled.

"Boys, break it up." Two police officers rounded the stage truck. One made for Tony, the other corralled me and Sam.

I tried to shake the pain from my hand but it remained, a dull throbbing soreness like a toothache in my knuckles.

"You okay?" I asked Sam. And a smile crept across his bloodied and bruised face, framed by all the spinning colors of the festival behind him. The light made his sandy-blond hair—bangs fluttering in the breeze—look like flames licking at the night sky.

~

At Vincenzo's café, the police officer instructed us to sit down in the front corner booth. His partner had taken Tony to the rectory. The café grew quiet. The patrons watched the cop remove his hat and approach Vincenzo at the counter. The two spoke in hushed voices. We sat on our knees and leaned over the seat backs, trying to hear what they were saying.

Vincenzo shook the officer's hand and poured him a cup of coffee, then motioned for us to join them at the register.

"Tony was harassing David," Sam blurted.

"Take it easy," the cop said, sipping his coffee. "That boy did a number on you, huh?" Then he knelt down at eye level with Sam. His forearms all scratched up and bloodied. His lower lip bruised and swollen. "Tony jumped you, isn't that right? And your friend here." The cop thumbed at me. "Your friend stepped in to help."

Vincenzo patted my cheek and said, "He tells me you got him good."

"I did," I said. Then I rubbed the bruised and swollen knuckles of my fist, like they were a prize I'd won from one of the game booths at the festival.

The officer finished his coffee and put his hat back on. "Ice that," he said. Then he winked at me and left the café.

Patron voices rose in his wake, layers of conversations in Sicilian mixed with English words. Some of the men wanted to know what was wrong with Sam's hair. They wondered whether the barber had been drunk when the boy got it cut. Other men whispered in conspiratorial tones that no bad tree bears good fruit.

Vincenzo chopped the air with his hands held together as if in prayer. "What do we got in here," he said, "a bunch of old ladies?"

The idle chatter ended. The hum of benign conversation returned. Sam and I took turns in the bathroom, cleaning the dirt and blood from our faces and hands. My father arrived and waited at the bar for me to finish. He motioned with his hand. "Come here," he said. He sized me up as if he'd never seen me before this evening. He studied my face, took my hands into his, and turned them over.

"What're you doing?"

"Eh, looking," he said. Then he held his own bigger hands next to mine and nodded yes, an answer to some question that only he had heard.

"Am I in trouble?"

"No." He smiled, his face brightened, and it made him look younger. "Go. Enjoy the festival."

~

At the concession tent for Italian ice, I ordered almond ice and Sam ordered lemon. Then we sat on the bench near the ticket booth. Inside, we saw the man who had exchanged the tickets for cigarettes at the café. He tipped his hat to us. I waved to him and then said, "Let's go on a ride." I jumped up from my seat. "We've got all these tickets to use."

19

The unveiling of the statue of Saint Sebastian took place on Saturday afternoon. A line formed in front of the side altar and snaked all the way to the confession booths at the back of the church. At the entrance, Brother Calogero handed out safety pins from a collection basket. Zia Nella and I waited in line. When I was little, Vincenzo brought me here before the crowds formed. *First in line,* he'd say, and then he'd lift me up so I could reach the statue with the dollar bill he gave me. *Oh, you're so heavy,* he'd say. *Pretty soon I won't be able to pick you up.* Then I'd ask him, *Will I be big like my daddy?* And he'd say, *Bigger.*

"Zia," I whispered. "Tell me about the Vassallos."

Her walnut eyes grew wide, my question cracking open those two hardened shells. She pulled me into her blouse, smelling of almond paste and powdered sugar. "That family is gone," she spoke low into my ear, a lie. "There are no more left." She kissed my bruised knuckles before letting me go.

Father Salafia pulled the cord that opened the red curtain, revealing the plaster saint. It stood on a pedestal, arms pulled back around a white Roman column. The feathered ends of arrows, hand carved and painted green, stuck out of the statue's chest and its left flank, thigh, and upper arm.

"Look," Zia Nella said. She showed me my mother's picture from the bulletin tucked in the handbag under her arm. It wasn't the small, grainy headshot from previous years. This was the color photo my father had the night Halley's Comet swung by Earth. It was larger, more like the way I remembered her. It brightened the page.

"That came out nice," she whispered. "I found the picture in your father's laundry basket, in one of his shirt pockets." She handed me the bulletin. "Keep it."

The line moved forward. Soon, it was our turn. Zia Nella rested her hands on my shoulders, steering me toward the statue. I pinned the five-dollar bill my father had given me to the saint's red sash.

~

After Mass the next morning, Zia Nella and I sat at one of the sidewalk tables outside Vincenzo's café. We ate slices of her almond cake. People congregating on the sidewalks spilled out onto Washington Street. My father and Ziu Frank sat inside at the bar, sipping espresso. Sam filled the refrigerated case with bottles of Orangina from the stockroom. This was the first time in years my father had come even this close to the festival with me.

"Here they come," Vincenzo said. He propped open the door with a splintered wood wedge.

A fervent army of men, women, and children ran down Washington Street. They wore white shirts, white pants, and white socks, though some were barefoot. Red diagonal sashes crossed their chests from right shoulders to left waists. They held bouquets high above their heads while chanting, "E chiamamulu paisanu. Prima Diu e Sammastianu." He is one of our own. First God, and then Saint Sebastian.

"Salvatore," Zia Nella said. "Frank. Come out here."

"You know how many times we've seen that," my father called out from inside the café.

The runners stormed the church.

"What are they doing?" Sam asked. He sat down next to me. Nella cut him a slice of cake.

"Declaring their loyalty to God and the saint," Vincenzo said. "They are saying, the saint is one of them, a paisanu. You know what that word means? It's like the way you and David fought for each other. You understand? It's the same thing."

Sam nudged me and said, "Hey, paisanu." Then he blew at his bangs. They floated up and came back down in front of his face.

I fake elbowed him in his side. He scrunched up his face in mock pain and threw himself off the plastic chair in slow motion. The chair kicked out from under his feet and fell on top of him.

Zia Nella scolded us for fooling around.

Vincenzo told her to let us be boys.

"You okay?" my father asked. He stood in the doorway.

I righted the chair and said, "We're fine."

Sam sat up, chewing the ends of a few strands of his hair. "I'm cool," he said.

Across the street, men carried the statue of Saint Sebastian on a wooden pallet out of the church. And a mass of the faithful followed close behind them. "Be careful," my father said.

∾

The festival crowd thinned out by midafternoon, the last hours of the three-day feast. In our little enclave, my father was the first to leave. He didn't want to lose the light of the day. There was work in the garden that needed his attention. "Don't let Vincenzo keep you too late," my father said. He marched up the street, hands clasped behind his back, head turned toward home. He rounded the corner, and I lost him behind a row of houses on Pearl Street. Everything he ever needed in life, he grew from working the soil. His plants, the peppers and tomatoes and greens, those were all the words and thoughts he wanted to tell me but could not.

Sometimes, when you no longer see a person, you begin to see them more clearly.

Soon, my zia and ziu said their goodbyes. She kissed my cheek and he pinched it. Her amaretto scent lingered in the air long after she was gone. Then Sam's mother called the café looking for him, and he had to go home, too. I stood in the doorway. Vincenzo and a few scattered customers remained.

The man from the ticket booth came in and sat down at a table by himself. He took off his flat cap and held it in his hands in his lap. Vincenzo sat down beside him. They made small talk. Under the table, Vincenzo dropped two cigarette packs into the cap. In one quick motion, the man flipped the hat back onto his head. Then he fished in the breast pocket of his tweed blazer for tickets. He put them down on the table under the cover of his palm. Vincenzo slipped his hand over the tickets as the man stood up to go.

"David." Vincenzo called me over to him. He slid his hand off the table and into his shirt pocket. "All set for tonight," he said with a wink. "Our last spin on the Ferris wheel like always, eh?"

The sun glinted off the café window into my squinting eyes. My father worked the soil alone under the heat from that light. "Maybe I should go home," I said, "see if my father needs anything. You wouldn't mind, would you?"

"No," Vincenzo said. "Go. Be with your papà."

～

At home, I found the hose hooked up to the outside spigot and snaked across the lawn. A garden rake leaned against a wheelbarrow at the edge of the garden beds. My father stooped between tomato rows. He stabbed the soil near the root of a weed with his hand weeder. Then he pushed down on the handle and tore up the root.

"Dad," I said. "Papà, you need help?"

He looked over at me, tossing the weed into the wheelbarrow. He picked up a hand rake in the dirt by his feet and gave it to me. I crouched in the row beside him. His thick, calloused hands loosened the roots of a dandelion that hadn't bloomed. He pulled it out, shook off the soil, and dropped it into a brown paper bag. "We eat these," he said.

I answered him by freeing a dandelion with my rake. Seeds from the white seed head sailed on a breeze. He lifted his head for a moment and watched them sail over the wire fence into the neighbor's yard. I tossed the weed into the wheelbarrow. He turned to me with eyes tight like the spiral arms of two distant galaxies seen head on. He grunted his approval.

We worked together in the garden in silence until the work was done.

20

I didn't see Tony in school the next day. Chris stopped me in the hall between classes and told me how Tony's father had beaten him, whipped him with the buckle end of his belt for picking a fight with me at the festival. Chris saw it all, standing in the flower bed outside their open kitchen window. Tony's mother got between Rocco and her son. She held her arms up in the air and pleaded with her husband that the boy had taken about as much as a boy his age could take. Rocco slapped her. She fell back against flat-paneled plywood cabinets. Then he chased Tony out of the house, and Tony tripped on the back-porch stairs and broke his left arm in the fall.

"It's your fault," Chris said. His backpack, dangling at the end of his right arm, swayed back and forth like a criminal on the gallows. "It's true, what they say about you. You're bad luck."

"I guess you better stay away from me then."

He stepped back. "It was all Tony," he said. "You know that, right? I have no beef with you. We're cool." He handed me a slip of paper.

"Love notes," I said. "From you, or Tony?" I crumpled it up without reading it and tossed it back at Chris.

～

That evening, Tony showed up for our final Catechism class. He had a swollen, crooked nose, purple bruises on his face, and his broken arm in a fresh plaster long arm cast. He sat alone in the last row of bingo tables at the far end of the church basement. Chris sat in the front. Several minutes before class ended at seven o'clock, Father Salafia joined us. He strode to the front of the room in his black suit and clerical collar, Buddy Holly glasses, and a comb-over that wasn't fooling anyone. He cleaned his glasses with a white handkerchief, held them up to the fluorescent lights for inspection, and set them back on his nose, marbled with broken capillaries. Then he launched into a meandering speech on the importance of the sacrament of confirmation in our lives and in our relationship with God. He closed with a reminder about confirmation rehearsal the following week. Then he dismissed everyone except Tony and me.

"Why can't I go?" I asked.

Father Salafia took hold of my upper arm, pulling me out of my seat. He walked me to Tony's table and sat me down across from him. Then the priest tilted the nearest folding chair on its back legs, dragging it to the head of the table. He sank into the padded seat with a sigh.

"Boys," Father Salafia said. His breath smelled like onions and coffee. He lectured us about how we had disappointed him. How we'd disappointed the Lord, our families, and the church. How we'd let down our confirmation sponsors—our spiritual guides. Then he leaned back in his chair, patted his potbelly, and asked us if there was something we wanted to say to each other.

Tony scratched under his cast with the eraser end of a pencil and said, "This isn't over."

"Looks over to me," I said. "May I be excused now?"

Father Salafia threw up his hands. "You may go," he said. "I will continue this conversation with both of your fathers and your sponsors."

I bolted from the church basement and crossed the street to Vincenzo's café.

"What's chasing you?" Vincenzo said. He looked out the window and pursed his lips when he saw Tony leaving the church. "Tell you what," Vincenzo said with a hand on my shoulder. "What do you say we close early and make dinner? We'll give your zia a rest tonight."

We dragged the sidewalk tables and chairs inside the café, and then went out again. Vincenzo locked the door. He pulled down the red security grille and fastened it with a padlock. We walked home in the warm evening light. He asked me about school. I told him Sam had invited me to spend the coming weekend at his father's house by the water in Stony Creek and how I didn't think my father would let me go.

"I'll see what I can do to maybe steer your papà in the right direction," Vincenzo said. He mussed my spiky hair and then left his hand on my shoulder, guiding me home.

At the card table in the kitchen, I finished my homework. Vincenzo cooked rigatoni with rapini and sausage in spicy tomato sauce. He looked silly wearing Zia Nella's pink floral-print apron, and he knew it and he didn't care. He did a little dance while adding basil leaves to the saucepan and sang "O Sole Mio" into his wooden spoon. He made the house feel light, made me feel light, the way a dancer pirouetting on stage made an audience forget gravity.

"Is it true," I asked, "what Rocco said about us? That we're cursed."

"Don't ever say that." Vincenzo spun from the stove, wagging the spoon at me as he whirled. Sauce splattered the table edge. "Don't even think it."

I flinched away from him. You could forget gravity, but gravity wouldn't forget you. "I'm sorry," I said.

He looked at the spoon as if just realizing it was in his hand, then at the speckles of strained tomatoes on the table. He let out a sigh, a balloon deflating. "Superstition," he said. "Don't give this idea power over you. It does not deserve your belief." Then he wiped the tabletop clean.

❦

When my father's car pulled into the driveway, I cleared my school-books and papers from the table and set out the plates. Vincenzo dished out the servings. My father clomped in through the cellar, hefting the weight of a fat jug of wine, red like old schoolhouse bricks. He turned with the bottle in his hands, as if to show us a newborn in his arms, so we could see my name on the strip of masking tape. "Want to try it?" he asked me.

Vincenzo raised his eyebrows, nodding at the gallon glass jug. The strip of tape had yellowed and dulled with time. But there was a fire in my father's perfect curling letters, a fire that time could not dull or put out.

"Okay," I said.

My father set it down on the counter. He removed the cork. "Let it breathe," he said. He washed the factory from his hands at the kitchen sink. Then he poured two fingers of wine into a half-pint jam jar for me, and filled mason jars for himself and Vincenzo. We stood there, the three of us, and I wasn't that seedling anymore.

Sometimes my father told me how much he cared with just his body. I couldn't see this before. I wasn't looking. His body gave voice to all the things left unspoken between us. You could read it in the worm-ing age lines on his face and in his knotted muscles, in the way they relaxed and went slack. The prose of tight-lipped men.

They held the jars up to the overhead light fixture. I did the same. The light brightened the hazy brick edges. The sediment settled. "This has a nice color," my father said. Then he dipped his nose into the mouth of the jar and inhaled. "Smell," he told me. It smelled like old leather and damp earth and overripe blackberries. "It was a good year," he said.

"That it was," Vincenzo said. "Salute."

"Salute," my father and I said.

We tried the wine. They let it sit on their tongues before swallow-ing. To me it tasted bitter, but I didn't want to be the boy who made a vinegar face. So I finished my glass and held it out for more, and my father laughed and said, "Two more fingers. But take it easy, make it last."

At the table, we ate the meal Vincenzo had prepared for us and drank the wine my father had made for me. They hunched over their plates, chewed with mouths open, lips smacking together, lifting their heads for the wine. Vincenzo got my father talking about the old days, the good days, as if there had once been a time when they could sink their teeth into the juicy flesh of a Saturn peach and never find a pit. When my father had sopped up the last of the sauce with a crust of bread, Vincenzo signaled me with his elbow and a nod of his chin.

"Papà," I said. "Sam invited me to spend the weekend with him at his dad's place in Stony Creek. Can I go?"

He furrowed his brow. "What's his last name?"

"Morris," I said.

My father repeated the surname, testing the foreign word on his tongue. He made a sour face. "What if something happens and I'm not there?"

"Nothing bad is going to happen," I said.

He held his index finger up to his lips and shushed me as if I were inviting misfortune into my life. "Don't say that," he said. "You don't know for sure."

"Let him go," Vincenzo said. "The boys, they look after each other."

My father reached over the table and gave my bicep a gentle squeeze. "Mizzica," he said. "Wow, your muscle, it's like a stone." Then he patted my cheek and said, "Okay. You can go."

21

The notes from Tony stopped. The constant put-downs, the shoving in the halls, the spitball taunts on the bus, all of it stopped after our last Catechism class. I felt relieved but skittish, like a rescue cat in a new home. I caught glimpses of him at school, his red zipper jacket disappearing around every corner—in his wake, the rubble of classmates who took the brunt of his anger in place of me. He was the planet killer on *Star Trek*, the doomsday machine set in perpetual motion, and his maw chewed up all matter in his path. Between classes, Sam witnessed him calling people names and pushing them around with his good arm. But he was alone now. Chris Cardella had abandoned him.

At home, my father's mood changed again, like a change in the weather, a low-pressure system moving in. Twice that week, Father Salafia phoned him. Twice my father argued about that no-good Morello family, how they were all the same bad eggs from the same sick hen. The tin-can voice of the priest buzzed through the telephone receiver, a garbled lecture from the teacher on a Peanuts cartoon. My father interrupted him with a chorus of *No, no, no,* and ended each call with a slam of the phone so hard the little bell inside chimed.

Friday, in school, Tony cornered me in the second-floor bathroom before lunch. I turned from the sink and was cranking the paper towel dispenser when I saw his reflection in the mirror, standing behind me.

I faced him and he took a step forward, backing me up against the urine-colored tile wall. A foot of space separated us. The left sleeve of his "Thriller" jacket hung empty. He didn't have a friend who would sign his cast.

"Did you send that priest after my dad?" He spat when he talked. "You trying to cost him his job, you little freak? You'll regret it."

"Whatever," I said. I brushed past him to the door.

"Piece of advice, Marconi," he snarled at my back. "Don't be around when this arm heals."

I flipped him the bird before the door swung shut behind me, then hurried down the stairs into the safety of the crowded cafeteria, where Sam had saved me a seat.

~

That evening, when my father came home from work, he washed his hands in the kitchen sink and mussed my hair. The day he'd had at the factory fell off his shoulders. And there it was, in the same silence, the words his body made, the ones I'd only just learned how to read. He warmed up the last piece of Zia's leftover sausage and rapini scacciata and gave it to me steaming on a plate because he knew it was my favorite. He sat with me at the card table but didn't eat. He would eat later, he said, with Vincenzo, after Sam and his father picked me up. He made me write down the address and phone number of Sam's father's house in case he needed to reach me. He reminded me for the hundredth time to be careful. "I know," I told him. But he shook his head as if there was no way I could know. Then his body changed. His face and shoulders snapped taut like a frayed rope stressed to its limit. His jaw sawed back and forth.

"Papà," I said. "I'll be fine."

My father spoke through his teeth. "When you come home, you stay away from Morello's boy. He bothers you again, you come to me."

"But you told me to fight back," I said.

"Doesn't matter what I told you before. Now I tell you something different."

~

Sam's father—Mr. Morris—took Route 9 south out of Middletown. He drove faster than mine ever would, the windows of the pickup truck rattling in the wind. Sam sat in the middle of the bench seat, playing DJ with mix tapes he'd made. I leaned on the armrest in the door, cheek pressed against the glass. When I was little, the way my zia spoke of how my father worked construction, you'd think no one else had been on the job. She made it sound like he single-handedly paved all the roads and built all the bridges in the state. I used to ask him which roads were his, which bridges, and he shrugged off the questions. *A crew of men made them,* he'd say, *and a crew of men were as strong as concrete.*

We passed under an overpass, the blue beams flecked with rust. I imagined him, kneeling in the median strip, arms stretched wide, completing the span. The immigrant holding up the New World. That was how I wanted to think of my father.

The highway soon sliced through wooded hills, walled in by exposed layers of rock in the roadcuts. A star could only show us a glimpse of its long life in the light that reached us here on Earth. But these rocks laid their whole stories bare—the how and the why and the when—if only you knew how to read them.

~

In Old Saybrook, we took the exit for Interstate 95 south and followed the shoreline highway. I'd never been on 95 before, never gone farther down Route 9 than Old Saybrook. I'd gone fishing there a couple of years ago, off a causeway with Vincenzo and my father. They caught a bucket of flounder and snapper blues, while my line got stuck and snapped in jagged rocks in the brackish waters below.

Mr. Morris turned off the highway at Branford, just as the setting sun reached the treetops. He took a scenic route down a wooded road with large homes set back at the end of long driveways, and then turned onto Thimble Islands Road and gave me a tour of the seaside village of Stony Creek. We drove past an antique store, a market and pizza place, and a small public beach with a gazebo. We pulled over onto the side of the road opposite a seafood restaurant and a bait and tackle shop. The truck idled at the curb. Mr. Morris folded his arms over the steering wheel and rested his chin on his wrists. In silence, we watched the boats come in, the sun dipping low over the islands that dotted the water. A group of teenage girls hung out on benches by the shore, but I didn't spot Jamie's Mohawk among them.

"Do you like it?" Mr. Morris asked. "The water, the boats, I mean."

"Yeah," I said. A dark-blue hazy line spanned the horizon.

"That's Long Island," Sam said, reading my mind.

"It's amazing."

"Sure is," Mr. Morris said. He backed the truck out and made a U-turn, and we were on our way again. Soon, we parked in the driveway of a stone-and-shingle waterfront house off Prospect Hill Road. The house looked like something out of *Grimm's Fairy Tales*, with ivy climbing the worn stones of the arched front door and two-story exterior chimney. Mr. Morris ran a bed-and-breakfast here. It had been a tumbledown house when he bought it, and he'd completed most of the restoration work on his own. After the divorce, he converted the garage into a one-bedroom for himself. Sam kept his room in the B&B for when he visited every other weekend.

The sun burned the horizon and bled into the clouds and sea, a scarlet wound soon healed by the deep-blue night. On a secluded beach east of the house, Mr. Morris built a small fire. His white Jimi Hendrix T-shirt hung on his lanky frame, billowing in a breeze. At the edge of the firelight, we gathered smooth triangular stones. They taught me how to skip the stones across the water with a sidearm toss. "Nice one," Sam's father said, and Sam shouted, "Awesome!" at my first four-bouncer. "Beginner's luck," I said. The tide would return the stone to shore, and the waves that rolled over it would roll it back into the sea.

"Hey, Sam," two teenage girls called out in harmony from the rocky end of the beach. They walked along the waterline, heading in our direction, one of them waving. Two smudges against the silver line of ocean and sky.

"Okay, Dad," Sam said, elbowing his father. "Time for you to make like a banana and split."

Mr. Morris laughed and started walking away from us and the girls. "Just don't get me into trouble with your mother," he said. "You need anything at all, you know where to find me."

Jamie and another girl came into high relief. Shapes carved on the surface of the night. Both girls wore black jeans, black tank tops, and piles of silver jewelry and silver-studded black leather jackets. They each held a backpack slung over one of their shoulders. Jamie's dorsal-fin Mohawk—now dyed sailfish blue with black tips—crested from the darkness to greet us by the fire.

"You're a sailfish," I said. "Cool."

"It's a crime you had to shave yours off," Jamie shot back. "Parental units."

In the firelight, the smoky lines of the new girl's Eye of Horus makeup wavered on the white of her skin. Tousled black hair fell around her collarbones. She smiled, and her cheeks dimpled. She pulled at me, at the raw materials of stars within me, cooked some billion years ago in a stellar nursery in some distant part of the galaxy.

"Never saw a girl before?" she said.

"No. I mean—" I stammered.

"David, right? I'm Em."

"You two just gonna stand there?" Jamie teased over her shoulder. She and Sam were dragging a Y-shaped driftwood log to the fire pit for a bench. "We could use some help here."

Together, we hauled the log into place and then went back for one more, a two-seater. We sat down beside the fire, Jamie and Sam on the smaller log, Em and I on the letter *Y*. Em unzipped her backpack and took out blue plastic cups and a bag of ice.

Jamie held up a four-pack of wine coolers. "Topping for your ice?"

We passed around the cups, ice, and wine coolers. Sam took one of the twist-top bottles and a handful of ice and poured his drink like he'd done it a hundred times before. He fell into easy conversation with Jamie, their shoulders touching. She quizzed him about life in Middletown since Butterfield.

The cap on my bottle was slick under my sweaty palms. "Let me," Em said. It twisted right off in her hands. Silver rings on her fingers glinted in the light. She handed the bottle back to me, each of her black-painted fingernails a period at the end of an unspoken sentence.

"Thanks," I said. I sipped my wine cooler, trying to think of something interesting to say. The drink tasted sugary and fruity, much better than the wine my father made. I sifted sand through the fingers of my free hand and quoted Carl Sagan, "'The total number of stars in the universe is larger than all the grains of sand on all the beaches of Earth.'"

"*Cosmos*, right? I love that show."

"So, you're into astronomy?"

"Astrology mostly. But it's all the same thing, right? The study of stars."

It wasn't the same thing, not really, but in that moment I didn't care. "Did you see Halley's Comet?"

Across the fire, Sam and Jamie started kissing. Em rolled her eyes. "Get a room," she said. Jamie answered with her middle finger.

"Classy," Em said. She elbowed me. "Let's go for a walk."

I took a long drink from my cup and set it in the sand beside Em's, then followed her down to the water's edge. We stood at the damp tide line where the sea rolled in, looking out at the horizon. Waves slapped against the shore. Pebbles tumbled forward, carried by the waves. The water soaked my sneakers and socks and the olive-drab canvas at the ankles of her combat boots. The sea tugged at my feet as it rushed back in a slow build toward high tide.

"Did you feel that?" I asked.

"Listen," she said.

Pebbles crackled like cereal flakes in milk.

We took off our wet shoes, rolled up our jeans, and waded into cold water up to our knees. The pebbles were slippery smooth under our bare feet as we made our way to the far end of the beach. Em had known Sam and Jamie since second grade. A dinosaur's age, she called it. For as long as she could remember, they were more like brothers and sisters than friends. But all that changed when Sam's parents divorced and he moved away. Jamie and Sam's status became amorphous. There were days when they acted platonic and days when they couldn't keep their hands off each other. But they never spoke about it, not even with Em. "It's gross," she said. Then she splashed me and asked about Vincenzo and his café, since Sam had gone on and on about it the last time he was in town. I told her about the old men and their cigarettes, the smell of coffee and Italian pastries. We talked about nothing but it felt like everything.

She splashed me again and this time I got her back, and we chased each other out of the water and sprawled out on the sand far from Jamie and Sam and the crackling fire. The heat of Em's body simmered inches from mine. Above me, scant clouds and stars, a grinning moon. Staring long enough gave me a floating feeling.

Em took my hand.

Our fingers locked, as if our hands were carved from the same piece of stone. With her free hand, she pointed out a long *W* in the sky. "That's

Cassiopeia," she said. Then she drew a straight line in the air from the W to the North Star. "Polaris," we said in unison, and she smiled her dimpled smile and made a second line high in the sky. "The Big Dipper."

I followed the curve of her moon-pale arm back to her shoulder, her neck, the line of her jaw. She rolled on her side to face me. Her black eyeliner swept out to her temples from the crinkled corners of her cat eyes. My ears felt hot. A static charge building up. I touched the curved tail of the Eye of Horus, traced it to its swirling end high on her cheek. She didn't pull away. She smelled like salt and lavender. Her lips tasted like candied peaches.

~

Back at the fire, after the girls had gone home, Sam and I wore Cheshire grins. The firewood snapped and popped, sending sparks trailing up into the sky like falling stars in reverse.

~

Saturday morning, Mr. Morris cooked a full breakfast for the guests of his B&B—a honeymooning couple and four seniors. He set the table in the dining room, serving farmers' omelets with home fries and bacon, buttered toast, and tall glasses of orange juice.

In the kitchen, Sam showed me how to make pancakes. I cracked eggs into a bowl and whisked them with a fork. I was still smiling from last night. Sam added flour and baking powder. Then, as if reading my mind, he said, "Sailing's not their scene, but maybe they'll swing by later tonight." He poured the milk and melted butter into the bowl. "Stir that," he said. "But keep it lumpy."

We cooked the pancakes until both sides were golden. Then we piled them on plates, enough for his father and us. I set the round glass-top table. Sam brought out the maple syrup and a bowl of strawberries.

When his father returned from the dining room, he sliced two bananas and added them to the bowl. "You boys did a great job," he said.

After breakfast, we walked to the wharf where Mr. Morris kept his twenty-foot sailboat docked. When I boarded the *Molly Brown*, I felt the water beneath my feet, the deck swaying this way and that. Sam put on his life jacket, and then he helped me put on mine. He asked me if I knew how to swim, and I lied and told him that I did. His father ticked off a memorized checklist of safety rules for me to know before we could leave. He showed me how to stop the boat in the event of an emergency by releasing the lines controlling the sails—the mainsheet and the jib sheet. He told me where to sit so that the boom, the pole along the bottom of the mainsail, wouldn't hit me if it swung from one side of the boat to the other. He explained how to shut off the outboard diesel motor, pointed out where he kept the fire extinguisher, and taught me how to radio for help.

We left the pier under power of the outboard motor, moored boats waggling in our wake. Sam helped his father remove the sail cover. They worked in silence, sensing how the boat carried itself through the water. If they spoke at all, they spoke two or three words between them. They anticipated what came next, tuned to the cadence of the other's presence. The way my father knew when I was on the porch roof or waiting for him at the edge of his garden.

I squinted overboard at the hull, frothing the water white. A breeze sprayed a salty mist in my face. Clear of the harbor, Sam's father directed the boat into the wind while slowing our speed. They raised the sails and shut off the engine, setting it in the up position. Sam watched the coast pull away from us. He trailed his fingers in the Long Island Sound. An estuary, he called it, a place where fresh water mixed with the salt of the ocean.

"You know," his father said, scratching the scruff on his chin. "In the old days, I'm talking before radio, before the sextant, before the magnetic compass even, sailors relied on the natural world for navigation. Take the stars, for instance. The way Scorpio chases Orion across the sky. That was their compass. A perfect balance of rising and setting stars." He sounded zen, like old Ben Kenobi from *Star Wars*. "You can find that harmony all around you. Just look at the ocean, how it's shaped into swells. These guys, they could read the water the wind had written for them. They paid attention to the position of the sun, the movements of the clouds, even the birds. They didn't set sail in search of land. They listened and read the signs, and that brought the land to them."

Sam brought his cupped hand up out of the water, and the water rushed through his fingers and mixed back into the sea. Crests sparkled in the sun. Far out, at the curve of the Earth, the sea touched the sky. Out here life became infinite, measured in starlight. My chest tightened as if my lungs were fuller than they'd ever been before.

22

We sailed through the Thimble Islands, passing a motorboat full of tourists. They waved at us. Snatches of their guide's narration carried over the loudspeaker: "Adriaen Block discovered the archipelago in 1614 . . . They were named after a fruit, the thimbleberry . . . Locals nicknamed Wheeler Island, Ghost Island." And then we were out of earshot. When I turned back to look over my shoulder, I saw a forlorn house on its own lonely isle—little more than a rocky perch— and I understood why the locals had given Wheeler that nickname.

"Captain Kidd had a hidden harbor here," Sam said. He sat down next to me.

Sam's father pointed off into the distance. "His cove will be over there once we clear Governor Island," he said. And he guided me through labyrinthine waterways, and said the name of each island we passed. He spoke as if the water held their names and stories in its swells, written there by the wind. Stories of Captain Kidd's treasure buried on Money Island during his mad dash to outrun the British navy in the 1600s, and Little Miss Emily, the P. T. Barnum circus performer, whose love affair with General Tom Thumb in the 1800s was somewhere still inscribed on the granite of Cut-in-Two Island.

Seagulls hovered over the water, sinking and rising on currents of air. Waves rolled against the hull, sails rippled in the breeze. The music of the ocean. The siren song of the edge of the world. I imagined myself way out at sea with Em and her smoky Eye of Horus makeup. We'd sail the void, set our course by the silver cords that tied the constellations and stories together. Like stars, we'd rise and sink with the speckled gulls and dapple the water with our light.

~

Back at the B&B, Sam and I washed the dinner dishes. Then we sat at the table on the flatbed truck his father used as a porch for the converted garage. Sam had just finished tuning his guitar when the phone rang. He leapt up from his seat, handed me the guitar, and ran inside yelling, "I got it!" I hunched over the instrument, craned my neck toward my fingers on the fret board. I formed a D chord, the way Sam had shown me, and the steel strings dug deep into the pads of my fingertips.

"That was Jamie," Sam said. The screen door slammed shut behind him. "Em got drafted into babysitting her little brother tonight. Jamie's over there now keeping her company. But they totally want to hang out next time you visit." Sam took the guitar and sat back down. "Check this out." He strummed the opening chords to a song.

"What is that?"

"'Boys Don't Cry.'"

"It is? Let me hear it again."

He started over, playing the chord progression twice. It sounded nothing like the song until Sam began singing the first verse, off key, and even then, it didn't sound much like "Boys Don't Cry" at all. I didn't have the heart to tell Sam. He was in a fantasy all his own—eyes closed, foot tapping and head swaying out of time—and it made this world, his divided home, unreal to him.

I knew what it was like to have that fantasy crushed. Tomorrow, when Sam went home, his mother would greet him at the door and pepper him with questions about his weekend. Tomorrow, when I went home, I'd want to talk to a mother I knew wasn't there, whose voice I couldn't even remember—my mother and her stars on the ceiling of my bedroom. I wanted to tell her about my weekend. I wanted to tell her about Em. Tomorrow, I would go back home, but for now I needed to pretend that I was never leaving.

"That's really good," I said. "Did you figure that out by yourself?"

Sam grinned. "I've been practicing all week."

The sun smoldered at the rim of the world, slipping further below the horizon. A dusky brown-and-orange sky hung over everything.

~

The rain began around three in the morning. Droplets pattered against the house and the leaves of the trees. Soon, a downpour drummed the roof and driveway. By five o'clock, the trees outside Sam's window swayed and bent in gusts. Branches creaked against the side of the house.

At the first thunderclap, the windowpane rattled. I pulled on jeans and sneakers and went outside. Flashes of sheet lightning made lavender flashes of twilight. Rain sprayed onto the front porch like mist over sailboat railings. The wind howled. Lightning flashed inside a charcoal billow of clouds, and then the sky went dark again. Thunder broke.

"What are you doing?" Sam said behind me.

"Watching the storm."

He looked up at the porch ceiling as thunder rumbled overhead. "You can work out how far away it is," he said, "by counting the seconds between the thunder and lightning."

I leaned against the wooden railing, tipped my head into the rain, and lifted my feet from the floorboards. Teetering there like a seesaw, I waited for the charge of electricity, and then counted for the thunder-clap. "This one's getting close," I said. My arms trembled. They were getting tired from balancing my weight on the slippery rail. "I wish we didn't have to leave." My feet set down with a thud. I jumped the three steps to the sidewalk and said, "You coming?" Then I ran off across the lawn with Sam's footsteps splashing behind. I stopped against a tree, leaned into its bark, and waited for him. The Long Island Sound showed in a flash of light. Thunder rolled overhead.

Sam called out.

"Catch up," I said. Then I scrabbled over granite boulders and loose rocks, down to the beach and into the water up to my ankles.

In the distance, anchored boats swayed on their spines—port, then starboard. A jagged line of lightning streaked and split into branches near the horizon. White foam waves crashed in around me. The lights of the islands flickered across the choppy water. Residents stayed shuttered inside their homes, waiting it out. Maybe they watched the storm through window slats, the way Sicilian fami-lies did in the war. Maybe in the hours after the Allied invasion began, the wartime skies looked like this. My father had run halfway around the world to try to escape that war and this sky, and even he could not break free. He saw an explosion so bright, the remnant of that light in our skies might never extinguish. He tried outrun-ning it, but there is weight in light as well as heat, and he burned, caught up in it.

"You shouldn't be in the water," Sam said. "Not with the lightning."

Breaking waves surged up the beach. Knee-high walls of crashing foam and water knocked me back a step and then seized my legs in retreat. Stones and barnacles tumbled into the sea, ammunition for the fight, for when the sea came back at me again. Shells and pebbles pelted my feet. My blue jeans stuck to me. They were heavy from being wet. Lightning flashed and a ground-shaking thunderpeal broke overhead. A larger wave struck me in a thunderous, spraying crash and knocked me down into the sand. The water washed over me. It receded into white foam crests out to the horizon and left me with the taste of sea salt in my mouth and the feel of the sea—thick and briny—in my lungs.

23

Low, heavy clouds covered the morning sky out to the horizon. After lunch, we packed our bags and loaded them into Sam's father's pickup. Tires turned over wet asphalt. Windshield wipers squished and chattered in time with the rain pattering against the truck. I felt small and heavy. Smaller and heavier with each mile marker we passed. We pulled off Route 9, into downtown Middletown, and turned down my street. Father Salafia stood on my front porch. He opened his black umbrella, hurried down the steps. His shoes splashed in the puddles pooling on the sidewalk. I felt like one of those pebbles on the beach worn smooth by tidewaters. *Pick me up,* I thought, *give me a good sidearm toss, and skip me across the waves.*

My father sat on the tattered flower-print couch in the living room, his face drawn and tired. The checkerboard on the tray table set up for a game. He had brought out a wooden bowl of walnuts and an empty dish for the shells that he cracked in his fist. When I walked through the door, he pulled the ladder-back chair out for me. "You all right?"

I kicked off my soaking-wet sneakers and dropped my backpack in the front hall. "Fine," I said. "I'm black?"

"Eh, sure," my father said. He pointed at the red pieces in front of him.

We played checkers.

"Tomorrow night at your confirmation rehearsal," my father said, "you say sorry to Morello's boy." His voice didn't have any kick in it, like he didn't mean what he was saying.

"I don't understand," I said. "Why?"

My father jumped his red piece over one of my black ones, removing it from the board. Then he placed my captured man crown side down on the tray table and said, "Doesn't matter why. I'm your papà. You do what I say. There is no why."

I studied the board. My father had forced me into a move that would give him a king on his next turn from a triple-jump play. He waited for me to move. My weekend stretched out behind me. A smudge of light in the dark.

~

That night, I sat on the floor at the windowsill in my bedroom with the light turned off. The rain marbled the windowpane, framing the outlines of the shed, garden, and wire fence in thick brushstrokes running down the glass. The pink cloud of the mimosa tree in bloom, a halo of color against all shades of darkness.

My father slept in the adjacent room, his back curled to the place where my mother would be if she were with him. I used to sleep there, after she died, every time it stormed. That frightened and shivering boy molded against the curve of his father's back. His forehead nuzzled in the dip where neck meets shoulders. The little hairs there tickled his nose. *Big boy like you,* my father used to say under his breath. I wasn't the boy he'd hoped for, this son who slept with his father during thunderstorms. But still he indulged me. And I understood how my father could love the stranger I had made out of his son.

I took the festival bulletin from my desk and opened it to my mother's picture. In the wan storm light, I could just make out her features. Her skin, pale like a ghost's, pale like mine. I had my mother's skin. My hair was coal black from my father. He had said life was like this—a raised fist. I had broken Tony's nose with mine. I thought that's what my father wanted.

Vincenzo once told me that my mother's red hair would come later, when I became a man. In my beard I'd see her, highlights among my father's sooty scruff. I wanted those highlights to come. I wanted to see the red brightening up all that coarse black hair.

24

Monday, by midafternoon, the rain had stopped but the sky did not clear. After school, Sam and I hung out at Record Express on Main Street. *Spleen and Ideal* by Dead Can Dance played on the store stereo. This was what empty church pews sounded like when no one was around to sit in them and make them creak. It was a cold sound, a sound for snowflakes. It demanded nothing, but you gave it reverence anyway.

Sam held The Cure's single compilation, *Standing on a Beach*, up to his face so that the album art of an old fisherman's large craggy face replaced his own. "You reckon we're old enough to watch for Halley's Comet yet?" he said, in imitation of an elderly man's voice.

When I didn't answer, Sam lowered the album and tucked it under his left arm. "What's up with you? You've been down all day." He pushed his blue-streaked bangs out of his eyes. From a freestanding display, he handed me a cassette in its long plastic security case. *Black Celebration* by Depeche Mode. "This is killer," he said. "I'm getting this for you. This'll cheer you up."

"I still don't have a tape deck."

He put his hand on my shoulder. "Dude, that is sacrilege what you just said. I've got divorce-guilt cash from my dad to burn, so let's fix this right now." He walked up the aisle toward the front counter.

"You don't have to do that," I said.

He spun around, walking backward, all cool and grinning. "I know."

Sam bought the two LPs for himself and the cassette for me, along with a silver-and-black portable tape player. "I still got five bucks left and some time to kill," he said. "What do you want to do, paisanu?" He handed me the plastic bag with my gifts inside.

Cry, I thought—but the words that came out of my mouth were cold words. "Italian ice."

At Vecchitto's, we both got the same flavors we'd had at the festival—almond for me and lemon for Sam. He staked out a spot at the table by the window and started planning our next trip to Stony Creek. I'd come out for a week in July when he spent the month at his father's place. Sam leaned forward on his elbows, legs bouncing up and down on the toes of his sneakers, and mapped out our summer. He narrated it like an adventure film serial, our sequel to Butterfield. The film promised more Wesleyan tunnel expeditions and Foss Hill nights before Sam left. It detailed our week together in Stony Creek, out on the water and on the beach with Em and Jamie. We'd form a band together, Cog and Pearl, with Sam on guitar and me as the enigmatic front man.

Beyond the train tracks and Route 9, the Harbor Park pavilion sat at the elbow of the Connecticut River. The river caught the pewter light of clouds and held it, a mirror for this overcast day. Silent and cold, the silver ribbon of water emptied into the Long Island Sound. It passed long-lost names and hearts etched in stones on its rocky beaches.

"So, Em," Sam said. He kicked me under the table. "She really likes you."

I shrugged as if to say, with a question, *I guess.* Then I ate my almond ice fast for the icy shock of brain freeze. Sam had unspooled a thread for me to follow—a way out of this labyrinth—and I held on to it even as I knew our Ray Harryhausen days couldn't last. Nothing did. "How long do you think it takes for a broken arm to heal?"

"I don't know, a month, maybe six weeks." Sam looked up at the tin ceiling and checked his mental calendar. "I'll be gone by then at my dad's, the whole month. Dude, I didn't even think about that." He reached across the table and put his hand on my shoulder. "Why don't you come with me?"

"A whole month? My father would never go for that."

"What're you going to do?"

"Hit the troll until he stays down. What choice do I have?"

"Tell someone. Tell your dad."

I checked the time on the clock over the counter. "I have to go," I said. "My father and the priest are making me apologize to Tony tonight. In their minds—" I mimed washing my hands. "Problem solved."

~

A fleece of clouds spun out west. The skies clearing where the sun would set. The sun burning a clear path to its rest. My father and Vincenzo should've been at work, but they were arguing in the kitchen when I came home. Their voices carried through the screen door to the back porch.

"You can't make him do this, Sal. No way. No godson of mine should have to ask forgiveness from that stronzo."

"That old crow knows how to call a man on his debts." My father's voice dropped in volume. I put my ear to the screen. The porch creaked under my feet. "David," he called out to me. "Stop listening and come in here."

The back door wheezed as I pulled it open. Vincenzo leaned against the doorframe to the front hall, arms crossed. My father pressed his palms to the countertop like he was trying to crush it. He stared down into the yellow laminate. "You remember what I told you last night?"

"Come on, Sal," Vincenzo said. "Don't make him do this. Let me talk to the priest again."

My father banged his fist on the counter. "Basta! Stay out of this, Enzo. He will apologize and then he will get confirmed and that will be the end of it."

"For Christ's sake, Sal. Not a day goes by that rotten Morello kid hasn't sent our boy a note promising to hurt him. David's too proud to even tell you."

"Is this true?" my father asked me. He still stared at the laminate as if reading from a script in a kitchen-sink drama. The blue vein at his temple throbbed.

"What does it matter now?" I said. "I took care of it. I took care of him."

My father let out a long puff of air, like he'd been holding his breath for years and just couldn't hold it any longer. He whirled on Vincenzo, his arms knocking the toaster over, freeing the plug from its socket. The toaster fell at his feet. "My son told you and you said nothing to me?"

"I didn't want you to worry. I kept an eye on him. Haven't I always kept an eye on this family?"

"This is what you do? Better you left us in Syracuse where you found us. My sister and me, we had a good life there. You should have left us."

Vincenzo pressed his hands onto the back of a folding chair, leaning into it. "You don't mean that, Sal."

Watching them argue was like peering into a shoebox diorama that someone else had made. Two paper men, frozen in place, around them a black-and-white backdrop of bombed-out buildings, piles of rubble, dead soldiers, and a barefoot boy squatting in the filth—a snapshot of an argument older than me. The big bang, the detonation that gave birth to all our stars, set them ablaze and in fierce motion.

My father threw his hands up into the air as if in surrender. "You should've told me."

"Boys fight all the time. I would've told you if it got out of hand."

"What's the matter with you?" my father said with uplifted pinched fingers. "You don't know what could happen with a Morello."

They fought as if I were not here, in this kitchen, where just a week ago we'd shared a bottle of wine, drunk from jars together. My piece of star burned in me, every cell in me igniting a chain reaction. I stormed upstairs into my father's bedroom and took the shoebox from his closet. When I marched back into the kitchen, they were still going at it—all of us now caught in a slow gravitational collapse. I threw the box onto the card table.

"I know you've been lying to me," I said.

The box landed on its side and the lid flipped off. The tarnished silver cross clattered on the table. Old pictures staggered out in stacked layers, fossilized remains of another age. The photo of the Vassallo family at the festival—the one with all their names on the back, the one with Rocco—lay faceup on the table.

My father approached it on unsteady legs. He flattened the mountain of photographs with a sweep of his hand. "What do you think you know?"

"I know you changed your last name," I said. "I know it used to be Vassallo."

Vincenzo shook his head, warning me off this path. But I could not stop even if I wanted to, and I didn't want to. No one could alter the course of the trajectory I had set for myself. "I know you broke Rocco's fingers. I know you're not from Syracuse. I know you lied to me about who you are and where you're from. Did you lie to Mom, too? Is our whole fucking life a lie?"

"Sta zittu!" The mark of my father's hand burned red on my cheek. My hand shot up to the place where his had been. I tasted blood in my mouth where I had bit my tongue.

"Jesus, Sal," Vincenzo said.

My father stared into his hand, as if he still felt the sting of my cheek there. "Go," he said. "Get out. I do not want to see you right now." His voice low, defeated. The furious backward sweep of his arm doing all the shouting for him: *Vai via. Go away.*

I ran out the back door and into the yard. Bumblebees buzzed, their faces buried in the silky whiskers of pink mimosa flowers. A blue jay bobbed up and down on a branch high above me and tolled a bell-like note.

Vincenzo came out onto the back porch. The bird bristled its pointed crest into a blue-black Mohawk. On the street somewhere, an unseen car honked its horn, wheels screeched. I jumped for the lowest branch, my feet scrabbling against the bruised and peeled bark. The jaybird squawked. In a flash of brilliant blues and whites, its wings unfolded and caught a lone patch of clear azure sky.

"David," Vincenzo called.

I climbed higher. The ridges of the bark dug into my palms. The branches dipped under my weight. Leaflets brushed my cheek, cool against the sting. Vincenzo called for me again, "Get down." The blue jay hawked a dragonfly in midair, and I kept on climbing.

25

"David, get down from there," my father yelled. "Now!" He was angry and impatient, but there was something else in his voice. Something in his face I could not read.

I sat in a thicket of leaves—the mimosa tree loomed over him, growing from the stone of his head, taking root in his mind. The overcast day had turned into a hazy evening, the sun a blood-red fireball that hung low and fat in the sky. Earlier, before my father came outside, my zia and ziu and Vincenzo each took turns trying to lure me down with bait. Zia Nella stood under the tree, a steaming dish of spaghetti and meatballs in her hands. She had made the tomato sauce from last year's garden tomatoes, my father's tomatoes. From the back porch, Ziu Frank proposed a game of checkers if I'd only be a good boy and go to rehearsal. But checkers was the game my father and I played together when he had no one else to play with. And going to rehearsal meant apologizing for him. "I don't care about getting confirmed," I said.

Zia Nella covered her mouth with her hand.

"Your father paid good money for that confirmation suit," Ziu Frank said.

"No one asked him to buy it," I said.

"No one had to ask him," Vincenzo said. He pleaded with me to go, and in return offered pastries and Orangina, all the sweets I wanted from his café. And I said, "No," as if that would be the end of it and I'd stay in this tree until this tree felt like my own bones, until blue jays alighted on my branches, and bumblebees drank my blossoms, and the land that bore me turned basalt-rich and weathered, and my father cultivated that soil for me.

My zia turned to the house and hollered for my father to come out here and talk to his son. But he did not come outside. He did not even come to the window or the door.

Comets went around the sun in unstable, elliptical orbits. This was mine. While in Stony Creek, I had reached my aphelion—the farthest point from the sun in my orbit—and now that I had returned to my perihelion? What now?

"David, get down from there," my father yelled. "Now!"

Zia Nella had gone into the house and shamed him into being a father, and I had my answer. Gravity. He didn't lure me out of the tree so much as he pulled me down out of the sky without laying a hand on me.

~

As soon as I'd gotten down from the tree, my father dismissed his sister and brother-in-law. He sent Vincenzo with them to wait for me at their house across the street. My father insisted there was still time to help him clean before I had to leave, and handed me the extension tube for the vacuum.

We spent an hour shuffling furniture around, folding kitchen chairs and stacking them in the front hall with the couch from the living room. "Hold it from the bottom," he said.

"I got it."

"Use your legs, not your back."

"I said I got it, Dad."

"Watch your fingers. Okay. Put it here. Bonu. Bonu."

Then he cleaned each room in silence as if nothing had happened. He thought that with enough soap and water and scrubbing on his hands and knees, enough suction power from the vacuum cleaner, he could erase all traces of that other world recorded in old photographs in a shoebox that even now sat in his closet. He mopped, scrubbed, scoured, and vacuumed his way around that house, around me, around the slap. It was his house. It had never been mine. Like the name, Vassallo.

When the rooms were back in order, he scratched his head, looked at the floor in the front hall. "You scuffed the tile," he said.

"It'll come off," I said, and I knelt and rubbed it with my thumb. "See? It's coming out."

"Do it right," he said from the kitchen. "Use a towel paper."

"They're called paper towels."

He came back with the whole roll. I took two and went to work on the scuff mark. The back door closed. The porch floorboards creaked. I bore down hard, put my elbows into it. "Tile's clean," I called out into the empty house.

26

Vincenzo waited for me on the steps of Zia Nella's front porch, leaning forward, elbows on his knees, nursing a glass of rosy wine. He stood when I crossed the street, brushed the creases from his dark slacks and white button-down shirt. He thumbed at my blue striped crew neck and jeans and said, "That what you're wearing?"

"I don't even know why I have to do this," I said.

"It's important to your papà that he sees you get confirmed. He never had the chance. So go easy on him."

The front door opened, and Zia Nella came out and grabbed me in her arms. "Don't do that again, David," she said. "You scared me half to death."

"Okay," I said, so she would let me go.

She held me at arm's length. "You have to forgive your papà. He didn't mean it."

I shrugged her hands off my shoulders. "We're going to be late," I said.

Zia Nella stepped back and pressed her hands together, fingers intertwined, and watched us leave.

Vincenzo and I walked several blocks without one word spoken between us. The argument with my father played again and again and again in my mind. I was the needle caught in the groove of his scratched record. The record warbled and crackled. The needle skipped through scratches, back to the night we roasted peppers, the night he caught me in my lie.

That night, my father told me to stay away from the man who fought when he knew he could not win. This was his lesson, the lesson of the fasces, the strength in the bundle of sticks, and the warning.

Finally, Vincenzo. He looked after us, that's what he'd said. He was the soldier, the Fascist Rocco spoke about, the one my father hid behind. I asked Vincenzo once if the Italians lost the war because they did not stay united, and he said, "Mussolini's one mistake was making an alliance with Hitler. The people went against him for that."

We were those men my father warned me about, the men who liked to fight anyway. This was what happened to Rocco's fingers.

Vincenzo lifted the needle from the turntable in my mind. "Long ago, I gave your papà my word. All a man has in this life is his word. His word is his currency."

∽

At confirmation rehearsal, we sat paired with our sponsors in the front pews. The girls sat on one side of the center aisle. The boys sat on the other side. Father Salafia explained the procedures of the Mass. Tony leaned forward and mouthed the words *You're dead.* His sponsor yanked him back by his jacket collar. Vincenzo patted my knee and whispered, "Ignore him." Then we went over the readings and practiced the anointing process. After rehearsal, Tony's sponsor walked him up to the priest with a rough hand on the back of the boy's neck. They waited at the side altar of Saint Sebastian. The church emptied.

The priest called out to me.

Vincenzo put his arm around my shoulders. "This is something you have to do for your papà," he said.

We stood up together and joined them at the altar of the saint. Tony's sweatshirt stretched taut over the cast. He cradled the broken arm in front of him. A scowl crossed his face under his crooked nose. We had a history, Tony and I, a whole shoebox full stashed under my bed, a chronicle of his unending bullying, and I hated him for that. I hated him for everything he'd ever done to me, every hurtful word he'd ever uttered, and I wanted to tell him. I wanted to tell him how much I hated him. I wanted to scream, *Fuck you!* But my father's broken record kept spinning, and what choice did I have but to skip along those grooves?

"I'm sorry," I said.

Tony stared down at his Reeboks—the fat white tongues of his sneakers sticking out at me. His downcast face hid his smug satisfaction from the priest. My apology was a victory for him. He tormented me, and the one time I fought back and won, I had to apologize for it. "Yeah," he muttered. "Me, too."

Father Salafia's face set into a cracked frown like molded clay stiffening and losing water as it dried out too fast. "Tony," he said. "Your father is next door in the rectory. Do you want to tell him why you can't receive the sacrament of confirmation?"

"No, sir," Tony said. He straightened his shoulders and stared me down. He waited for me to blink before saying with a smirk, "I'm sorry, David."

"Okay, boys," the priest said. He clapped his hands together. "Good. I will see you both this Sunday."

27

That night I lay on my bed, eyes closed and ankles locked, biting my fingernails and listening to Depeche Mode on my headphones. If you could make ash and embers sing for you, these were the songs they would sing. Throwing sparks from a dying fire. And if you could be those songs, you would know what it was like to feel those red-hot embers trailing off you, floating around your body.

My father shook my foot.

I sat up, pulled my headphones down around my neck. "Don't you knock?"

"How can you hear anything with those things on?" My father hovered at the foot of my bed like a helicopter trying to land in rough weather. "Where did you get that anyway? I thought you gave that thing back?"

"Did you come in here to make me apologize to Rocco next?"

My father moved to the window and shut the blue curtains. Then he opened a fat astronomy book on my desk and flipped through its pages. He was still hovering, unsure how to stick this landing. "One time," he said, "my papà showed me a picture in this book he kept with him during the war, and he says, *Turiddu, tell me what you see.*" My father scowled at the swirling eye of Jupiter scowling back at him from the page. "It was the winged head of Medusa, David, with three ears of wheat and three bent legs. Your nonnu had told Vincenzo that this was Sicilia, a jewel, a star, but it was the hair of snakes that I saw, you understand? The gorgon, she turned me into stone. I was scared, David. I couldn't see what your nonnu could. You think you know Tony, but you cannot know what he sees. You cannot know what trouble he brings. Better you leave him alone now."

"Whatever," I said. I put my headphones back on to drown out the world.

~

When my father told me that story, he was trying to tell me how my nonnu once thought of Sicily as a bright star in the night sky, and how all men's wars would one day end, but the sky and those stars, they were infinite. He was trying to tell me to let it go, to do what he could not. This proxy war with Tony would die down, it would end, and our family—like Sicily, that three-pointed bright star of the Mediterranean—our family would endure, it would be safe. My father believed my apology would stop the bullying, but he didn't see Tony the way I did, didn't recognize the wounded, cornered animal Tony had become. Tony and I, we had a history, it didn't belong to us, but we had made it ours. We had made monsters of each other, and of ourselves. In Tony's story, I was the troll. For as long as he could remember, in all the stories he'd ever told himself about me, I was his nemesis.

My nonnu was wrong. Stars were fires and they burned like wars burned, and they ended, too. My father and Tony's father had started this war long ago in Melilli, in the village where they were born—Typhon trapped under the mountain, spitting embers, embers seeding other fires, songs of ash, songs of smoke—but it would be their sons who ended it.

~

Friday, I wrote my own note, slipped it into Tony's locker at lunch: *Sunday. Harbor Park. Midnight.*

135

28

Saturday, Em called.

That morning my father drafted me into helping him in the garden. He showed me how to prune tomatoes—pinching off the side shoots that sprouted from the armpit of each branch. I went up and down the rows plucking out tender shoots until my fingers were sticky and smelled of sweet greens. Past the beets and the romaine lettuce, my father squatted over a bed of garlic in his white sleeveless undershirt, the front and back stained with sweat, and snipped spiral stems from their stalks with shears to make the bulbs grow bigger and stronger. Later, he would wash and slice the garlic tops, fry them with liver, onions, and potatoes.

Zia Nella was in the house doing the work that my father and I would never do. She had stripped the sheets and pillowcases from our beds, put on fresh sets, and hauled the bundle to the washing machine in the basement when the phone rang. She called to me from the back-porch door, the beige handset pressed into her blue floral blouse. I wiped my hands on my jeans as I climbed the stairs.

"There's a girl on the phone for you," Zia Nella said. She spoke in hushed, conspiratorial tones so my father wouldn't hear, and her voice betrayed the little girl locked away inside her from before the war changed everything. Her hips swiveled to some memory from her youth. I imagined an accordion folding air into music—an old love song from the dusty streets of Sicily. She held the handset out to me and asked, "Who is she? She sounds nice."

"Someone from school," I said and grabbed the phone from her hand. I hoped it was Em, and when I said, "Hi," and she said, "Hi" back, my face got hot. I hurried through the kitchen, into the front hall, and up to the top of the stairs, stretching the coil cord as far as it would go.

"Sam gave me your number," Em said. "Hope that's okay."

Even though Em was in Stony Creek, she sounded so far away that she might as well have been on another planet in some distant star system.

"He did?"

"He said you wouldn't mind. But if this is a bad time or something, or if you don't want to talk to me—"

"No," I said. My voice cracked and I winced, hoping she didn't notice. "This is a great time. I'm glad you called."

"Oh, good. So, how's Middletown?"

"Not as good as Stony Creek," I said.

She laughed, and I pictured her black eyeliner crinkling at the corners of her eyes.

"You wouldn't say that if you lived here," she said. "God, I'm so bored. There's this cool band playing a party in Mystic tonight and my parents won't let me go. What's your sign, anyway?"

"Pisces," I said.

"I knew it," she said. "A water sign. I'm a Scorpio. Anyway, Jamie has this whole plan to go out to Middletown next weekend and go spelunking in the tunnels. I mean, that's what she's calling it. But, I wanted to see if, maybe, you'd want to hang out, too?"

I ran my fingers over the taut ridges of the telephone cord. "I love those tunnels," I said. "You could get lost for hours just checking out all the old stuff, seeing where the next bend takes you. It's like this whole other world down there."

Through the banisters I spied a flash of Zia Nella's blouse. "Hold on a second," I said to Em. I leaned over the railing and shooed my zia back into the kitchen. As I sat back down, the stairs creaked. The phone felt slick in my damp hand. I was sweating more now than I had been working outside in my father's garden.

"David?" Em's voice crackled up from the receiver. An electrical signal carried from miles and miles away, and still it zapped me.

"I'm here," I said into the phone. "Sorry about that."

"So, how about it? Next weekend. Is it a date or what?"

"Yeah," I said. "A date."

~

After Em had hung up, I sat on the stairs and rubbed my ear sweat from the receiver with a thumb. I bet Em had a phone in her bedroom, where she could close the door and wouldn't have to shoo her family away like nosy pigeons pecking at the window. In my mind, her room looked a lot like Sam's—poster-covered walls and shelves lined with cassettes and records. But she'd also have dog-eared books on astrology, stacked on her nightstand and desk. Maybe she was reading her horoscope right now, comparing our astrological charts, using the stars as guides to understand whether we were meant to be together.

Zia Nella stood at the bottom of the stairs. She wore bright-yellow rubber gloves dirtied with oven grease. "Do you like her?" she asked.

"We're just working on a science project together," I said. Zia Nella followed me back into the kitchen where I returned the phone to its wall-mounted cradle.

"You know," Zia Nella said, "your ziu Frank and I used to study together, too."

"It's not like that," I said. I took a walnut from the wooden bowl on the counter and cracked it open with the V-shaped silver nutcracker.

"David," my father bellowed from the back porch. "What are you doing, David? There's work outside."

Before I had a chance to lie, Zia Nella lied for me. "Sam called him," she said, "to talk about schoolwork."

My father stepped inside and wiped the sweat from his forehead with a paper towel. He filled a glass with water at the sink, downed half the glass before taking another breath. "Outside," he said. "While we still have the light."

∾

Sunday—the day of my confirmation—my father was up at dawn. He made a pot of coffee and hard-boiled eggs and burnt toast. Then he threw open my door and hollered at me to get up and eat something. He showered while I stumbled downstairs to the kitchen. I wanted it to be next weekend already. I wanted to wander the tunnels with Em, her hand in mine. Our evening would end with us stretched out on Foss Hill, kissing under a vault of stars.

My father yelled at me from the top of the stairs to tell me the bathroom was free. I showered while he banged around in his bedroom, getting into his suit. Soon, the doorbell rang. He barked at me through the bathroom door for taking too long. The doorbell rang again, and he stomped downstairs to answer it.

He'd laid my navy-blue suit out on my bed—a nicely dressed flat boy, with a fluffy pillow for a head.

Zia Nella pinched my cheek in the front hall when she saw me in that suit and tie. "So handsome," she said. She took my picture with a Polaroid instant camera. It ejected the photo like a tongue wagging at me. She shook the picture, blowing on it like it was a mug of hot coffee, and watched an awkward boy, fidgeting with his clip-on tie, appear in the image. "One more," she said. "This time stand straight."

"Leave him alone," Ziu Frank said. He patted my shoulder with an approving smile. "Look," he said. "Look." He led me into the kitchen and showed me the box of cannoli in the refrigerator. "For after."

Vincenzo came up from the basement with a bottle of wine. He poured two fingers' worth into two half-pint jam jars. Then he held one out to me and said, "This will make it go easier."

"That's a lie," I said. "You drink it."

He poured my jar into his own. "Salute," he said, and drank the wine.

In the front hall, my father slapped his hands together. "All right," he called out. "Come on. Let's go." He held the door open, sweeping his arm in the air to get us moving. "You have to respect the time," he said.

On the way out of the house, Zia Nella slipped the Polaroid into my suit-jacket pocket and whispered, "For your girlfriend."

~

We stood in front of the wide stone steps of the church, the five of us in formation like suspects in a police lineup. Two altar boys latched open the center double doors, and out stepped Father Salafia—a sentinel beside the impassive stone stare of the witness.

My father hitched up his pant legs and squatted in front of me. He flattened his palm against the first cool step and shot a sidelong glance at all the other steps. The church bells pealed and his eyes watered. This was the sound of my father crying. He cried for imported Sicilian stone—not for me, not for my mother—stone cut into the image of the church he left behind in Melilli.

Before I could squirm beyond his long reach, he'd licked a finger and slicked back my cowlick. He smiled at my embarrassment, straightened my shirt and jacket collars, examined my clip-on tie. "I should've bought you a real one," he said, "taught you how to tie it like a man." He patted my chest. "Beh, you look good." Then he followed Zia Nella and Ziu Frank inside.

Vincenzo and I waited in the line of boys with their sponsors in front of the smaller door on the right. The girls with their sponsors lined up on the left. Rocco and his wife arrived with Tony and his sponsor. Rocco dropped his cigarette and snuffed it out under the heel of his dress shoe. Tony glowered at me—a slow burn meant to wither the troll who dared summon him. He'd gotten my note. He'd be there tonight. His father smacked the back of his head and pulled him close and whispered in his ear. Tony stood ramrod straight, staring at the back of Chris Cardella's head in front of him, eyes boring a hole through his skull. The line started moving. Vincenzo placed his right hand on my shoulder. We walked inside the church, the echo of our footsteps like the sound of the ocean trapped in an empty seashell.

~

It was eleven o'clock that night when I pulled on my denim jacket and snuck outside with my shoebox of notes from Tony and the photograph from my father's closet—the snapshot of his family in Melilli at the festival, with Rocco in the background. Middletown looked deserted, dark except for the bright moon, quiet but for the far-off insect calls and the occasional car. The tall, flat columns and sweeping, curved top of the church towered against the sky in a wash of floodlights. The church looked beautiful like that, lit up at ground level with the arched doors and flourishes all dark.

A police car sped up Washington Street, and I ducked behind a tree. The taillights disappeared around the corner at High Street. Then I walked to the café, the sidewalk tables and chairs stacked inside behind the storefront window and the red security grille. Light seeped around the yellowed edges of the drawn shades of Vincenzo's second-floor apartment windows. I went around back and threw the box into the dumpster. My father and Vincenzo and Zia Nella, all their secrets—I didn't want to be like them.

I crossed Main Street to the lower end of Washington and cut through a parking lot, deserted except for an old man. He struggled to push a shopping cart filled with plastic bottles and dented cans. The cart's front left wheel wanted to go its own direction. The empty highway stretched out on either side of me, a concrete river. Pools of light from the streetlights rippled on the asphalt. I took the stairs down to the pedestrian tunnel. It ran beneath the highway to Harbor Park and the Connecticut River. At the bottom of the stairs, weeds grew through cracks in the graffitied walls. Plastic bags and paper bags and soiled fast-food containers all littered the yawning tunnel entrance. The air smelled of urine. The rusted gate stood ajar, the lock broken. Inside, someone's singing washed in the reverb of the tunnel, but I couldn't make out the words.

"Who's there?" a man's voice boomed from the darkness.

The thin blade of a pocketknife glinted. My eyes adjusted to the underground. A man in an olive-drab jacket and torn blue jeans sat slouched against the wall. He squinted at me. "A boy," he said. The left corner of his mouth twitched. He folded the blade into the handle and pocketed the weapon. Then he covered his bare feet with a tattered blanket. When I didn't move, he waved me over to him. "Shake and Bake won't hurt you," he said.

"I'm just going to the river." I stepped through the gate.

"This is my place." His voice thundered around me. He held out a dirty hand and looked sideways at me, clicking his tongue through a gap-toothed grin.

I searched my pockets and found the two dollar coins Vincenzo had given me. I inched forward. Shake and Bake had bits of food trapped in the wiry curls of his thick, sandy beard. He smelled like hard, pungent cheese. I gave him a coin. I'd paid the ferryman.

He pocketed the dollar piece and began to sing again, the throaty mumbling song of a man lost in his own world.

The melody reverberated through the tunnel and followed me out the other side. Past a pedestrian path, a hexagon-shaped pavilion stood in the center of a wide patio, a mishmash of brick and asphalt, with grass sprouting up from every crack. Shattered glass sparkled beneath two unlit lampposts. A steel railing and narrow strip of boardwalk marked the river's edge. I sat with my legs dangling over the side, heels bumping against the steel bulkhead, arms drooping over the lower railing. My sneakers hovered over the moon on the water. The water was higher than usual from all the rain these last weeks. In the distance, anchored boats swayed in the river. The sky curved overhead like a movie screen showing a three-dimensional film, and I had the glasses that made the images pop. I felt like the stars were right in front of me. I could reach out and touch them, trailing my fingers through the ocean of sky the way Sam trailed his through the waters of the Long Island Sound. The stars felt that close.

In the myth of Pisces, mother and son transformed into fish and swam away together. In the myth, the sea saved them both. The water drummed against the bulkhead. Shake and Bake's crooning echoed in the night, repeating the same troubled refrain, and I didn't hear Tony climb over the Route 9 guardrail or scuttle down the grassy embankment to the boardwalk until he was on top of me.

29

Tony punched the back of my head, and my forehead slammed against the steel post of the boardwalk railing. I dropped the photograph. "What the hell do you want, Marconi?"

My back curled into a crescent moon, and I held a hand over the egg-shaped bump swelling above my left eye. Pain spiked through my skull. My vision blurred. My father's picture floated on the water. "Vassallo," I said. I stretched an arm out through the bars. "My father's last name."

"Your father's name isn't Vassallo," Tony said. "They're all dead because of him, because of what he made my father do."

"No. You need to see." I got down on my belly and hung over the edge, holding the post with one hand and reaching out with the other.

Tony grabbed my shoe with his good arm. "Are you crazy?" he said. "It's just a stupid picture. Leave it."

The photo drifted and I shimmied further out, Tony pulling against me. The cement lip of the boardwalk pressed into my thighs. My fingertips brushed a corner of the photo. It bobbed beneath the water. "Let go," I said. "Almost got it."

"Stop, you're going to fall." He tugged my ankle.

"Get off!" I kicked my foot out of Tony's grasp. My fingers, slick with blood, slipped from the railing, and my head slammed against the rusted metal of the bulkhead and then the water—a burst of freezing wet.

I struggled for a moment, but only a moment—my arms and legs were lead weights on a broken fishing line. Tony's face wavered, a distant moon that gave off no light. *Help me.* He didn't hear me, but maybe I didn't speak. Maybe I only thought the words. My mouth filled with too much water—the taste of silt and mossy stones. I knew who he would become. He would run. He would pretend he was never here. He would carry his own secret now, too.

"It was an accident," Tony said—his voice disembodied, floating in the dark like me. "It was an accident. My father didn't mean to shoot them."

30

The water closed over me. The world shimmered in blue flaring light. The light contracted and the world grew dim and flat, and then the light flared again, and the world shimmered with the heat from the fires of a billion stars all going supernova, all winking out one by one. In the hot, blue light of the last star burning out above me, my father as a boy from one of his stories sat in a cave hulling almonds with his brothers and sister, father and mother. The sounds of war so close, they shook the stones of the world. Bits of dirt and rock fell on top of them. The boys buried their faces in their father's shirt. They hugged him tight. Outside, the Allies pushed the German army through the streets all the way to Mount Etna. *Don't look,* their father said. *Saint Sebastian will keep us safe. He always keeps us safe.*

An enormous inky blackness unfurled around me, so thick and dark as it crept east and west like the black sickled wingspan of Typhon—storm-demon and fire-monster of the ancient world. *Better if Etna destroyed everything,* my father told me when he told me about the cave. *That's what we should've prayed for,* he said, *for the volcano to come down on our heads.*

~

On June 1, 1986, I made the sacrament of confirmation in Saint Sebastian Church. The bishop led the renewal of baptismal promises. He performed the laying on of hands and said a prayer. I approached the altar with Vincenzo, my sponsor. He stood behind me, putting his right hand on my shoulder. The thurifer swung the thurible containing the smoking incense. The bishop anointed my forehead with chrism, calling me by the confirmation name I had chosen.

"Salvatore, be sealed with the gift of the Holy Spirit. Amen."

"Peace be with you."

"And also with you."

I left the altar with my new name, my father's name. I had made it mine. I slouched against the wooden backrest and looked at the painted stars on the ceiling. Early man engraved his stories on the sky with imaginary lines to trace the outlines of the constellations and to keep them there forever. I was like that—the imaginary thread, tracing the outline of memories that told a story of a boy who followed his father into the mouth of a volcano, into the heart of a curse.

SALVATORE

1

When we came here out of Sicily, we left behind the bones of our father and mother, and the bones of their fathers and mothers, and the bones of the land we came up in. This new country was good. We settled down. I bought this house, grew a garden, made you. My son. My David.

I did what I could, raising you on my own. I did my best. I put a roof over your head, kept you from going hungry. I made sure you had shoes on your feet, clothes on your back. Made sure you went to school. It wasn't easy, on my feet all day, eight hours of grinding metal and breathing in the metal dust. I gave you life, tried to make a man out of you. I was the vine and vinedresser and you—picciriddu—you were the fruit.

2

The day you left me, I looked everywhere for you—the porch roof outside your window, all the rooms in the house, the attic, the basement, every inch of the yard and shed, even up in the mimosa tree—but you were gone, the sun only just starting to come up. You snuck out of the house again, I told myself. That's what I wanted to believe. What haircut would you come home with this time?

I banged on Nella's door. Frank answered, on his way to work, a foreman at a construction job an hour away in Plainfield. He asked if he should stay. "Go to work," I told him. "One of us shouldn't have to lose a day."

Inside, a ceramic rooster figurine stood on a little table in the front hall for good luck against danger. In the story of the rooster, a family hired assassins to kill a rival family, but the crowing of the birds woke them up and saved them from the plot. When I told your zia that you had snuck out of the house sometime last night, she paced the kitchen and fingered the rosary beads in her pocket. She started every sentence with "what if." "What if he's hurt?" "What if someone took him?" "What if it was—"

"Enough," I said. I sat down at the table and took the lids off her ceramic sugar and cream rooster and hen. "Call his friend. The kid's last name is Morris. Look it up in the phone book."

Your zia's English was always better than mine, and her eyes were better, too—she could read the small print in the white pages. She found the right number on the third try. She spoke to Sam's mother for twenty minutes. Your zia's face had gone white. She sat down next to me. "David didn't go out with Sam last night," she said.

"Boys lie. Call Jimmy at the factory. Tell him I won't be in today."

"His mother said we should call the police."

"Call Jimmy. I'll wait for you in my car."

We drove around the neighborhood, out by the library and around Wesleyan. I went slow and we craned our necks out the windows at nothing, and I asked myself, "Where did I go wrong?"

I did not realize I spoke the words aloud until your zia, she made a little joke, if you can believe that, she said, "Turiddu, where do you want me to start?"

And I said, "At the beginning," and we laughed—tight, nervous laughter—driving down Main Street, and I decided then, David, that I wouldn't be mad at you, I wouldn't yell or slap you, I'd let you keep whatever crazy hair you came home with, if you just came home, I'd hold you at arm's length and ask you, *Please, please don't run off again.*

In the North End, at the traffic light on Main Street before the on-ramp to the Arrigoni Bridge, by some unspoken agreement, I turned right and went past Saint John Church and the old cemetery to Rocco's house by the highway under the bridge. Nella stood outside the car, arms folded like a boss. I rang the buzzer. When Rocco first came to Middletown, he rented a room in this house. Now he owned the whole building, lived on the first floor, rented out the other two. On the opposite side of the door Rocco cursed, his deformed fingers fumbling with the knob. Finally, he opened it halfway, leaned his bare forearm against the doorjamb, and looked at me and Nella and my car parked at the curb. He spoke Sicilian. "Who else is with you?"

He checked around the porch. "Where's your little soldier? What do you want?"

"David went out last night," I said, "and he isn't home yet. I want to talk to your boy, see what he knows."

"Antonio was here all night. He doesn't know anything." Then Rocco started to shut the door, but I stopped him with my foot.

"I want to hear him tell me," I said.

"Minchia!" Rocco opened the door wide and hollered over his shoulder for Tony. The boy stumbled out of his room in his underwear and complained that it was too early yet for him to get up. He spotted me on the porch, and then darted back inside his room to put some clothes on. "What's he doing here?" he said.

I called out into the hallway in English. "Have you seen David?"

Tony stepped back into view, wearing jeans and a loose-fitting sleeveless shirt. He cradled his cast with his good arm. "I haven't seen him since confirmation yesterday," he said.

"You better not lie to me," I said. I showed him the back of my hand, but the boy's mother, watching from the kitchen, made me feel ashamed, and I lowered my arm and fell quiet.

"My son answered your question, Sal. Now, you leave him alone."

I stepped back from the doorsill and Rocco slammed the door shut. One of the concrete pylons of the Arrigoni stood a few feet from the little porch, and I craned my neck at the steel and cement underbelly of the bridge. The dull highway noise, the thunk and grind of vehicles overhead, all our days spun out like worn tire treads kicking up dirt on the asphalt.

At the car, Nella put her hand on my shoulder. "Let me call the police," she said. I opened the door for her. She sat down in the passenger seat. "The police can help us."

I leaned into the car. "No," I said. "David is fine. David will come home. I know he will. Maybe he is home right now, getting ready for school."

"Sal, look." She pointed back at the house.

Rocco had come outside onto the porch. A lit cigarette dangled from his lips. The strong Morello build in him, buried under the flab of soft years spent working for the rectory.

"It's a terrible thing," he said. He tapped the ash from his cigarette. "I hope you find him, but you brought this on yourself, Turiddu."

3

The house felt different, like it had changed overnight. It felt bigger somehow, and somehow smaller. In the kitchen, I fixed a pot of espresso with the Bialetti Vincenzo had left here years ago, right after you were born. Forgetting to take it home with him—that was his way of giving your mother and me a gift.

Outside, I sat bent over my knees on the back-porch steps. I blew steam from the little cup in my hands. You wouldn't like it. One taste and you'd make a face and complain it was too bitter. But you would grow to like espresso. The taste for it, that comes with age.

Dio mio, you were growing up fast. You did a good job pulling dandelions with me after the festival. You worked hard that day. I think that was the first time you joined me in my garden without my asking. We made a good dinner together from those greens, didn't we? *The food you grow and care for, it has a better taste than what you buy in the store.* I told you that while we sat at the table and ate the simple meal we had cajoled from the earth with our own hands.

I kept that time spent with you and my plants all for myself, let myself hope that maybe there would be more time like that for us.

~

The doorbell rang. Two police officers stood on my front porch. They took off their hats and held them at their sides. Across the street, Nella stepped out of her house. Her skirt billowed around her ankles. She stood with her hands palm to palm, covering her mouth.

"Mr. Marconi," one of the officers said. "May we come in?"

"No," I said and shut the door.

He knocked. "Mr. Marconi," he said, "we understand your son is missing."

I went out the back door and uncoiled the garden hose. I brought the pistol end to my garden and adjusted the spray to a mist. The two men walked up the driveway.

"Mr. Marconi," the officer started again. "My name is Milardo." He placed his hand over his heart. "Angelo Milardo. I helped your boy, David, when he got into that fight at the festival. I'm sorry to be the one to tell you this, but—"

I sprayed them. "Get off my land," I said.

They raised their arms to protect their faces, and then turned away. I let go of the nozzle's trigger. They left a trail of footprints down the driveway from the wet soles of their shoes. I turned the hose on my garden. My plants were thirsty. They needed me. At the curb, Nella stood with the police. They helped her into the patrol car after they told her what I could not hear. I studied one of the pole peas, how it divided into thinner stems, becoming spidery as it grew around the wood. I wet my hand with the hose, wiped the leaves and the thick stems, careful not to unravel the twining smaller ones.

The police car pulled away from the curb. I wiped sweat from my brow with my shirtsleeve. I felt light-headed. I sagged to my knees. They pressed into the damp loam. My fingers like the roots of some old tree drawing water from the earth. The wet soil soaked through the canvas of my pants, the knees stained with dirt.

Oh, Dio mio, figlio mio—when you were just a child, before your mother got sick, you followed me while I worked the garden, asking question after question. You wanted to know the names of the plants and how they grew. You wanted to know what they ate and drank, if they felt pain when I pruned or picked them. You spoke English mostly, your mother's influence, with a Sicilian word woven in here and there. Always mispronounced.

"They are for eating," I told you. "Now watch where you step."

"But they're alive," you said.

"Beh, sure they're alive," I said. And then, because I thought your questions would never end, and because I was tired from a full day of working at the factory, I lost my patience. I raised my voice. I said, "You want to learn or you want to make up stories about the basil?"

And you cried for your mother.

I remember how you cried, so many nights after your mother was gone, cried and never let me sleep. So many nights I sat with you to keep the bad dreams away.

Still, I could not protect you.

4

On the evening of your mother's death, I gripped the steering wheel and watched moths spiraling around the lights in the hospital parking lot. I didn't know how long I'd been there until a guard tapped on my window with a flashlight and shined it on me. I covered my eyes with one hand, started the car with the other, and the radio came on, playing some American pop song. It started to drizzle. The guard walked back to his booth. *I love this song,* your mother had said. I turned up the volume, but I could not bring myself to look at the passenger seat.

In the kitchen, I had a beer. Nella washed the dishes and pans that I had left piled up in the sink. I put my head down on the table.

"David's in his room," she said.

"You brought him here? Why?"

"He wants to see you," she said.

I walked upstairs and looked in on you, your face and palms against the windowpane. "Get away from there," I said from the doorway of your bedroom. "The window's dirty."

"I'm trying to see the sky," you said.

I knelt beside you, and you spoke to my reflection in the glass. You said, "Where's Mommy? Is she coming home soon?"

"If you turn off the light," I said, "you can see outside better."

You turned off the light, and we sat in your room in the dark.

"I still can't see," you said. "Where did the stars go?"

"Behind the clouds," I said.

"Make the clouds go away."

"I can't, David. Only God can do it."

"When will Mommy come home?"

"Your mother is gone."

"Where did Mommy go?"

"God wanted your mother in heaven."

"Can we go see her?"

"I don't think so," I said. "Come downstairs with me. Your zia, she is waiting."

You followed me downstairs and ran into Nella's arms. She kissed your cheeks and hugged you tight. "He's just a baby," she said in Sicilian, "he doesn't understand what he's lost." Her eyes reddened and watered. Then she held you at arm's length for a good look. She brushed your hair from your forehead and planted a kiss there, and you made a shy face and tugged on my pant leg and asked me if you could sit outside on the porch.

"Go ahead," I said. "Your zia will be right out." Then I turned the outdoor light on for you, but you asked me to turn it off.

You perched on the top back step. You held your head in your hands and peered up at the clouds.

"I need him to stay with you for a while longer," I said.

Nella cupped her hand over her mouth and began to cry.

"It's better this way," I said.

~

Maybe I should've let you see your mother in the hospital. Maybe I was wrong keeping that from you—keeping you from her. But I didn't want you to see her like that, and I was used to keeping secrets anyway. I cleared the house of all your mother's belongings so that you wouldn't see her everywhere. You were so young, younger than me the day my brothers died—what that did to me and my parents, the way we let them haunt us, I never wanted that for you.

5

Summer came early the year you left, a heat wave the second of June. In the evening, maybe there would be thunder, a storm to cool things off. Several hours of this heat and already I missed winter. At least then I could put more layers on, more shirts, a sweater, a long warm coat. Summer in America, it wasn't like the dry climate of home with the breeze that blew off the Mediterranean and cooled the coast. It wasn't the warm, dry summer of Sicily. In America—mannaggia l'America—the heat made clothes stick, sometimes as early as the second of June, and then all the layers got peeled away, down to the bones.

6

It was August 1943 when the Allies captured Sicily. Men and women—children, too—all applauded defeat, all gave thanks to God and to the saints. In Melilli, we danced and cheered and cried, tired of hiding in caves, glad to be rid of German and Italian soldiers. I was a boy then, nine years old. I had come from the cave with my family to celebrate in the piazza. A man ran down the steps of Saint Sebastian Church shouting, "He's safe! Our saint is safe!" The crowd cheered for the statue and for the four descendants of the original bearers. "Bring him out," they chanted. "Vassallo, Morello, Cardella, Santangelo, bring him out!" My father, along with these three men, went into the church to answer the call.

My mother hugged my sister and then me. She went to hug my brothers, but British jeeps rumbled by, and we all turned to look and clap. When the convoy was gone, she shouted for Emanuele and Leonello, but the twins were lost in the crowd. She took us each by the wrist and dragged us along the cobblestones, through stomping legs and feet. She called for her sons while looking out from the top of the church steps. My father came to the door and asked what was wrong, and she yanked at my arm and said, "Salvatore didn't keep an eye on the twins, and they've run off."

My father mussed my hair and said, "Turiddu, find your younger brothers." The men inside the church called to him. "Raphael," they said, "hurry up." And he winked at me before going back in. I heard their voices, "One, two, three!" And then a groan, and the people roared as my father came out again, shouldering the statue with the other bearers. They clamored down the steps and parted the revelers as if it were the Feast of Saint Sebastian, when they dressed in white and wore red sashes and marched through the streets chanting, "He is one of our own! First God, and then Saint Sebastian!" They went around the rubble at the corner of Via Marconi, where our house once stood. There were no more homes there after the Allied invasion. Only foundations. Family plots filled with stone.

So I ran from the celebration and found my brothers in our father's almond orchard. The twins sat facing each other in a clearing among the trees. They banged rocks on an unexploded shell set between them. "Emanuele!" I yelled, turning off the dirt road and running into the orchard. "Leonello, what are you doing? Get away from there!" They turned and smiled—that's all I have of them before the flash and crack like the brightest lightning and loudest thunder, before the tinny ringing in my ears, before the shock that came through the ground, up my legs, and into my chest, before the force of it knocked me down and drove the wind out of me.

All these years later, and I still smell that day in my sweat—a smell so thick it is in my throat. The choking stench of rotten eggs and smoke, a dry smell like something overcooked. It still turns my stomach.

When I opened my eyes, the clouds looked like the bowls of curd my father made from milk and lemon juice. Everything moved around me except for the ground flat against my back. There was a low throbbing in my head, and a ringing in my ears like the handheld Sanctus bells that the altar boy rings at the consecration during Mass. I threw up.

"Emanuele?" I said. "Leonello?"

I looked at where my brothers had been and couldn't understand what was wrong with what I saw—an arm by a patch of dandelions. Then I looked at my hands and saw the blood there, and I knew what was wrong—that arm in the grass was bent at the elbow the wrong way. And I wasn't sure I understood how it got that way.

I rubbed at the corners of my eyes, feeling dirt caught there, but the feeling would not go away. I kept on rubbing—it was all I could do to stop thinking about what was in my eyes and about the fumes and what they'd carried into my lungs.

I don't know how long I sat in the orchard before I saw my father. He had been on the dirt road from the cemetery when it happened. He left the men and the statue, and the rest of them redistributed the weight of it on their shoulders. He approached, slowly, and then dropped to his knees at the edge of his land, mouth agape. No sound came from his throat. He was only an image of a scream. A crowd gathered as my mother rushed by and stood in the orchard. She swayed, turning in circles, her dress billowing around her like an umbrella spinning in the storm of dandelion seeds set free by the explosion. She knelt among the naked dandelion stalks to pick up a hand, cradled the bloody palm against her cheek, and began to wail. I wondered which twin the hand belonged to, and if a mother could tell the difference.

7

We had two pieces of property, one above the village and the other in the valley below—that was the almond orchard. In the rocky land above, we cultivated carob trees and figs and prickly pears, and we had a small farmhouse and a well for fresh water. This is where we lived after Sicily was captured, after the bombardment destroyed our house in the village. I loved the view from the fig trees up by the farmhouse. You could see the whole world from there. Rows of red-tiled rooftops staggered down to the cemetery, almost at the base of the mountain. Farther out, the concrete German bunker stood sentinel over the waters of Megara Bay. And above it all, Mount Etna in the north, trailing gray smoke from its mouth. That volcano was always smoking.

But the view I missed most of all was the view into our cemetery. It was a little walled city with an iron gate. Inside, mausoleums housing long-forgotten families and headstones topped with angels lined narrow cobblestone roads. All the newer plots had flat markers like the ones my father engraved for my brothers the night of their wake.

Everyone in the village came to our home to pay their respects that night. They brought us food, generous in those lean times. The Morellos, fishermen by trade, made a fish stew from that day's catch, with crusts of stale bread soaking in the salty tomato broth. The Cardellas, a family of shepherds who had lived in these mountains long before Melilli even had a name, carried a casserole of roasted lamb and potatoes. The Santangelos, who tended the mountainside olive grove that hid the entrances to the caves from prying eyes, baked lemon olive oil cakes, sweetened with the last of their rationed sugar. Everyone gave what they could—some families came with a jug of wine and a little basket of figs, a plate of salami and cheese—and they offered their condolences and prayers and they sat with us, eating and talking in lowered voices.

Palms and flowers and little statues of the Virgin Mary and Saint Sebastian surrounded the small coffins opposite the fireplace. A silver crucifix hung from a nail on the wall above them. My mother kept closing the shutters as people opened them—she did not want the souls of her children to find their way out of the house. She did not want them to leave her.

When the Morellos arrived with their fish stew, Concetta—Rocco's mother—covered the mirror my father used for shaving with a black cloth, and then opened the shutters of the window with the view of the water. My mother rose to close them, but Concetta placed a hand on her forearm. "Giuseppina," she said, "leave at least one open."

My mother collapsed, wailing, into Concetta's arms. Concetta guided her to the chair beside Nella, sat her down, and then knelt before them both. She took my mother's hands in her own, speaking soft words of comfort. Nella wept and buried her face in my mother's skirt. Concetta's eyes welled with tears.

I stood in the doorway, because I could not bear to stay inside—my mother's wailing cries filled that small stone house—and I could not bear to go outside where my father worked on the flat marble and my mother's cries echoed through the mountain, more terrifying than the nights of heavy gunfire during the worst of the fighting.

The men stood around him, smoking cigarettes, keeping silent company. Rocco made coffee and brought it out to my father and the others, and then he joined me. He leaned into the doorframe. Rocco was two years older than me, a head taller, and shared his father's curly, dark hair and round Greek face. He held out a palm-sized paper tube. "American candies from a British soldier," he said. "I saved them for you, Turiddu."

"We can share," I said.

My mother's sobs quieted. Concetta sat beside her now, an arm across her shoulder. Rocco's father squatted and brushed stone shavings from Emanuele's name while my father began carving Leonello's.

Rocco thumbed open the cardboard lid and poured candy-coated chocolate pellets into my hand, and I called Nella to me and split my candy with her.

The Santangelos were the first to leave that night, and like the others who would soon follow, they did not go home right away. They took their time on a long, winding path around the village so as not to bring death into their house. We watched them go, and when they were out of sight beyond the rows of prickly pears and past the snaking stacked stones that marked this lot of arid land as my father's, Rocco said, "Don't worry, my father and I will be here through the night."

~

In the morning, before the funeral Mass, Rocco and his father helped us load the coffins and the two flat stones, a shovel and a bucket of water, into a donkey-drawn cart. They walked with us to the church and carried the coffins inside, and then went home to wash up for the service. I knelt with my father in front of the twins to pray. He made the sign of the cross and clasped his hands together. He bowed his head, resting it on his knuckles. I thought his head would roll off his neck and onto the floor if it weren't for the support of his praying hands, balled together into one giant fist. I looked up over his head at the statue of Saint Sebastian at the side altar and shrine, and I wanted to ask him what it felt like to be pierced with arrows like that. It must've happened so fast— Roman guards tied him to a tree, archers bent their bows, arrows shot through the air and into him—and I wanted to know how he survived. Why did God save Sebastian, only to have him later stoned to death and thrown into a sewer? Maybe God didn't save him at all. And maybe the martyr never had the power to keep us safe. If it was just a lie, then the statue came to us for no other reason than the storm. The rest was made up, a story. It was all just make-believe.

8

Outside the church, my father took the shovel and my brothers' stones from the cart, and he said, "We walk," and I followed him to the cemetery with the bucket of water and a dented tin cup. While he dug the graves in the hot sun, I sat in the shade with my back against the stone wall. It was cool and rough, and I pressed my back against it. I tapped on the bucket and watched the cup bob inside. My father stopped and looked at me—the sole of his right boot on the end of the shovel blade, a white-knuckled grip on the handle.

"Get me some more water," he said, and he drove the shovel into the ground. It made a lonely sound, tearing into the earth that way. He took off his T-shirt and tossed it at the wall.

I walked between the rows of graves to hand him the cup. He drank some of the water, poured the rest over his head, and handed me the empty tin.

"Now go back to the shade, out of the sun," he said. "It's too hot."

During the service at the cemetery, I stared at the two wooden coffins suspended by ropes over the holes. The statue-bearers had carried the coffins down from the church in procession after Mass, and the rest of us followed behind. Near the marked gravesites, the men hesitated.

"Which one goes where?" Morello whispered.

"Ask the priest," Cardella said.

My father shut his eyes.

After the service, Don Fiorilla shook my father's hand and told him to be strong. Then he told my mother how sorry he was for her loss, and that she must find comfort in the knowledge that God had called her boys back to heaven. I asked him why, and the priest got down on one knee, and gripped my arms as if to shake the Devil out of me.

"Ours is not to question God's plan," he said. "These are the paths laid out for us. The best you can do is to remember your brothers." As he stood up to leave, he laid his hand on the top of my sister's head and said, "Look after your brother now."

My mother squeezed Nella's shoulders while my father went to work, lowering the coffins, shoveling dirt over the graves, stopping to wipe his brow with a handkerchief from his back pocket and to gather strength for one more shovelful, for the last. His job wasn't finished until he'd filled their graves. My father measured his care for his children in hard work.

When everyone had gone, my father sat down on the ground beside my brothers' graves. He smoothed over each fresh mound with his hand, patting them down. He looked at my mother, and then turned away. I waited for him to cry or to say something. I looked to him for a clue for how I should be acting. My mother cleared dirt from the flat markers. Nella whispered to me that the flat stones were like pillows at the heads of their new beds. I took my sister's hand in mine and we stayed that way, watching our parents. We dared not move until they stood up and brushed themselves off.

∼

That night in my dreams, my brothers erupted into a fireball. I felt the blast of hot wind and the wet hail of torn-away body parts—so fast and hot in the air that the fire and my brothers became one. The force hit me, pushed me down, and my brothers entered me. We were all together again.

I knew that to dream of the dead was a bad omen, a sign that someone in my family would die soon. But I didn't tell anyone about it, not even Don Fiorilla after Sunday Mass or in the confessional. I prayed that morning. I balled my hands together into a tight fist, and I prayed to God that it was just a dream, that this omen was just more make-believe.

9

For a week after the funeral, the shaving mirror stayed covered and Concetta came in the mornings, long after my father had left for the orchard. She did the housework and opened the shutters my mother had closed, and sprinkled salt around the house to ward away the contamination of death. My mother was not well. She did not rise until noon, and then only to make her daily pilgrimage to the cemetery with a bucket and a washcloth. She poured hot soapy water over the twins' markers. Steam rose from the earth as she scrubbed the stones. She scrubbed around the letters of their names and around the dates, used the wet cloth over her finger to clear dirt from the engravings, the way she used to wash the fleshy curves of their ears.

Even after Concetta stopped coming, my mother did not get better. In the mornings, she hid away in bed while my sister and I had a glass of fresh-squeezed orange juice and biscuits or a slice of bread with butter and jam. My father let his black coffee get cold, listening to the news broadcaster's voice over the hand-crank radio. He wanted to know what had happened since the king ousted Mussolini from power, but the crackling voice talked about food and water rationing, the Allied invasion of Italy that September, and the Italian surrender a few days later. The war had passed over us like a hurricane, and now we were in its eye.

All afternoon, my mother stayed down in the cemetery, and my brothers suffered her wailing—the sound that came from her throat like the keening of a wounded dog. It filled the streets and made people uneasy. They feared for the souls of my brothers, that my brothers would hear their mother's cry and never leave. But more than that, they were angry at how she reminded them every day of the people they, too, had lost.

Evenings, on my father's way up from the orchard, he took her home, and she closed the shutters and picked at the simple meal I had made for us with Nella's help. She ate like a bird and told stories about the twins. I left the house because I could not listen—when you talk of the dead you risk summoning them back.

I sat in the orchard at night and pressed my back against the bark of one of my father's almond trees to force myself not to slouch. I looked at where it happened—where I knew the star-shaped crater was, with a ring of burnt grass around it—and I was glad that the dark swallowed up that spot. I tried imagining our family before the war came to Sicily, when the fighting was just something we heard about from the radio. We had listened at dinner to the newscasts about what was happening in Europe and in Africa, and our father nodded and said, "Remember what I told you about planting. You have to care for the seeds in good soil for them to grow. And if you take good care of them, they will take care of your family."

The earth did take care of my brothers. But I could no longer picture them as they were before the war. I could only see the twins buried in the cemetery with the dirt around their coffins, cradling them like they were babies again. And each night when I closed my eyes, I saw the accident in my mind. I saw the unexploded shell on the ground between them, and I tried saving them. But I knew that I wasn't fast enough to reach them in time, and even if I could, I wasn't strong enough to carry them. So even in my imagination I could not save them.

"Go home," my father would say when he came to get me. "Your mother is worried." But I wouldn't move. I couldn't pull myself away from that place or out of that moment. I wanted him to talk with me about what had happened. I wanted to know if he blamed me. I thought he did.

He pulled me to my feet and I went home, and he stayed behind. "Don't worry your mother" is all he said to me then.

10

Life went on in the land—in the planting, in the watering, in the spreading of the piles of manure. Life was in the almond and carob and fig harvests of those last years of war. Those last years of living in Melilli. Soon, families began rebuilding their homes, but we did not. We stayed in the little farmhouse, the charred foundation and rubble of our home on Via Marconi left fallow. The school reopened. It was Nella's first year, and in the mornings and afternoons, I walked her to and from class. While she attended school, I worked the land with our father.

One morning, in April 1945, my father cranked the radio at the kitchen table with his head low to the speaker while my mother left with her bucket and washcloth. When the news came that partisans had captured and executed Mussolini—his body on display in Milan, hung by his feet from the girder of a gas station—my father's hands shook and he held on to the table edge to steady them. It was the same spot, the man on the radio said, where Fascists had killed fifteen civilians one year ago.

"Take your sister to school," my father said to me.

Then he got up and went out to his garden. He knelt down next to the tomato plants and wiped dirt from their leaves. He spoke tenderly to them, and I knew—even then, I understood—that these were now my father's sons, back from playing hard in some field, hands and faces dirty. He washed them up, his green boys.

When I left Nella at school, I went to the church before working in the orchard, and I stood at the altar of the statue of our patron saint—the ancient stone face, cracked and pitted and scarred like one of the elaborate tombstones from the cemetery, marking the grave of a man dead for centuries whose name on the stone had been erased by time.

Behind me, the doors opened. Rocco walked up the center aisle, hands in a fist held at his waist. He took a seat in the first row of pews. "Turiddu," he said. With a wave of his arm, he beckoned me to join him.

I sat down beside him, but I could not take my eyes off the statue.

"My mother," he said, "she's borne six children and lost five, and I asked her, *How? How can you be so strong after losing so much?* And she says to me, *You are the miracle. The others, I gave them to God.*"

"But they got sick," I said. "There was nothing you could've done."

"We prayed, didn't we, Turiddu? Your family sat with mine, and we prayed together in this spot. You are like my little brother now, and Nella, she is a little sister to me." He put his hand on my shoulder and squeezed. "Don't be too angry with the saint. He protects us, he does, in ways we cannot always understand. You will see. I promise."

"Do not talk to me of promises," I said. "What I see is nothing but stone and childish stories."

Rocco crossed himself. "You don't mean that. Don't let anyone hear you say that. People are already starting to talk."

"What people say is not my concern."

∽

The war ended. Men again left on ships bound for America. They left for Middletown, but we knew of it as Little Melilli. Families from our village had been going there since before the First World War. We even heard that they had built a church over there and that someone had carved a statue of our saint from memory. They left Melilli, chasing the promise of good-paying jobs and a better life. They left to forget war, forget poverty, forget hunger, and forget the bodies of the loved ones they lost. But they would not forget their saint.

In time, my mother resumed caring for us, cooking the meals and doing the housework. Still, she spent her afternoons at the cemetery, cleaning the stones—her wailing faded to feeble whimpers—and she spoke of the twins and nothing else. And there was never another May Feast of Saint Sebastian for my family. Rocco Morello, the eldest son among the four families, held my father's place as one of the bearers. My father, he never carried the statue again.

11

By 1946 the whole village was talking behind our backs like a drove of braying donkeys. They blamed us for their own misfortunes and later for strange fires that no one ever witnessed save for those who reported seeing them. In the three years since the twins died, Santangelo's olive trees produced less and less fruit, Morello's blue-and-white fishing boat went missing—disappeared from the locked stone boat shed down by the shore—and a pack of wild dogs started killing Cardella's sheep. Then, this past season, all the chickens in the village fell ill and died, and crop yields were low except for our crops. We were lucky. Our harvests were bountiful. Strange, after everything, we were lucky in this.

The spontaneous fires began in September. First reported by Cardella—he claimed flames leapt out from a hole in the ground and almost cooked his legs, and he held up his burnt pant legs as proof of what he saw. The story passed from person to person like influenza until everyone in the village had a similar story of narrowly averting catastrophe from a burning hole that opened up under their feet, and they went to the priest and demanded he take action.

I'd heard it said many times how our family brought this evil to Melilli. Our mother wasn't right in the head, they said. She had a sickness in the brain. Our father, too. So it was only a matter of time before

Don Fiorilla paid us a visit on an evening in December near the end of that year.

When Nella stood up from the dinner table to answer the door, our father stopped her with a stern look. She sat back down in her chair. He opened the door.

"Good evening," Don Fiorilla said. The priest took off his saturno, held it by the wide circular brim. He asked us to pardon him for the interruption, but he wondered when my father would return as a bearer in the festival. "It isn't good," he said. "Your family, they need the saint's strength now more than ever."

"Please, leave us in peace," my father said.

"Raphael," Don Fiorilla said. And his voice grew softer. "I hear you are sleeping in the orchard. In the spot where the boys—"

"Where I sleep is my business," my father said. "Good evening, Don Fiorilla."

My father shut the door and sat back down at the table without a word. He pushed his fork around his plate of spaghetti with runny tomato sauce. He had made the sauce over the summer with onions and basil and stored it in lidless jars in the sun to dry. He stirred the sauce over three days while it thickened and reduced to a paste. Then he sealed the jars and stored them in the farmhouse closet. Later, with oil and water, we'd dilute the thick paste back into sauce.

The tines scraped the dish.

"What's this?" he said. "This is water. You ruined my sauce."

"Then don't eat," my mother said.

She took his plate and upended it over the garbage. He pushed himself away from the table. The chair legs scraped against the floor.

"Turiddu," my mother said. "I can see the war on your face."

I had finished eating, but I held on to my plate.

She tugged it, but I did not let go. "It's in your eyes," she said. "You have a hard face for a boy." She pulled the plate from my hands. "Last night I dreamed a knock at the door, and I knew it was my Emanuele

180

and my Leonello." And I asked her, "How?" And she said, "Because a mother, she knows these things."

My father got up and went into the other room, the one we all shared as a bedroom. My mother stood at the sink, washing dishes. "I could pick your brothers' voices out from among the other children playing outside," she said. She scrubbed hard at the plates, at stains that were not there. "Such good boys, always coming when their mother called. Why didn't they come? The years would've given them sweet, deep instruments. All the men in our family have nice baritones, but none of them had those eyes. They shared my eyes, my very long eyelashes, so long that people mistook them for girls when they were infants. This made your father mad."

Emanuele and Leonello were good-looking boys. Not like me. I had a nose as large as a man's, a Roman nose, and a scowl. Back then people always thought I was angry. They asked me what was wrong. Years later, and they still asked me. I kept this boy's face even as creases in my forehead and around my eyes and mouth all pulled my frown off the bone.

My father walked out of the bedroom carrying a pillow and a hunting rifle. "Get your jacket," he said to me.

12

In Melilli, almond trees bloomed white in February. In December they were green, getting ready to bloom again, and they had to be shaken by a pole to free them of mummies, leftover nuts that bred disease. In the orchard, my father took two poles from the shed and handed the shorter one to me, and we knocked the mummy nuts to the ground.

"Look here," my father said. "Look. See how the seal of the shell is bad?" He held one in his free hand. "They'll rot the whole tree. So do a good job while there's still some light left."

I whacked the tree limbs hard. The mummies pelted me.

"Easy," my father said. "You'll break the pole."

In half an hour, it was dark, and my father walked with me along the dirt road leading from the orchard. I watched the dust kicked up by my shoes and my father's larger ones. A full moon crested. And through the shadowed bars of the cemetery gate, the dust settled into the moonlight.

"There's a light in the window of a mausoleum," I said. "What do they need a light for?"

My father told me it was nothing but the moon, then took me by the arm and pulled me down the road.

"It's not the moon," I said, and I struggled in his grip.

When we reached the edge of the village, my father said, "Go home." And then he turned back toward the orchard.

I kicked a pebble, and a cloud of dirt trailed around my ankles.

After my father was gone out of sight, I circled back to the cemetery and climbed over the gate. That was the first time I had been in there at night. It was easier to walk among the tombstones this way, without the sun to show me the names of all the people buried there. I looked at the stones—some of them were taller than me—and at the dark shapes of the mausoleums further inside. Where was the one with the light in its window? It had seemed like it wasn't so far away from the road outside. Then I saw the light in the distance, and I went after it down the main cobblestone street, onto a dirt path, deep into the cemetery.

I walked on, never quite reaching the mausoleum. I stopped to get my bearings. All around, headstones stood or leaned like shadows across the rows of burial plots, but I could no longer see the cemetery walls. This place seemed bigger than I remembered. I was lost, and the light was lost to me, too. But I had to go on. I had to know why the light was there and why the dead needed it.

I wandered off the trail, stepping over graves, until I came back to the dirt path. I knew I had been this way before because I recognized the cracked and half-fallen stones that lined the edges. Then I saw the light again, and I hurried after it.

At the mausoleum, I stood on my toes to look through the round stained-glass window. But I couldn't see into the tomb because of the black-and-gold picture of the martyrdom of Saint Sebastian.

I tried the metal doors but they were locked. And then I heard bushes rustling, the laughter of children. I followed the sound around to the other side of the mausoleum, but no one was there. The laughter stopped. I looked at a row of bushes cut close to the marble wall. Here, the moon lit up a stained-glass window identical to the one on the other side. I reached up and touched the glass where the light went into the tomb, my fingers like the arrows into the saint's side.

The laughter came again, only this time it was further down the path. I followed it to my brother's graves, where I knelt and touched the damp grass.

~

Sometimes it felt like I'd been following my brothers my whole life. But I never caught up to them. Sometimes in my garden, finding my way among the rows of vegetables, I could almost see them. Then a breeze would blow, and the leaves of my garden would move, their shadows restless under sunlight. And I would know I was alone.

Did you see your mother, David, in spite of everything I did to prevent her ghost from visiting you? Did she stay with you the way the twins stayed with me? For you it wouldn't have felt like a curse. I know that you would say this. I know as if you were here with me now.

~

Back on the dirt road outside the cemetery, I walked to the orchard and found my father slumped beneath an almond tree. He was looking into his hands and muttering to himself. I inched closer, crouched behind a line of rough stones, the footprints of an old farmhouse long gone. He was off somewhere in his mind, trying to make order of his thoughts and failing. He pulled at his hair, buried his cheeks in his knees, folding into himself as if he were a child and not the man of his house.

At the howling of a dog, he raised his head, his right arm falling along the side of his leg to the ground. He stared at his hand, flattening the grass blades. He leaned back against the tree, fingertips grazing the butt of his rifle. He slid it out from under the pillow, checked the chamber, and placed the barrel in his mouth.

The instinct of a spooked animal possessed me. I wanted to run, but my feet took root in the ground. In the place where my brothers died,

I saw them made whole and playing. Still those smiling boys, my little brothers. Then that light and that sound like no light or sound I had ever seen or heard before, or since. And those hands—the fingers curled a little with the palms facing up at the dandelion seeds that speckled the air. Those feet that had nothing to support.

I went cold. I felt as though every drop of blood rushed out of every vein in my body and went down my legs in search of an outlet, as if trying to escape through my toes. I don't know, maybe my father was frightened by the taste of metal with a hint of gunpowder, but something made him look, something made him see me. He took the rifle out of his mouth, hit his head against the almond tree, and cried out. He put his hand on his forehead and kept it pressed there as if he was trying to hold everything in, all of it bleeding between his fingers to the corners of his eyes and down his face.

That's when I ran as fast as I could, without knowing where. I ran without knowing that my hands covered my ears. I looked back at how far I'd gone, and I knew it wasn't far enough. How far did I have to go? How far to outrun that sound, and everything?

I didn't slow down until I was out of breath and cramping up. I doubled over, pressing my hands against the pain in my side, chilled from sweating in the cold. I wished that my father had never told me the story of how the statue came to us.

～

That stone had been around a long time. Who knows where it came from or who the man was that shaped the rock into the image of the saint, and why? What vision he thought he saw when he first saw the slab of stone. The important thing is that a man carved the statue, and it was a man who told the story. We can't know anything beyond that. We try. We think we do. And that is how we get into trouble.

13

Weeds came up through small cracks in the domed concrete bunker, and long stalks of grass grew wild around its outside perimeter. I stepped down into the trench that led to the metal door. I pushed it open, creaking the hinges and sending an empty bottle wobbling across the dirt floor until it clinked against empty food tins. In the corner, I found a musty blanket and wrapped myself up in it. Slats of moonlight shone through three sea-facing gun ports. I crouched there, at the middle port, and looked out from where soldiers had attacked enemy ships at sea.

Half the night passed. Maybe more, but I could not tell from the cold. I could not tell from my breath on the air in the gray light of the bunker. A stray dog padded outside in the brush. I shut the door, turned the wheel, and locked it. The animal sniffed and growled. A deep thunder rumbled.

Cold air came in through the gun ports off the sea. In the sky, a sheet of fast-moving clouds blocked out the moon and stars. Soon, the darkness swallowed me. I lay on the ground with my eyes open, unable to sleep. During the bombardment, I had wished for daylight to stop the bombs and gunfire from lighting up the night sky, from filling it with sound. Now, I wished for this night to never end, for the thunderclaps to mask my father's rifle blast.

I thought of my father in the orchard. Did he ask where his saint had gone, what he did to make Saint Sebastian turn his back on us? I listened to the storm outside, wondering about every thunderclap, wondering if God had caused the sound, or my father. I should've known better than to think I could run away.

Outside, the dog barked. His two eyes looked in at me from one of the gun ports. The space was too small for the animal to squeeze through, but that didn't stop him from trying. He wanted his shelter back, to get out from the storm. I reached my arm out, fingers feeling the dirt floor for a stone. I felt a can and threw it at the eyes. The tin clanged against the concrete. The dog yelped and ran off.

I shivered through the night. I was awake when the rain drummed against the bunker, awake when the thunder broke so loud it made me think it was right on top of me, still awake when the storm passed at first light. But even the storm couldn't last forever. I knew it wouldn't, because I had wished it. Outside the gun port, the sky was clear. There was no sign of the dog. Daylight would show me if my father had taken the top of his head off. I turned back to curl up in the blanket again. Next to an empty ammunition canister, a pocket-size leather notebook lay in the dirt, a nameless soldier's journal. The cracked leather was the color of a saddle, with a matching strap to tie it shut. Some of the pages were water damaged or faded, entries in black ink smudged and illegible. A matchbook marked the last entry. And what I could read there told me everything. It changed everything. At the time, it felt like fate had revived me, given me a sense of purpose and power. But I know now it was the curse of my brothers still moving against me. They had not yet let me go, would not, until they had taken everything from me.

1943. Melilli, Sicily.
The British overran Noto. Many Italians surrendered or fled into the mountain villages to hide among the locals there. But I made my way north, traveling only at night and never on a main road, for I believed the enemy only two, maybe three days behind me. I met up with three

Germans, and together we retreated to defensive positions in a village called Melilli.

In two days the enemy will be on top of us, maybe sooner. The shelling draws nearer. The Germans and I have prepared for the worst by making improvised grenades from discarded food tins and packing them with gunpowder, tying nails around the cans, and sealing the edges of the lids with clay. We used cotton twine soaked in water and coated with gunpowder for the fuses.

I have little hope this position will hold.

∾

I took the tin that I had thrown at the dog. Bits of dried clay crumbled around the rim of the lid. There was a hole in one end where the fuse must've been. I took the lid off. The tin was empty. It should have been full of explosives, like the shell that killed my brothers. What were they thinking when they banged on it? Did they know that there was a fire inside and that they were letting it out? That same fire should've taken me. My hands would've touched my mother's cheek. My grave would've been washed every morning. That's how it should've been.

But I lived. Maybe you could say that I had been blessed, that Saint Sebastian had saved me, but I say that it would've been better if the statue had never come to Melilli.

∾

So I stood on the rocky outcropping at dawn and looked out at the desolate bay and at the sea, calm despite the cold breeze. A plume rose above Mount Etna, blown into a long dark line across the sky. Old men in the village told of a monster trapped there under the mountain in a constant struggle to break free. But that was a story told to children.

I held my hand in the air over Etna's crater, and the dark smoke issued from my fingertips. There was no monster. Etna was just a volcano—a great windpipe in the Earth feeding oxygen to powerful fires that burned deep underground. Those fires, so strong they melted stone. The day the twins died, I swallowed a piece of that fire, and it had burned in me ever since. In the same way caring for the vegetable garden nurtured my father, the way the plants sustained him, gave him life, each breath I took fed the fire inside me, made me stronger.

∼

I walked back to Melilli with the journal in my pants pocket and the tin in my hand. I took the road that went around the opposite side of the hill to avoid passing the orchard. I didn't want to see what my father had done to himself. At the back of our farmhouse, I saw my mother leaving with my sister, and I watched them from behind a fig tree. My mother had her bucket and washcloth, my sister her schoolbooks. After they had gone, I ran to the house and into the bedroom, opening the soldier's journal on my cot. I took my father's toolbox and canister of rifle ammunition from the closet. Then I pried open the casings with a knife, poured the powder into the tin, and tied nails around the outside of the can. I made the fuse and dried it out, passed it through the hole in the top of the tin, and sealed the rim with clay from my father's garden. Then I hid the journal under my mattress and wrapped the grenade in a blanket, cradled it in my arms.

In the piazza, Rocco helped the old chestnut grower—Longu Castagna—set up his cart for roasting chestnuts. It used to be that every morning, Rocco would be out on the water with his father before dawn, but since Morello's boat had disappeared, his father now sold his labor to an estate owner far from the village, and Rocco went to work for Longu, harvesting and selling his chestnuts. Old Longu Castagna and the Morello family, they went back a long way. Some said they went as far back as the finding of the statue. They said that Longu was one of the sailors on the ship that ran aground. But that would be impossible. That would make him over five hundred years old. That was just another story. More likely, the old man belonged to a family—one of many families—whose ancestors came from far away to see the statue that had washed ashore, and followed Morello and the other bearers when they carried it here to this spot.

The people of Melilli gave him the name Longu Castagna: *Longu* because he was one of the tallest men in the village, almost five-eleven, and *Castagna* because long ago the old man had brought back a chestnut-tree cutting from the slopes of Mount Etna and from that single branch had cultivated a grove at the edge of the village. No one remembered his true name or age anymore, and if you asked him, not even old Longu could tell you.

Rocco set a stone beside each of the two wooden wheels, brought the fire bin down from the cart, and then started cutting *X*'s into chestnuts on a flat board. "If you're here for chestnuts," Rocco said to me, "you are early."

That day in the church when we sat before the statue of Saint Sebastian, Rocco had told me not to be angry with the saint, that the ways the saint protected us were not always for us to understand, but I could not remember the prayers our families had made for his five lost siblings, and I could not replace them. No one could.

"I'm not here for chestnuts," I said.

Old Longu whistled a tune I did not recognize while he got the fire going. He turned the cylinder over the fire bin. The flames leapt up, cleaning the metal container. He stoked the fire with a stick, and then turned the handle of the cylinder as Rocco dumped a full bowl of cut chestnuts into it.

"What have you got there?" Longu called after me.

The inside of the church glowed in dim oranges and blues from rows of windows near the high wood-beamed ceiling. Seams from the wood slats broke the clouds and angels painted there. My footsteps echoed down the center aisle, through rows of empty pews and gold-trimmed arches and up to the broken angels.

This was Melilli.

Safe in his pillared side altar, with a golden metal disk for a halo, the martyr Sebastian leaned against a marble tree trunk. His arms were bound behind him, his body a pincushion of arrows. He gazed down on me with imploring eyes as if he knew my mind. If he could speak, he would tell me to have faith, the way he had faith. This twice-martyred saint. He turned his back on us, if he was ever with us at all, if he was ever more than just old stone.

I touched an arrow where it entered his chest, fingered the chiseled wound. The wound. I felt it in my own chest, here, a pressure behind the breastbone. A fire inside me ready to bloom a flower of flames.

I knelt before the statue of our patron saint, set the makeshift grenade at his feet. Dust spiraled upward around the rusted, filthy tin. "Did it hurt?" I asked the stone, and the stone replied with stillness.

So this was Melilli, this wound we shared in silence. We were all broken at the seams like the painted scene of heaven above me. But they closed their eyes and covered their ears just as the saint had done the day my brothers played with that unexploded shell, and every day after.

I took the matchbook from my pocket. My eyes stung and teared the way they did when I was chopping onions from my father's garden. I cursed the half-domed altar, sliced like an onion and cracked with jagged white lines of peeling plaster. I rubbed at my eyes. Bits of clay pocked with gunpowder clung to my fingernails and the folds of my knuckles. My brothers had broken apart like stone under a sledgehammer and left behind a little crater in the orchard. Now I would make another.

I struck the match. Today, today they would hear me and the weight I carried in the heavy clop of my shoes. I struck the match, and it was the ruin of everyone around me.

14

I ran for cover behind the second row of pews before the grenade detonated. My heart was racing. My ears rang as the saint's body blew apart into fragments of stone and dust. When I stood up, my legs shook. I leaned against the pew in front of me. My throat was dry from the dust, and I coughed phlegm into my hands. I felt chalk and bits of stone in between my teeth. Sebastian's torso lay on the floor in front of me. His arms, still tied to the tree, broken at the elbows. A fire consumed the white cloth that had covered the altar, now split into two charred halves. The flames licked at the walls of the shrine, and the wood ignited with a splintering crack.

"Turiddu," Rocco shouted. He ran up the center aisle and fell to his knees and dragged the broken torso of his patron saint into his lap. He rocked back and forth with the stone as he cried, "Oh, Turiddu. Turiddu, what have you done?" He looked at me and asked me why, and when I had no answer for him, he pulled at his hair and wailed like a lost mother mourning her child—and that was as good an answer as any that I could give.

But I felt no grief, no guilt, not even shame. I felt nothing at all except for the desire to run. So I ran—I ran out the side door of the church. Smoke billowed out after me into the sky. A woman's scream echoed around the piazza, and I knocked into old Longu's cart. The cart, the fire bin with its burning red coals, and the chestnuts toppled over, and I hurried to the mountain road with the old man cursing me from below.

Church bells rang out in alarm. Rocco's words chased me up the mountainside to the farmhouse. *What have you done?* I pushed open the farmhouse door. "Mamma," I called out. I checked the bedroom. The house was empty. I opened the window and looked down the slope, into the village. Between tiled rooftops, people rushed through the narrow cobbled streets and into the piazza in front of the church. A commotion of shouting and swearing men marched up in a cloud of dust. Some of the men brandished guns. They made a pageantry of force on the road—the same road they had walked after the twins died, carrying solemn gifts of food to my family.

I bolted the door. The crowd assembled around the front of the house. They talked over each other, loud and confused empty talk. They did not know what had happened, only that the church had been attacked and the villains, whoever they were, now hid in the Vassallo farmhouse.

I peeked out the slats of the shuttered window.

"There's the criminal," cried old Longu. "Knocked me down running away. You saw what he did, Rocco. Tell them."

"It's true," Rocco said. He pushed his way to the front of the mob. "It was Salvatore Vassallo. He blew up our statue."

The howls of men demented answered Rocco's accusation. A fat man pounded on the door—Nunzio, the baker who bought our almonds for his pastries. "Come out!" he yelled and threw his weight against the wood. The hinges creaked. Other men joined him, calling for my surrender, calling me coward and murderer, as if a man can murder a piece of stone. It was my family that had brought the sickness of death to their lost animals, my family that had brought the mysterious fires. And now—I had taken their patron saint.

Don Fiorilla hurried up the road from the church, out of breath and waving his arms in the air, shouting for everyone to stop this madness. He paused under a fig tree and fanned himself with his saturno. "Please," he said. He was winded and had trouble speaking. "Let Turiddu go. It's not right, what you are doing. He is only a boy."

Some of the men stepped back. They sided with the priest. They wondered aloud in sheepish voices how a family could have done the things they accused us of, even as troubled a family as mine—maybe the people who saw the ghost-fires had too much to drink, maybe they saw only what the wine made them see, and hadn't they all lived and seen enough of this cruel life to know that animals sometimes got sick and some seasons were better than others? And this terrible business at the church, didn't it make more sense that a band of outlaws had been responsible for destroying the statue than a mere child?

"Let us send for the carabinieri," Don Fiorilla said. "If the boy is guilty, let them arrest him." The priest stepped forward, a man of reason, but a stampede of donkeys always tramples reasonable men.

When the mob broke in and dragged me out by my armpits with legs kicking, the expression on Rocco's face—I would never forget—like the chiseled stonework of the martyr.

"What is the meaning of this?" my father's voice called out. He and my mother stood at a distance beneath the curling pods of an old carob tree. In his hands, he carried the pillow he'd brought down to the orchard and a bushel basket of almonds stored from the last harvest. His hunting rifle hung by a strap from his shoulder. He was alive, my father was alive, and even as I struggled against the men who held me captive, I thanked God that day for my father's life.

"Salvatore destroyed the statue," Rocco said. "I saw it with my own eyes." His voice, like a crack of thunder the saints could hear all the way up in heaven. The cries of men rose around me, echoing Rocco's declaration.

My father threw down the pillow and basket. The almonds spread out, wobbling around everyone's feet. "Get off my land!" he shouted. He raised his rifle and trained it on random targets of men, staring each of them in turn down the long barrel.

My mother fell to her knees and wept, and through her tears she cursed them all—all the men who laid a hand on her boy. "Thieves," she said, "you want to take my only remaining son from me." She spat in the dirt and shook her crossed middle and index fingers at them. "May your hands fall off."

Rocco dragged me across the rocky ground by my shirt collar to stand before my father. "Look at your son's face," he said.

"Let him go," my father said. He leveled the rifle at Rocco's chest.

The men closed around us, making the horns of the goat with their fists to deflect my mother's curse.

Rocco released me. "Look," he said.

My father turned to me and searched my face, and he asked me, "You did this thing?" And my face gave away my guilt. The rifle sagged in his arms, the barrel dipped and pointed at the earth. In that moment, Cardella and Nunzio rushed my father. They grabbed for his gun. I panicked and ran. Behind me, the sounds of a struggle and then gunfire— two shots.

∾

This was what happened to people when they believed too much in stories. Those stories that we all loved, if we held the pages to the light, we'd see right through them. If we held them close enough, they'd burn.

15

Old women in their black mournful shawls stood in doorways crying at the smoke billowing from the church. Men pulled at their hair with both fists and shouted curses at the sky. I stopped in front of the schoolhouse and looked back to see if Rocco and the others had followed me, but I could not spot them through the commotion in the streets. A man rushed into the school, and I followed him to my sister's classroom.

"There's been an attack," he said. "Saint Sebastian Church is on fire." Then he ran to the boys' class across the hall. One of the girls screamed. The students jumped from their chairs and crowded around the windows.

"Calm down," the schoolteacher said. "Come away from the windows."

I told her our father wanted Nella to come home right away. The teacher said for us to be careful, and then I grabbed Nella's hand and led her outside. We ran to the opposite end of the village and took a goat path that wound up the mountain slope.

"Where are we going?" Nella asked when she saw that we were not going home.

We stopped behind a crumbled wall with a swastika painted on it. The mayor had lived there. When the Germans came to our village, he welcomed them. He sat at their table, ate food stolen from our stores. After the war, the people turned against him. Someone killed him in the night. The authorities never caught the one who did it.

"We're not going home," I said. "I'm supposed to take you somewhere safe."

"The cave," she said. "There's going to be another war, isn't there?"

"The cave isn't safe anymore, Nella."

She tightened her grip on my hand. "Turiddu, you're scaring me."

"Don't let go." I towed my sister behind me as I ran, bits of stone crunching under our feet and rolling down the slope.

The craggy path went up, almost to the mountaintop. We hid behind some prickly pears, and I peeked over the edge. Our farmhouse looked deserted, but the more I looked, the more I made out two bodies sprawled on the ground, not moving. And the more I stared at those bodies, the more I wished I hadn't ever seen them.

Two goats walked up the path. They must have wandered from the flock belonging to Fortuna or Russo—any number of goatherds from the village. Their creamy-white coats dirtied with brambles stuck to the long fur. They looked at my sister and me as if they were trying to figure out what to make of us. Then one lowered its head, and I thought it was showing me its long corkscrew horns as a warning, but it was only grazing on the low weeds. The second goat did the same. They stood there, chewing and watching us, as if this were a normal day. As if the world below us weren't going crazy with the shouts of men and the cries of women and that dark smoke rising above the church.

Nella tugged on my arm. She pointed at a group of men in the piazza with guns. "What happened?" she asked me.

There was something about those bodies in front of our farmhouse near the carob trees—the way they lay in the dirt and the way the dirt darkened around them. I did not want Nella to see. I grabbed her arm. "Come," I said.

We passed the way to the caves, following the goat path down and around the backside of the village. Someone shouted, "Check the caves." And I saw a cloud of stone and dirt as several men scurried up the steep, terraced mountainside. They startled the goats. One of the animals lost its footing and tumbled over the side, breaking its horn at the skull. The other animal butted a man as he came up on the path.

I turned away and said, "We have to keep moving."

And we did not stop to catch our breath until we were outside the village, crouching in the bushes by the highway. Rocco and Cardella stood on the road behind us. "What happened," Cardella said with a hand on Rocco's shoulder, "is no one's fault but the boy's."

"Who are they looking for?" Nella asked me.

I put my fingers to my lips until they had gone out of sight, back toward the cemetery. "Listen," I whispered. "There are men coming after us. We have to leave."

"But where are we going?"

I looked at the highway, read the sign, and said, "Syracuse. Our parents are meeting up with us there."

∿

Syracuse was twenty-three kilometers away—fourteen miles of rocky terrain in the early cold morning. It was a long day of following the highway and hiding behind limestone outcroppings from cars that drove by. We were hungry and tired. We stopped in an abandoned fort dug into the stone. Over the next terraced hill, an orange grove filled the valley. A farmhouse stood on the other side of the trees where two men loaded crates onto the back of a truck. I signaled to my sister to stay put, and then I snuck into the grove. I picked as many blood oranges as I could from the low-hanging branches, held the ends of my shirt out and filled it with fruit.

When we had walked a good distance from the grove, we sat under a tall and slender cypress tree. They lined the dirt road ahead of us with their tapering cones, like flames growing out of the earth. I peeled the thin red skins off two oranges and separated them into wedges on my lap. I made sure that Nella ate most of the citrus. I learned something that day about the strength I had inside of me when I had someone to look after.

16

My brothers followed me from the orchard to the German bunker. They stayed with me until the morning under the dark cloud that split the sky. We made our way to the church together, their lips pressed against my ears, whispering, their fingers pointing to the statue.

My brothers were there in our farmhouse when the men stood outside screaming. They were there when I ran, when the shots were fired. They followed Nella and me all our lives.

~

Syracuse was framed by the sea on one side and the curving base of the Hyblaean mountain range on the other. Men waited in long lines every day looking for work—maybe two or three got lucky with some small job. Women walked the rubble-lined alleys after dark, selling themselves for food or a few coins. War orphans wandered the streets like ants without their queen. Some of the boys—the smart ones—worked in groups. They circled a man, tugging at his shirtsleeves, pleading with their dirty faces for a handout to fill their empty stomachs, while one boy picked his pockets clean. I watched the boys that first full day in Syracuse. I watched them work, and I learned from them.

~

"Where are they?" Nella asked as we crossed a stone bridge to the island of Ortygia, the Old City, and walked by some crumbled walls and scattered columns.

"I don't know," I said. "They'll be here soon. But we have to eat, so when we find the market, I want you to cry."

"How do I do that?" Nella said. "I can't cry on command."

"I don't know," I said. "But you have to make it look real. Tell the merchant you've lost your mother."

Nella stopped walking, took my arm, and said, "Don't make me do that."

"You have to," I said. "Who can ignore a little girl crying for her mother?"

"You're the Devil."

"Nella," I said. "If you don't do this, we're going to starve."

We wandered the narrow streets, the winding alleyways, threading ourselves between pale stone buildings connected by gated arches, until we found a market tucked away on a side street. Vendors sang out their merchandise, fish fresh from the boats that morning, fruits and vegetables from the local farmers.

As we walked through the crowded market, I slipped a loaf of still-warm bread from out of an old lady's shoulder bag while she argued over the price of clams. I tucked the loaf under my arm as if it belonged to me all along, felt a rush of excitement, and whispered to Nella, "It pays to be small."

Nella crossed herself and asked for God's forgiveness.

"God won't feed us," I said. "But you see that merchant over there? He will."

"We have bread," she said. "Let's go. Don't make me do this."

"I'm all you have," I said. "Better pray you find me." Then I slipped into the crowd and made my way to an alley on the other side of the street. I stood, pressed my back against the wall, and peeked around the corner.

Nella called out my name, turning in circles and looking for me. Her voice grew louder. "Turiddu," she cried. "Turiddu. Don't leave me, please."

A woman stopped and wiped Nella's face with a small cloth from her handbag. They spoke, but I couldn't hear their conversation. Then the woman turned and asked the nearby vendor if he'd seen this girl's brother. The merchant came around from his cart, got down on his knees, and cleared strands of hair from my sister's forehead. He took her little hands in his bigger ones.

I crossed the street. But before I reached the cart, a man had the same idea as me. He grabbed a basket of the merchant's chestnuts and ran off with it.

Nella saw him, stamped her feet, and pointed, saying, "You're getting robbed. You're getting robbed."

The man turned around, saw the thief taking the chestnuts, and chased after him. Several men in the crowd followed—all yelling and screaming curses—and in the chaos, I threw a quarter wheel of hard cheese and a salami roll into a basket of almonds. Then I grabbed the basket, looked at my sister, and said, "Run!"

∿

In a bombed-out building, I sat on a collapsed wooden beam, cracking almond shells with a stone. Nella stood at the window with her back to me and took a picture of the Virgin Mary down from the wall. She removed the broken glass, setting the shards on the windowsill. "The frame is still good," she said. Then she blew the dust off, kissed the picture, and placed it back on the nail.

"Come away from there," I said. "Someone might see you."

She went through a cabinet and found some candles. Then she turned to face me and said, "Don't ever do that again."

I split a shell open with my stone. "That was quick thinking, telling the vendor he was being robbed," I said.

"I'm serious," she said. She arranged the candles on the floor at the foot of the picture.

"Here," I said. I cut a slice of cheese with my pocketknife. "Eat."

She stood up, took the slice, and ate it while admiring the little shrine she'd made. "Do you have matches?" she asked.

I dug into my pocket for the matchbook. The design on the cover showed the fasces set in the center of the green, white, and red stripes of the Italian flag.

Nella took the matches and lit the candles.

I tore the heel from the bread loaf and saved it for her in my lap because I knew that was her favorite part. Then I took another piece for myself and said, "That's not going to help you. It's better if you learn that now."

"Look at this house," she said. "Look how the whole second floor caved in." She walked to the cracked wall behind me and touched the shadow where a picture once hung. "Everything came down," she said. "Everything but the Virgin. Do you see?"

I cut into the salami roll and said, "I think you see what you want to see."

Nella threw the matchbook at me. And I stared at the Fascist symbol, at the bundle of wood bound together with red bands around an axe. "Keep it," I said.

∼

That night, we found wool blankets in a broken dresser and spread two on the floor. Then we huddled together with the rest of the blankets covering us, but Nella couldn't sleep. She wanted to know what happened to our parents, why they were late meeting us, and why we ran away from home. I told her I'd tell her in the morning, that I was too tired. But the morning came and went and another one after that, and still she never stopped asking. Almost a week passed before I told my sister what I had done. All those days of stealing bread and fruit, of living on the streets, I knew that soon my luck would run out. Someone would catch me. And then what would happen to us? They'd send us to an orphanage, maybe split us up or something worse. Nella deserved the truth before that happened.

So I took her to the harbor one evening. She liked sitting on the pier and watching the moored boats swaying in the water. But the longer we sat there, the harder it became for me to tell her. What would she think of me? What would you, David? How would I explain it to you if I could? At the woodpile, I tried to show you how we break. How a family splinters. There was a time when I thought we had that strength again, the strength of the bundle. But we had already lost too much.

Nella threw a pebble into the water. The water rippled out from where the stone sank. "They're not coming," she said. "And we can't keep stealing from the markets. One of us is going to get caught."

"I know." I blew into my cupped hands and rubbed my palms together. "Nella, I want—"

She held her hand over my mouth and said, "I have something to say. I found a job washing dishes at a delicatessen near the market."

"When did this happen?"

"You sleep late," she said.

"Nella, what did you tell them?"

"I cried about how my father died in the war and how my sickly mother couldn't work. The owner's wife took me in and fed me. While I ate, she pressed her husband to give me the job. It doesn't pay much, but at least we don't have to steal anymore."

"You didn't use Vassallo," I said.

"No," she said. "I used our street, Marconi."

I jumped to my feet and held out my hand for her. She took it and I pulled her up. "Let's stay here tonight," I said. I climbed into one of the small fishing boats, moored to the pier.

"It's better than the stone floor we've been sleeping on," she said. "But it will be colder, and we'll need to get up early so the fishermen don't catch us."

I helped her into the boat. We bundled up in some coarse sacks and looked up at the night sky. I felt glad that she had interrupted me. And now that I didn't have to steal anymore, maybe I didn't have to tell her the truth.

"What's happened to us?" Nella said.

At first I thought she was asking the stars, and I laughed, saying, "They won't answer."

She pinched my arm and said, "I was talking to you, stupid."

I slapped her hand away.

"Those men," she said. "They were looking for someone. Was it you?"

I sat up and hugged my knees. "If you knew what I did," I said. And I felt as if I had something caught in my throat. I tried clearing it. Then I spit into the sea. "You have to promise," I said, "never to tell anyone. Not even a priest, not even at confession."

She put her hand on my shoulder and said, "I'll never tell a soul."

So I whispered my crimes in her ear. The little clouds my breath made rose away from me, out over the sea. What harm could a few dark clouds do out there? I watched them go because I could not look at my sister.

Nella cried.

I wanted to comfort her, but she scooted away from me. "Where was that worthless saint when the twins died?" I said.

"I want to go home," she said.

"You can't," I said. "Those men who came after me up at the farmhouse, some had guns, and one of them—I don't know who—shot our parents. Maybe Cardella or Nunzio, it could have been any one of those men. There's no going back."

She bundled herself up with her arms across her chest and sobbed. Suddenly, a shoe clocked me in the head, and I turned around. The boat wobbled. We held the sides to steady ourselves.

"Filthy little hooligan," a man yelled from the edge of the pier. "Get out of there."

I pulled on Nella's arm, but she wouldn't move. I had to drag her from the boat. At the pier, the man grabbed my wrist. He smelled like a fish merchant.

"Are you all right?" he asked my sister.

She kicked him in the shin. He howled and grabbed his leg. The two of us ran down the wooden planks and into the maze of dark city streets.

Drunks staggered by, holding arms out against buildings for balance. A prostitute wearing a white nightgown stood in front of a half-opened door and made a *come here* gesture at me with her finger. We turned into a narrow winding alley between crooked rows of old buildings. All the roofs had collapsed long ago. I spotted a door. Its hinges creaked when I pushed it open. The room was as big around as the dirty mattress on the floor. The fisherman's one-shoed clop, like a limping horse on the cobblestones, drew near. I peeked out the door and saw him talking with the prostitute. She pointed at the alley.

"That whore gave us away," I said.

"What're we going to do?" Nella asked.

"I'll lure that old seahorse far from this place." I put my fingers to my lips to stop her from protesting. "I'll come back," I said. "I promise."

"But what if you don't?" she whispered.

"Then go to work in the morning," I said. "I'll find you there."

I put a stone in my pocket.

Nella touched my arm and said, "The delicatessen, it's at the end of the market on Trento."

I ran out the door, knocking over the garbage on my way. As I rounded the corner at the other end of the alley, I saw that the fisherman had taken the bait.

I stopped several times under lampposts and marked the poles with the pointy end of my stone. Then I waited for the fisherman to see me before running off again. At the bridge to Ortygia, I yelled, "Stupid donkey. Over here!" The crazy man waved his arms and shouted obscenities. I crossed over into the Old City. The streets became narrower. I walked between the tunnels of houses, marking each corner that I took, this way, then that—right into a dead end. I crouched behind some garbage cans and waited. All the little noises of the city sounded like a man coming after me. Shadows moved on the far wall. They took on the shapes of wild stallions with fish tails—beasts of mythology.

I came out from behind the garbage and peered around the street corner. Jets of water washed over nymphs, seahorses, and other strange creatures carved into the stone basin of a fountain. It stood in the center of a large piazza. Moonlight reflected on the pool. A fine mist wet my skin. The statues were beautiful. I drank from the fountain and splashed water on my face. When I looked up from the pool, I saw the main road that led back to the bridge. And on the other side, I thought I saw my sister.

"Nella," I called. But she didn't hear. So I ran after her, my shoes echoing through the narrow streets. Her pace quickened, she turned a corner, and I lost her. Then a light turned on in a window overhead, and a man shouted down into the alley, "Stay away from my daughter."

I ran from there as fast as I could go. It didn't matter where my legs took me, only that they took me far from trouble.

By the time I slowed down long enough to catch my breath, I had gotten myself so turned around that I couldn't tell north from south. The streets were empty and quiet. I tried following the smell of the sea on the air, but I couldn't find my way back to the water. I wandered most of the night, never seeing the markings I had left behind. And as the houses became less densely packed, I gave up the search. Nella was a smart girl. She would stay the night in that derelict house and go to work in the morning just like we'd planned. When it was light out, I'd find my way and meet her there.

I left the road and sat under an olive tree. In the distance, I spotted an almond grove in full bloom. But it wasn't time yet for them to blossom. I figured this was my mind playing a trick on me with some white stone. But I felt curious, so I crossed the field and another road. I found seats cut into the white, stony hill in the shape of a half moon. I sat down in one of the rows, pleased with myself for having reasoned out the deception. A lizard scurried over the seat in front of me and down the aisle, on its way toward the remains of a stage. Even in the dark, I could see that this old Greek theater stood in ruins with the stonework crumbling and falling apart. Lizards performed here now.

Looking out over the ridge, I saw the flowering almond trees again. And I rubbed my eyes, trying to blink away the vision. Still they stood just beyond the theater. Then I heard my brothers' laughter, echoing from that place. I jumped up out of my seat. They said my name in whispers from those trees, and I knew it was a lie, but I wanted it to feel real. So I followed their voices with my arms out in front of me, trying to catch hold of their bodies. They led me into an abandoned limestone quarry to the mouth of a large cave shaped like the cavity of an ear. Their laughter came from inside.

"Hello," I called out. And my voice joined their voices in an echo. I listened to it fade. A cool breeze came from within the cavern. I explored its winding spaces, its high, smooth walls, and my footsteps sounded like soldiers on the march—Roman guards. The cave had multiplied me into a legion.

17

A hand on my shoulder woke me. Daylight streamed in from the cave mouth, and a priest stood over me.

"What're you doing here, a boy your age?" he said.

I jumped up and backed away from him. "How did you find me?"

"Find you?" the priest said. "You were shouting in the Ear of Dionysius. The whole of Syracuse can hear you from this cave. Come with me to the rectory, and I'll tell you the story."

I looked at my shoes, the soles worn through at the toes. "I don't care to hear it," I said.

"What do you care for then?"

"I want to see my sister."

"Where is she?"

"She works at a delicatessen on Trento."

"Ah, in the market. Yes, I know it well," he said. "I'll send for her."

"I want for us to have a warm bath and a good meal," I said.

"Then you and your sister shall have both," he said.

"And maybe a new pair of shoes," I added.

The priest laughed. "What is your name? I am Paolo Giovanni."

At the rectory, I washed up and ate fried eggs and sausage with the priest. The busy sounds of the city—merchants pushing two-wheeled carts, horses clopping over cobblestone streets—battered against the shuttered windows like a storm. A car engine sputtered and died. Two men argued.

"What were you dreaming?" Don Giovanni asked.

"I don't remember," I said.

"Well, you're safe here at Saint Anthony's until we can contact your parents. Where are they?"

I told him the story my sister had made up, that my father died in the war, that there's no work in the village where I'm from, so my sister and I do little jobs in the city to bring money home for our sick mother. He asked me the name of the village, drumming his fingers on the table when I stumbled for an answer, so I covered up my lie with another one.

"My parents were both killed when the British came," I said. "I take care of my sister now. We've been on our own ever since, living on the streets and finding small jobs to do."

"There is room here for the both of you," the priest said, "if you'll work for it. What kind of work have you done?"

I looked at my hands and said, "I helped my father tend an orchard."

"Ah," the priest said. "So you know your way around a garden."

He took me to the courtyard and pointed out the sweet peas whose blossoms needed tending and bushes that needed pruning.

"Why did you feel the need to lie?" Don Giovanni asked.

I knelt down, tightened the laces of my shoes, and said, "I was afraid you'd send us to an orphanage."

He placed his palm on the crown of my head and said, "They are overcrowded. We have space for you right here."

Then he led me to a small plot of land tucked into a corner of the courtyard. "We want a vegetable garden here," the priest said. I knelt and rubbed the soil between my fingertips. He told me I could start that day, and showed me to my room.

18

That first year at the rectory, I made a vegetable garden, the best one I could. I planted tomatoes, peppers, and zucchini in the spring and artichokes, onions, and asparagus in the fall. My sister left her job in the Old City and worked in the kitchen. She had the room across the hall from mine on the second floor, both little more than closets. I often sat by the casement window eyeing the cars and people below. This was the best hiding place in all of Sicily. During the day I worked, and at night I read the Bible, most often the Book of Job. God took everything from him, and still he believed. I never understood why.

One night, while having dinner alone with Don Giovanni, I asked him about it. "That's really a question you would have to ask Job himself," he said. "But if I had to guess, I would say that Job understood that God had His plan. Job had a choice, like all of us, and he chose faith. Is there something you're grappling with, Salvatore?"

I pushed a piece of roasted zucchini around my plate with my fork. I could feel him looking at me, so I had to answer. "No, just understanding, Father."

"Perhaps if you came to Mass like Nella," Don Giovanni said. Then he commented about how the tomato sauce was very good. I thanked him and told him it was my father's recipe.

"If you ask Him," Don Giovanni said, "God will help you. But you have to ask Him."

I wanted to believe that living in the rectory and working for the church made up for what I'd done, but the nightmares of the twins, those terrible dreams, they never stopped, and every time I left the grounds, every time I opened those doors, it felt like the whole of Syracuse knew my secret, as if the cobblestones sensed the added weight I carried and whispered my crimes on the wind.

19

For my fourteenth birthday, the last day of April 1948, Nella baked an almond cake. She dusted the top with icing sugar and then scattered toasted almonds over it. We sat together with Don Giovanni. I told him that I would not prepare for the sacrament of confirmation this year, or any year.

Don Giovanni furrowed his brow, drank his coffee, and said, "I don't understand."

"He can't," Nella said. "He's not in a state of grace. Not after what he did."

I dropped my fork. It clattered on the plate. "Thank you for the cake," I said. I pushed the plate with my half-eaten slice away from me. Then I got up from the table, walked out of the rectory, and sat on the back steps. The trees were still bare. And I thought of my father's orchard, coming into bloom, and the color it made.

~

Later that night, I snuck into the kitchen for another slice, but my sister had thrown the cake away.

20

At fifteen, I put a boy in the hospital for making my sister cry. She had turned twelve the day before and insisted that she no longer needed me to walk her to and from school. I allowed it since the school was near the convent, three blocks away.

That day, I took a break from my work and sat on the stoop of the rectory, enjoying the afternoon sun, when she ran, crying, around the street corner. Three boys—younger than me by a year and a half—followed her. I'd seen them around the neighborhood before and didn't like the way they looked. The one in the lead, Aldo Fabrizi, teased her for being a war orphan. And he said other things, dirty things about how she looked older than most girls her age. She opened the little gate, ran past me, up the stairs, and into the house. The heavy door banging shut behind her. I charged Aldo like a bull, pushed him across the narrow street and into a pile of garbage in the alley, where I sat on his chest, punching his face until my knuckles bled. His friends shouted their support, but if Aldo landed any blows, I couldn't feel them. I was too crazy in the head.

When Don Giovanni pulled me out of the alley, with a hard grip for a priest, Aldo didn't move. He had one eye closed and the other half opened, a swollen, bloodied face, and a broken nose. His friends helped him get to his feet. He had an arm around each boy's shoulder as they brought him inside the rectory, setting him down on the sofa. Don Giovanni called his mother, and then he told me to go up to my room and wait for him. Aldo's mother arrived with the carabinieri later that night, and they spoke with Don Giovanni in his study.

Nella knocked on my door.

"It isn't locked," I said. I sat on the windowsill, looking down at the alley across the street.

She came in with a damp washcloth and cleaned my bruised fists. Then she sat at the foot of my bed with her arms around her knees, bent up to her chest. "Will you walk me to school tomorrow?"

"Yes," I said. "And I'll walk you home, too."

She let out a long breath, put her chin on one of her knees, and said, "This isn't home."

"I know."

Don Giovanni entered without knocking.

I looked at his reflection in the window and asked, "Will the boy be okay?"

"The pig deserved it," Nella said. "The foul mouth on him."

"Nella, please leave us," Don Giovanni said.

When she left, he shut the door and told me that the church agreed to pay for the boy's medical bill. Then he slapped me. I had seen his hand in the window coming at me, but I didn't move away from it. My eyes watered from the pain, and he told me that if I did anything like that again, he would send me away to the orphanage.

∽

The next day, while weeding the garden, my hands felt strange—rough and unknown to me. The lines on the palms looked like the scars from skin sewn together by an unsteady hand. Like my hands had been stitched together from some strange skin. I made a fist, released it. The bruised knuckles still red and sore from the fight. I picked a scab and watched the cut fill with blood. I dug the fingers deep into the good soil like roots looking for water.

I only wanted these hands to cultivate life.

21

Don Giovanni knew that Nella and I came from Melilli. He knew what I had done. I never figured out when he discovered my secret or how. But I've always suspected Nella broke her promise to me in confession.

It came out one evening after dinner. Don Giovanni and I had coffee while Nella cleared the table. "Aldo's nose has healed," he said. "I thought you should know that he forgives you."

"Then he is stronger than me," I said. "May I be excused?"

"No, you may not," Don Giovanni said. Then he reached across the table and took my hand, searching my face. "It would be better for you to go to confession," he said.

I pulled my hand away. "I will not."

He locked his fingers together in front of his face and said, "Thank you for the meal, Nella. I'd like to speak with your brother alone now."

"Yes, Father," she said. She glanced at me and then hurried out of the room.

Don Giovanni touched his forehead to his locked-together hands. Then he raised his head, looked at me over the knuckles, and said, "Tell me, Salvatore, how is it possible that your family once carried the strength of the soldier-saint in their blood?"

"That's just a story," I said. "It's not real."

He put his hands—palms down—on the table and got up from the chair. "The stories in the Bible are real," he said. "Are they not?"

"That's your profession, Father. I wouldn't know."

Don Giovanni brought his empty cup into the kitchen. "Sebastian was a real man," he said from the sink. "A sainted man. His exalted spirit—"

I got out of my chair, knocking it over as I stood up. "It was just a statue," I said. "Emanuele and Leonello, they were real."

My fists clenched, and the fire in my stomach gave me heartburn. But I had my garden and my sister to consider, so I held my breath, righted the chair, and let the air out of my lungs little by little.

"I'm sorry, Father," I said.

He stood in the doorway with a towel draped over his arm. "Your soul is like a pot of water boiling down," he said. "Do you understand, Salvatore? Let me help you."

"You've been good to us, Father," I said. "Good to me. And I thank you for that, but working in the garden is all the help I need."

"If you won't make confession here," he said, "go back to Melilli. Make the pilgrimage to Saint Sebastian's shrine and pray for his forgiveness. Ask him to pray for you. I'll go with you if you like. I've discussed this with Don Fiorilla. There will be no trouble."

"Don Fiorilla," I said. My legs felt weak. "Are my parents alive?"

He shook his head no and said, "I'm sorry, my son."

I dropped to my knees and took the priest's hand, kissed it, and held it against my forehead. I cried. For the first time in as long as I could remember, I cried. "I ran, Father. I heard shots, and I kept running. I was so scared. I ran like a coward."

"From the beginning, my son."

I looked up into Don Giovanni's face, crossed myself, and said, "Bless me, Father, for I have sinned . . ."

22

When I finished, I took the chair at the head of the table and sat down, feeling like the crack in the bottom of an empty bucket, feeling like I could sleep for days and never get enough sleep.

Don Giovanni studied the wall as if he read my penance in the grapes and vines stenciled over the plaster. His lips moved, but he did not speak. He lowered his head. "Prayer is good," he said. "God likes prayer, but for this—" He kissed his Saint Anthony necklace. "For this, God likes action better. You are to take a basket of vegetables from the garden to Aldo's family."

"Yes, Father," I said. I wiped my face with a tissue and blew my nose.

"Not one time," Don Giovanni said. "You must do this each week for the remainder of the season."

As I got up to leave, he said, "And, Salvatore. Make the pilgrimage. You will know when you are ready."

23

My first time delivering the vegetables in the morning, I walked up the three flights of stairs and heard Aldo's parents arguing over money. Their voices grew louder as I neared the top floor, with the mother saying they had nothing left to sell except for sheets and their wedding rings, and the father saying it was bad all over with so many men out of work and what more could he do.

I knocked on the door and the mother answered, a small, stocky woman. She let me in without a word, cupping her hand over her mouth.

They lived in one room with a window into the alley. The parents' bed stood in a little alcove with a curtain strung on a wire for privacy. Aldo slept on a cot beneath the window. His nose was crooked from where it healed wrong.

"At least our good-for-nothing son has brought us a bit of luck," the father said. "Bring the basket here."

I set the basket down on the metal folding table in front of him, his lanky frame slouching in the wooden chair. "These are from my garden at Saint Anthony's," I said. Then I turned to Aldo, who had thrown off his blanket and sat up in his cot. "I'm sorry I broke your nose."

He wiped the sleep from his eyes and shrugged, saying, "Forget about it." Then he grabbed a ball from under his cot and said, "You want to go outside?"

"I have to get back," I said.

In the stairwell afterward, with the door shut behind me, the bickering started all over again. I heard the father slap Aldo and say, "What are you doing, asking him to go outside? Give me that ball. You should be looking for a job." And it made me smile. At least they were together. A family, whole.

∿

The second time I delivered the vegetables, I asked Signore Fabrizi if he needed anything done around the house. And he smacked the back of his son's head, saying, "You hear that? You could learn something from this boy who broke your nose." Then he said to me, "You can start by sweeping the floor. The broom is in the closet."

Signore Fabrizi made Aldo watch. The boy sat at the foot of the cot, a dim look on his face like the lights behind his eyes had little power in them. I kept quiet and swept the floor, taking my time to do the job the right way. I got down on my knees, cleared dust from under the bed, and sneezed into the crook of my arm.

Aldo and Signore Fabrizi both wished me good health, and I thanked them. Then Signore Fabrizi slapped my back and said, "At least the boy hasn't lost his manners, eh?" And he helped me move the dresser to get at the dirt there.

When I finished, I collected all the dust with the dustpan and emptied it into the trash bin. Next, I saw that the dishes needed washing, so I set about washing them, wiping them down, and placing them on the drying rack in clean rows.

∿

One evening, in the middle of summer, when Signore Fabrizi had found a construction job, he stopped by the rectory with a deck of cards after work. Nella showed him to the garden where I stood watering my plants.

"So this is the famous garden," he said.

I turned off the hose and gave him the tour of tomatoes and peppers, eggplants and zucchini. Then we sat inside at the kitchen table and drank coffee.

"Do you know how to play Scopa?" he asked. He shuffled the cards, dealing three to me, three for him, and four on the table, faceup. "The goal is to get the most cards, though some are worth more than others," he said. Then he showed me the value of each card and explained the rules.

We played late into the night. I lost most of the games at first, but I caught on in the end. Then I walked Signore Fabrizi to the little gate outside, and he thanked me for the company. "My son," he said. "He won't play. He thinks it's an old man's game."

"Is it?" I asked.

"Beh, it's an old game."

~

For the rest of the summer and into the fall, I found myself looking forward to picking the vegetables—always the best ones from the garden—and walking the four blocks to where the Fabrizis lived. And with each visit, I started feeling better, lighter, not so tired. I slept easier. So when winter came, and I no longer had to deliver the baskets, I still visited them. I cleaned their apartment—it never looked cleaner than when I worked on it—ran errands for them, and played cards with Aldo's father.

24

"When are you going to Melilli?" Nella asked.

I set the box of nativity figurines down—it echoed in the church—and said, "Are you crazy in the head? I'm not going back there."

"I heard Don Giovanni," she said. "You're making the pilgrimage."

"You were listening," I said. "All those months ago, like a mouse waiting for a crumb to fall from the table." I waved her off. "Anyway, it doesn't matter. I'm not going. The past is the past." Then I gave her my back and took a figurine wrapped in newspaper out of the box. I removed the paper and wiped dust from the wood carving with a dry cloth. "This is our home now," I said. And I placed the little donkey in the manger.

Nella pulled me around, saying, "Don't turn your back on me." And I raised my hand against her. She cringed away from me, shielding her face with both arms. My hand shook. I had almost hit someone again—my sister, my family, the only one left in the world. And my job was to protect her. I grabbed the communion rail and sat down on the floor of the sanctuary, feeling sick in my stomach.

"Turiddu," she said. "Signore Fabrizi isn't your father."

"No, he isn't," I said. I buried my hands under my armpits. "I have no father."

She knelt down, cupped my face in her hands, and said, "Yes, you do. We have a father. Even dead, he is still yours and mine. We should be tending his orchard. A few more months and the trees bloom."

"We don't have an orchard anymore," I said. I looked at her face, framed by the shell-like dome overhead. "I'm sorry."

She kissed my forehead. "Get up," she said. "Finish the nativity scene. I have an errand to run this evening. Will you walk with me?"

～

Later, when I walked with Nella on her errand to a three-story building in the Old City, she asked me to come in with her. On the second floor, she pushed open a half-closed door. A young woman greeted us in the narrow hallway.

"I am Giulia," she said. "Come with me. Serafina is this way."

We followed Giulia into a little room. Serafina—a plump old woman—sat at a table by the window. Her hair as white as the pale stones of the city. Across from her, a middle-aged man, the age my father would've been, with thinning gray hair and a weather-beaten face, fingered his hat in his lap. Serafina said something about the opening of the eye, and then she stuck the pointed end of a pair of scissors into a soup bowl filled with water and oil set between them. I looked away. I didn't want any part of this business.

"Why are we here?" I whispered.

Nella shushed me.

I wanted to leave, but I remembered today, in the church, how I'd almost hurt my sister and how she forgave me. So I waited beside her.

In the corner stood a knee-high porcelain statue of the Virgin Mary with rosary beads hanging from her outstretched hands. A dusty painting of Saint Lucia, who held her eyes on a tray, hung from the cracked wall behind the old woman's chair.

"In the sink," Serafina said. "Be careful."

Giulia took the bowl and left the room, followed by the man—his hat still in his hands. He pushed past us and mumbled, "Excuse me."

Nella tugged at my arm and then pulled me along to the table.

When I sat down, Serafina studied me with her cloudy eyes. I wondered if she might be blind, but I felt her gaze going through me. She leaned to one side, looked over my shoulder, and said, "When we are children, our guardian angels are so loyal to us that they turn their faces from the sight of our misbehavior. In that moment, if we wander off while they are not looking, they can become lost. You have lost your guardian angel," she said. "I'm sorry. I cannot help you."

"Please," Nella said. She dug through her purse. "We'll pay more. I think I have enough." The coins tinkled.

"Okay," I said. "Let's go. I came with you, now we can go home."

Serafina took my hands and said to Nella, "Your brother, he is a strong boy." Then she turned them palm up. "And stubborn, yes?"

I pulled my hands away from her feather-light touch. I had expected her skin would be rough like sandpaper with all the wrinkles and folds, the large knuckles and crooked fingers.

"Do not be afraid," she said.

"I'm not," I said.

"No, you are not," she said. "Not afraid of me." Then she clasped her hands together with a loud smack, held them in the air, and looked at the ceiling. "But you carry something," she said. Her voice almost a hum, like music. "Something from long ago, something heavy. A weight not of this world." She put her arms down and looked at me. "This is what frightens you, this thing that you carry."

I gripped the table edge, remembering my father, his eyes the color of hazelnuts, his mouth a thin, serious line cut across his face, the way he carried himself when he walked, like he bore the statue with him everywhere he went. How the weight made him strong. His shoulders, his back, hard like lava stone. And I remembered how the accident in the orchard took that strength away from him, and me.

I turned to my sister and said, "What have you told this woman?"

"Nothing," Nella said. "I swear."

"Bring the bowl and the oil," Serafina said.

Giulia entered with the white soup bowl and an olive oil tin. She set them down on the table. Then she lifted a jug of water by Serafina's feet and filled the bowl.

Serafina added three drops of olive oil.

Beside me, Nella took a breath and held it in. We waited. Serafina, Nella, and Giulia, they all watched the droplets of oil coming together, producing an island on the surface of the water.

"Very bad," Serafina said, tapping out the words with a fingernail on the table as she spoke. "A strong curse."

Nella squeezed my shoulders.

"You see," Serafina said. "The oil is as one. This is a sign that the source of the malocchio comes from beyond the grave."

I couldn't look at this woman and her cloudy eyes anymore. I couldn't listen. I covered my ears with my hands as if I'd never heard of the statue of Saint Sebastian washing ashore, never once believed in its power, or in the name Vassallo.

Turiddu, Leonello called out to me. And the hairs on my arms stood on end. My brother's voice felt cold to me, colder than any winter chill I'd ever felt before.

Leonello and Emanuele stood behind the old woman. Their faces and clothes looked flat, faded and yellowed like an old black-and-white picture. Emanuele raised his arm in a jerky movement, the outline of his body flickered. He pointed at Saint Lucia's eyes on the tray in the painting. I blinked and rubbed my eyes, and when I looked again, my brothers were gone.

"This is nonsense," I said. Pushing my chair back from the table, I got to my feet. The water sloshed around in the bowl but the island of oil remained intact.

"You can help him?" Nella asked.

Serafina leaned back into her chair, her sides pushing against the armrests. "I cannot," she said.

"Why did you bring me here, Nella? Come on, let's go."

"Wait," Serafina said. "There may be a way. Tell me, what did you see? You saw something, yes? This could be important."

"I saw nothing," I said. "We're leaving." I took Nella by the arm, led her to the door.

Giulia cleared her throat and said, "Your brother should listen to my grandmother. She has helped many people." Then Giulia held out her hand for payment.

～

On the way home I said, "That was a waste of money."

Nella folded her arms across her chest. "You give me so little and hide the rest under your mattress. I'll spend what is mine however I like."

"Okay," I said. I slung my arm around her shoulder. "Where did you find that crazy old woman?"

"One of the girls in school," Nella said. "She had headaches, she complained about them all the time. And she felt tired in class, always yawning. She told me that her mother took her here and that Serafina cured her."

"Tell you what," I said. "If I'm sick, I'll go to the doctor."

She stopped and said, "You need more than a doctor. I know about the nightmares. I can hear you from my room. I just wanted to help."

"Help?" I took both of her hands in mine. "This woman, she steals people's money and tells them what they want to hear. You understand? Now we have a good home here with a nice garden. And I made my confession, delivered the vegetables. I thought you would be happy with this."

"I am," she said. "But it hasn't stopped the nightmares."

"Just bad dreams. Nothing more. They will pass."

"No," she said. "I don't think they will, not until you go back to Melilli with flowers for our parents' graves, and beg their forgiveness and the forgiveness of the saint."

I let go of her hands. "No more, Nella. No more talk about going back."

25

In the morning, I ran errands for the rectory, buying sausage, fish, and bread from the market. On my way back, I stopped at a street vendor who sold jewelry. "I want to get a little something for my sister for Christmas," I said. "What do you have?"

"My wife made these," the vendor said. And he showed me bracelets and necklaces, earrings and pendants, little charms and pins.

I looked through his cart and saw a Saint Sebastian medallion, big like the ten-lira coin. "That one," I said. "She'll like that one." I paid the man but hesitated before taking the medallion from him. I stared at the image of the saint. "Cover it up," I said.

The vendor nodded and wrapped the medallion in thin paper.

At the rectory, I found Don Giovanni in the kitchen with a pot of water boiling on the stove. He added pasta to the water, stirred it, and then took a can of sauce from the overhead cabinet. He turned and smiled as I entered. "Perfect timing," he said. "Fry up those sausages."

I put the fish in the refrigerator. "Where's Nella?"

Don Giovanni released the blade on the small opener on his key ring and said, "A GI gave me this. American boy. Protestant, but nice. Have you seen one like this before?" He punctured the top of the inside rim of the can and advanced the opener with rocking motions.

"No," I said. "Where's Nella?"

He tilted his head at a note on the table. "She left that for you."

I read the note. "You let her go back there?"

"Take it easy," he said. "I arranged for a driver to take her and bring her back when she's ready. She'll be well looked after. Now be a good boy and fry up the sausages, please."

I took the pan from where it hung on the wall, added some olive oil, and placed it on the burner. Then I cut up the meat and put the slices in the pan. "She's going back there because of me," I said.

Don Giovanni heated the sauce in a saucepan and drained the pasta in a strainer in the sink. "This is something she needs to do," he said. "Why don't you add some peppers? We still have a jar in the pantry. And get an onion," he called after me.

When lunch was ready, he brought out a bottle of wine and set it down on the table between us. Then he handed me the heel from the bread and took a seat.

But I couldn't eat. I read the note again, crumpled it in my fist, and said, "This was a mistake."

He opened my fist, took the note, and smoothed it out. "Let it go," he said.

"How, Father?"

"Eat," he said. "You won't find the answer on an empty stomach. And don't forget to take a bottle of spumante to the Fabrizi house."

~

After lunch, I looked in on Nella's room and saw the bed made and her slippers by the bedside table, and the little desk in the light of the sun coming through the window. A small gull perched on the ledge outside. It tapped at the glass with its beak. As I stepped into the room, the bird made a squawking cry. I put my hands up and said, "It's okay." And the gull looked at me sideways. Then I pulled out the chair from the desk and he backed off the ledge, catching the air with his dark-gray wings.

He hovered there for a minute and then flew away. I sat down, picked up my sister's pen—the one she had used to write the note.

The gull came back, tapping at the window. I could hear Nella telling me how this bird carried a message. Churches and priests, they weren't enough for her. She had to see God everywhere in the world.

"What do you want, eh?"

The bird made this laughing little cry and then flew off again.

I watched it cut the air. "What do you want to tell me?" I asked. "You're just a stupid bird pecking at its reflection in the glass. What do you know about Melilli? How's my sister?"

That dirty gull flew in circles and then went out like a shot, west. That message I understood. I understood what that meant. I remembered the superstition from my mother. It meant a storm was coming. My mother used to say, *The seagull that flies inland flies away from a storm coming in.*

~

When I dropped off the bottle at Signore Fabrizi's, he wouldn't let me leave without offering some food. We sat at the table, eating orange wedges and prickly pears.

His wife set a dish of cannoli on the table and said, "It's nice to see you, Salvatore. But you don't look well. Is everything okay? How's your sister?"

"She's good," I said. "We're fine. You know, we stay busy."

"Wonderful, wonderful," Signore Fabrizi said. "Not like our son, always out on the streets making trouble. Just last week he stole an old woman's purse. If it weren't for the men I know at work who have friends at the carabinieri, that boy would be rotting in jail right now. That was my first and last mistake," he said, holding up one finger.

"Maybe I can speak with him," I said. "Or Father Giovanni."

"Boh," Signore Fabrizi said. He threw his hands into the air. "He's no good, that son of mine." Then he bit his first knuckle.

"We try," his wife said. "But nothing makes a difference. How did you turn out so good, Salvatore?"

What would they think of me if they knew about the statue and how I let my sister go back there alone because of what I did?

"I know what you're thinking," Signore Fabrizi said. "You broke Aldo's nose. How could we think you're good? That was different. So don't worry about it. Let's play some cards, eh?"

"I promised Don Giovanni I'd clean out the cellar," I lied.

"Next time," Signore Fabrizi said. "Next time."

∾

Outside, the sky darkened as fat storm clouds rolled in from the sea. The air felt cool and heavy with a damp breeze. The streets emptied. People shuttered their windows. The wind picked up, whipping through the city, spinning newspapers and dirt into little funnels. "This looks like a bad one," I said out loud. And then the downpour hit. I pulled my jacket up over my head and ran. I thought of Nella caught in this mess with her driver—some stranger.

At the rectory, Don Giovanni sat inside by the window, watching the storm and smoking a cigarette. I went up to my room, dried off, and changed my clothes. When I came back down, he said, "What is your answer?"

"I promised myself I'd look after her," I said. "I must go."

He put the cigarette out in the ashtray on the windowsill, folded his hands in his lap, and said, "Good." Then he looked outside. "Bring your raincoat."

∾

Don Giovanni placed a call from his office. In fifteen minutes, a car idled out front. The driver honked the horn. I ran out and climbed into the little two-seater. In an hour and a half, we reached Melilli.

The rain eased up. I dismissed the driver, pulled the brim of my cap down over my eyes and slipped through the village like a ghost. The buildings, the olive trees and prickly pears, the stone under my feet, it all looked the same. But something felt wrong. I rocked on my heels, bounced a little on my toes, all to catch my balance with the earth, the soil. I knelt down, my fingers touching the wet ground, and I knew—immediately—I knew that I did not belong.

A nativity scene covered in clear plastic stood near the church. The church still dominated the piazza, but it looked old to me now, the writing on the stone worn down, and smaller, the way grief shrunk my father. It didn't look so big and powerful anymore.

The rain stopped, but the clouds did not break. A man slept inside a little black car parked off to the side. An open newspaper covered his face. I banged on the window. His arms shot up, knuckles knocking against the roof, and the newspaper fell to his lap. He looked around the inside of the car, confused. Then he saw me and rolled down the window. "What's the matter with you?" he said. "I'm sleeping."

"Where's my sister?" I asked him.

"Your sister? How the hell should I know? Get lost."

And as he rolled up the window, I put my hand on it, pushing down. "Nella," I said. "You drove her here. You're supposed to be keeping an eye on her, not sleeping. Where is she?"

He pointed at the church. "She went inside," he said. "When she came back out, she told me she'd be back. I don't know where she went."

A young boy, ten, maybe twelve years old, pushed a cart into the piazza. I recognized it as old Longu's. I let go of the window. The driver rolled it up as I walked away from the car.

"This is Longu Castagna's cart," I said. "I'd know it anywhere. Where is he?"

"Dead," the boy said. "It's my cart now. Would you like to buy some snails?" He took a lid from a pot and set it aside.

"No," I said. "What's under here?" I peeked under the tinfoil on a tray of arancini. "I'll take one. Are they fresh?"

"My mother made them this morning," he said. "They're still warm."

I paid the boy and said, "How did Longu die?"

"He was very old." The boy shrugged.

I took the road that went up to the farmhouse and bit into the top of the cone of deep-fried rice with saffron, almost getting to the chopped lamb filling. I never imagined Longu Castagna would die. He was old when my father was my age—that's how my father told it anyway. And all the other stories about Longu, I knew they weren't true, but still, the man was a part of Melilli, like the homes we built with stones from the mountain.

~

My father's farmhouse stood above the village, a mausoleum to a different time, with tiles missing from the roof and window shutters broken. The door hung from its hinges, the wooden frame rotting away. I finished the arancini and walked inside. The house smelled of urine and mold. A pool of water formed in the corner from a leak in the ceiling. Broken tins, jars, dishes, and cups littered the floor. A crack in the wall cut the stone in a jagged line through the nail hole where my father had hung the silver crucifix. I knelt where my brother's coffins once stood when families came to pay their respects. It felt colder here. Goose bumps prickled up my arms and down the back of my neck. And then I saw it—the crucifix—face down in the mess on the floor. I took it, wiping it clean with the end of my shirt and blowing dirt from the little crevices in the features. Then I propped it up in the windowsill. I heard a gunshot and flinched, moving away from the window. In the pencil-lead darkness of my shut eyes, voices shouted outside the house, but I could not understand them. Someone pounded on the door. When I peeked through my fingers, the door swung wide on one hinge and banged against the rotting frame in the wind. The gunfire, the voices, all of it was just in my head, echoing there and multiplying.

Out the window, down the side of the mountain and over the village, I saw the cemetery. I knew where Nella would be.

~

Three young men approached me on the road from the farmhouse. I knew one of them right away as Rocco—his hair thick with dark curls and his face round like his father's. People used to say how he looked just like his father did at this age or that one, and now, at seventeen, Rocco had filled out into the broad-shouldered, V-shaped trunk of a true Morello. But in his walk and on his face, he carried something different, a distaste for life—for his own or for others', I could not tell.

Rocco threw a stone at me. I ducked and it whistled past my ear. "You shouldn't be here," he said. Beside him stood the sons of Cardella and Santangelo, also seventeen. The beanpole Constantino Cardella had a heavy jaw like his father, and poor Roberto Santangelo, he turned out a pear like his mother. They blocked my way.

"I don't want trouble," I said. "I'm here to take my sister home."

"You don't have a home," Rocco said. He picked up another stone, tested the weight of it in his palm. The man who now threatened me hated the boy I remembered—that friend who shared his candies with me the night of my brothers' wake and stayed with my family until morning. I had done this to him.

The stone hit me in the shoulder, and Rocco reached for another, the other two following his lead. I cut off the road, a rabbit thumping through an open field. Three stones struck my back in succession, but still I ran. I tumbled down a steep slope of ferns and white rocks. I picked up the road again where it curved around the hillside and saw them at the bend, following me with murder in their throats. Roberto lagged behind, his pear shape wobbling a distant fourth in this mad race.

People watched from half-shuttered windows. Others stood aside and spat on the winding streets as I passed. Soon, I could no longer see my pursuers, but their pursuit echoed through the densely packed limestone houses.

At the gates to the cemetery, I felt the tug of my father's almond orchard, the roots of those trees buried deep in my bones. I wanted to care for the orchard, to see the trees in full white bloom again like the white-haired heads of old fathers and mothers watching over their children. But deep inside, the fruit did not forget—the fruit could not forget—that I had abandoned them. I looked down the dirt road to the grove in the distance, grown wild and dying with no one to tend to it. I wished someone had burned it to the ground and rid the place of all that rotting wood and stinking fruit.

I slipped through the gates and found Nella by the grave site of the twins. She knelt, dressed in black, her head bent toward the ground as if she no longer had the strength to lift it on her own.

"Nella," I said. I took her face in my hands and wiped the tears from her cheeks with my thumbs.

"You came," she said.

"Of course I came," I said. Before I could warn her that we had to leave, she showed me our own stones alongside the stones of our family. I touched the flat marker that had my name carved into it. We were all together here. My brothers. My mother. My father. I felt the pull of them on me, like the pull of too much earth under my feet. I pushed my fingers into the dirt of my father's grave—the soil cold and wet from rain.

In the overcast light, the cemetery spilled out around us like a charcoal sketch on a gesso board. Out of those grayscale lines, two old women dressed in black stared at us. Don Fiorilla stood on a ladder beside them with flowers for the top vault of a stack five high. One of the women murmured our names. The other woman covered her mouth in horror with her bony hand.

Don Fiorilla turned at the sound of our names. The ladder swayed beneath him. His arms flailed like a man drowning at sea. As the ladder fell, he caught hold of the lip of the vault, his shoes scrabbling against stone. Flowers fell from their holders. "Salvatore," he cried, dangling from the roof of the crypt. "I tried stopping them."

The widows crossed themselves and called upon the Madonna for the safe delivery of their souls from the forces arrayed against them.

"Help him," Nella said, and when I gave her a stubborn look, she slapped my shoulder and said, "Go."

I righted the ladder and helped the priest down. He held on to my shoulders and took each rung one at a time, and with each step he thanked me, called me "My son."

"Tell me," I asked him, "what happened?" The words tumbled out of my mouth. "Who killed my parents?"

The old women scurried away like mice. They passed a small lot where Rocco and his two compatriots moved like sidewinders among the sunken crosses and uncut grass.

Don Fiorilla stepped off the ladder, got down on his hands and knees, and kissed the cobblestone. "I couldn't stop them," he said. He balled his hands together, shook the balled-up fist at the clouds, and asked for God's forgiveness. "Forgive me," he begged, "for I could not stop them." Then he turned to me, clutched the ends of my coat. "They are good people. Only a few"—the priest held his hand out, palm up as if weighing how many souls he carried there—"a handful, got swept up in their emotions. They love their patron saint."

"Salvatore," Rocco said. "It was you who plunged the knife into their hearts."

"Leave him alone," Nella said.

"I have no quarrel with you, Nella. Do not get in my way."

"Step aside, Father," Constantino warned the priest, but the priest refused. "I will not," he said, standing up and brushing off his pant legs.

Rocco stabbed the air with his finger, pointing at me. "I sat with your parents," he said, "until the end." He blinked back tears. "Your father, he refused to believe, right up to his last breath, he denied what he knew to be true, that it was you who broke his heart, you who killed him. It was you."

"I destroyed the statue," I said, pounding my chest. "The statue. But you." I spat at Rocco's feet as he neared me. "You let them murder my parents, and for what? For stone. No, worse than stone. For the fairy tale that held the stone together."

Roberto tugged on Rocco's arm and said, "Look at his face. It's true, what they say, he has the malocchio. Let's go before he puts the curse on us."

Rocco jerked his arm free. "It's too late for that. Isn't it, Salvatore?"

The priest shouldered between us. "Rocco," he said, "that is enough. This is not like you."

"You do not know what I am like, Father."

"Come, let us go to the church together, and you can tell me. Or, if you prefer, put me in the ground next to Raphael and his family. It is your choice, my son."

Rocco backed away—pushed by the priest's words—and his friends followed. He was no longer a Morello of old, no longer of a line of fishermen. He hadn't been in a long time. The sea did not show in him. He did not have the salted, leathery face or the watery eyes of a man who wrestled the sea for its treasures.

"Wait," I said, and they stopped, and I said, "Rocco," but he cut me off, a sliver of cut stone shone in his eye, and he said, "Pray I never see you again." Then the priest took his arm and steered him away to the gate.

"I'm sorry," I said. But I did not know if I had said it for Rocco or my parents, the twins or Nella, or Saint Sebastian and God.

"You were right," Nella said. "There is nothing for us here."

~

In the car, the driver made a cushion behind the two seats from some towels he had stored back there. Nella, because she was the smallest, squeezed into that tight space.

I looked at the church through the window of the front seat and said, "You went inside."

"I asked the saint to pray for you," Nella said.

"You saw the statue? How can that be?"

"The saint didn't look the same," she said. "It's possible they repaired the damage. Or they made a new one. What does it matter now?"

"Maybe everything," I said. "Maybe nothing. Do you think he heard you?"

She leaned forward, put her hand on my shoulder, and said, "My brother came back, didn't he?"

It rained again as the driver turned the rickety little car around in the piazza. I looked out the back as we left and saw the cross at the top of the church—the last thing I ever saw of Melilli—against all those rain clouds.

26

We spent that Christmas and New Year's with the Fabrizis at the rectory, celebrating with big meals of fish and lasagna, cannoli and buccellati—biscuits filled with pistachios and almonds and other dried fruits—and at midnight of the new year, 1950, we popped open a chilled bottle of spumante. We ate around the same table each holiday, like a family—the Marconis, the Fabrizis, and Don Giovanni, together.

And, like a family, I taught Aldo how to care for the garden. He never did get his act together, but he didn't make too much trouble. He listened to my instructions and watched me work. He lacked patience and a delicate touch, but in time, he learned. And, little by little, Aldo became a fine gardener.

27

On Holy Saturday, 1952, the altar in Saint Anthony's had been stripped in preparation for the Easter Vigil. The church stood empty and dark. Don Giovanni prepared for Mass in the rectory. I sat on the steps to the courtyard with a glass and a new bottle of wine, my gardening tools in a canvas bag by my feet.

After sundown, the congregation would come. They would wait in the church in the dark. They would wait for the priest to light the Paschal candle and carry the light into the church. I always slipped in after him, after the light, to sit beside my sister in the last row.

The gate across the courtyard creaked open. A man with a pack slung over his shoulder limped up to my garden. When he knelt at the row of artichokes, I told him to back off.

"These are good," he said. "The leaves are tight."

"Don't tell me about my own garden," I said.

The man stood up slowly, favoring his bad leg. "I need to find something," he said. "Isn't Saint Anthony's where I go to find something?"

"It's not good to go looking for things," I said. "That brings trouble."

"Like the trouble at the bottom of that bottle?"

A sediment cloud swirled around the bottom of the wine bottle. "The only trouble is this is the last bottle."

"I'll share that one with you and buy you another," he said.

I got a second glass from the kitchen, and we sat on the steps, sharing the last of the wine. He told me how he had been a soldier during the war, how the war took everything from him, the house he grew up in, his parents, his sense of belonging to the city of his birth, of being Roman. "Now," he said, "I work and travel all over." Then he made his first two fingers walk across his lap. "More like this," he said. And the soldier gave his walking fingers a limp.

I emptied the bottle into his glass with the last of the sediment. He stretched his legs out in front of him, and I could see that the soles of his work boots had lost their tread long ago. I looked at how mine were new, a Christmas gift from Don Giovanni. They were the priest's boots for working his soil.

People had started gathering at the foot of the church steps, holding their white unlit candles. The soldier drank the wine and watched them. "A man will look for God his whole life and never find him," he said. "Even when he thinks he has."

"Is that what you're looking for, God?"

"No," he said with a frown. "Nothing like that." He faced me. "You don't remember, do you? Well, how could you? You were very young, and the men I was with, the soldiers, they were not good men. You took me to see your father in the cave."

He'd been filthy back then, during the war, but then again so had I. We all were. He had not had that limp, and I hadn't destroyed the statue yet. I finished my wine in one bitter swallow and shot up from my seat on the steps, afraid that he had seen, in my face, the face of the martyr.

"I found a journal in the bunker," I said. "An Italian soldier's. I wish to God I'd never found it. You were there, fighting. Do you know whose it was? Was it yours?"

The soldier swirled the empty glass, stared at the long red tears staining the sides, like he was staring into the past. He shook his head no in long, slow movements, like a bell in a tower tolling out the notes at a funeral. "It wasn't mine," he said. He spun his finger around the inside of the glass and licked the wine off his finger. "It was chaos. I barely made it out alive. The journal, it could've belonged to anyone."

The last of the congregation disappeared into the unlit church, my sister among them. Don Giovanni stepped out of the rectory. His white vestments draped the ground. He moved slowly, floating like a spirit. He held the white Paschal candle, inscribed in red with the year, MCMLII, and the Greek letters alpha and omega. The deacon on the sidewalk got a fire going in a tin drum. The priest blessed the fire, and then he lit the candle from its flame. His lips moved as he uttered words I knew by heart but could not hear from this distance: *Yesterday and today, the beginning and the ending.* Inside, the congregation waited in the dark. He would bring the light to them, and they would light their candles from the one he carried, and from each other's.

The soldier rubbed the knee of his bad leg. "I told your father that it wasn't safe to stay in Melilli, but he wouldn't leave, and I—I should have stayed with all of you. His faith was as strong as stone. I should've listened to your father. If I had taken off the uniform and lived as you lived, life might be different for us both."

"I remember," I said, pinching the bridge of my nose. "I wanted my father to take your pistol. I was afraid, and you were a soldier like our soldier-saint. But nothing could have saved them from what happened, from me."

"You were just a little one." The soldier held his arm out four feet from the ground to show how small a boy I had been in the war. "You made a mistake."

"How can you know what I did?" I felt my brothers somewhere just out of my sight, like a headache coming on above my eyes. "You weren't there when the twins died. When I—"

"Don Fiorilla told me what happened to your family. That's why I've come to see you. He asked me to take you and your sister to America."

"America," I said. The name did not sound so foreign in my mouth, because it came from Italy. It came from Amerigo Vespucci, the best navigator in the whole world, an Italian so great they named two continents after him. In America they said a man could buy a house with a nice piece of land if he worked hard for it. But it couldn't be just any land. It had to be home. There had to be a second chance for me in Middletown, in Little Melilli, and why not? They had their new church, their statue carved from an old man's memory. I had my new family name. I could put down my roots, produce good fruit in that kind of soil. As long as there was a new Melilli to make a life in, a place where the statue had always been whole, then the boy—Salvatore Vassallo—that boy, he never had to exist.

28

We needed documents, passports. I asked Don Giovanni about this when I made arrangements for the soldier, Vincenzo, to stay the night. Don Giovanni told me that he knew a man who could make them for us. They had worked together helping young men escape the country before the war started. He looked at recent portraits of me and my sister on his desk. He took the frames apart. He said he had prayed for me since he found me in the cave, a prisoner in the Ear of Dionysius.

"I would like to hear that story now," I said.

"The cave," he said, "was so big and the echo so great that a man outside could hear even a whisper from someone inside. The tyrant Dionysius imprisoned men here and learned of plots against him from their amplified voices."

I laughed and said, "Who am I plotting against?"

"I pray for you that someday you will learn to be free," Don Giovanni said.

~

I knocked on my sister's door. She stood in the doorway in her nightgown, the Saint Sebastian medallion I gave her for Christmas a few years ago around her neck. At fifteen, she was beginning to remind me of our mother before the twins died. It was in the way Nella started putting most of her weight onto her right leg and keeping the other bent slightly at the knee. I told her that we were leaving in a few days.

"Where were you?" she asked me. "I waited in the church and now you knock on my door and talk about leaving. Where are we going?"

It was in her voice, too.

"America," I said.

She snapped her fingers and said, "Just like that. Oh my brother, you are crazy in the head. Who put this idea in there?" And she knocked in a playful manner on the side of my head as if it were a door.

"There is a man downstairs," I said, "and I think the saint sent him to find us. I think you were right about the saint. He heard your prayers. He's given us a chance at a new life."

"And you still can't say his name," she said, fingering the medallion. "Who is this man?"

I wanted to. I wanted to speak the name of the saint out loud. But I couldn't. I avoided it, like I avoided speaking about the past. Instead, I settled for silence.

∾

Outside, the night was calm, quiet except for insects calling one another from the darkness. I pulled at my sleeves and looked at the rectory's wood trim. Some of it was rotten, and birds made nests in the hollowed spaces. Last summer, a sparrow had nudged its young from a nest in the trim boards. One of them fluttered to the ground, wings beating, and a black cat pounced. Many times over those hot months, I had fed that cat when it cried outside my window. I looked at where the nest had been. A few twigs still hung over the edge of the dark hole.

∾

Easter morning, Nella checked in on me. She sat on the edge of my bed, wiped the night and its dreams from my forehead with her hand. "I made coffee," she said. "And I met Vincenzo."

I propped myself up on my elbows and asked, "What did you think of him?"

She stood up and looked out the window. "He has an honest face," she said. Then, turning around, she walked to the door. "It's late for you to still be in bed. We have a lot to do."

~

Nella insisted on consulting the old strega—Serafina—before leaving. So we brought a ricotta cake covered with honey and candied fruits to the Fabrizis' house, wished them a happy Easter, and said our goodbyes.

Signore Fabrizi shook my hand while patting my shoulder and said, "America, eh? Good for you."

"Aldo can have my job at the rectory if he wants it," I said.

"You hear that, Aldo?" Signore Fabrizi yelled at his son through the closed bathroom door. He waited a minute, and then pounded on the door. "Hurry up," he said. "Say goodbye to the man who just gave you a job."

His wife brought out a plate of pastries and said, "When he's eighteen, the military will take him off our hands. That will straighten the boy out. Have a cannolu," she said.

"No, thank you. We can't stay," I said. But she wouldn't take no for an answer, so I split one with my sister.

When Aldo walked out, drying his hands on a towel, I told him that he was the new gardener at Saint Anthony's. "Do a good job taking care of Don Giovanni's vegetables," I said.

"I will," he said. "Thank you."

At the door, Signore Fabrizi put his hand on my shoulder and gave it a squeeze. "You turned out a fine young man," he said. "What are you, eighteen?"

"A few more weeks," I said.

He waved a half-limp hand in the air between us and said, "My goodness. A fine young man."

Nella kissed Signore Fabrizi's wife on the cheek and we said our goodbyes again, and then we made our way to Serafina's house in the Old City.

~

Nella knocked on Serafina's door. Giulia let us in and told us that we couldn't stay long, that her grandmother was sick. The old woman sat in bed, supported by pillows. She coughed into a handkerchief and wiped the corners of her mouth.

Nella took the seat at the table by the window. I stood with my hand on the backrest of her chair.

"Ay, ay, ay," Serafina said. "Come closer. Here." She pointed at a bedside chair.

When I sat down, her eyes grew wide. "Are they always with you?" she asked, pointing with a trembling, crooked finger. "This is what you saw the night you came to me."

I looked at where she pointed, but I saw nothing. "What?" I said. "Tell me, what do you see?"

Then she grabbed my shirtsleeve and said, "They are like demons now. And they will haunt you for the rest of your life unless we rid you of this evil."

I pulled my arm away and asked, "How could they?"

Serafina shrugged. "You wouldn't let them go," she said. She took out a pair of scissors from the bedside table drawer. "Spirits who stay too long in this world become envious of the living. You understand?" She recited a prayer to Saint Lucia and made the sign of the cross.

Giulia set a bowl of water and a tin of oil down on the bedside table. Serafina poured three drops of oil into the water. When the droplets came together, she pierced it with the scissors and said, "I put out this malocchio. Go no further." She leaned over and studied the bowl.

"Is that it?" I asked. "Is it finished?"

"Boh," she said. "Who can say? Now you must do your part. You must let them go."

~

The call came Tuesday afternoon that our passports were ready. Don Giovanni picked them up, and then he walked us to the bus station. The sun had come out from behind some clouds. Women sat by opened windows and said, "Good day." Vincenzo tipped his hat to them. Horses clip-clopped on the cobblestones, donkeys brayed. Car engines sputtered with grinding gears and honking horns. The air smelled damp like in the rectory garden. I took my sister's hand in mine.

"Thank you," Nella said. "I know what you think of women like Serafina."

"You prayed for me," I said. "And you asked the saint to pray for me. Look at the good that came of it. What I think of the strega doesn't matter."

"Try," she said. "Try to do what Serafina suggested."

"I will," I said. "I promise."

Before we boarded the bus for the airport, Don Giovanni recited a short prayer for a safe journey. Then he placed his hands on my shoulders and said, "Salvatore, you must understand, I wanted to make sure you were well looked after, so I made a phone call to Don Salafia, the parish priest in Middletown. If there is any trouble, anything at all, go to him. He can help you."

"Thank you, Father," I said.

"You have good jobs in construction waiting for you and Vincenzo," Don Giovanni said. "And there is an apartment for all of you when you arrive, a two-bedroom." Then he looked at Vincenzo and said, "One of you will have to take the sofa."

Vincenzo slapped my back and said, "I've slept on worse."

"Nella," Don Giovanni said. "I've secured a place for you in Saint Sebastian School." He put his hands up before she could speak and said, "I will wire the tuition money, but you must promise me one thing."

"Anything, Father," Nella said.

He wiped her tears away with the hem of his sleeve and said, "Write to me on occasion. I know your brother will not."

~

The plane moved fast down the runway. Nella shut her eyes and squeezed my hand as the land angled and then dropped away from the window. We dipped and turned low over the slope of Mount Etna. The plane carried us away from the citrus groves and the lobes of prickly pears at the base of the mountain, the flowering sapling vines growing up the slope through the terraces of black stone, and the rows of chestnut, pistachio, and almond trees. Old rivers of cooled lava cut through groves of oak and pine. Here and there a tree stood alone, thriving—its roots buried deep in the lava beds. Then we were alongside the smoking, snow-capped crater, moving out over Sicily to the sea sparkling in the sunlight. Never again would I see water as clear as the Mediterranean. Never again would I taste better fish than the fish from that sea.

Nella crossed herself and prayed, and when Vincenzo laughed at her, she said, "It's not natural, being in the sky. We're not birds."

"We swim in the ocean," he said. "Are we fish?"

There was the mountain, so small now that I could crush it in my hands. And yet, I knew it was a lie. My ears popped. Small ice crystals formed on the window. I put my hand there. The glass felt cool. We were in the clouds—like a fog—then we broke through the clouds, above everything.

I was as close to God as I'd ever get.

29

I should have told you everything.

When we came to Middletown, we didn't lose the feelings we had for our family or for the land we came from. We came from a long line of Sicilian farmers and bearers of the statue of Saint Sebastian. We were the best farmers, and the men in our family, they were the strongest men in our village, and our soil was the best soil in all the world. The land, she gave us everything: almonds in the orchard, grapes on the trellis in my father's garden, with a few fig and carob trees, wild prickly pears, tomatoes, and onions between the trellis rows. I wished you could've seen it as I did. Felt it. We didn't lose these things. We carried them with us like we carried the saint, deep in our bones and just as strong.

I stood at your bedroom door, opened it. The air in your room was cooler than in the rest of the house. The white shades were down, the curtains drawn. Stress fractures spiderwebbed the blue plaster walls.

On your desk were a stack of books written by men with foreign names—names like Sagan and Asimov. These were not Italian men. I found places for them on your double-stacked shelves. The particle-board sagged under the weight of volumes of astronomy and mythology hardcovers and paperbacks. I could feel then, in the heft of all these pages, how you had been looking for something.

You should've heard it from me—that our family name was Vassallo. And that before I came along, there had always been a Vassallo in Melilli, a hardworking man who carried the statue for the feast and cultivated the almonds in the orchard—a servant of Saint Sebastian and God.

That was in your bones, too.

I opened the curtains and rolled up the shade. Clouds moved through the sky at a steady pace. I lifted the sash and it was like an oven door opening—the heat hit me, thick and stifling. I crawled out your bedroom window. The sun beat down. The shingles, hot. I dug my heels in, leaned against the window frame.

I wished you could've seen the place where I grew up. The house on Via Marconi where I was born. I had wanted to name you after that place, after Guglielmo Marconi. Did you know about this man? Did they teach you in school that it was Italians like him who made the world? He was the father of radio. He won the Nobel Prize—the son of a Giuseppe and an Irish wife. I had wanted to name you Guglielmo, but your mother, she had her heart set on David.

All I ever wanted from life was a nice piece of land with good soil to till, and a son to till it with me. That day in the garden with you, that day was the second-best day in my life—the first was when you were born. I was a lucky man. A lucky man.

I should have told you everything. I should have been the pole and the support string when your little pea shoots reached out from the soil. You could have been like one of the great men, like Marconi or Vespucci. I was wrong. I wasn't the vinedresser. I was an old pole in a discarded woodpile, and you, you were the sprig in the garden, and this, this was how a boy came to grow like a pea without a pole to climb on.

30

The pink, threadlike flowers of the weak-wooded mimosa tree were in full bloom. The trunk had split in the high winds of an ice storm years ago. The branches bent and swayed, but the tree, it did not break. Not completely. It had some strength left in it—strength enough to hold you when I could not.

One day, rain might upturn that old mimosa. Or a hurricane would take it. One day, that tree would break. *I should take it down soon before it damages the house, or worse. I should take care of that tree before someone gets hurt.*

Voices drifted up from the lawn. The hairs on my arms and on the back of my neck stood on end. Emanuele and Leonello watched me from my garden. They still had the eyes of boys, clear of the struggles of life, wide but not wide enough to take in the true color and light of the whole world. "I cannot help you," I said, and I waved them off. I never could.

There were the sounds of a car door shutting and delicate footsteps on the driveway, the car pulling away from the curb, and Nella crying, "Turiddu, Turiddu." Her cries were the cries of a young girl, lost in a market in Syracuse.

"Here," I called out to my sister, and we looked at each other—her look saying what words could not say and my look saying, *Are you sure?* And she nodded yes, her hands in a fist over her heart, her long graying hair hiding her face from me, and I turned to my garden, but my brothers were gone.

VINCENZO

1

Salvatore came to see me at the café the day he lost David. It was in the afternoon, the heat wave hadn't let up, and I had no customers. I turned from the sink when he entered. His shadow cut across the floor and tables, and crept up the opposite wall—a long, dark line that grew and snaked around the room as he walked. He sat at the bar but couldn't get the words out. His head fell like a stone into the circle of his arms on the counter.

"What's wrong?" I asked him.

When he finally spoke, he spoke into the Formica, a low rumble from his throat in the thick dialect of his village.

My hand shot up, cupping my mouth. I stumbled back into the metal sink.

Salvatore raised his head into an oblong of sunlight that stretched from the storefront window and over the wall to the bar. In this light, his gray hair thinned, and I could see the dry scalp. The crown of his head.

"Have you eaten? Let me make you something. You have to eat."

I made a simple meal of dandelion greens and pasta. But Salvatore couldn't hold down the food. When he ran to the bathroom, I followed and stayed with him, my hand on his back, his head over the toilet.

He wiped his mouth with a hand towel and said, "He was a good boy, my David, wasn't he?"

"The best," I said.

"He was smart, too," Salvatore said. "The best in school."

"The very best," I said. "He was one of our own."

∿

I closed the café for the remainder of that week. I stayed with Salvatore, slept on the living room sofa, checked in on Nella. I was there that Thursday afternoon when Salvatore and Nella received the news that the coroner had ruled David's death an accidental drowning. He had struck his head and fallen into the river. Maybe he had slipped, leaning over the railing. The policeman stood on the front porch, sweating in his uniform in the heat. Salvatore still would not let him come inside. The officer asked if David had been depressed, if he had been acting out or was upset about something at home or in school. The man didn't say the word *suicide*, but we all knew what he was trying to tell us, and in our answers, we saw the pattern in the weave. David had never learned to swim—why else would he have been alone down there at that time of night? Maybe he had wanted to fall.

Salvatore had heard enough. He went out back, left the officer standing on the porch. His sister, close behind, called out to him. "Turiddu," she said, and he said, "Let me work, Nella." Little brown blotches from a lifetime of hard work under the sun covered his arms and the backs of his hands—calloused hands, dirty and cracked. He filled an empty bucket with water from the hose. He carried the bucket to the garden, set the bucket down, hard. Water sloshed over the plastic rim onto his boots. "I'm his papà," he said. He wet his hand and wiped the leaves of the peas. He called out to his sister and she spun around, and they looked at each other from across the yard. "The work," he said, "it's good for me."

~

It was a long, hot summer. Salvatore's face and arms became even more tan and leathery from hours under that sun. His garden grew so many tomatoes and peppers, cucumbers and zucchini, he kept coming to the café with overflowing boxes of produce. When I told him *No more, I can't eat them fast enough, they go bad,* he took them across the street to the church. Father Salafia accepted all the vegetables and herbs Salvatore grew, and what the priest didn't keep for the rectory, he donated to the soup kitchen on Main Street, in the North End.

That August, Sam came by the café one last time, two girls with him—friends who knew David—and told me he and his mother were moving back to Stony Creek. The girls, Em and Jamie, they had come to the service at the D'Angelo Funeral Home. They were strange-looking girls who sat quietly in the back, the one with the tall blue hair comforting the delicate, raven-haired one. I never knew David had such good friends as these.

It was late in the day, the day they came to visit, and I brought them chilled Orangina and cannoli and we sat in the corner booth—David's favorite spot. They stayed a half hour and we spoke of David only once. Sam brought him up, and Jamie held his hand to give him courage. "I should've been there," Sam said. "I could've . . . David tried to tell me, but I didn't listen. Why didn't I listen?"

"Put that out of your mind," I told him. "What happened, it was not your fault. No one is to blame."

~

That fall, after school started back up and Sal's last butternut had been harvested, that was when I first noticed the Morello boy, Rocco's son, Tony, sitting on the church steps night after night. I watched him while I cleaned the café. Sometimes he stared out at nothing. Sometimes he studied a slip of paper in his hand for hours on end. Then he'd look at the café with dread and longing, the same way a man might look up at the stars, feeling small and alone.

Even when the first snow of the season fell, three inches in the second week of November, Tony still loitered on those steps. It was a Tuesday, early evening but already dark. The snow had eased a little, gusts of it swirling powdery white under the streetlamps. Tony had cleared a spot on the steps with his shoe, and sat shivering, his red leather jacket too thin, made for show more than warmth.

Business had been slow all day, and my last customer had cleared out over an hour ago. On the church steps, Tony blew on his bare hands. "That stronzo," I said to myself, "he will catch pneumonia out there."

I put on my sheepskin-lined overcoat, gray with a fat charcoal fur collar that was warm against my neck, and crossed the street. I had picked it up at the military surplus store just over the Connecticut River. I'd gone with David. What a pair we made marching out of that store, David in the peacoat I bought for him and me in this. The clerk told me it was genuine Soviet issue, as if that sort of thing mattered to me. I just wanted something that would keep me warm. Quality material, he said. They knew how to stay warm, those Russians.

"What are you doing out here?" I shouted, throwing my arms wide.

"None of your business," Tony said. His thick black curls stuck out wild from his head, shaggy and dusted with snow.

"You just made it my business." I motioned for him to follow and started back toward the street. When I didn't hear him behind me, I turned around and said, "Don't make me drag you."

"You wouldn't dare," Tony said. "I'd tell my father."

"If you think I'm afraid of your father, then you've learned nothing. So go ahead, bring him down here. Maybe he can tell me what the hell you're doing every night on these steps, watching my café."

Tony hugged himself, rubbing his arms. "Please, don't."

I recognized the desperation in his voice, the need to find a way out of a hole he'd dug for himself. He was asking me to pull him up out of that hole but was too stupid to know it, or too proud.

"You'll get sick if you stay out here dressed like that," I said. "Come inside. I won't ask again."

This time, he followed me back to the café. We tracked snow on the tile floor I had just mopped. "Before you leave," I said, "you're cleaning that up."

Tony slunk into the front corner booth.

Behind the counter, I poured a glass of wine for myself and ladled the last of my fish stew from the pot on the hot plate for Tony. I cut a lemon in half and picked out the seeds with the tip of my paring knife.

"This will warm you up." I squeezed both lemon halves into the bowl and sat down across from Tony. He slurped a shallow spoonful of broth. He looked thinner than he had the day he and David had fought. "David always sat there," I said, "in the spot you're in now."

Tony dropped the spoon and it clattered on the tabletop. Flecks of parsley mixed with olive oil and lemon juice splattered his jacket, but he didn't wipe them off. His skin turned ashen except for his nose and ears, still red from the cold. The boy needed me to push him.

"You gave David such a hard time," I said. "You never left him alone, never let him breathe."

Tony took a slip of paper from his jacket pocket and held it in his lap. "It was an accident," he said. He slid the paper across the table. "That night. I was there. I tried to help him. I did. I swear. You have to believe me."

∾

I made Tony repeat what happened that night at Harbor Park. And then I made him tell me again. By the third time his eyes were red and his nose snotty and he couldn't get to the end for all his blubbering.

Somewhere, during it all, I'd crumpled David's note in my fist so tight that the knuckles bulged white and the blue veins on the back of my hand stood out like routes on a map.

"You're sure he said Vassallo?" I asked him. What I meant, what I couldn't say, was *Are you sure he was there because of us?* But I already knew the answer. It had been there all along, in the shoebox and the pictures and the slap that I couldn't stop or undo. In that moment and all the mistakes that led up to it. Those mistakes weren't Salvatore's alone. Not even Rocco's. It had begun with me.

"I'm sure," Tony said. His voice was scratchy.

"And I'm the only one you've told all this to?"

Tony wiped his nose with a napkin and nodded yes.

"Good," I said. "The mop is in the back."

"You were serious about that?"

I knew this kid, better than he knew himself. Better than even his own father knew him. That man was hard on him, but hard in a mindless way. A boot on the neck must be a guiding force. "If I have to get up—" I said. I bit the side of my hand, a wordless threat that warned, *If I catch you, I will ruin you with my hands.*

Tony cleaned the floor. Outside, fat snowflakes fell as slow as turtles. Snowdrifts curled into the corners of the windows. Veins of ice crept across the glass. I poured more wine. David's crinkled note sat on the table in front of me. A torn piece of blue-lined notebook paper. His tight letters bled at the sweat-stained edges. My promise to Salvatore and Nella to guard our secrets, my word—my currency—it made me a poor man in the end.

2

In this life, you were both the boot on the neck, and the neck. This was the essence of discipline and war. The boot promised purpose and direction. It demanded obedience, provided order. I was a man with a talent for killing other men. This was the one thing in life I was ever good at. Lift the pressure on the neck even a little and you set a man like that adrift. This family, they never stood a chance. Not with a man like me in their life. David's death sentence was set the moment I found his father as a boy in the scope of my rifle.

It started on that day in Melilli, late July 1943. I ended up there by chance, falling in with three German soldiers after escaping Noto. We were not much of a fighting force, more like ragged dolls some child had outgrown and tossed aside.

I took the sniper's position at the second-story window of an abandoned farmhouse above the village. I swung my rifle scope around the panorama of houses with hand-chiseled walls of dry stone enclosing each parcel of rocky land where groves of prickly pear and pistachio and fig trees grew. A boy of eight or nine years old squatted behind the flat spiny lobes of prickly pears with his pants down around his ankles. He saw the Germans—Lieutenant Krause and his two men—drag the corpse of an American soldier outside and drop it in the dirt by a dry well. A paratrooper by the look of his uniform, scattered far from his unit like a leaf in the wind. The boy pulled his pants back up in a hurry. He shielded his eyes from the sunlight glinting off the lens of my scope. I placed my finger to my lips and motioned for him to stay down.

Lieutenant Krause signaled up at me that he was taking his men to the bunker we'd spotted by the shore on our first sweep of the village. When the Germans were out of sight, I waved the boy inside, but he shook his head no. I leaned my rifle against the wall and went out to him. Filthy clothes hung like rags off his thin frame. He wore a hard look on his face, dark eyebrows drawn together and lips pursed tight. I pinched my nose and said, "Who made that stink? Was it you?"

The boy didn't crack a smile. I licked my thumb and tried wiping dirt from the boy's cheek, but he turned his head away from me. And I saw in the set of his scraped chin, in the way his fists clenched at his sides, the lines of boys from my own childhood standing at attention at the parade grounds of the Fascist youth brigade—the Balilla—in Rome. That same combination of pride and courage and determination.

"Where are your parents?" I asked him.

When he didn't answer, I took a chocolate bar from my jacket pocket and waved it in the air. The boy reached for it, but I pulled it back from his grasp and repeated my question.

"The cave," he said.

I gave him the chocolate. He tore into the wrapper. Then I held out my hand for him and said, "Come. It's not safe here."

The boy led me up an ancient footpath, bordered by terraced rows of dull-green olive trees, the trunks knotted and gnarled, the branches twisted into monstrous shapes. They looked like sculptures coiling from the rugged earth. Caves dotted the mountainside path. Music drifted down from one of those caves, a cheerless guitar and the low, throaty voice of a fisherman. He sang of an invasion at the marina and lamented his broken shoes, worn out from fleeing the invaders. Women gathered clothes off clotheslines strung between the trees. Men smoked cigarettes and stood doleful watch over their unfurrowed fields in the low-lying land beneath the village.

"Salvatore." A man stepped out from behind the trunk of a centuries-old olive tree. He had a rigid, pockmarked face, black hair, and a bulbous nose.

Beside me, the boy ducked his head. The man, his father, grabbed him by the neck of his torn shirt. "What are you doing out here?" He held his son's face, turned it left and right, examining the chocolate stains around the boy's mouth. Then the man looked up at me, took me in—my ragged uniform, my haggard face, and the pistol holstered at my hip. "Get inside," he snapped at his son. "And wash up."

Salvatore took two steps into the cave that was, up until now, obscured by the enormous tree, and then stopped. He stood in the darkness, one shoulder pressed against jagged limestone, and watched me.

The man introduced himself as Raphael. He thanked me for seeing his son back to him.

Artillery shells thundered in the distance, a tragic percussion for the old folk song, a warning in the melody. "Soon it won't be safe," I said, "not even in these caves."

Raphael waved my concern away. "Soldiers came to our village last week," he said. "We prayed for help, and you know what happened?" Raphael gave a crooked-toothed grin and said with admiration, "An American fell from the sky, pulled out of the clouds by the saint. He was one man against half a dozen men."

"The American is dead," I said.

Raphael nodded yes. "But we are still here. You understand?" Then he ushered me inside the cave. We sat on wooden crates by a stone fire pit. He shared a meal with me of almonds and stale bread and good red wine from a tray on a crate set between us. His children gathered from the dark corners of the cave. Raphael broke crusts of bread from the hard loaf and handed them out. Then he retold the tale of their patron saint. The little ones like wild-growing olive shoots around the feet of their father.

The twins each tugged on one of their father's pant legs and begged him to tell it again. Nella and Salvatore agreed with their siblings. They never tired of hearing about their saint, as I had never tired of my father's stories from Greek and Roman mythology.

Raphael laughed and said, "Another time. Another time." Then he led me through a narrow, bending passage. Salvatore followed at my heels. I stooped into a low-ceilinged chamber where candle drippings crusted the stone floor. Raphael held his lantern aloft. It threw a flickering light on a prehistoric painting of a stick-figure man on the far wall. The washed-out oval head listed to one side. The forearms were missing. The figure stood on spindly legs the width of one pigmented finger stroke. Lines drew outward like the rays of the sun from the figure's chest.

Salvatore took my arm and pulled me toward the cave art. "See the arrows?" he said. "That's Saint Sebastian."

Stories possessed an uncontested power over the young. I knew this well from my own life at that age—recognized the wide eyes, the jaw hanging open. How that story must have played in his mind like some film spooling off a reel in a dark cinema.

3

Outside, the music had stopped. The guitar player now sat in an old chair in the shade of an olive tree, legs crossed. He held his instrument close, bent his ear to the strings while working to adjust them back into tune. An older man stood over him and implored the young musician to please play something else. The same song, all day, every day, since the American died, it was too much. It was driving him mad. "Pasqualino," he said. "Why don't you play something upbeat for a change? Something, I don't know, happy."

"Something happy? Nino, what is there to be happy about, eh?"

Raphael stood—resolute and surefooted—at the mouth of his cave. He lit a half-smoked cigarette and watched the two men argue. Over his shoulder, the shadows of his family wavered in firelight. A barrage of distant gunfire echoed throughout the mountain village.

"Take this," I said. I unholstered my pistol and offered it to him.

"You think I don't know what's coming." Raphael exhaled cigarette smoke out of his nostrils. "I know, more than you think." He took a thick book from the satchel that hung at his waist. The leather binding was old and torn, the stitches loose. He had painted the cover in white folk sigils. These old symbols of protection he redrew each year to renew their power. "My father gave me this book," he said, opening it with great care. The pages curved in waves, rough like the wicked sea that had carried me here with hundreds of soldiers just like me. "His father gave it to him, who got it from his father. It has always been so, so it has always been." In the book, he showed me an image of an ancient banner, the reds and yellows fading. "This is Sicily," he said. "My father called it the star with three points." He touched the three legs bent at the knees and joined in the center by the head of Medusa. "The jewel of the Mediterranean, beautiful and cursed." Soil was caked under his fingernails and around the cracked cuticles. His head bowed under the weight his eyes held for the precious stone that bore him up, his island. "And this," he said. He turned the page to a picture of their patron saint and kissed it. "This is Melilli."

"Pictures," I said. "Pictures will not save your children when the bombs fall."

"The bombs," he said. "The bombs are not for us. They are for you. Take off that ugly uniform. Put on some good clothes, hardworking clothes."

Pasqualino began to play again, the same song on his guitar. Nino covered his ears and petitioned heaven to intervene. "Raphael," he said, when it was clear that heaven would not answer. "He will listen to you. Everyone listens when Raphael speaks. Make him play something else. I beg of you."

"It was not so long ago that you wore the black shirt," Raphael said. "Do not ask me for favors."

And with that, Nino ripped the guitar from Pasqualino and smashed it against the trunk of the olive tree. The musician shot up from his chair, and the two men fell wrestling to the ground.

Salvatore emerged from the darkness of the cave like some ghost of my childhood, black eyes burning in his dirty face. "Take the gun, Papà." His words, thin and anxious.

Raphael dropped his cigarette, grinding it into the dirt with the toe of his boot. "Go," he said to me. "You'll lose your life out there. And for what?" He waved me away with a violent sweep of his arm. Then he took Salvatore by the shoulders, his hands a bridle, and led his son back into the cave. They rejoined the wavy shadows of their family. The boy's voice echoed from the cave mouth, "Why didn't you take the gun, Papà?" and the father's voice followed, "Better to be a swine than a soldier, Turiddu."

≈

If I had only listened to Raphael, I could have disappeared among the people of Melilli. To the British I would've been just another Sicilian peasant. And when the Allies liberated the island, that day in the orchard with the twins, I would have been there still. Maybe I could have prevented that tragedy, or the ones that came after. But I did not stay.

Back at the farmhouse, I stood over the bloated corpse of the American. Flies swarmed the face and the bulging eyes. The mouth hung open and the flies crawled inside. The soldier regarded me with an opaque, milky-white stare. One man against half a dozen men. I placed two flat stones on his eyes and returned to my place in the house by the window on the second floor. I found the Germans in my rifle scope. They climbed up the goat path. I followed them. The curved butt of the gun fit smoothly against my shoulder like it was a part of me. And it was a part of me. I fingered the trigger. I could take maybe two of them out before the third got me.

Lieutenant Krause waved as they drew near, his fair hair dazzling in the afternoon sun. I set the rifle aside and went out to greet them. We were low on ammunition so we fashioned grenades out of food tins, nails, and gunpowder from hunting rifles left behind by the peasants. The lieutenant told us the British name for them—jam-tin grenades. We found enough spare material in the neighboring houses to make one for each of us. Then we headed to the bunker and took up defensive positions there. Krause believed a division of German soldiers would be here soon. But I had a feeling—someone like Nella might call it a premonition—that the enemy would be here before long. Two days, maybe less before we would be uprooted and lost like so many trees before the fury of the flood.

"And if the British get here first," I said. "What then?"

"We kill them," Krause said to me in Italian. "Or they kill us. There is no alternative. We will not let them murder us with our hands in the air. Or have you forgotten what I told you about what the Americans did at Biscari?"

Krause had been at Biscari, hidden in one of the airfield's outbuildings. He'd watched Americans massacre Italians and Germans who had surrendered. It was a wound still fresh in his mind—and he made it our own, too. If we were to die, he wanted us to die fighting.

~

Night fell. Tracer fire crisscrossed the sky. A barrage of artillery rumbled up from the low ground around the village. Two batteries, by the sound of it, and who knows how many infantry, lurking in the brush and cratered terrain. I dropped my journal and covered my head with my arms. The mountain trembled and then shook like an earthquake. The blasts of those big guns rattled me from my boots all the way to my teeth. We would not last long. If the Germans did not get here soon, we would die having never seen the faces of the men who killed us. They were out there, just as blind as we were. Men who dispatched death with heavy mortars, who readied the next shell in time with each tremendous jolt of those damned machines. These were men with just one idea.

The barrage came in waves. We hunkered down, waited it out. Time passed, maybe an hour, maybe more or less. It was difficult keeping track. A minute here was a lifetime when shells whistled overhead and cratered the earth. Explosions like that, they were always bigger than you ever imagined. The war stories that captured your youth never made it personal. They were never meant to kill you, those stories, only trap you. It was fantasy for bullies and small men.

Moonlight filtered through the gun ports, laddered with cement dust from the ceiling. Outside, a German platoon crept along the mountainside from the south. Krause believed that now we had a fighting chance. But the white glow of a flare arched overhead and soon proved his chimera false. The platoon scurried for cover, frantic under Allied fire from the high western ridge.

Krause shot wild bursts out the gun port, and the pop and prattle of small arms fire answered him in the night. His men joined the fray, but their efforts were futile. The enemy had already cut the Germans to pieces. We could do nothing but listen to the dying cries for help from the men not killed outright. The shelling that followed was a mercy for me. They whistled overhead. Brackets of mortar fire like dogs on the hunt, sniffing out our position. It was only a matter of time now. Each explosion grew closer. The last one sent a rain of dirt and debris through the gun ports.

The muzzle blast of an enemy howitzer flashed. And Krause emptied his submachine gun at it. That was it. The fool had just a pistol now with its eight bullets. These Germans were like blindered horses. They saw only the path in front of them, and that led to one place.

When the shelling subsided, Krause scanned the ridgeline with his binoculars. His men clutched their MP40s in slick, sweaty hands the way toddlers clutched blankets. Like the pharaohs of ancient Egypt, Krause would have his men die with him, entombed in this slab of concrete. A mausoleum to fools.

"This is madness," I said. I picked up my journal and stuffed it in my pack, slung the pack over my shoulder.

Krause drew his Luger on me. "Where are you going?"

"We're just four men," I said. "Against a battalion. This is suicide. I don't want to die for nothing."

"My men do not desert," he said. "Run and I'll kill you."

"Take it easy." I moved to set my pack down, but then swung it at Krause. It hit him square in the chest, knocked him back a step.

I ran from the bunker, pulled myself up and over the embankment, my legs kicking out behind me. But I was too slow. Krause shot me from the doorway. Pain ripped through my knee, muscle torn away from bone. I hit the ground, screaming. I had never heard a sound like that come from me before. It filled the bay, as if the bay itself had shrieked at the sight of blood so close to its shores.

Krause's men sprayed the tree line with covering fire so he could reach me. "You coward!" he shouted over a hail of bullets. My face wet with his spit.

I drew my pistol and shot him. The bullet tore into his belly. He slumped over, hands covering the hole I'd made in his abdomen. The widening patch of blood flooded the canals between his fingers.

The other two scrambled out of the bunker trench. An enemy rifle blast rang out, striking one of them. The side of his face sprayed across the soil. The other crept through the trench, hunched down, helmet bobbing in and out of view. His arm swept up and he tossed a grenade at the tree line. Then he swung himself over the embankment and rolled onto his belly. He wormed his way forward while the whole area drew fire.

Krause tried to speak but only sputtered bubbles of blood and spit at the corners of his mouth. His pupils dilated almost to the size of marbles, the way an animal looked when it knew it was about to die. He reached out to me but I recoiled from his touch. His eyes rolled back in his head to show him the blackness of what came next. His eyelids fluttered. He choked out his last breath, and when he died, he hissed like a snake slithering unseen through tall weeds.

When the last German reached me, I still held the gun in my hand, still pointed it at Krause. He was a kid, no more than nineteen. He stared down at his dead lieutenant. "Please," he said in his simple Italian. He wasn't fluent in my language, and I did not speak his, but I knew what he meant. He wanted to live, same as me. I holstered my weapon, watching him for signs of betrayal. None came, but that could change in an instant if faced with a choice between his own life or mine. I knew what I would choose.

4

Under cover of darkness, we made it to a stream and rested beneath the canopy of a massive fig tree, its slender branches drooping down around us. My head pounded in time with the pounding ache in my leg. I cut the pant leg open. The wound wasn't as bad as it looked—or felt. The bullet had torn up the side of my knee, grazed the kneecap on the way out, fracturing the bone. At least it was not shattered. The German said something as he cleaned and dressed my wound. He knew I could not understand him and yet he spoke anyway in that dirty, guttural voice, full of spit and scorn. A cat coughing up a hairball.

I scanned his face for some clue that would translate his words for me. His eyes darted around our position. Was he running the numbers, working out the odds, asking himself if I would slow him down, get him killed? How long would he wait to take me by surprise with a knife to my throat in the night? Or would he take the easy way out and turn me in to the next German unit we found? A weak smile crossed his lips. He'd made his choice.

My fingers searched beside me, feeling the earth, an above-ground root snaking out from the trunk, and then a stone. My arm came up fast with the stone in my grip, striking the side of the soldier's head. He went down. And I struck his head over and over again until it split open like the shell of a soft-boiled egg with all the yolk oozing out.

I took his pistol and his pack with its ammunition, rations, and the map of Sicily he'd stolen from some municipal building during his scramble to escape the British. I gave no thought to the pack I'd left behind in the bunker in Melilli. I did not think of the journal inside, the one that spelled out exactly how a boy in pain could make a bomb. One soldier's pack, it seemed then, should be as good as any other.

I covered the German's face with his blanket. The sight of his skull cracked open like that made me sick to my stomach. But this, this was the only way I knew how to live.

~

Four days I hobbled north with a walking stick cut from the fallen branch of an almond tree. I felt like an old man, older than my twenty-four years. In Adrano, a village at the foot of the volcano, I attached myself to a new Italian regiment. Their medic checked my wound, said I was lucky it hadn't been worse. He patched me up the best he could.

Three more days and the regiment broke under Allied assault. But I didn't hear bombs dropping, or bullets whizzing over my head. No mortar fire. No cries from the wounded or frightened soldiers. I heard nothing at all, not even my own beating heart. Silence shrouded me. And I remembered the myth of the hundred-headed monster buried deep inside that mountain. Looking around at all those helmeted men, I saw how the story might be true, how their heads—our heads—made up that creature.

5

We retreated through the rocky backbone of the island, my new regiment in tatters, and made contact with German positions in an abandoned village called Randazzo. It would be in flames before the week ended, bombed out and burning. At night on the narrow, winding road down the mountain—another withdrawal in a long line of withdrawals—Etna smoked and spewed lava, and you couldn't tell the molten glow of the mountain's fury from the dying embers of Randazzo.

On the coast, in Messina, a military evacuation of the island was underway. Allied mortar fire pursued us from one position to the next as we pulled back. The bastards knew even the places where we tried to steal a few hours of sleep. Their shells whistled overhead and the thunder sounded, all day, all night. Boom. Boom. The ground always shook. We lost several good men in a barrage of machine-gun fire the day we learned the king had deposed Mussolini. From that moment on, the Germans looked on us with suspicion. They wondered if we would go against them now, and for good reason. Even our king knew the end was coming.

But these Germans were smarter than Krause. They understood that the earthworm cut in half grows a new tail. We set our jaws and disappeared into the mountains. We traveled off road and only at night, without light. Following the ridgeline, we came to Messina. Dirty seagulls circled the ships in port and greeted us with their cries. We were not soldiers, mere food for gulls.

6

I escaped into the Italian countryside before the Allies crossed the Strait of Messina and landed on the mainland. Outside the fishing village of Scilla, I found a derelict farm among the olive trees, the stable and the sheepfold deserted. I stole civilian clothes from the farmhouse. The shirt fit loose in the shoulders, and I had to make an extra notch in the belt with my knife to keep the pants from falling down. The jars of preserves and honey and dried figs lasted a week. The Allies controlled the village, and the distant gunfire became more sporadic and indistinct as the Germans abandoned the toe of the Italian boot.

In the piazza, I stood in line as Americans handed out rations and supplies to the local population. A soldier glued a placard to the wall of the municipal building. In Italian, it decreed all citizens to surrender their weapons and ammunition in two days. The mayor, a man with a round belly that spoke little of the hardship around him, introduced himself to the lieutenant in charge. They spoke through an interpreter. The mayor complained about the rations, and the lieutenant scolded him, told him that the days of eating well at the expense of his neighbors was over. The mayor raised his hands and cried, "You misunderstand. I am no Fascist. Ask anyone here and they will tell you, that man, he is no Fascist!"

I stepped forward in line, accepted the meager provisions. What would Raphael think of me now—unwashed in dirty peasant garb like some peripatetic puppet in an impromptu street show.

∽

The next evening, four soldiers arrived at the farm—I was the last stop on their house-by-house sweep of the farmlands surrounding the village. A skinny Italian American asked if they could come inside. His Italian was pretty good, though his three compatriots didn't speak a word. They appeared haggard and worn, shaken as if each man sensed his own impending death. The price for taking Sicily from us. I asked the Italian American if he thought the war would be over soon. His expression told me that it would be a long hard slog up the boot. The Allies had suffered heavy losses at the Salerno beachhead, and the Germans now occupied Rome. And then the bad news, it got worse. It turned ugly. The whispered talk of death camps jittered on his lips. I told him to stop telling me rumors and nonsense. Then the soldier slid a picture across the wooden table at me.

"Got that from a German photographer," he said. "Can you believe it? The last decent Kraut in this world, and he had a camera."

My stomach curdled at the dull and grainy mound of the dead piled one on top of the other, skin and bones and nothing more. Did he think that I knew about this barbarism? How could I have known? It was impossible for me to know of such a thing as this. I pushed the picture back toward the soldier. "Germans," I said. "They have no honor. They've brought nothing but death and destruction to my country."

From the cupboard I took a loaf of stale black bread, traded from a boy whose father wanted Chesterfields. The soldiers spoke in English behind my back. Did they see through my disguise? Could one soldier see the soldier in another man, beneath the swine? What was it my father used to say? *Better to eat black bread at home than white bread in someone else's.* My parents warned me, but I didn't listen. They understood nothing good would come of this war. My mother cried the day I left. She held the back of my hand up to her cheek and begged me. *Flee Rome,* she said, *go into the country, hide. Your father and I, we'll help you.*

What was a nation if not a family? And when your family needed you, would you not do your best for them? Give them whatever you could, even if that meant spilling blood, your own or someone else's? When my country called my name, I stood at attention, proud and ready to fight. But I had no country now. This alliance with the Germans had seen to that. My right as a young Italian man, a son of the she-wolf, to carve his place in this world had come to nothing. That the king betrayed Il Duce and approved the armistice disgusted me. This was true. But I had betrayed my own parents when I chose my nation over them. Against those two powerful forces in my life, caught between Scylla and Charybdis, what was I to do? Maybe I should've run when my mother asked me to. It was an impossible choice.

Where were they now, my mother and father? Were they still in Rome? Were they even alive? I could only hope that my parents had moved somewhere safe, that they had gotten out of the city long before the Allied planes dropped their bombs, the streets filled with gunfire, and the Germans occupied the capital.

The pain in my bad knee flared up. I staggered back to the table and fell into the old, creaking chair.

"You hurt?" the skinny Italian American asked.

I broke the bread with unsteady hands. It was hard and bitter, too salty. "A goat," I said. "My last one." I held up a finger and shook it. "I tried to milk the stupid animal and she kicked me. I got so mad, I killed the ungrateful beast with a stone to the head. My last goat. I never ate so well again."

He translated my lie for the others, and the man with the medic's armband craned around the table to get a look at my knee.

I waved him off. "I'm fine," I said. "I just need to stay off my feet for a bit."

"Let him take a look at it," the Italian American said.

"This," I said. "This is nothing. Don't waste your medicine on me. You'll need that where you're going."

The medic sat back in his chair. There was no need to translate. He understood enough. He pulled a pack of cigarettes from his breast pocket and offered one to me. I declined but the others each took one. Soon storm clouds of smoke hung over our heads. The Italian American nosed around the room. There wasn't much: a wood stove, a sink—no running water—and a pair of rough-hewn wooden cabinets. My soldier's pack was in the bedroom, stowed under the cot. If he found it, they wouldn't kill me right off. No, that would come later, after the interrogation. Maybe they would do it here, a bullet to the head, or maybe I would die from some unknown disease in a prisoner of war camp, packed with other prisoners like sardines in a can, marinating in our own oils.

The Italian American leaned on the frame of the open bedroom doorway and poked his head inside. "You live alone?" he asked. Flecks of ash fell from his cigarette with each word.

I could take the medic with the bread knife on the counter, maybe one more, before the Italian American shot me. If I was fortunate, he would miss, but I was not a fortunate man.

"Wine," I said to him. "In that cabinet over there. Please." I rubbed around my kneecap. "Bring the bottle and some glasses."

The wine was just this side of vinegar, but the men did not complain. Together we finished the bottle, and when they left, I watched each of them in turn get swallowed up in the long shadows of the low evening light. Then I shut the door and barricaded it with a chair. By candlelight, I sewed a pillowcase from the bedsheet, large enough to hide my pack.

I spent the rest of the night on the thin naked mattress, one hand inside the pack inside the pillowcase, clutching my pistol. The wolf locked in the jaws of the hunter's trap. I could wait for the end to come, or I could chew my paw off and hobble away, the way I'd always done.

I was the troublemaker I'd told David about that time on the Ferris wheel. I was a poor student and a terror, always stealing and fighting, always misbehaving. My parents, they couldn't handle me. My youthful crimes made priests blush. You had to make boys like me respect you. That was the first thing I learned in the Balilla. They beat some sense into me, their black shirtsleeves rolled up in virtuous labor. You see, I was nothing but formless, delinquent clay, and with their fists, they molded me into finest marble—chin high, shoulders straight, right arm held out and up, leading the others in singing the Fascist anthem "Giovinezza." *Hail, O people of heroes, hail O immortal fatherland, your sons are reborn with faith in the idea.*

But boys got their strength from their mothers. This was the one truth the Balilla swept away. After David lost his mother, I read to him each evening, the way mine did for me before I turned my back on her. I read some of my favorite stories from Greek and Roman mythology, and I took requests. David loved hearing the story of Persephone trapped in the underworld, reuniting with her mother on Earth for a few months out of the year, and how that reunion made spring bloom.

When I'd stand at the door and turn off the light, he'd ask me in a voice muffled from under the blankets to leave the light on. *Please, Enzo.* And I'd turn on the light, say, *See, there's nothing there. Nothing to be afraid of.* But I didn't see what he saw. I couldn't see, not with my eyes. But his young eyes saw the movement of monstrous shapes in the shadows, the kind that crept out at night from closets that were left even a little bit open. So I'd sit with him until he fell asleep. I was the same at that age—all boys are—until the Balilla made a man out of me.

The pistol was slick in my grip, night sweats and I had not even slept. We should've ground the world under the heel of the Italian boot, like the filthy butt of a cigarette. All those men who never made it to Messina, did they still believe, still fight even in their graves? What song would their bones sing to us, ground up as they were under the heel of the world?

~

The fighting dragged on. By October, the Allies controlled southern Italy. Their advance slowed by German defenses and heavy rains in the unforgiving terrain of the Apennines. In those mountains with winter coming, the way north would not be safe for a long time.

It was June 1944 when the Germans withdrew from Rome and the Allies captured the city, and I finally returned home. I don't remember how long I walked under the summer sun. That scorching heat beat down and ironed the shirt on my back—dripping in sweat—the darkened cuffs rolled up at my elbows, the collar stained. My feet blistered in dirty socks with holes at the toes and heels, and the soles of my boots worn through, with breaks in the leather along the seams. I didn't know the time of day or the day of the week when I stood in the road—lined with the wreckage of German legions—waving down an American military convoy that rumbled past. The last truck in the line stopped and I pointed north. "Rome," I said and the driver handed me a canteen and thumbed me into the truck bed. I sat between stacked crates of supplies, savoring the metallic taste of the warm water.

~

When I set foot in the deserted streets of my old neighborhood—the working-class neighborhood of San Lorenzo—leaflets fell on the city from gray-bellied planes overhead. It looked almost beautiful, like snow, if not for the sporadic gunfire in the distance, the bombed-out railroad yards at Stazione Termini, the scorched and damaged houses, the shells of buildings standing in the rubble of their own guts, and the ruined facade of the Basilica di San Lorenzo fuori le mura—the Basilica of Saint Lawrence outside the walls.

I walked past the playground—the field burnt and littered with debris—and, further out, down a little cobblestone street the bombs had

284

missed. I stood at the end of the block of shuttered three-story houses. The block where my parents had raised me up, where I'd scraped my knees as a boy. In the twilight, this place looked like the picture in my head. But the picture in my head had sounds, it had life, laughter, bickering. The quiet here unnerved me, as if the street itself was in mourning. I limped along the pavement. I picked up my pace. I wanted to see my parents again, eat a home-cooked meal, and sleep in my own bed.

A dog barked from inside one of the buildings. "Fico," an old woman said. "Be quiet, Fico." And then I saw her, backing away from the first-floor window, half the shutter broken and hanging from the hinge.

When I turned back from the woman at the window, I noticed a break in the row of houses. The muscles in my jaw tensed. The image my eyes showed me blurred for a second. And in that second, it was as if I fell out of this world into a nightmare where someone replaced the house I grew up in with this charred stone frame standing in front of me, three stories of burnt bones in the middle of a quiet block.

A hand touched my shoulder and a gentle voice asked, "Are you okay, Signore?"

"I was born there," I said.

The voice belonged to a beautiful young woman with long black curls. She cradled a paper bag in one arm. A long loaf of bread stuck out from the top.

"I'm sorry," she said. "This war has been a curse on us all. Is there anything I can do? Do you need a place to stay? Some food?"

I remembered that I hadn't eaten all day. And I searched deep within myself for some sign of hunger, a grumbling stomach or a light-headed feeling, but found none. "No," I said. "Thank you for the offer."

"The city is still dangerous," she said. "Please take care." Then she hurried away, her heels clicking on the cobblestone street. And as she rounded the corner, I wondered what losses were behind the sadness in her voice.

Inside the house, the floors above ground level had collapsed. And with the roof gone, I looked up at the leaflets floating down from the sky. I snatched one from out of the air. *Rome is yours!* it declared. *Your job is to save the city, ours is to destroy the enemy.* I dropped the paper, looked at the flyers all around the rubble. I got on my knees and sifted through broken furniture and dishes, burnt hardback books of poetry and novels, the curled and coal-black pages crumbling to ashes in my hands. I thought of the people who had lived here—the bickering old couple on the top floor, the poor widower who kept to himself on the first—and I thought of my family's pictures on the walls, the bedroom where I had dreamed as a boy, my father's favorite reading chair, my mother's prized kitchen. How she loved cooking for the three of us, sharing conversation and good wine. I missed her cooking. I missed them both.

I had no relatives, no other family, and couldn't think of where to go. I cleared debris from the floor, curled up on my side, and slept like a baby in his mother's womb. And in the night as I slept, Raphael came to me. We used the pages of some book for kindling and made a fire of a mound of collapsed floorboards. He spoke to me in the flickering light, but he made no sound. Or I could not hear the words.

The next day, people spilled out of their homes and mobbed the streets, welcoming the American army with flowers and hugs and bottles of wine. The sun hurt my eyes. I stayed in the shade of shop awnings and avoided the cheering crowds and the columns of marching soldiers, the parade of tanks and trucks towing big guns, all heading north. I found an abandoned first-floor apartment in an alley and washed the soot from under my fingernails. A message scrawled in dried blood on the mirror read: *You die, you disappear.* The soot whirled down the drain. And I felt hollowed out, like some nameless beast had gnawed away at my insides, picked the bones clean.

7

That evening, I found Silvio Rosi—a friend of my father's—at his little café tucked away on a quiet, narrow side street. Two round mosaic tables fit into the tight space to the left of the smashed door-length window where the old man stood with a dustpan and broom, sweeping up the glass. He had a horseshoe ring of gray hair around the sides of his head, and he looked thinner than the picture I had of him from my memory.

"Excuse me," I said.

He turned around and his face went white. His mouth fell open. And the broom dropped from his hands. "Enzo," he said. "Enzo Giordano." Then he hugged me and kissed my unshaven cheeks. "You're the spitting image of your father," he said.

I took a seat and he sighed and said, "You've seen the house."

"What happened, Silvio?"

He wiped his brow with a hand towel hanging from his back pocket and sat opposite me. "The Germans," he said. Then he spit into the street. "The Fascists," he said, spitting again. "They accused your parents of harboring partisans. Can you believe that?"

I buried my face in my hands, not sure if I could hear any more.

"I don't know," Silvio said. He waved a hand in front of his face as if swatting a fly. "I don't know if it was true or not. Your father, he denied it, of course. And the soldiers, they searched the house three times. That last time your father came to me. Right here at this table a few hours before curfew." Silvio tapped a finger on the tabletop. Then he looked over his shoulders, leaned in closer, and said, "He told me they were leaving the city, him and your mother, that it wasn't safe anymore, and that they'd be back as soon as possible."

I lifted my head from my hands. "He didn't tell you where they were going?"

Silvio lit a cigarette and shook his head no. He blew smoke out of his nostrils and said, "That night the apartment building burned down." He reached out and patted my hand on the table. "We searched the place. Everyone from the neighborhood pitched in. But your parents, well, they must've got out in time. I'm sure of it." Then he slapped his hands on his thighs, stood up, and said, "I have a room upstairs. It's tiny." He held out his pinkie finger. "But a bed is better than nothing. You can work off the rent in the café. They'll come back. You'll see."

The café stood in eerie silence in the hours before dawn. By the time Silvio arrived—around seven in the morning—I had already unlocked and pulled open the folding steel gate, put the two tables and chairs outside, and received the delivery from a black-market courier, a ten-year-old boy on a bicycle. He delivered one loaf of bread, a tin of olive oil, a box of spaghetti, and four cans of ground American coffee. I paid him with money from the shoebox under the loose floor tile behind the counter, then I brewed a fresh pot of coffee.

Silvio and I sat together, sipping our coffee until it got cold, dipping in crusts of stale bread left over from the day before. We waited for the morning rush that never came.

～

At lunch, we ate the spaghetti with the olive oil and bread. Then I wiped the tall, round tables and stools that lined the walls all the way to the counter in back. Silvio swept the black-and-white tiled floor for the second time that day, and he straightened the pictures of his family that hung on the wall—his wife and two unmarried girls, his father and mother and in-laws. Then he dusted the frames with a worn cloth.

Midafternoon, we had customers. They arrived in twos and threes, and I searched their faces for my father, for the pointed chin, the patch of gray at the temples, the round glasses—the serious and studious look of my father. But I didn't see him. I saw men walking in with dazed and haunted faces, drawn long and pained, and with just a few lire notes in their wallets. They bought one cup of coffee and nursed it for hours. At first the men stayed quiet, beaten down by a day of looking for work and finding no jobs available. But as the shadows grew longer outside, and the tables filled up inside, they began talking. They talked about where they had looked for work, and the long lines they had waited in. Their voices grew louder. Finally, they argued and made jokes and told stories. Finally, the café came alive.

~

Each day that followed held the same rhythm. And as the week passed into a month with no sign of my parents, I grew more restless. I knocked on all the doors on my parents' street, visiting people I had not seen in years, and asked them about Carlo and Anna Giordano. I asked everyone who walked into the café the same questions. I felt sorry imposing my troubles on them. They had their own problems. They'd survived the Allied bombing of the San Lorenzo district when so many others had died. And I'd heard stories from the men in the café of Germans stealing their coal for the winter, and looting the city for food and supplies. But no one had seen my parents since the night of the fire.

8

The night I met Sergio Romano—a partisan who had fought against the Germans and the Fascists—he sat alone in the corner of the café, smoking Lucky Strikes and dipping biscotti into his coffee. Men at the other tables whispered his name. They spoke of Sergio's prison sentence in the late thirties for crimes against the state, the torture he endured there, and how, upon his release, he took on three Blackshirts in an alley not far from here. He stood his ground, unarmed against three armed brutes, and he won. During the German occupation of Rome, he printed anti-Fascist leaflets from his basement and led a resistance group.

Sergio came into the café an hour before closing and stayed until all the customers had left for the night. I cleared the two tables outside, wiped them down with a damp cloth, walked back inside, and shut the narrow door behind me.

"Stop asking about your parents," Sergio said. He didn't look at me when he spoke. He stared straight ahead. "That's not smart."

"Do you know where they went?" I sat down at his table.

Sergio snuffed out his cigarette in the ashtray, his head turned to the window. He checked up and down the street. Smoke curled out from around the scar on his lips as he spoke. "Your father delivered messages for me. One of my best couriers. You should be proud."

I pounded the table with my fist, rattling the ashtray and cup. He never even flinched, but it made him look at me just the same.

"Your father got careless," Sergio said. He lit another cigarette. Then he tapped a finger against his temple. "I told him to use his head, that he risked our entire operation, but he wouldn't listen. He had to hide some young man who had run from the Fascists." Sergio shrugged his shoulders and gave me a blank stare. "Beh, at least he was smart enough not to give me a name." He stood up and left some money on the table. "Your father had a good heart," he said. "But it was too big. Don't make the same mistake. There are still Fascists out there settling old scores. Don't go looking for your parents."

~

In my little room above the café, I lay awake long into the night, hands clasped behind my head. My feet hung off the end of the fold-up aluminum cot, only half covered by the blanket. Silvio had salvaged the cot from a building the Germans abandoned when they pulled out of the city. The thin mattress pad sagged where he'd tied the broken springs to the frame with chicken wire.

Yellow light from the street pressed through the window slats, cutting shadowed rungs on the plasterwork wall. The wall looked like the earth cracked from years of drought. Pictures grew from those cracks. I saw the white flowers of almond and citrus and olive orchards, the trees heavy with bloom. In the harbor of a seaside village, fishermen tied up their little boats and hauled in their fish. They brought the fish to market in carts pulled by donkeys. The fishermen had carved and painted the panels of those carts with such magnificent skill and spirit. But they had traded in the traditional bright reds and greens and yellows for lifeless black and charcoal gray. Instead of chivalrous knights and castles, there were soldiers and corpses in the rubble.

I had carved my place in a colorless world.

~

The next day, I hired a man who printed missing persons leaflets. All I had was a small, grainy portrait of my parents. Even this wasn't mine. It belonged to Silvio. That Saturday, I took off from work and bought a bicycle. I pasted the leaflets on the walls of buildings all over the San Lorenzo district. On street corners, I shoved them into people's hands like a mad beggar. Each weekend, I covered the walls of different districts and stood on busy corners. But always the reactions of the people were the same. The men with their evasive eyes and coarse temperaments shooed me away like a stray dog. The women left in a hurry, saying, "Sorry, I can't help you." Children took the leaflets and held them out to their mothers, crying, "Read it for me, Mamma." But the mothers gathered their little ones and left without a word. They shied away from me, reluctant to take the paper I pushed at them, as if accepting it meant they accepted responsibility for the war and all the terrible things that happened because of it.

But in war as in peacetime, man committed terrible acts all the time. He could be a ferocious animal if he had to be, and sometimes he had to be. That was nature, nothing more. No more aberrant for a man than the duties of motherhood for a woman.

My search for my parents reminded them that we were a beaten people. It exposed their fears that perhaps this had been our fate from the beginning. But the blame, the blame was not ours. Our disasters in Sicily and Greece, and in other places, rested with our leaders. Their strategy and planning had been poor. Mussolini's goals were vain goals, not glorious ones.

This was not to say that a man with honorable intentions always won out. Fortune played her part in a man's life, too. She was the squall and the calm, the fickle mistress and the unrequited love. You could never stop chasing her, never bear parting ways with her.

The odds were against me ever finding my parents. My heart knew this. Every beat was a beat closer to accepting a life without answers. My dream of a Rome with my parents still in it was just that, a dream. I could never know the price for their troubles.

Yet my belief in my own infallibility kept me searching. Vincere, e vinceremo. To win, and we shall win! It was a fool's marriage of force and passion. The notion that a man could bend the arc of destiny to his will by brute strength alone.

As it turned out, Fortune had other ideas for me.

9

If you could stand untouched by the passage of time around you on a balcony overlooking the walls of a playground in the San Lorenzo district, you would first see a fraternity of boys gathered in the sweet comfort of youth. You might even see me, shy at first and quiet, a mouse of a boy with no friends to call his own. In time, I'd push my shyness down the well of my heart and hide it from the world behind ramparts of false bravado. I'd rule that field with fear and violence until I was no longer allowed back. When I next returned, I would return in the uniform of the Balilla. You might not notice me at first among the camaraderie of uniformed children. We would march in fraternal lockstep, clutching rifles to swelled chests.

From your balcony outside of time, you would see Allied bombs hit the neighborhood in 1943. Afterward, on that damaged field, a mass of frantic civilians would congregate. Perhaps you would see my parents there, consoled by the Pope himself with trucks of food and water.

In another year, one hot July night, I pedaled past that empty playground near the café. I wonder if you would recognize the children from the playground in the men who rushed at me from the shadows. They knocked me down off my bicycle. My bad knee struck the cobblestones, then my shoulder, and then the bicycle fell on top of me.

"What do you want?" I shouted.

And they answered with the shoes on their feet.

I covered my face with my arms and begged, "Please, stop."

One of the men held something long in his hands. He raised it against me. I heard the whoosh of air as the object came down and connected with my head. Then the world went black.

~

Sunlight glowed around the edges of a window shade, drawn and yellowed. My head throbbed. I tried sitting up, but the pounding in my head grew worse, and a sharp pain shot through my left side. It was sore to the touch. I took short, staggered breaths.

"You're awake," said a woman at the door. "Don't try to move," she said. Then she placed a cold, damp towel on my forehead.

In the dim light, I saw her curls falling around her face and shoulders and around the delicate lines of her mouth.

"Where am I?"

"You're safe now," she said. "Here, drink this."

She tilted the smooth rim of a glass of water against my lips. I swallowed a sip, and then another, until it seemed like I'd drunk the ocean dry.

"I know you," I said. "How do I know you?"

"My name is Maria," she said. Then she pulled up a chair beside the bed and sat down. "What do you remember?"

I told her about the house, and that was when I remembered how I knew her. "You were right," I said. "The city, it is still dangerous." Then I let her know how my parents went missing, my search for them, and the strangers who attacked me.

Maria crossed the room to where my jacket hung from a hook on the back of the door. She pulled the folded map of Sicily from the pocket. "You were stationed here," she said. Then she flattened out the map and handed it to me. "I lost my husband in the war. I didn't want to believe it at first, but I knew it had happened even with him so far away in Africa, I knew. It sounds crazy, but I felt the bullet that took him from me." Maria held her hands over her stomach and said, "This is where they shot him. I felt it here like a piece of darkness slipping into my blood."

"It's not crazy," I said. "I envy you, Maria. I learned the hard way."

She pulled her hands away from her belly. "I think I have some eggs left. It's almost noon. You must be hungry."

"Thank you," I said. "But I should be getting back to the café. Silvio must be worried sick."

"Stay," she said. "Rest until you are better. It's no trouble."

When Maria returned, she propped my head up with pillows and set a tray on my lap. She brought me two hard-boiled eggs and a cup of black coffee. "I hope you don't mind," she said. "Milk is hard to come by these days."

"I don't know if I even remember the taste," I said with a half smile. But a smile like that was no smile at all. A smile was only true in the whole face, in the eyes. A person became a lighthouse that way.

She took my hand in hers and said, "Eat. Life will get better. You'll see. Soon we will be swimming in milk."

"We can only go up from here," I said. And for a moment, our faces lit up and pierced a hole in the blackness brought on by the howling gale of war. For a moment, she was a beacon on that dark coast and I, I was her keeper.

∽

Maria left to find Silvio at the café and tell him what had happened. Alone, I spread the map out on the tray in front of me—the map I had taken from the young German's pack, the one I had killed. I traced its creases with my fingers, felt the way the paper curled as if it were trying to find the curve of the land. A water stain darkened the mountains around Palermo. My faded bloody thumbprint smudged the topography of one of Sicily's smaller island neighbors. Penciled lines guessed the routes of armies. This map, it was my skin.

My hands tremored in regret like the land in the aftershock of an earthquake. I reached for a pen in the drawer of the bedside table. On the reverse side of the map, I wrote the names of my parents: Carlo Giordano and Anna Giordano. They had wanted nothing more for their son than for him to desert the army, to live. But he stayed when he should've run, ran when he should've stayed. He was a coward, two times. In Rome. In Melilli. And that cowardice had a cost.

The room spun like I'd just returned home from a night of heavy drinking. I placed one foot on the floor to keep me anchored, keep me from spinning into sickness. Then I added the German names: Krause and his two men, Lang and Vogel. And I pressed on with even more names, the names of the Italian men at Noto and Adrano, the men who stayed and fought.

All those names, each one, it seemed had settled in the bones and around the damaged cartilage of my knee. All those names, each one a fracture, a crack, a torn ligament. I had the knee of an old man now. It ached, a bottomless pain, an old man's weather-forecasting knee. It sensed a change in temperature, a cold front moving in.

All those names, and this pain, they were the terms of a debt I now owed.

10

That afternoon, Silvio closed the café for an hour and paid me a visit. He had a board for dama Italiana—Italian checkers—tucked under his arm, and he carried the red and black pieces in a brown paper bag. He set up the game on the mattress and said, "You gave me a scare this morning. At first, I thought you overslept, but when I checked your room . . ." His voice trailed off.

Maria set down two coffee cups on the bedside table. When she left, Silvio shook a limp hand in the air and whistled. "You have a nice view in here," he said. "Better than the hospital."

"They're not coming back," I said. "My parents."

Silvio patted my hand. "At least you're okay," he said. "That's what counts. That's what they would've wanted." Then he pulled on his hairy earlobe and said, "Well, let's play."

~

In the evening, Maria insisted on sleeping on the sofa in the other room. I felt too tired to disagree but made a half-hearted protest in a show of good manners. She wouldn't hear of it—"It's no trouble," she kept repeating—so I gave in after a few minutes, satisfied that I'd made the proper effort, and expressed my gratitude for her kindness.

Her bedroom was long and narrow with one east-facing window, offering warm bright light in the mornings. Dust fell from cracks in the gray plaster walls when the occasional truck rumbled down the street. A menagerie of elegant wood carvings of giraffes, lions, donkeys, and gazelles with long curved horns stood on her dresser.

Maria doted on me the entire week I spent recuperating at her apartment. She sat with me for coffee in the mornings before leaving for her secretarial job at the local Catholic school, came home for the lunch hour, prepared our meal, and ate beside the bed. She even helped me to the bathroom down the hall like someone's invalid grandfather. And in that week, the loss connecting us grew. It united us like two flies trapped on flypaper. She confided in me about Arnaldo, her barrel-chested husband, her clumsy giant—a carpenter's apprentice by trade—who carved those little wooden animals as gifts for her birthday. I told her about my skinny father, always reading a book when he wasn't working at the brewery, and my round little mother's love of cooking. And I spoke about Sicily, about Raphael and the cave, the statue and the customs that gave them strength. Even with nothing, lives carved by the agency of outside powers, they were stronger than us.

Our common loss bound us up in shared nightmares confessed to the cracks in the plaster walls in the middle of the night. I slept light in this strange bed without my pack stowed underneath. So when Maria woke in the other room from a bad dream, I woke, too. I heard the startled cry caught in her throat and pictured her bolting upright on the sofa, clutching her pounding chest. I heard the sighing, the pillow fluffing, and the stifled sobbing. Sometimes she came to the bedroom door and put her ear to the wood, listening for my breath, for the assurances my breathing gave her.

~

The following week, when I got back on my feet, back to work at the café and the little room I rented from Silvio, I began seeing Maria. It started that first night after work. She walked through the door as I prepared the café for closing. I looked up from my broom at her smile and shapely form, worn down by war and poverty. Dark bags hung under her eyes, and worry lines creased her forehead. She reminded me of an ancient Roman statue, her sober beauty disfigured by time and the elements but still breathtaking like those marble women from antiquity.

"I wanted to check in," she said. "See how you were doing."

"Are you hungry?" I leaned the broom against the corner. Then I poured a glass of wine Silvio bought from the priest down the street and set the bottle and the glass on a nearby table. "Here," I said. "Sit, sit." I pulled the chair out for her.

From the cupboard, I took the dandelion greens Silvio had found growing in a bombed-out lot on his way to the café that morning. I soaked them in a bowl of water, fished them out, and sautéed them in olive oil in a skillet on the hot plate, adding garlic and the leftover spaghetti from my dinner.

"You didn't have to go to all this trouble," Maria said.

"It's no trouble," I said. I lit a candle on the table and poured myself a glass of wine. We sat in the café for hours with the night swirling around us, and it was like it had been those days in her room while I was getting better. We were together and that was enough.

~

Maria stayed with me that night. I hadn't been with a woman since just before I left Rome for the war. She reminded me how nature made bodies for more than just pain.

I woke in a sweat in the middle of the night, confused. I tore the covers away from me, reached under the bed, fumbled for my pack. But then I heard Maria's voice, shushing me. "You had a bad dream," she said. She took me into her arms and we slept until the sun pushed through the slats in the shutters.

11

News of the liberation of Florence that August and of the heavy fighting along the Apennines in the north gave Maria hope that soon our country would be whole again. Whole and at peace.

Women sought the lie of peace to build their nests. But it was men who struggled to make those nests possible. For a man, life was war. Even if all the nations of the world no longer fought against each other, you could not rid life of conflict. Men existed cut off from the promises of a world at peace. Sicilian women understood this lie, and that made them as dangerous as a man with a gun and the passion to fire it. Their hearts were just as guarded as their men's, bound in tradition and fixed in soil. And that is who they would always be, no matter who won this war or the next to come.

I had walked in lockstep with Rome. I had carried a plague of men with tanks and guns to foreign shores. And for what? It was only a matter of time now. Soon this disastrous war would come to an end and Maria would inhale the opium of peace. What then? If I stayed, I became just another small man fighting for a nest to come home to. For the comfort of a woman's lie.

As summer passed into autumn, and autumn into winter, I saw my parents at every turn. Each face I passed on the street, I searched, wondering, *Was it you who my parents protected? You they tried saving because*

I had refused? The ghosts of the city haunted me in the daylight hours and in the long hours of sleepless nights, imagining the ways the Fascists tortured my parents. The images wouldn't stop. Even in my dreams the pictures found me, flickering in grainy black-and-white newsreel fashion. My mother's voice begging for mercy. My father's begging for my mother's life. And always the dream ended on the dirty face of Raphael's boy with his pants down around his ankles, defecating behind the prickly pears. He was the face of yet another path I had not taken. Not even Maria beside me, not the touch of her skin or the melody of her voice or the strength of her words, could stop these shadows.

$\sim$

Spring bloomed in Rome. Sheets of white linen fluttered high above narrow streets on ropes strung between buildings. Flower sellers pushed their carts of mimosas and sweet-scented violets through the cobblestone maze. We heard rumors that the war for Italy would be over soon. Any day now. Perhaps, even tomorrow.

Word finally came on the breath of our black-market delivery boy. It was near the end of April when he burst into the café shouting the news of Mussolini's capture and execution by partisans in the north. The café erupted with cheers. Men and women jumped up from their stools, shouting and crying and hugging one another. Silvio dusted off a bottle of red wine from behind the counter. "It will be over soon," he said, as he pulled the cork out and held it, wet, up to his nose.

As sure as Maria was thinking of me when she heard the news, my thoughts turned to Raphael and his family in Melilli, those simple people who had stayed with me so long. I bore their memory like a tree bore fruit. Did they celebrate the death of this man the way these people in Rome celebrated? I imagined the people of Melilli treated today with more reverence. Today, in Melilli, the feast day for their saint came early. In my mind, Raphael carried the statue with the other bearers. They carried it out of the church to the fevered cries of the men and women and their children who crowded the piazza with hands thrown in the air, crying and asking Saint Sebastian to pray for them so that some small fortune might one day bless their families. The bearers carried the statue down dusty streets by all the little houses and down into the lower parts of the village around the old cemetery and back again to the piazza where they had started. The dust they raised—like a little storm cloud—following those men wherever they went.

The delivery boy tapped my arm for a sip of wine. He held my cup with both hands and drank from it and gave it back empty and ran outside.

"Your shoe," I said, standing at the door. "Tie up your laces."

He knelt down and tied his shoe. He smiled up at me through the legs of men and women spilling out from their homes, crying and talking about the death of Il Duce. Then the boy darted off, disappearing into the crowd of children playing in the street. But still I heard him, and the news, for good or ill I could not say, carried by his boyish, squeaky voice.

∽

When you finish the game, the king and the pawn end up in the same box. This was something my father told me often growing up, and it stuck in the back of my mind now as I waited for the end.

12

That night, Maria and I stumbled up to my room and fell into each other's arms. She was drunk on wine and possibility. Some men cried under the influence but not me, not this man. He was always a happy drunk, content to forget himself. My tears were a vestige of lees at the bottom of a bottle. When the smell of brewed espresso woke me in the morning, my mouth felt dry and my head thick from the wine the night before. Maria was up, sitting at her favorite table in the back by the bar. I sat down across from her, sipped the steaming cup of coffee, and watched her read the paper. She held a finger under the words and her lips moved while she read. Her eyes narrowed and her brow creased as if she'd just found the keys to the secrets of the world buried somewhere in the newsprint. I opened the rolling shutters and squinted against the thin morning light. The streets were still, like the quiet after a storm.

Maria looked up from the newspaper. "Vincenzo," she said. "Where are you?"

"Here." I walked back and sat down. "I'm right here."

She reached across the table, took my hands in hers. "Only a part of you is with me."

The low throbbing of my hangover grew, pulsing as if powered by the beating of my heart in my throat. The lingering din of air-raid sirens and antiaircraft guns sounded in my head. Sicily all over again. No medicine could ever dull that headache, and even if such a pill existed, I would not swallow it. Other boys younger than me, and some older who had seen combat in Africa, deserted or surrendered. For those men, the sirens howled a warning, but for me and men like me, we could not resist their lure.

"I love you, Vincenzo," Maria said. "We can make a life together now, a home, a family. You love me, don't you?" Her eyes watered.

I didn't answer because I didn't know how to find the truth in the words she wanted to hear.

Maria dabbed at her eyes with a napkin, crumpled the wet tissue in her hand. She gave me a stone-blank stare. All the warmth in her face drained away. "I thought you were a better man," she said. Then she folded the newspaper and tucked it under her arm. She took one last sip of her espresso and stood up from the chair.

Without another word, she walked out of the café.

～

After the last customer left that evening, I walked the dark streets to Maria's house and stood outside her building, the curtains of her second-floor bedroom window glowing in a dim light. I rushed up the flight of stairs, knocked on her door. "Maria," I said. "Maria, let me in."

"Go away," she said through the door. "Please, Vincenzo, just go."

Outside, I paced the cobblestones. If only Maria had left well enough alone, left things the way they were. If only she hadn't asked of me the impossible. I approached the stairs again, my stomach churning. I pictured her thick black curls, her shoulders like weathered marble. The look on her face when she'd left this morning, like she had seen through to the dark place I felt inside me even now.

Maria's light went out. I turned away, remembering all the times we had stumbled down these streets on our way home from the café, our heads and hands pressed together, as if together we could hold back the past.

~

I spent the night reorganizing my pack. The clicking of the high heels of the staggering prostitutes and the voices of their drunken customers echoed from the street below, filling the four walls of my little room. At sunrise, I pulled a chair up to the window and watched the orange light catch in the clouds. I watched men and women leave their homes to earn a day's wage, or to find one. Then I opened the café, made espresso, and stepped outside with my cup, waiting for the delivery of black-market goods from the boy on his bicycle.

13

The weeks that followed were filled with the lives of the men and women who came to Silvio's café. They came in the morning before work, they came on their lunch hour, and at night they stayed almost until closing. There were young men and couples, old and new. There were grandfathers who sat outside marking the time they had left in this world by the position of the sun and moon. Smoke curled around their yellowed fingers, cigarettes burning out in their hands. I waited on them all, smiled, and made conversation, my life moving in step to the rhythm of their lives. But I was not a part of them.

On the second of May, the German army in northern Italy surrendered. That night, I saw Maria—statuesque Maria—for the first time since the day she left. She passed the café, walking hand in hand with another man. In that moment I wanted nothing more than to beat him to death with a stone, the passion of the jealous Cyclops. But Maria was even more beautiful than the nymph Galatea. And I would not risk making their love immortal by taking this man's life.

Everything I had tried to forget was there, in her. It was in the way the black curls of her hair bounced against her back, the way she tilted her head just so. In my mind, she had sprung from the chiseled stone of some ruined temple, and that was where she had gone. Back to stone. She was a cruel trick of the gods or perhaps a god herself, a mere myth, nothing more. But there she was, as warm as flesh, and I was the one who was cold.

She glanced at me and abruptly turned away, leaning into the man's ear. I was a ghost to her, standing in the window twisting a damp dishrag in my hand. Just another one of the missing or the dead.

~

When the war in Europe ended, I slung my pack over my shoulder and bid Silvio farewell. I found work as a truck driver in Naples, smuggling cigarettes the length of Italy from the Gulf of Taranto in the south to Trieste in the north and into the Balkans. Anywhere but Rome. I went where the work took me, long hours driving alone in the cab with nothing but music on the radio.

I roamed through landscapes decimated by men who had labored long hours in the pursuit of destroying what other men labored longer to build. I slept in boardinghouses overrun with these men. Creatures who, like me, wandered the Earth to find some distant corner of it free from troubled dreams.

In the end, there were other women—late at night on rainy streets or in run-down bars thick with the unsettled and the lost—but none like Maria. Other families who shared their bread and wine and stories with me, but none like Raphael's family. I didn't know then what became of them. But the debt I owed, the pain I felt in my knee, I understood now how to repay it—how to finally live with that pain.

14

Silver-gray olive trees lined the terraced ridge, pockmarked with neolithic caves. My feet still knew the way up this ancient path that Salvatore had led me on when he was just a boy. It overlooked the mountainside cluster of homes and the church of Saint Sebastian. Off in the distance, the waters of the deep bay between Augusta and Syracuse glistened in the sun. The people of Melilli called this bay by its ancient name, Megara—a Greek colony ruined and rebuilt many times over many catastrophes, until the Romans came and destroyed it for all time—but outsiders knew it as the Gulf of Augusta.

By 1952 when I returned to Melilli, this wide-open bay had turned into a major oil and gas port. Tankers and tugs and pilot boats dotted those blue waters. Refinery smokestacks cut into the evening sky like the spires of some new church. A breeze whistled from deep inside the cave where I had met Raphael and his family. I stepped through that dark mouth of the Hyblaean mountain range. The mountain sighed like a ghost that couldn't go to its rest until it had told its tale to the living.

My flashlight shone on a small ring of stone singed by fire. At the deeper end of the cave, in the arc of my sweeping light, stood a firewood rack with timber cut to lengths. I carried logs back to the ring. Then I dragged a jumble of dead branches from outside, piled them up in a heap, and got a fire going. Firelight flickered off the limestone walls and disappeared where the ceiling vaulted into darkness. A rhythm of shadows mirrored the dance of the fire.

I sat on a stool and warmed my hands over the flames. Still I heard the rising and falling breath of the mountain coming from the low back passage. The draft felt cool on my face. I stooped through the tunnel and entered the cave-art chamber. The porous limestone wall had trapped the pigments of this prehistoric painting. The diminutive lines dulled by time like the delicate fluted bones of another age dug out of the earth. The augury of their saint fixed on a rock face, his heart put out by Roman arrows.

15

The sun dipped behind the mountaintops far in the west, bathing Melilli in a citrus light. Crows speckled the sky. Pairs of old men strolled the narrow streets, smoking cheap cigarettes. Peasants returned from the fields with braying donkeys hauling carts into the lower village. The grocery had closed for the evening. A baker swept the floor of his bakery, pausing at times to drink from a clear bottle. I knew what this man was after—the courage to face his troubles. He wanted God to come to him and whisper into his ear all the answers he would need in his lifetime.

Inside, I set my pack at the foot of the countertop, pulled a stool close, and sat down. The baker set out a tray of cookies and cannoli and long, thin loaves of bread.

"Nothing for me. Thank you."

He took his bottle of grappa and a shot glass from the shelf behind him, and placed them on the counter in front of me. "That kind of day," he said. He did not smile. He nodded without changing his hard expression. Like stone. It was sharp, and I thought it could never change. "You are Italian," he said, filling my glass.

"From Rome." I nodded.

The baker took a glass for himself and filled it. "To your health," he said.

We drank, and then he asked me about my leg. I told him that I was injured in the war. Then I pushed my empty shot glass toward the baker, and he filled it. I could feel the grappa more than my bad knee now. "Do you know where I can find Raphael Vassallo?"

The baker looked out his shop window. "I don't know that name," he said.

"But I met him here during the war." I swished the grappa in my glass, downed it, and pushed the empty glass toward the baker for more.

He took up his broom again. "We're closed," he said.

As I left, I passed a fat man wearing a long black coat. "They're closed," I told him. But he smiled and waddled in anyway. His coat was unbuttoned, and through the opening, I saw the white tab collar of his clergy shirt.

~

In the piazza, I looked over the ruins of the old church of Saint Sebastian. The freestanding facade stood among the rubble like a gray monument to the martyr. Weeds grew around the outer boundary and through crevices in the rough-hewn limestone. The 1693 earthquake had destroyed this place. People felt that quake as far away as Malta. It cracked foundations, collapsed homes, demolished some forty towns, and killed thousands of men, women, children, and livestock but not the statue carried here. That statue, it didn't have a scratch on it. Not a one. And the survivors, they called it a miracle. So they rebuilt Saint Sebastian's church—bigger than the first one. Sicilians were a stubborn people, a passionate breed. The qualities of rocks and ashes. It was what made their soil rich. Some called Sicily an island on a sea of light. I thought of it as a fire extinguished, cooled, and hardened into stone.

16

The sky darkened. The land and sea set against a blood-orange horizon. An evening fog moved into the lower village, shrouding trees, houses, and the old cemetery in an eerie stillness. A light rain tapped out its rhythms on the tiled rooftops like distant drums marching out a war beat.

The priest from the bakery stood outside the church with a tall, lanky young man, preparing the Easter fire in a rusty tin drum. A refurbished American army jeep pulled into the piazza. The young man wiped rainwater from his face with the sleeve of his jacket. Then he strolled across the way and banged the faded white star on the hood of the vehicle. The driver climbed out of the jeep. "Constantino," he said. They shook hands and hugged one another. They looked close in age. Their low conversation, a whispering echo that died along the mountainside.

"Signore," the priest called out. He beckoned me to follow him. Inside the church, he dipped his hand into the basin of holy water and crossed himself. Then he waddled down the center aisle under a painting on the wood-paneled ceiling of their saint, praying while angels took his crown, helmet, bow, and arrows to the Madonna. I followed the priest to the side altar where the painted statue—chipped and pitted—stood under a domelike canopy carved from limestone into an ornamental crown with four twisting columns of gilded vines. Before

I was aware that my arm was moving, my hand touched the statue's rough, chalky surface.

"This is plaster," I said.

The priest studied me. "The real statue is not for public viewing, not anymore," he said. "We only take it out for the May festival." He walked past me, and I followed him to his office. He sat behind his wooden desk and poured olive oil from a tin into a bowl. Then he took a loaf of bread from a brown paper bag, broke off the heel, and handed it to me.

"Thank you," I said. I tore into the dark, crunchy crust and read the nameplate on his desk.

"Why are you here?" Don Fiorilla asked. He took a piece of bread for himself and dipped it in the oil. "Pilgrims come in May to see the statue," he said with his mouth full of the oiled bread. "But you, you are no pilgrim."

When I finished telling the priest who I was and why I had come, he stood up, walked to a large wooden door, and took a ring of keys from his pocket. They jingled in his hand until he found the key to the bolt. Then he opened the thick door. A locked gate of elaborate ironwork blocked a narrow staircase that disappeared into darkness. "I know the family you are looking for," he said. "I baptized them all." He took another key from the ring and unlocked the gate. "Come," he said. "Their story is at the top of the stairs."

The priest tugged on a string hanging from the ceiling of the staircase. A dull light came on. He put one foot on the first stair, pulled on the wobbling wall-mounted handrail—the flathead screws turned in their brackets, squeaking loose from the wall—and he hauled himself up, took a breath, and then continued. I climbed the steep, creaky staircase with my arm against the wall for support, my lousy knee throbbing each time I set my full weight on it.

At the landing, the priest took out a handkerchief and mopped his brow. Then he unlocked another door. Several ornate archway gates blocked our passage. He found each key with great care and patience, unlocking one gate after another. In all, there were seven, counting the one at the foot of the stairs, seven gates protecting a small dusty chamber beyond. When he entered, he pulled a string to light the room.

The statue stood locked up in a cage bolted to the wall. The stone figure looked old beyond time, like the dried-up skin of a frail man nearing the end of an impossibly long, hard life. Necklaces, medallions, and pendants all hung from around its neck in a chain-mail shirt of gold. And a red cloth with the saint's name embroidered in gold thread was wrapped around the feet.

Don Fiorilla bowed his head. His chin disappeared into the folds of his neck fat. He rested his praying hands on his enormous belly and spoke softly about the statue, how it came to them and what happened to it. While fingering rosary beads in his pocket, he told me about the Vassallo family, that Leonello and Emanuele, Raphael and Giuseppina had all died because of the war and what it had left behind. He told me just enough so that I would see what I needed to see—two lost children standing at the foot of my need for redemption.

A faintness overcame me, and I fell back against a support beam. Dust snowed down from cobwebbed rafters. The muscles in my bad leg seized up and I sank to one knee. Flakes of dust settled in my hair and on my shoulders and at my feet. The dirt had passed out of those upper shadows, sifted through the low light cast off from the naked bulb.

The priest touched my arm. "What's wrong? Can you stand?"

When I shook my head no, Don Fiorilla withdrew his hand in terror. He turned to the statue, made the sign of the cross in the air, and mumbled a prayer.

"You misunderstand," I said. "I got shot in the war. The leg, it's never been the same." But the priest wouldn't listen. He believed that I was sensitive to the sacred presence of the statue. Like the bearers in their folktale, he thought I felt the weight of its divine power.

Don Fiorilla kissed his hand, wiggled the fingers between the cage bars, and touched the statue. He told me where I could find Salvatore and Antonella. His eyes watered. He fingered the rosary beads again and shifted his weight from one leg to the other. "I've prayed for them," he said. "For years I've prayed, and now those prayers have been answered. You will take them away from here to America. You will help them build a new life, a better life."

I dug into my pack, fished out the map of Sicily. It fluttered in my hands from my hand tremors and tore at the edge of the crease line. I added the names Raphael and Giuseppina Vassallo, Emanuele and Leonello Vassallo. I had failed them, too. Then I stood, stretched out the kink in my calf muscle.

Don Fiorilla clapped and exclaimed a miracle with his wrinkled, smiling face. Then he grabbed my arm in a firm grip and said, "Don't tell anyone who you're going to see in Syracuse."

~

Outside, Don Fiorilla introduced me to Rocco Morello—a son of Melilli, home on furlough from his military service. A fortuitous turn, the priest called it, and with great enthusiasm arranged for the man to do him this one small favor: take his friend Vincenzo to Syracuse and hurry back.

We drove out of the piazza and down the mountain through the fog that had settled in the low places around Melilli. The light rain stopped. Pipework and oil drums from the refineries in the bay towered over the little fishing villages along the coast. I looked out at the wild horizon of wine-dark sky and sea. I held the windshield and leaned my head into rushing salty air, refreshed by orange blossoms from the valley.

"Did the Allies give you that lame leg?" Rocco asked me.

I brought my head back inside the jeep and patted the dashboard. "This is a fine American machine," I said. "I think you got a better deal out of the war than I did."

Rocco didn't look that much older than the young German soldier I'd killed with the stone—and I recognized the fear in him of being made to feed the lower appetites of our nature. "Do not worry," I said. "There will not be another war like that one, not for a long time yet." And then I asked him how long until the end of his service, and he told me his service ended in June, and he shifted gears and drove on through the countryside in silence—his white-knuckled grip on the steering wheel never loosening.

He dropped me off at the Greek theater. I thanked him for the ride and wished him luck. Then I set out on foot with my pack slung over my shoulder and followed the directions Don Fiorilla had given me. I did not think I would see Rocco again.

17

At Saint Anthony's that night—the night of the Easter Vigil—Salvatore did not remember me at first. On the steps of the rectory, we shared wine and conversation. When he asked if I'd known an Italian soldier who'd left his journal in the bunker, I felt that madman Krause staring me down again. My fear, my desperation—the price of running was higher than I'd ever imagined. So I lied to Salvatore. What else could I do? He was older now, but inside of him crouched that same little boy who had begged his father to take my pistol all those years ago at the mouth of the cave.

Later, I stood in the back of the church and watched the service and listened. The priest brought light to those who waited in the pews in darkness. He chanted the Easter Proclamation. But Salvatore wasn't sitting in the church with his sister. He didn't hold a candle lit from the candle carried by the priest. Salvatore sat alone in his bedroom—his silhouette in the square of dim light from the top-floor rectory window. He watched a fog move through the streets, hugging the stones, and I watched him from the stony church steps. Two bombs had torn apart his family, and one had come from me, from the knowledge he found in my careless words. Without that, could he have destroyed the statue? Would he have ever thought to even try?

I carried the weight of those questions alone, not knowing where his guilt began and mine ended.

∾

That April, I used my savings to buy our way to Middletown, Connecticut—that was Salvatore's choice, his Little Melilli, the boy in him believing that the world could give you a second chance. We moved into an apartment the church had found for us—a two-bedroom on Ferry Street in the Sicilian neighborhood on Main Street's north end. Salvatore and I had jobs and Nella had school. We minded our own business. We didn't bother other people. We kept our heads down and worked hard, not wanting too much from life except for a quiet one. My life was honest work now, the hard labor of construction. Building roads and bridges built me anew as it covered me in a sackcloth of sweat and concrete dust. For Salvatore and Nella, the world was an as yet unnumbered possibility. Seeing this for them made me see it for myself, a sight I had not enjoyed since childhood, since before the Balilla. A vision of my life as infinite.

In this part of Middletown, in the tenement blocks of the North End, parents spoke to their children and to each other in the regional dialect of Melilli. On these stoops, women traded gossip and comfort while scolding their children misbehaving in the streets. Men, smoking too many cigarettes, played cards on overturned vegetable crates and argued with their hands as much as their words. On these streets, fierce love—the only kind of love a Sicilian knew how to express—was always on display.

I didn't miss the old country, but there were days when Salvatore scuffed at the cement with his boots and shook his head in wonder at how anyone could cover up and hide away so much good soil. Days when Nella came home from school and slumped on the sofa, fingering her Saint Sebastian medallion. Once I found her in the kitchen, eyes closed, nose pressed into the yellow petals of an early wildflower. "It doesn't smell the same," she murmured. Then she shook off the thought and placed the flower in a mason jar of water on the counter.

The three of us, in the days and weeks that passed, we formed our own family unit, our own little village in the larger one around us. I slept on the sofa bed with my pack stowed away behind the backrest—imagining my service in the war behind me. My war dreams nothing more now than groups of boys fighting in the playground over a swing set. But each night I'd startle awake in an unvoiced panic to the sounds of Salvatore, panting and calling out from his nightmares. I'd throw the sheets off and plant my feet on the carpet, holding a jittery vigil in the dead of night, and I'd listen to Nella, in the other room, shifting in her sleep, her footsteps padding to her brother's door, her voice small in the dark. "Turiddu, are you all right?" she'd say, and his voice, gruff like a parent's voice when scolding a child, "Go back to bed, Nella." Then he'd punch the pillow and untangle himself from the sheets, the box springs squeaking.

Nella would linger at the door—even after he chided her—her palm flat against the wood. "Oh, Turiddu," she'd say, "you promised." The squeak of the box springs and creak of the hardwood floor allayed my disquiet. He'd come to the door, stand in the slant of light from his room, and tell her that he had not forgotten, that he was trying his best, and that this was all he could promise her. Then they'd both settle back into their beds, their breathing easing into a steady rhythm, the night passing uninterrupted until morning.

There was freedom in the sounds of those two siblings sleeping safely, freedom in the gravity of it. Because I was a part of them—the good, the bad—and they, me. And with them, in the duty of looking after them, my life again began to feel full. But like all hungry men who finally sit down to a good meal, I imagined I could have more.

One night, sitting up on the sofa bed under the soft light from the side-table lamp, I wrote Maria a letter.

> *I'm in America now. I brought two war orphans from Sicily with me—Salvatore and Antonella—my own version of a family. You would like them. Salvatore, he is a remarkable young man, eighteen, with a talent for gardening. And Nella, she does well in school. She is fifteen years old and already smarter than me, I think.*
>
> *I've missed you, Maria. I made a terrible mistake, I know that now, and I hope you can find it in your heart to forgive me. Life here, it's a good life, finally. One day, I'll have my own café like Silvio's. You'll see. It will be our own little piece of Rome. Please, say you'll come.*

18

In May, during the Saint Sebastian festival, we sat on the stoop of our building and watched the band advancing down Ferry Street ahead of the men in white who carried the statue. Crowds of people came out of their homes and lined the sidewalks, crying out the saint's name, crying out, "Pray for us." Women and their children rushed into the street as the statue passed, clapping in time with the music as they joined the parade. Men ran up to the band with cups of wine. The organetto player dropped out of the tune first, knocked back the drink, took up his squeezebox, and found his place again in the Sicilian peasant song. The marranzanu player dropped out next. He tossed back the wine with a flick of his wrist, held the jaw harp against his parted front teeth, and played the hypnotic, droning melodies of his instrument. Each musician took his turn with the offered wine, with some of the players stumbling their way back into the song.

I stood up to check the mail for the second time that day when Salvatore held my arm and said, "It's Sunday."

"Beh, a man can't stretch his legs on Sunday?" I said.

"What are you waiting for that you keep checking the mail?"

"Nothing," I said. "I told you, it's my legs, I can't sit down too long." Then I nudged Salvatore's shoulder and motioned with my chin at the parade. "Let's go," I said. And we picked ourselves up and followed the crowd as it turned the corner onto Gilshannon Place, and then Green Street and Main Street, looping all through the Sicilian neighborhood. The music warbled and faded, the tempo slipped, but then the tune wheezed its way into a crescendo in a fit of drunken delight at the steps of Saint Sebastian Church.

Salvatore took his sister's hand. They watched the men carry the statue into the church. The bells rang out from the recessed niche in the facade in honor of the saint's return. The peal of the bells brought Nella to tears. She leaned into her brother's shoulder and whispered in his ear.

"Will you come inside with us?" Salvatore asked me.

We were first in line for the veneration of the statue, the first to pin money on the red sash tied around the statue's waist. Salvatore fumbled with his wallet. His sister steadied his hands. Together they pinned a ten-dollar bill to the sash. Then Salvatore placed his palm over the chest, as if he felt a heart beating beneath the plaster. "Pray for me," he said.

Back outside we bought squeeze cups of Italian ice. We stayed for dinner, eating big plates of lasagna with grilled sausages, peppers, and sweet onions on a long folding table set up under a tent on the church grounds. We stayed for the late Mass celebrated by the Bishop of Norwich. And we walked home under a clear night sky, lit up with stars and a shining half moon.

19

Three weeks later, I found a letter from Rome on the kitchen table. It had been a long, hot day on the job—unseasonably hot for early June, according to the foreman. My shirt stuck to my back, the armpits stained and damp. Salvatore won the coin toss and took the first shower. I stood in front of the fan on the counter, pinching the edges of the envelope.

Nella stood at the sink, washing and slicing radishes for the salad. "Who's that from?"

"An old friend," I said. I picked a cherry tomato from the bowl.

She slapped my hand away. "After dinner will you help me with my English?"

I nodded yes, poured a tall glass of water, and sat outside on the stoop. Beads of water condensed on the glass. The letter from Silvio, written on paper as thin as the skin of an onion, stung my eyes just the same. Maria had come by the café, married and happy with a beautiful daughter and another child on the way. *The train does not pass two times,* Silvio wrote.

There was more in the letter about how his health was failing, how his two girls and their husbands would soon take over the business the way he had from his father. Silvio was at least seventy by then. Around the age my parents would've been.

I sat on the stoop a long time, folding and refolding the letter, tracing a finger along the edges of the paper until I'd given myself a paper cut that did not bleed. I might have sat there forever, a granite monument, if Nella hadn't come out to tell me the shower was free.

When I didn't get up, she asked, "Is it bad news?"

She dug the toe of her shoe into the doorjamb rot, her long black hair pulled back into a messy bun, her cheeks flushed from the heat, her eyes—fierce eyes the color of walnuts—aging her far beyond her fifteen years. She was almost a woman grown, with a delicate beauty like the statue of the saint restored after its destruction.

"Someday you'll find a good man, and you'll start a family of your own," I said.

Nella's face darkened. "I don't want children," she said. "I won't bring our family's curse on them."

∼

After dinner, I helped Nella with her homework at the kitchen table. She was in the eighth grade at Saint Sebastian School, and all the kids in her class were a year or two younger. That didn't bother her. Nella was determined to learn the language so she wouldn't have to repeat the grade again.

We puzzled over the pronunciation guides in her lesson book together, the way English words were spoken and the way the words were written. When we'd had enough of *knock* and *knife* and *knight* and all the others, Nella went to bed and I walked up the street for a drink.

The café was long and smoky with a low tin ceiling painted white. Men hunched on stools at the mahogany bar, their backs curved like the blades of sabers. A pair of young men sat at the small front table, talking and laughing too loud. One of them tall and lanky, the other thick and pear shaped.

At the bar, I ordered a shot of grappa and took Silvio's letter from my jacket pocket. The bartender, an older man with thin gray hair framing a shiny bald spot on the top of his head, raised his eyebrows at the paper in my hands. "A woman?" he asked in Italian.

I held out my glass for another shot and then another, stumbling through the story of my time in Rome after the war.

"But you are here now," the bartender said.

"Beh, here I am. You lose one thing, you gain something else." And the more I drank, the more I ran my mouth and said things better left unsaid.

"Melilli, you say?" The lanky young man from the front table leaned against the bar beside me. How long he had been standing there, I did not know. "You look familiar," he said.

"You must be mistaken," I said.

"Constantino," his friend called out to him from the table. "It's late. We should go."

"This man says he knows Turiddu," Constantino said. "But that's impossible. Isn't that right? You must be seeing ghosts."

I pushed my drink away, unable to finish it. "Let's step outside," I said. I took the young man by the elbow and led him out the door. Despite my drunkenness, or perhaps because of it, I had him up against the brick wall with my left forearm pressing on his Adam's apple before he knew what was happening. "Better you forget what you think you know," I said.

He held up his hands. "Take it easy."

I let him go. He walked calmly back into the café, where his friend stood wide-eyed at the window.

That night, lying on the pull-out sofa in a drunken melancholy, I touched the glow of the streetlights that cut across the living room. The room swayed. The scene in the café, the bartender, the altercation with the lanky young man—it all seemed hazy and distant, unreal. Snapshots from a dream. One of Salvatore's nightmares clouding the grappa. The trouble at the bottom of the glass.

Maria, she was gone to me. The mother to some other man's children. I had been so brash as to try to grasp at the vision of my life as infinite, the one Salvatore and Nella had made me want to believe in. But I'd found instead a wall, built by my own hands, unintended yet still impenetrable. On the other side was the life I could've had, but for who I was and what I had done, what I could not leave behind. Salvatore and Nella, they were all I had left in this world, all the world would ever let me have. They were all that mattered.

20

The following Saturday at Public Market—the Italian grocery store on Main Street around the corner from where we lived—Salvatore wandered the vegetable aisle, inspecting the green and red peppers, the artichokes and string beans, the cauliflower and broccoli, the yellow and green zucchini, and the meaty Roma tomatoes. "These are good," he said, taking two heads of cauliflower and holding them up to his nose. "But they're not fresh."

"What are you talking about?" I said. "They have good food here."

"I'll have my own garden someday," Salvatore said. "Then you'll taste the difference."

"That's a day I look forward to." I eyed the capicola, the soppressata, and the other deli meats at the end of the aisle in the back of the store. "I'll pick up some cold cuts."

At the meat counter, old Sicilian women in black dresses and black shawls, with dark upper-lip hair, waited for their orders in the line ahead of me. They talked in whispered tones about a boy who'd cursed his family and took into his heart the malocchio—the evil eye. One of the women pointed with her whiskered chin at Salvatore among the vegetables, picking potatoes from a wooden basket. She made the mano di cornuto—the horned hand—from her clenched left fist hanging at her side. The other women made the sign of the cross. They talked but kept their distance.

~

In the afternoon, I sat with the young priest at the rectory on Washington Street. Don Salafia listened while cleaning the lenses of his black-rimmed glasses with a tissue. Then he put on the frames and told me how he was disappointed in my lack of judgment with the bottle. "Boh, what can you do?" he said. He pushed his glasses up the bridge of his long nose with his first finger and answered himself. "You can do nothing about the past," he said. "My papà, God rest his soul, he was from the old country, and he used to say that what happened over there didn't matter. It's what you make of your life here that counts. The good people of Middletown, I know they feel the same." He patted my shoulder, indicating our conversation was at an end.

As he held the front door open for me, he said, "Constantino and his friend are here to make new lives, like the three of you. They are not looking for trouble. That was a different time, a different world."

~

I spent late nights at the café with the hope that I'd run into Constantino again, but I never saw him or his fat-bottomed friend—the one who was shaped like an old mother. Nights at home, the wall clock in the kitchen ticked away the seconds of every minute, every ticking second twisting in my gut, a countdown to the Devil's hour when Salvatore cried out from his sleep and Nella came to his door to quiet him.

21

That summer, Salvatore and I worked on an overpass on Route 9, south of Cromwell, with a construction crew of Sicilian Americans born and raised in Middletown. We had been on the job two months when the foreman, Fat Joe Corvo, introduced a fresh crew of men. The first was Frank Lombardo, a local. Frank stood about five feet with a stocky build. He had a thin mustache and a crop of wavy, dark hair cut close around the ears and the back of his neck. The second and third I recognized from that night in the café—the long-limbed Constantino Cardella and the thick Roberto Santangelo. The fourth young man stood a few inches taller than the others, well built with a serious face. He looked familiar, but I couldn't place him until I heard his name: Rocco Morello.

Salvatore and Rocco stared at one another like they'd each seen in the other a long-dead enemy returned to the world of the living.

"I got to get that forklift working," Salvatore said. He never took his eyes off Rocco.

"Vincenzo, why don't you show these boys around?" Then Fat Joe wiped sweat from his brow with a handkerchief and walked back to the shade of his trailer, out of the furnace of the sun.

"You should've told me you were going after him," Rocco said. He watched Salvatore under the forklift hood. "You remember me from Melilli, don't you?"

"I remember thanking you for the ride," I said. Then I gave him a little slap on the cheek, made him look at me. "We're here to work. What are you here for?"

~

Salvatore and I took our lunch break on the median strip away from the worksite and the other men. Nella had fixed us sandwiches of mortadella, provolone, and thinly sliced tomatoes with olive oil drizzled on the bread slices. We sat in the grass, napkins on our laps. We shared warm coffee from a thermos. I shared my concerns. "Those boys," I said, "are trouble," and Salvatore said, "You worry too much, like a woman," but I could see that they worried him, too. We got to our feet when Rocco approached, followed by Constantino and Roberto. "Let me handle this," Salvatore said to me.

"Constantino told me," Rocco said, "but I didn't want to believe him. Of all the places you could've crawled off to, you had to pick Middletown. You just couldn't let it go. Didn't I warn you what would happen if I ever saw you again?"

Salvatore stood wordless and with an unruffled look.

"This is for our saint," Rocco said. Then he punched Salvatore in the stomach. Salvatore doubled over, and Rocco knocked him down with a blow to the side of his face. Constantino took me out with a solid kick to my bad leg, and I fell to one knee. Roberto came up behind me, held my right arm bent against my back in a hammerlock hold, and pinned me to the ground.

"This is between them," Constantino said. "It does not concern you."

"Get up and fight, you coward!" Rocco yelled.

Salvatore touched the cut on his cheek, and then he looked at the blood on his fingers. "Let Enzo go," he said. "Roberto should be holding my arms back."

"On your feet," Rocco said.

Salvatore stood—hands at his sides—as if he were offering himself up to the Lord. Rocco struck his face again. Salvatore took the blow, but remained standing.

"What's wrong with him? Why doesn't he fight back?" Constantino said.

Rocco came at him again with both fists swinging. Salvatore took those punches, and more.

The construction crew watched from a safe distance. Frank stood beside the foreman and argued for him to intervene. When Salvatore's strength gave way, he dropped like a stone from a great height. His right eyelid cut and bruised, his face bloodied. "Bastards," I cried, and I rolled free from Roberto's hold. "I'll kill every one of you."

"I knew this was a bad idea," Roberto said. He waddled like a baby duck to its mother, the foreman.

Salvatore winced when I took his head into my lap. "I'm sorry," I said.

"It's over," Constantino said. "Look at him. It's finished."

"Maybe for you," Rocco said. He spat on the ground, walked down the median strip, and entered one of the blue portable toilets lined up on the other side of the worksite.

In the weight of the stone of Salvatore's head, I felt the push and pull in him of the boy he once was and had buried long ago. An untended seedling with girdling roots that dug deep into the earth, deep into the past. Neglect had made it grow wild and sick.

"This is my fault," I said. "I had too much to drink one night and—"

"Enzo," he said. "No. I deserved this." The ghost of the boy he had been stared up at me through half-closed eyes, discolored and bruised and already swelling up. He tried to say more, but his words were lost in a fit of coughing.

"You are as strong as a mule," I said to Salvatore. "As strong as a mule and twice as stubborn."

"Take these," Frank said. He stood over me with his hand out, the keys to the forklift dangling from his index finger.

"Stay with him," I said. Then I climbed into the forklift, started it up, and drove down the closed lane of the highway. The foreman jumped up and down, waving his arms over his head. His shirt came unbuttoned and his hairy gut flopped out. The workers laughed. I turned into the dirt clearing and picked up the toilet with its door flush against the load backrest, trapping Rocco inside. His muffled screams brought out a cheer and more laughter from the men.

"Minchia!" Rocco shouted from inside. He thrashed the door against the backrest. "I'm doing my business in here," he said. He cracked open the door as far as he could. His head just fit into the gap. "What the hell is going on? Are you crazy?"

"You don't go near Salvatore again," I said. "You understand me?"

"Vincenzo, put me down."

I jerked the lift, and the portable toilet pitched front to back. Rocco slipped and fell. The door clattered shut.

"Porco Dio!" He battered the door against the backrest and shouted a litany of curses. He insulted the saints, blasphemed the Holy Trinity, even profaned the Virgin Mother. But soon the fool tired himself out. He grew quiet. There was a long pause before he finally spoke again, a subdued animal in a filthy cage. "Okay, okay, okay," he said.

"Now you understand me?"

"Si," he said. "Please, let me out," he pleaded. "I'm wet like a baby."

I set the portable toilet down. Then, as I backed the forklift away, the door opened, and out limped Rocco. A Rubicon of urine ran in a dark stain down the leg of his blue jeans.

∾

Frank helped me get Salvatore up the flight of stairs and into our apartment. Nella was home from school for lunch. She went white when we brought her brother through the kitchen and into the living room. The steeple of her hands, palms pressed together, covered her mouth. We set him down on the sofa and told her what happened. She dampened a towel in the sink and wiped blood from his brow and face. He winced and scolded her to take it easy. "Turiddu," she said. She knelt at the sofa with her forehead resting on her brother's chest and her long, thick black hair splayed out.

He put his hands on her shoulders and said, "Nella, I'm fine."

She turned her ear to his heart, closed her eyes, and listened. Color came back into her face. The same stone-cold features she shared with her brother now softened by the song of their blood, and for her it was the sweetest music ever made on this Earth.

Nella blinked and looked up from her place at his chest and touched her own cheek where his was bruised like she was looking in a mirror. She touched the same hard bones that made up his face, only it was her face she touched, her bones, and they were under a thicker skin.

She straightened up and finished cleaning him. Then she took the quilt draped over the back of the sofa and covered him with it. "Stay with him," she said.

"I took care of it," I said. "Where are you going?"

When Nella had gone, Frank drew up a ladder-back chair beside Salvatore and took his hand. "I'm sorry I didn't step in sooner," he said. Salvatore eyed him with his good eye, and a smile cut across his bruised and purple face, and he laughed so hard that he held his side from the ache.

~

The next day, the foreman came to the apartment. He walked carefully, dabbed at the mustache of sweat on his upper lip. "Rocco worked you over good," he said. "I'm sorry. You believe me. There was nothing I could do." He took an envelope out of his jacket pocket and gave it to Salvatore. "Take the week off. This will never happen again," he added. He looked at Nella, and then me. "You have my word. Those boys, they're gone. I fired them."

The foreman left the room and Salvatore turned to his sister. "What did you do?"

"What kind of man doesn't defend himself?" Nella asked. "You would've been happier if that brute killed you, is that it?"

"There will be no killing," Don Salafia said through the open door. He had his hand on the foreman's shoulder. "Go in peace, my son," he said. And the foreman hurried down the steps. "May I come in?" The priest entered. He sat in the armchair beside Salvatore on the sofa. "How are you?" he asked.

"I'm fine, Father," Salvatore said.

"Of course you are," the priest said. "You are one of God's strongest children. You as well, Nella. And you will carry on, the both of you, together, as you have before when God tested you." The priest took off his glasses, closed his eyes, and pinched the bridge of his nose. "I have faith in you," he said, "but I need your faith in return." He put his glasses back on. "I know the history of this conflict, but I ask you now as I have asked Rocco, let it go." Don Salafia leaned over the space between the armchair and the sofa, placed his hand on Salvatore's shoulder, and said, "There can be no winner in such a contest. Understand?"

"I didn't lift a hand against him," Salvatore said. "And I never will."

Don Salafia smiled. "You are like the saint now," he said. "There will be no more trouble from Rocco or his friends. You have my word on that." Then he stood up and turned to go, stopped, and said, "I hope to see you all at Mass. I'll be reading from Isaiah, a sermon on forgiveness."

22

Frank came over every day after work that week while Salvatore recovered. He came with a bottle of wine, or a bag of groceries under his arm. He looked in on Salvatore and helped Nella around the apartment, keeping the place clean and making sure the garbage went out on time. The construction crew was his first job straight out of high school, but he didn't mind studying alongside Nella, quizzing her about English words and American history. I knew Salvatore appreciated the kindness, and the attention Frank gave his sister didn't bother him either. I could tell because his face brightened when Frank came around.

But still, Salvatore was very much Nella's brother and he wanted to protect her, to do right by her. Those evenings after dinner, Salvatore and I sat in the living room playing checkers. He sat on the sofa with a view over my shoulder of Nella washing the dishes and Frank beside her, drying them. I won those games.

One night I told him, "You're not paying attention." Then I jumped my red piece over his black one and into the empty square beyond it, and over the second and third piece. "King me," I said. "Again."

He studied the board and frowned. Nella laughed at something Frank said to her, and Salvatore looked up.

"Your father would approve," I told him.

He nodded his head in agreement, pointed to his eye, and then placed his finger over his lips to say shush. He was playing the role his father would've played, the silent watchful eye, the chaperone marking boundaries. It was his duty to make sure everyone did things the right way. That was something David never understood. Our fathers, they were here to show us where to step, how to walk tall in this world.

23

Salvatore carried himself like a tall man, taller than anyone I knew, even me. Sometimes, I'd even forget that I was taller than him when we were together. His father was the same way. I don't know where it came from, maybe it went all the way back to the statue, maybe to that painting in the cave. Some distant ancestor saw something there that lit a fire inside him, and he kindled it down through the ages, one generation to the next, learning too late how all fires end.

I saw this fire in the way Salvatore stood his ground when Rocco came at him. I saw it in the way he grew restless as his strength returned with each passing day. Also, in his laughter, the way it lit up a room and consumed him into silence. The way he laughed when I suggested he enroll in night school to improve his English. He held his side where it hurt, howling and snorting through the pain at the idea of sitting behind a school desk. "I learn from you," he said. His whole body laughing until he could no longer breathe. Then his lungs let out a wheeze, his shoulders sagged, his face darkened, and the light in his eyes smoldered.

At the end of the week of Salvatore's convalescence, on a Saturday night, as I was walking home from the café, I saw Rocco loitering in front of our building. He craned his neck at the second-floor windows.

Then he took something out from under his jacket, stepped back into the light from the streetlamp.

I limped faster along the sidewalk. "Rocco!" I shouted.

He swung a Zippo down against the leg of his jeans, flicking the lid open, and dragged the wheel of the lighter across the denim. The Zippo sparked a tongue of blue flame. "E chiamamulu paisanu," Rocco intoned. "Prima Diu e Sammastianu. You don't get to come to Little Melilli and start over as if nothing happened. You cannot erase what you have done."

In his other hand, he held a bottle with a white cloth hanging from out the neck.

"Rocco," I shouted again. "No!"

But he was a Morello—a bearer of the statue from a long line of bearers like the Vassallos and the Cardellas and the Santangelos, all the way back to those first men who carried the saint home. And he had that same damned ember smoldering inside him, set alight and fanned into a blaze the day Salvatore destroyed the statue. I should've known better than to accept the word of Don Salafia. Priests and their gentle ways, they cannot put out that kind of fire in a man. A man like that, his breath is the engine that fans those flames.

Rocco lit the cloth and lobbed the bottle. A light came on in the second-floor window of our apartment. I tried to run, but my knee gave out and I fell to the pavement. The glass shattered with a loud pop. Then the curtain went up in a bright blaze. Nella cried out, and then Salvatore. I pulled myself up using the brick wall of a building for support. Rocco scurried down an alley and into the shadows like a cockroach.

∾

Inside, I found Nella seated at the chair opposite the two street-facing windows. She cradled her right arm, her nightgown singed and torn.

She flinched as her brother turned her arm. He examined the burn and the lacerations from shards of glass that had torn through her flesh. Beside him, an empty pan of water used to douse the flames.

Soot and debris littered the windowsill, and the wet curtain fluttered in a breeze. "I'm sorry," I said. "I'm sorry I couldn't stop him."

"Rocco," Salvatore said. And the name caught in his throat. He spit it into the empty pan on the floor by his feet, but you could not spit out a bitter taste like that. His forehead curdled, wrinkles creased the corners of his mouth and eyes. His jaw became a rictus of bone and taut skin. "Forgive me," he said. His head dropped into his sister's lap while he wept.

"Shh," Nella said. She brushed his black hair back from his forehead with her fingers. "Turiddu, shh," she said. And the tightness in his face ebbed.

I called a local doctor that we knew, a Sicilian. In fifteen minutes, he arrived with his leather bag. I greeted him outside and rushed him upstairs. Tenants stood in their doorways, some from the third floor leaned over the stairwell railing. A few had been shouting about their interrupted sleep since the disturbance began. But their eyes grew wide when they saw the doctor. And they asked if everything was all right, if we needed help.

"Mind your business," I told them. "Go back to bed."

In the bathroom, the doctor held Nella's arm under the cool running water of the tub. She grimaced as he cleaned the cuts and scratches and washed her wounds with antiseptic cleanser. "She's lucky," he said. "The burns could be worse, but she should go to the hospital."

"No hospital," I said. "Take care of her here, and never speak of this again."

The doctor sighed and nodded his head in agreement. He applied a cream over the burned skin and then covered it with dry, sterile gauze. "Give her aspirin for the pain," he said. "I'll be back in the morning to check on her. Make sure the blisters don't break open."

After the doctor left, Salvatore swept up the broken glass in the living room. Then he sat in the chair by the windows like a carabiniere on guard duty. I poured wine into half-pint mason jars and sat at the kitchen table with Nella. She drank with unsteady hands. Her black hair was plastered against her ears and neck, her face pale.

"You should sleep," I told her.

Nella stood up. She moved like a tree buffeted by strong winds. All these years she'd bent and sighed through her brother's and parents' countless storms. And finally, I could see, she might break.

"Sleep," she said. She faced the cabinets. "Who can sleep like this, with that figgh'i buttana walking around out there as free as air and water?" She banged one side of the counter and then the other, saying, "We can't live in Melilli, we can't live here." Then she raised up her hands and looked at the ceiling. "God, I wish you'd tell me where we are supposed to go. We paid for our sins with blood—twice over. Why are you doing this? Why is Rocco? What wrong have we committed against him? The saint is more than a piece of stone."

I placed my hand on Nella's shoulder. "I'll take care of it," I said.

She spun around, wagging a finger in my face. "Like you took care of it before?"

"If you hadn't gone to the priest—"

"I made a mistake," she said. "Going to the foreman and the priest for help, it was a mistake."

"Beh," Salvatore said from his perch at the window. "The first mistake was mine."

"You were just a boy," Nella said. "And our parents—after the twins died—we needed them. Where were they? They loved the ghosts of those boys more than they loved their own living flesh and blood. You were right to be angry, Turiddu. With one arm the saint takes you under his protection while his other arm strangles you. You were just a boy, but that bastard, Rocco, he is a man." She took a hammer from the utility drawer and started toward the door. Her wounded arm hung limp at her side, an injured bird with a bad wing.

Her brother blocked her path. "Where are you going with that?"

341

She stood firm. I knew that scorch-eyed look, and the silent understanding that passed between them. It was like the silence at Adrano at the foot of Mount Etna when I saw in the faces of the soldiers the many faces of the monster on the mountainside.

"Oh, Nella." I shook my head no. "Not you," I said. "You don't need to do this." I crossed the hall and stood beside her, placed my hand over hers on the handle of the hammer, eased it from her grip.

"I made a promise to Don Salafia," Salvatore said.

"And where is the great Don Salafia now?" Nella said. "The priest, he cannot protect us. Open your eyes."

"Your sister's right," I said. I set the hammer down on the little table by the door. "This cannot go unanswered."

"I started this," Salvatore said. He tried his best to sound strong and sure, but I heard the uncertainty in the tenor of his voice. I saw it in the forward pitch of his eyebrows. He was losing a battle within himself.

"Let me do this for you both," I said. But I did not say what I should have: that the fault was mine as much as anyone's. My journal had provided the ammunition that broke Salvatore and Rocco apart, that split a family and set a village against them. In the bunker, outnumbered more than two to one, I had told Krause that I did not want to die for nothing. But now, for these two, I would do anything.

Salvatore shrugged me off. "I brought this on our family. I should be the one to finish it."

"Turiddu," Nella said. Her voice almost pleading, but whether for him to go or stay I could not tell. I don't think even she knew.

Salvatore swept Nella's hair away from her forehead and planted a kiss there. "Lock the door behind me and go to bed." Then he walked out into the hall and hurried down the stairs.

"Enzo," Nella said. She grabbed my wrist as I followed her brother out the door, her fingernails digging into my skin. "Don't show that bastard mercy. Do it right this time. And bring my Turiddu back to me."

24

Rocco rented a room on the top floor of an old house on Bridge Street under the Arrigoni Bridge. We followed the train tracks through weeds and rusting freight cars, out by the old cemetery and Hartford Avenue, over where Portland Street turned into Bridge Street, and where concrete columns rose up to meet the steel of the Arrigoni.

The house stood dark except for a lighted window in the corner of the top floor. On the porch, Salvatore raised a fist to pound the front door, but I pulled him back. I rolled up my shirtsleeves, knelt, and inserted a hairpin into the lock. Pushing the pin down, I jiggled it back and forth until the tumbler moved. Then I bent the pin into a tension bar and pulled it to the right. The lock clicked.

"You learn that in the war?" Salvatore asked me.

"After," I said. Then I motioned for him to be quiet, and we slipped inside.

A black phone sat on a table by the wall opposite the staircase. The numbers inside the finger holes had worn off. I took my knife from my back pocket, opened the blade.

Salvatore whispered, "What are you doing?"

I cut the wire to the wall jack. Then we snuck up the three flights of stairs.

The crack under the old wooden door at the end of the hall glowed. We checked the other two rooms: a toilet and a furnished, empty bedroom. Then I pressed my ear to Rocco's door, heard him praying. He was too stupid to think we would come for him here, too stupid or too devoted in the power of his saint's protection.

Salvatore waited a step behind me. There was something in the way he stood-one leg forward, chest out, and fists clenched at his sides-something in the deathlike pallor of his face lit from below. I saw in him the ghost of the boy I knew from Melilli. *Go home,* I wanted to tell him. *Go home to your sister, be like your saint. You don't have to do this. I could give this to you. I owe this to you.* But Salvatore nodded his chin toward the door. There was no going back.

Inside, Rocco bolted upright from kneeling at his bed and smiled—he had wanted us to follow him. Salvatore rushed at him like a bull to a matador. In one graceful move, Rocco stepped aside and knocked the wind out of his opponent with a punch to the abdomen. Salvatore doubled over, hands on his knees.

I picked up a wooden chair by the window and struck Rocco over the back with it. He hit the floor with a thud. Then I shut the door behind us and locked it.

"What did I tell you?" I said. "You remember?"

Rocco pushed himself up with his arms and shook his head like a dog shaking off water.

"You came to my home," Salvatore said. "My sister is hurt because of you." He grabbed him by his armpits and pulled him to his feet. "Face me like a man," he said. "This is what you wanted."

"I didn't hurt her," he said. "You did." His solid left hook sliced open a cut on Salvatore's brow. Then he went for an uppercut, but Salvatore ducked and landed a blow of his own. They danced around the room, trading insults and throwing jabs with counterpunches.

Rocco taunted Salvatore, observing his wide, even stance, how he charged, what side he favored. But Salvatore was no longer the bull in this fight, and Rocco, he was no bullfighter. This time, when Rocco stepped aside, Salvatore stepped with him and barreled him into the wall. The plaster cracked. Rocco covered his face with his arms while Salvatore kneed him in the chest and drove them both crashing to the floor.

Salvatore sat atop Rocco, a leg on either side of him, and pummeled his face.

A man pounded at the door. "What's going on in there?"

Salvatore pressed his hands over Rocco's mouth.

"Mi scusi, Signore," I said through the door. "My friend, he is drunk. I helped him home and tried to put him to bed, but he fell taking off his shoes." Then I slipped several ten-dollar bills under the door. "For your trouble," I said. "Buona notte."

When I heard the man walk away, I turned and saw that Rocco's face was bruised and swollen. His left eye was swollen shut and the other darted around in its purple socket. He squirmed under Salvatore's weight. His arms were splayed out, fingers scratching at the floorboards, feeling under the bed frame. Then his hand came up fast with a knife in his grip.

Salvatore elbowed Rocco's wrist. The blade clattered to the floor. He kicked it away as he stood up. "Sceccu," he said.

I bent the little finger of Rocco's left hand backward until I heard the snap of the joint forced apart.

"Sammastianu," he cried.

"Who do you think sent us?" I whispered into his ear. Then I went further until the bone cracked and Rocco howled in pain.

"Vincenzo, my God, that's enough," Salvatore said.

I cut a strip of cloth from the bedsheet with my knife. "You don't have to stay," I said. "Not for this. There is no shame in you leaving now. We won't speak of it again."

Rocco spat blood on the floor at our feet. "Still a child," he said. "Poor Turiddu plays with matches and gets scared when there is a fire. Go, run and hide behind your sister's skirt. Let a man clean up your mess."

"You see," I said. "He is like an animal. Next time we might not be so lucky. Next time we could lose Nella. I could lose you both."

Salvatore knelt beside me, his mouth set in a grim line. "I'll finish it," he said. He tied a large knot in the middle of the strip, shoved it into Rocco's mouth, and pulled the cloth tight between his teeth and around his head, tying it off in the back. "We are no longer children," Salvatore said. "This is a serious business, what you have done, so now we talk serious." Then he broke the ring finger on Rocco's right hand.

Rocco gnashed his teeth around the knotted gag. He let out a low moan. He looked up at us with his one good eye, wet with pain and anger.

"Don't test me," Salvatore said. "Come near my sister or my home again—" He broke another of Rocco's fingers. "I'll kill you. Understand?"

Rocco nodded yes. But he was like that young German. He would betray us. Already, he fixed his gaze on a meteor shower out the window. It flared over the Connecticut River—a streak of fiery lights—and Rocco, I imagined he took it as a sign from his saint.

"I don't think you do," I said. "Not yet." Then we dragged him by his arms to the window.

He squirmed and thrashed, kicking out his legs.

We backed him up against the sill, and Salvatore trapped him there with the force of his body. "This is your language," I said. "This is how you learn." Then I slammed his fingers in the window.

A spiderweb of capillaries bloodied the yolk of his eye. The eyeball bulged and watered. His head lolled sideways with a bulging blue vein in the middle of his forehead and a line of snot swinging from his nose.

When we released him, he hid his crushed fingers under his armpits and rocked back and forth. I loosened the gag, and through his misshapen mouth Rocco uttered, "Raphael, do you forgive me now?"

"You don't get to ever speak my father's name," Salvatore said.

"I'm sorry," Rocco said. "I'm sorry. Forgive me. Please. I never meant to do it."

The fight had gone out of him. The inflamed feelings—the dead weight that is the settling of old scores—had finally left Rocco.

"You had an accident at the machine shop," I said. "The shop out on Newfield Street. That's where you work, isn't it?" Then I leaned into his ear and whispered, "The lights in the sky, they were your saint, sending me for vengeance."

~

Outside, we lingered in the backfill beneath the bridge. Rocco's sobs thrummed in my ears. Salvatore fell back against the concrete column and slid down its rough and pockmarked surface. He squatted in weeds, his arms flopping limp over the tops of his knees. I knew he didn't mean for this to happen, that he wished he could fix things. If ever a son needed his mother, he needed her then. Casa mia, matri mia. She held the family together. She was its heart. Only she heard the troubles of the mute, as the old saying went.

The sky loomed over the river—the impermanent stars and moon set against all that blackness. In my dreams about the war, I dreamed of a boy huddled in that void, trapped in the moment of his own unmaking.

Bloodshed swelled me up like an intoxicating breath of cleansing sea air. There was no sense in denying nature. My wine was violence. It always had been, long before I trained and marched in formation in quickstep parades of boy Blackshirts. And long after I became Balilla, an obedient boy, a strong young Italian. A Fascist one. A delinquent in a uniform. The vicious dog trained to follow orders was still a vicious dog.

An ambulance wailed in the night. The low, rumbling hum of a car passed overhead. Rocco's window went dark. I toed the dirt with my boot and sent gravel scattering into the black. The dark had settled dense and thick as fog around me. And I could not shut it out.

25

"I heard a siren," Nella said. She sat in the dark by the broken window, looking out into the night.

"It's finished," I said and locked the door behind us. "We took care of it."

"Not like before?" She watched the street below as if expecting Rocco to return.

"No," I said. "Not like before."

Nella turned away from the window. "Turiddu, you're hurt." Her brother winced as she touched the cut on his brow. "Let me clean that."

He pulled his head away. "It's nothing," he said. He took her hands into his hands and said, "We won't speak of this again."

She turned his hands over—the knuckles scraped raw—and hid his bruised fingers in her closed fists. "No," she said. "We won't speak of it." Then she led him to the medicine cabinet in the bathroom and left me standing in the slanting beam of a streetlight through the broken window.

～

Each night, the beam flickered and dimmed in the blue before sunrise. Each day, I worked the Route 9 overpass with Salvatore and Frank. We broke for lunch together and in the evening sat down for dinner at the apartment with Nella. We pretended that night never happened. We had our quiet life. What we had done—the price we had paid for it—it was the only thing that could be done. And for a time, the world agreed with us. But it wore on Salvatore. Mornings before work, he began tending seedlings in long plastic trays set on the kitchen counter by the window. Evenings he transplanted the young plants into larger ceramic planters set in front of the big living room windows. In our apartment, he grew a forest of hot and sweet peppers, and Roma tomatoes. He never stopped long enough to look at his hands. He always stayed busy.

Nella kept the red and raised scars on her arm hidden with long sleeves or a shawl draped over her shoulders, just another secret. That year, she graduated from Saint Sebastian School. She wrote to Don Giovanni in Syracuse to thank him and tell him that she would be attending the public high school in the fall. And in four years, in 1956, at nineteen, she married Frank Lombardo.

After the ceremony, Salvatore and I sat at one of the bingo tables lined up in the church's basement hall. We drank red wine and ate pastel-colored Jordan almonds from little white mesh bags. For that night, the wariness lifted from Nella's face, and she carried herself as if she'd lived her whole life here, in this little American town where bombs and wars were something that happened to other people. She and Frank chatted with their guests, and I could hear Nella's laughter across the room. It was everything Salvatore had wanted for his sister, for himself.

A man with an organetto walked on stage, followed by a mandolin player. They greeted the audience and asked them to leave the tables for the dance floor. Then they played and we clapped out a beat and watched as the older couples locked elbows and danced in circles and the younger men whirled their dates around the floor, and the girls gathered the corners of their dresses and swung them left to right. I wondered about Maria, then, if her wedding had been this full of hope and promise. I hoped it had.

Salvatore and I hung back. The dancers moved and swayed like an ocean tide. Fulvia—a widow in her early thirties—stood from an empty table, dangling her high heels by their straps from one long finger. She danced. And the way her feet touched the floor, the curve of her arches, the hem of her black dress brushing against the chiseled beauty of her ankles, she reminded me of the streets of Rome, how they narrowed and curled around blue-shuttered buildings of the finest stone and around fragments of age-old temples and statues.

I nudged Salvatore's shoulder.

He made that disapproving face of his, the one where it looked like he'd bitten into a bitter orange peel. "Go if you want," he said.

I joined the circle that formed around Nella and Frank, who were dancing, and we held each other's hands above our heads, moving one way and then the other, Fulvia's long braided hair swinging against her back as the tarantella got faster.

The pain in my knee, it burned like a stoked campfire shooting sparks. I hobbled to the nearest table and sat down, masking the ache with more wine.

"You're a good dancer," Fulvia said. "It's a shame about your injury."

"This," I said. I waved my hand as if swatting a fly. "This is nothing. You Italian Americans, you're soft like balls of dough rising on the counter."

"Is that what you think?" she said. "What if I told you that I'm not looking for a husband? What would you think about that?"

"Perfetto," I said. "I am not looking for a wife."

A mop and bucket bumped against the edge of my chair. "Scusi," Rocco said behind me. I stood up and pushed in my chair. Then he saw me and quickly looked at his shoes. His awkward grip on the mop handle slipped and the wood clattered to the floor.

"Vincenzo," Salvatore called out from two table rows over. "You all right?" He approached us.

Rocco fumbled with the handle in his damaged fingers, cursing under his breath. He flinched when Fulvia touched his back.

"You poor man," she said. She knelt down and helped him.

He leaned the handle against his shoulder and mumbled his thanks. Then he kept his head down and pushed the mop and bucket across the room. He hunched over a child's spilled soda while the altar boys cleared the empty plates and dishes from the long tables and refilled the ceramic rooster pitchers with wine.

I gripped Salvatore's arm. "He can't hurt her now," I said. "Look at him, a lame dog on the priest's leash."

Salvatore's jaw muscles clenched and he ground his teeth together. "A lame dog still bites," he said.

Fulvia finished my wine. "I don't want to know," she said before returning to the dance floor.

~

After the wedding, Frank moved into the Ferry Street apartment, where we all lived for a number of years before he and Nella bought the house on Pearl Street. They had postponed their honeymoon to save for the down payment. And then, they just never got around to taking one.

By 1964, I'd opened my café. Soon after, I got in touch with my old employers from Naples. They arranged a little job for me with their friends in the tri-state area. In two weeks, a man started making regular stops at my café late at night. The trunk of his car was full of bootleg cigarettes—American and sometimes even Italian brands if he could get them. I sold the cigarettes out of the storeroom in back, always selling out the Italian packs first. Sometimes I went down south with the man and drove a truckload of cigarettes back to Connecticut. That's when I made real money. Soon I had saved enough to buy the building and move into the apartment upstairs. Finally, I had my little piece of Rome. I had my customers, the rhythms of their lives, old men passing the time, children on their way home from school, and families coming in after church services. Some evenings when Fulvia stopped by, I'd cook us dinner and brew espresso afterward, and we'd laugh about things that were not funny.

26

Salvatore had a difficult time with the Sicilian girls in town. The ones he liked whispered about him behind their hands. The ones he didn't approached him because of the stories the others whispered. The American girls turned up their noses at his calloused hands and broken English. I worried he might end up a priest.

And then he met Eileen.

A July night in 1972, he burst into the café to tell me about her. I had made fresh espresso and wiped down the tables, preparing for the after-dinner rush.

"She's a seamstress," Salvatore told me. He took a seat at the bar, then shot up and leaned against the counter, drumming his fingers on the Formica. He smiled and looked up at me. "She's fair skinned with this red hair, red like red wine grapes," he said. "An American, but she did a good job fixing the hemline on my suit pants."

The next day Salvatore ripped the armpit on one of his good button-down shirts and brought it in to the tailor's where she worked, as an excuse to see her again. It took Salvatore three carefully torn dress shirts to work up the courage to ask her out. She told me later how his thickly accented tongue tripped over some of the English words, and how she blushed and said, *Yes*. She had accepted, she said, because she could tell that Salvatore had ripped his own shirts. And because that made her laugh.

They had their first date at my café on a warm summer evening at one of the tables outside under the stars. I liked them together, instantly. Some people made beautiful couples. And you could see, in their beauty, why they were together. Then there were couples that just made sense. Salvatore and Eileen, they were like that. They made sense.

She was the first to fall asleep that night, according to Salvatore. Curled around him, her fingers grazing the dark arm hair from his shoulders to his wrist. She drifted off with the steady music of his heartbeat in her ear. In the dark, he felt her body close against his, and he closed his eyes and listened for her slow breathing.

In early September of that year, they married in a small ceremony at Saint Sebastian Church and bought the house across the street from Frank and Nella. Eileen was young, not yet twenty-six, and Salvatore was thirty-eight. Six months after that, David came into this world.

I never saw Salvatore happier than the day David was born. Sitting there in the hospital room, perched on the edge of Eileen's bed, holding his son in his arms, I think he believed Eileen had sewn up the mistakes of his life with her needle and thread.

27

For Nella, the days passed away in growing apprehension over the baby's well-being. She pestered Salvatore about his nightmares, wondering if they still troubled him, and when she got nowhere with her brother, she quizzed her sister-in-law. Eileen told her that everyone has nightmares. But Nella was sure Salvatore's nightmares were more than just bad dreams.

So she hung strings of garlic over the crib and pinned the Saint Sebastian medallion her brother had given her to David's undershirt. Eileen thought Nella's concern for David was sweet, the folk traditions of the Sicilian peasants endearing. Though Salvatore complained and sighed, he didn't have the heart to go against his sister. But when she brought a strega to the house, behind his back, he'd had enough of Nella's superstitions.

On a Saturday, Salvatore and I had just returned from West Hartford, where we bought an old-fashioned wine press from a Portuguese man who was clearing out his grandfather's basement. On the ladder-back chair in the living room sat a wizened, shrunken woman, her back bent like a vine pulled down by a ripe tomato. The tray table stood to one side with a bowl of water, a shot glass of olive oil, a saltshaker, and a pair of scissors. Eileen sat on the sofa, holding David cradled in her arms while Nella paced the width of the room.

"Maronna mia," Salvatore said. "What the hell is going on?"

David let out a thin wail. Eileen shushed the boy, bouncing him in her arms. "Whatever happened to the two of you during the war," she said. "Whatever happened to your family, you don't have to tell me. You know that, Sal. But if this puts Nella's mind at ease, where's the harm?"

The strega tossed up her hands. Wiry strands of her hair wormed out from under her black shawl like the snakes of the Medusa. "I must have quiet," she commanded.

Nella eyed her brother. She implored him, her hands together in prayer. It was an old argument, one he had put to rest in Syracuse all those years ago when he made a promise to his sister to do his part as Serafina suggested. To let his brothers go. But he couldn't. I knew he couldn't. What kind of man could let go of his family?

The tension eased from Salvatore's shoulders. "This is it," he said. "After this, no more." His hand cut a straight line through the air.

Nella agreed.

The strega dipped her thumb in the shot glass and held it upside down over the bowl, dripping the olive oil into the water, one drop at a time, while reciting some secret prayer passed down to her from her mother on Christmas Eve in the long tradition of the stregoneria. She leaned over the bowl, studied the dispersal of the droplets, and saw no eye-shape among the oil. "No malocchio," she finally pronounced.

Nella threw her arms around her brother's shoulders.

"Okay," Salvatore said. He embraced his sister. "Okay." They exchanged kisses on the cheek and when they separated, he held her arms and said, "You see? Nothing to worry about. David is fine."

The strega hacked into a skeletal hand. She wiped phlegm from her palm with a tissue. When she caught her breath, she cleared her throat. "There is evil in this world," she said. "It can come from anywhere, anyone." She tugged on her lower eyelid as if to say, *Watch out. Be vigilant.* Then she dipped her thumb in the oil and made the sign of the cross on David's forehead. "You can't be too careful."

28

When David was three months old, we took him to the festival of Saint Sebastian. I stood at the foot of the stone railings of the church with Frank and Nella, Salvatore and Eileen. She cradled David in her arms. We had on our Sunday clothes from the eleven o'clock Mass—pinstriped suits for the men, nice long skirts and blouses for the women. This was our Little Melilli, made by the first Sicilian immigrants to Middletown, the stonemasons and stonecutters and carpenters who worked without charge building this church, building for themselves a new world.

And at the center of that world stood the three days of the Feast of Saint Sebastian, when they spilled out into the streets and called back centuries of history. Three days when no distance existed between the stone and mortar, the brick and steel of Middletown and the limestone village of Melilli cut into the craggy mountainside.

The congregation lined the sidewalks as a sea of barefoot men and women dressed in white with red sashes converged on the church from lower Washington Street and from family plots at Saint Sebastian Cemetery. They chanted, "E chiamamulu paisanu. Prima Diu e Sammastianu." And they shouted out, "Pray for us." They streamed up the stairs and through the open doors of the church, carrying red and white flowers in honor of the soldier-saint.

When the bearers brought the statue—held shoulder high on its pallet—out into the street, the crowd erupted into cheers. Confetti rained down from a bucket lift. Some of the men threw their flowers at the saint's feet. Women kissed their hands and touched the statue. Parents held their infants aloft for the saint's blessing.

"Lift him up," Nella said. "Up," she said again, pushing her own hands palm up toward the sky.

Eileen raised her son to the statue as it passed. He cried, held high over everyone's head. David's fat little legs kicked the air, and his plump little arms flapped like chicken wings. His stubby fingers opened and closed, grasping at the air between him and the statue. Then he wet himself, his cries grew louder, and Salvatore laughed, a big-bellied laugh. He doubled over and held his knees. His eyes watered. That got Eileen giggling and David, with pee running down his leg, wailing.

Frank and I joined in, and Nella crossed her arms over her chest and gave her brother a look, the kind that felt like a biblical stoning. Then a smile cracked her face and she broke down laughing, and her laughter turned to snorting. Soon all the people around looked down their noses at us. But we couldn't help ourselves. David was every bit his father that day. He may not have been born Sicilian, but he was cut from that stone.

Across the street, I unlocked the café door. Eileen brought the baby inside and set him down on a blanket on one of the tables. Nella helped change his diaper, and then she asked if she could hold him. When Eileen nodded yes, Nella wrapped David in his blanket, cradled him in her arms, and walked toward the storefront window. She bent her head close to his, watching the street.

"You should've seen your nonnu during the festival in our village," she said. "If I close my eyes, I can still see him carrying the statue through the streets with the other men. So proud. He carried our saint for all of us. For you. He was a good man, your nonnu, a fine man. In another world you would've shared his name."

29

That spring, the first after Salvatore and Eileen bought the house, he plotted out almost the whole backyard as a garden. Eileen played with David on a blanket on the grass while Salvatore measured and built the garden beds out of lumber and galvanized screws. He spoke to his son about the plants he would seed, the lettuce, basil, bell peppers, and zucchini. He pointed out the poles and the chicken wire, drawing a picture in the air with his hands to show the trellises he would make for the cherry tomatoes, snap peas, and green beans. He poured everything he had into that soil, his hands finally doing the work they were meant to do.

In August, on a hot night, Salvatore and Eileen had everyone over for dinner. They sat the guests—Nella and Frank, me and Fulvia—at the picnic table out back, and they served up salad fresh from the garden, a bowl of roasted peppers with garlic in olive oil, pasta with zucchini and green beans, and the tender meat of grilled rabbit. For the last two days, that rabbit had been at Salvatore's crops. Two days Salvatore tried catching the animal. He bought a trap, laid it out with a mess of carrots, lettuce, and apples. But the rabbit ignored the caged bait for the run of the vegetable garden. That morning, Salvatore had cornered the rabbit by the woodpile and caught it with his bare hands.

Eileen rocked the white wicker cradle next to her chair. David was fast asleep. She had grown up in an orphanage, never known her parents, so we were her family as much as she was ours. We ate until our stomachs ached and drank until we ran out of Chianti. We even finished off the dusty, old squat bottle in the straw basket, the corked wine from Don Salafia. He had given it to Salvatore and Eileen as a present on their wedding day.

After dinner, we sat in the living room. Nella had David in her arms, her hand cupping the back of his head. Fulvia tickled his belly. The baby smiled, his eyes wide. He grabbed hold of her long braided hair. Eileen went into the kitchen to get dessert, Salvatore to get a bottle of grappa and shot glasses. Frank stepped outside for a cigarette.

In the front hall mirror, Salvatore brushed a strand of hair from Eileen's face. She smiled up at him, pecked him on the cheek, and walked out of view. She returned to the living room with a plate of cannoli. Salvatore set the bottle and glasses down on the tray table. He poured my glass, handed it to me, and said, "This fall we make our own wine."

~

At six months old, David started talking in a stream of consonants and vowels strung together with gurgles and sighs. Salvatore couldn't shut up about it. He memorized that boy's babble even though he couldn't understand it himself. And Salvatore grew impatient, wanting to know when he could talk with his son. But Eileen, she acted as if she understood the endless words and funny noises David made. Those two, they spoke their own language from the beginning.

Next summer, on a bright Saturday morning, Eileen set David down on a blanket between two of the raised garden beds. He played with his wooden toy car, spinning the wheels and banging it on the ground, and he talked in a slur of words and shrill sounds. Eileen filled a basket with snap peas and lettuce, responding to her son in a lyrical voice. Their voices like a song of simple words and made-up ones in glissando tones.

Salvatore stood hunched over his garden, pruning basil. "David," he said. "Watch." Then Salvatore showed his son how to pinch back basil above a set of leaves with his fingers. "To make the plant grow bushy," he said.

I sat on the back porch, trying a glass of the first batch of our red wine. It was thin in my mouth. Maybe next year we'd get it right.

David pushed himself up to standing, and toddled toward the peppers. Then he hoisted himself over the garden bed, trampled through the plants, and plopped down in the dirt. The boy took fistfuls of soil and threw them into the air. He put his dirty fingers in his mouth and gibbered. He uprooted a pepper plant.

"No!" Salvatore yelled. He lifted David up out of the garden bed and held him out to Eileen. "You have to watch him," he snapped. "He could get hurt."

David cried, holding out his arms for his mother.

Eileen took him into her arms. "Shh," she said. "It's okay." Then she turned to Salvatore. "There's no need to yell."

Salvatore surveyed the damage to his peppers and shook a limp hand in the air. "I wouldn't sit down for a whole week if that garden belonged to my papà."

"It isn't your father's garden," Eileen said. "What's going on with you?"

"Boh," he said, conceding to her with a wave of his arm.

She set David down on the blanket and combed her fingers through his fine hair. "My little gardener," she said. "You take after your old man, don't you?"

Salvatore grinned. "Old man," he said. He flexed his biceps. "I'm young and strong like the bull. Let me show you." He pinched her ass and she jumped into the air, squealing. Then he chased her around the garden beds until they collapsed into the grass by the blanket, with David climbing on top of them and pulling at his father's hair.

30

When David was four years old, Salvatore came to my café, his face cut into a frown. He told me how he'd spent the day in the garden with his son, teaching him about the soil and the plants. But David, he just wanted to play. When his father wasn't looking, the boy had wandered into the shed and climbed onto the lawn mower, trying to reach the hanging garden tools.

"I turned away for a minute," Salvatore said, "a minute and he was gone."

"But you found him," I said. I put a hand on Salvatore's arm. "He's okay."

I closed the café early and walked Salvatore home. In the kitchen, Eileen had left dishes covered in foil on the table for him, and a heart drawn and shaded in with pencil on a slip of paper torn from a yellow notepad.

"Eileen," he called upstairs, but there was no answer.

We found her and David stretched out on the grass in the backyard, staring up at the autumn stars blooming in the night sky. Eileen must've heard us, but that didn't matter. Nothing could interrupt her time with her son. She kept talking with David, her voice expressive and clear.

Salvatore sat down on the folding chair on the back porch. I went inside for a bottle of our red wine from last year. We'd gotten the blend of red and green grapes just right after a few seasons of trying. The wine had just a hint of the pressed skins, giving it that nice rose petal blush. I added a splash of club soda to my glass and returned to the porch. When I offered Salvatore the wine, he shook his head no.

"Can you find our constellation?" Eileen's words carried across the lawn.

"There," David said. He pointed out the *V* of stars up above. "Like in my room, stickers on my ceiling."

"That's right," she said. She took his hand into her larger one, and she held it up to her cheek.

"Tell me the story again," David said.

And Eileen told him the story of Pisces, of gods and monsters, of how a volcano came into this world.

Salvatore leaned forward, his elbows on his knees and his face rapt as if he, too, were a boy just beginning to come into a world of light and wonder. A world where stars had names and stories, and where boys had the time to learn them all.

31

The bottle of wine sat empty on the table. Several burgundy droplets stained David's note. Outside the café, the morning sun glared off the snow—a pristine, white landscape, save for a few furrows of tire tracks in the road from early risers who left for work before the dawn. Soon, salt and plow trucks would come and make a mess of all that quiet beauty.

Sunday. Harbor Park. Midnight.

David had written these words alone in his bedroom. The letters spelled other words if you knew how to read them, hidden there behind the tight hand: *fear, anxiety, hope, excitement, anger,* and maybe even *love* for the raven-haired girl that had come to my café.

I didn't know what I would say, what I would do when Tony arrived after school today, if the boy even had the courage to come back at all. I wished he'd never told me.

Nella rapped a gloved knuckle on the glass door. She was bundled in a black wool coat, a blue scarf wound around her neck, and a blue knit hat pulled low over her ears. She had a lemon look on her face, like she'd just tasted something sour, and it said, *Have you been here all night?*

As I stood up from the table, I slipped David's note into my pants pocket. I opened the door and she bustled inside, peeling off layers.

"What are you doing here?" I asked her.

"Frank saw the light on and the grille up on his way to work," she said. "He called me from the foreman's office."

"So I had a little trouble sleeping last night," I said and waved her off. Behind the counter, I began grinding coffee beans.

Nella took the empty wine bottle to the sink. "How long has that been going on?"

I packed coffee grounds into the filter and started a pot brewing. "Do you want a cup?" I filled a plate of almond biscotti from the bakery case. She rinsed the empty bottle to return to Salvatore.

In all her life, Nella had never missed a day caring for her brother, not even after David's death. She made all the funeral arrangements, picked the casket and the flowers and the palm cards. She dealt with the church and the cemetery. She kept her brother's house spotless, even David's bedroom, everything the way he left it. She prepared pots of tender lamb stew and loaves of spicy sausage and broccoli scacciata. She stayed with Salvatore in the evenings to make sure that he ate. In the mornings, they sat together on the back porch with coffee and little almond cakes, still warm from her oven.

I dunked a biscotto into my cup of black coffee. She wet a clean rag and began wiping down the tables. "You don't have to do that," I said.

It would ruin Salvatore to know the truth about David. But Nella, that woman had an armor against life.

"Go take a nap," she called from the front of the café. "I can take care of things down here."

"You," I said, "get my café ready?" I smiled to show her that I knew my café was in good hands.

Nella pushed the thick sleeves of her snowflake-patterned sweater up to her elbows. "How hard can it be?" she said. "You do it every day."

"Eh, va bene." I finished the biscotto and took my cup upstairs to my apartment.

～

I slept until noon. When I came downstairs, Nella was tending to the midday rush of customers. I stepped behind the counter. The workspace was immaculate, everything in its place. There were no dishes in the sink, the refrigerated case was stocked with glass bottles of soda and Orangina and sparkling water, and the bakery case was filled with neat rows of that morning's delivery of fresh pastries and cookies.

Nella tapped the counter and held up her index finger. "I need one cappuccino and one cannolu, chocolate dipped."

"Coming right up," I said. Then I filled the grinder with espresso beans and got to work.

～

By midafternoon the café had emptied save for a few regulars—old men from the neighborhood playing cards and smoking unfiltered cigarettes. At the bar, Nella and I shared a plate of soppressata and pecorino, roasted red peppers and green olives.

"I should hire you," I said. "You looking for work?"

Nella laughed. "You've made it on your own this long."

"Beh, sometimes I had help," I said.

Nella's face deflated, her smile pressed into a thin, flat line, and she nodded her head in agreement. I took the last green olive and chewed the meat free from the pit. Nella propped her chin in the heel of her hand, elbow on the counter. She studied the framed map of Sicily. "Did we make a mistake," she asked, "not telling him?"

"A mistake? No," I said. I stood up and pushed my stool back under the lip of the bar. "No," I repeated. My bad leg was stiff, the knee sore. "Freezing rain tonight," I said. I limped behind the counter and filled a small brown paper bag with pastries and cookies.

"Sometimes, I thought about taking him there," she said. She stood and pulled on her jacket and buttoned it up. "His father would never go back, but a part of me wanted him to know where he came from."

I fingered the torn edge of the note, still crumpled in my pants pocket. "He came from America," I said. I handed Nella the paper bag of sweets. "Besides, there's no going back, not for us. We are like your brother's tomatoes, transplanted from one home to the next. This is where we live now. What we did, we did for him and for David. We did what was best for them," I said. "Don't ever think different."

She held her gray-streaked hair up while she wound her scarf around her neck. Then she opened the bag, held it up to her nose, and closed her eyes, inhaling the smell of sugar.

∽

Late in the evening, I sat by the window with a cup of coffee and a plate of tricolor cookies. The last customers had left hours ago. The streets were a mess of dirty slush under the dark, starless sky. Closing time had come and gone with no sign of Tony. I wouldn't blame the boy for not coming. He was a Morello, after all. I popped a cookie in my mouth as a mix of sleet and freezing rain crackled outside. Then I sipped my coffee. When I looked up again, Tony's red jacket cut the darkness.

I let him in and then relocked the door behind him.

"Shouldn't we go upstairs?" he said. He paced the length of the café, eyeing the large storefront windows.

"Take it easy," I said. "Your father's not out in this mess. Where does he think you are, anyway?"

"Does it matter?"

"Sit down before you make me nervous," I said.

Tony grabbed a handful of napkins from the counter and dried his face. He pushed his dark flat curls out of his eyes and slouched into the booth. "I should tell someone, shouldn't I?"

I slid the plate of cookies in front of him. "You told me," I said. "But maybe I should, I don't know, tell the priest."

"The priest, he will have to go to the police."

"Shit," Tony said. "I'm in trouble, aren't I?" He scratched the back of his left wrist, already covered in raised red lines, a phantom itch from a cast that was long gone.

I grabbed his right wrist to stop him before he broke the skin. "No one's telling the police," I said. "No one's telling anyone. You hear me? You've hurt this family enough. If people knew you were there that night, think what it would do to David's father. Is that the kind of man you want to be, the kind that kicks another man while he's down?"

Tony's head drooped and he sank deeper into the seat back. His mouth fell open. His lower lip quivered. He sniffed back snotty tears. "No," he said.

I patted the back of his hand. Rocco's boy needed me to comfort him now, to tell him that everything was going to be all right. And I needed him to keep his Morello mouth shut.

"Good," I said. "Eat."

Tony took a cookie from the plate and nibbled at it like a mouse.

"You need to trust me," I said. "Everything will be all right as long as you do what I say."

32

That spring, Salvatore gave in to his sister and began attending Mass on Sundays. He went with Nella and Frank, and afterward they would all come to the café for coffee and pastries. Salvatore never stayed long, his garden always called him home. In the winter months, when he didn't have a garden, he took long walks by himself from the café down to Harbor Park. He sat under the pavilion until the moon's silver face shone in the river, and then he'd return to the café just before closing time, and we'd share a glass of wine in silence.

Once every few weeks, Tony came to my café, too. He came late in the evenings after all the customers had gone. He sat in the spot where David should have sat. He asked me the questions David should have asked me. They were questions I never thought I'd hear a boy like Tony ask—questions about first crushes and first heartaches, the things he could never tell his father. If there was a hell, I imagined this would be mine, sitting there with Tony, explaining life to the wrong boy.

Tony grew into the broad-shouldered giant one would expect of a Morello. His voice deepened until he shared the same gruff timbre as his father. But the way Tony spoke, the curve of his shoulders, the way he walked in the world—it all showed how he carried that night with him. Sometimes he tried to bring up David. He did it shamefaced and full of the need for me to tell him that it was okay, that what he put David through was just what boys do, that he wasn't to blame. I wouldn't give him that, because I couldn't give it to myself. No, he wasn't responsible for the choice David made to go to Harbor Park that night. But David would've never been there if Tony hadn't driven him to it. In this way, Tony and I were alike. He was forever bound up with David's life as I was with Salvatore's. Only Tony would never get a chance to set things right, and that would eat him up, if he let it. I didn't have to like Tony, but I wouldn't let a man's curse condemn another boy.

He kept coming to the café, kept sitting in David's booth, kept trying to make sense of what he'd done. And I let him.

∾

I thought I was being careful, that Salvatore and Nella would never know about Tony's visits. But one evening, Nella came by at closing with a look on her face that spelled trouble for me. Without a word she poured herself a glass of her brother's wine and, standing behind the counter, stared at David's corner booth.

"I saw you last night through the window," she said. "You and Tony."

"He's been coming around," I said. "I didn't know how to tell you." I braced for her anger. She would hate me for letting that boy sit in David's place, the way I hated myself.

"The way you were with him—so cruel." She shook her head, mouth filled to the brim with distaste and scorn. She set the wine on the counter untouched. "He's just a boy, Vincenzo, a boy with the wrong last name. That cannot be his fault. Whatever happened between us and Rocco, Tony isn't to blame. David is gone. Salvatore is broken. Tony is the only boy left to protect."

"I protect David's memory," I said. My fist came down on the counter, like a weight dropping. "What that boy did to David, the notes and the humiliation, it wasn't right. What his father did to you and Salvatore—"

"Is in the past, Vincenzo," Nella cut me off. She covered my fist with her hands. "Tony was terrible to David, yes, and to lots of other boys. But he's stopped all that. I hear he even stopped making trouble at school. If he comes to you again, I beg you, forgive him." She pressed her palms together in front of her chest, a prayer for me. "Show him some compassion. God knows he sees none at home. We know better than most the price a boy pays when he is made to account for his father's sins."

~

I could not do what Nella asked of me. I could not forgive Tony. The best I could be for him was his own Balilla. I would not teach him to fight. But I could show him what it meant to have respect and loyalty, a sense of purpose—all the things his own father lacked.

The next time Tony came to the café, I handed him a mop and told him he had a job. He could start by cleaning the floors.

"You going to pay me?" Tony asked. The mop was a foreign object in his hands. It was clear to me then that he had never done an honest day's work in his life. Salvatore had always taught David about work, taking care of the house and the garden, helping me in the café. Salvatore had done right by his son.

"This is your first lesson," I said. "Never do a job for free. Of course I'll pay you. Now get to work and don't get smart with me."

I sat at the bar, drink in hand, stool turned to watch him. I told him what I expected. He would arrive on time. He would do as he was told, and he would do it well. He hadn't even cleaned half the floor before the complaints started. His back hurt, his feet hurt, when could he sit down and take a break.

"Why do I have to work while you're sitting there having a drink?" he whined.

"No job is too small to take pride in," I said. "It does not matter if you are the janitor or the big boss on top. How well you do your job is a reflection of the kind of man you are."

He was fifteen then. On weeknights he came well after closing. He organized the stockroom, washed the dishes, cleaned the floors and tables and countertop. Soon the complaints went away. He found himself in the work, in being able to set something right, even something as simple as a dirty floor. I didn't know what he told his father about where he was, and I didn't care to know. I could not give Tony love, but I could defuse the bomb his father was trying to make him become.

The summer before his senior year, after he'd finished cleaning one night, Tony set a worn hardback book on the table in David's booth. *The Martian Chronicles*. "I found it in the library," he said. "I read the whole thing. Three times. I still don't get what he saw in it. But I know he saw something."

I opened the book, took the check-out card from the sleeve in the back cover, and there was David's name. He'd renewed it twice. "I would've bought it for him, if I'd known how much he liked it. How did you find this?"

"He tried to read it on the bus. But I never let him. Why didn't I let him? I thought, maybe, if I read it—" Tony turned the book over and stared at the cover, a desolate red landscape. He flipped through the pages. He was looking for something. He was looking for David—not the bullied boy, but the person Tony never saw.

I knew that regret. It never left you. We were all children of our fathers' curses.

33

Two months before what should've been David's high school gradua-
tion, Tony walked into the café on a Sunday evening. There was only
one customer left, a long-haired boy from Wesleyan University nursing
an American coffee, thin nose stuck in a paperback. I'd set two glasses
on the counter and a bottle of wine, expecting Salvatore to return from
his afternoon in the garden any minute, when Tony sidled up to the bar.

He stood a couple of inches taller than me now and had lopped
off his black curls for a short military haircut. "I screwed up," he said.
He scratched behind his ears like that rabbit had, just before Salvatore
caught it all those years ago in his backyard.

I came around the counter and led him by the elbow into the
stockroom. "I'd say you did," I said. "What the hell are you doing here?"

"I didn't know where else to go." Under the bare bulb of the stockroom, Tony appeared jaundiced.

"What's so important that it couldn't wait until tomorrow night?"

Tony leaned against a metal shelf of canned coffee and folded his
arms across his chest. "My girlfriend's pregnant," he said. "She wants
to keep it."

I wiped my hand over my face. "On a Sunday," I said. "This is why
you come to me? Christ. Go tell your father."

"No way, he'll kill me. That's why I came to you."

"I'm not your friend, Tony. I'm not your father. That's not what this is." The words were as hard as any slap. And as soon as they were out, I wanted to stuff them back in my mouth. *Show him some compassion.* That's what Nella had asked of me.

The boy's jaw clenched and his back stiffened and he spoke through clenched teeth. "Fine," he said. He opened the door, but I grabbed his bicep and held him back.

"Do you love her?" I asked him. I let his arm go, patted him on the shoulder. I didn't know what he was to me, but I didn't hate him. Not anymore. He was more than his father's son, at least he was trying to be.

"I guess."

"If you love her," I said, "don't run away."

~

That night I told Salvatore about Maria. I told him he was lucky to have had Eileen for as long as he did, and David, too.

34

Long ago—so long now that no one alive remembered—men ran naked through the streets of Melilli with only a cloth to hide their modesty. In this way, they commemorated Saint Sebastian, who was clothed only in his faith the day he died. Sicilians called these men the Nuri. They ran from every village and city in the province to join the men of Melilli in the festa dei Nuri—the festival of the naked.

But those old times, they were gone. Now the Nuri covered their bodies with white clothes and dressed their heads with white scarves. They wore red sashes from their shoulders to their hips and tied them around their waists to mark the places where Roman arrows had pierced their saint.

David should've been there when his father finally carried the statue. David should've known. He should've known how his father was a Nuri in the Saint Sebastian festival before the end. How Salvatore had swayed in the wind of that crowd. They lifted him up, just like the breeze lifted tree limbs, made the trees taller.

NELLA

EPILOGUE

May 2000, the last day of the festival of Saint Sebastian dawned, and the sunrise did little to warm the chill settling into Nella's bones. A boy of about nine years old climbed over the sagging wire fence in her brother's backyard. She watched him from the end of the driveway—his dark, wild hair, his thin shoulders under a too-big T-shirt—setting down in the fallow garden.

Nella called out to him.

"Shit," the boy said. For a second he looked at her, and she recognized the straight line of his nose, the thick, curly hair—Tony Morello's son.

"Wait," she said. But the boy was already scrambling back over the fence. His shirt caught on a broken loop of rusty wire and tore as he lost his footing and fell into the opposite yard. He picked himself up, dusted off his blue jeans, and then darted away. The downy parachutes of dandelion seeds swirled in his wake.

Salvatore's house had stood locked up and empty now for a number of years she dared not count or remember. People in Middletown, they talked of hearing strange noises coming from the property—the howls of a child sobbing long into the night, the back screen door clanking shut, creaking footsteps.

Nella never heard or saw anything out of the ordinary. She wanted to believe that Tony's son was just here for the ghost stories, to see the truth for himself. But there were other stories that might have drawn him here. Other truths.

She found the front door open and called out for Vincenzo. The house answered her with a creaking floor joint. She walked down the hall, trailing her fingers against the wall, tracing a crack in the plaster. So many times she had come here to see Salvatore and David. They were both boys still in her mind, boys she had fed and cared for the way Salvatore watered and cared for his garden. Or at least she had tried. And now—now all she had left of them was their silence.

Taped cardboard covered a square of windowpane in the back door. A plate of new glass cut to size leaned against the wall where Frank had left it for Vincenzo. The toolbox sat open on the kitchen counter.

She took a pair of work gloves from a drawer and stripped away the masking tape. Then she removed the cardboard and cleared glass fragments from the sash bar. By the time Vincenzo arrived, clomping unevenly down the hall, she was fitting the new pane into the frame.

"Let me do that," he said by way of greeting.

Nella waved him off. "Sit," she said without turning around.

Vincenzo pulled up a folding metal chair. Nella held the glass in place with one hand, while pressing glazier's points into the frame. She asked for the thin wooden stops and held out her hand. He passed them to her one at a time. She tapped the stops into place with nails as delicate as needles.

When Nella was done, she stood and surveyed her work. The new pane was cleaner than the others. Through it she saw the garden where Tony's son had stood, a blade of young grass among her brother's weeds.

"Go on then," she said. "Tell me what you think."

Vincenzo shook his head. "Not sure what you keep me around for," he said. He knelt before the door, pressed his palm against the glass in the glare of the sun. The sparse strands of his white hair swept back off his high forehead. Time had creased his face like a crumpled paper bag. Still she saw in him the shape of that young soldier who came for her and Salvatore in Syracuse. The one her brother was sure the saint had sent to guide their path to a new life.

But she was old now, too. Sometimes, she forgot that. Sometimes, she looked at herself in the mirror and wondered what strange old woman this was, staring back at her.

"Tony's boy was here again," she said.

Vincenzo's shoulders stiffened. "He knows he shouldn't be here. His father and I agreed. This place, it isn't good for him. I'll talk to Tony."

"He's just a boy," Nella said. The words felt familiar on her tongue. She'd said them to Vincenzo so many years before about Tony. "Let me handle it."

"He's curious, the way David was curious." There was a tremor in Vincenzo's voice, the slightest crack. But he swallowed back the moment, took control of himself again. He dusted off her work with a rag. "Maybe next time it's not just a window that breaks. Maybe he gets hurt. Maybe he hurts someone by mistake."

Sunlight filtered through the pane. She saw their reflections in the window, and in the window the faint morning star—always brightest in the twilight hours before dawn—the star that never set.

"I miss them," Nella said.

Vincenzo nodded his chin at her.

∼

Nella went home, leaving Vincenzo at her brother's house to clean up after her. She dressed for church—a peach sweater set and matching paisley skirt down to her ankles with a brown knitted lace shawl—and walked to the rectory. She carried a pan of ricotta cake for the church auction. Every year she baked a cake or a tray of cookies to help raise money for the church, and no one but Vincenzo ever bid, no one wanting to risk the taste of her family's curse. He sat in the front row, away from the tables under the tent. His liver-spotted hand, the only hand that ever shot up at the cry of the auctioneer. Twenty dollars, no more. Every year. Still, she made something special for the feast. She helped Saint Sebastian Church in some small way, and that was all that mattered.

She left the cake with Don Salafia. He took the pan and thanked her and closed the door. He was in a hurry to prepare for the eleven o'clock Mass. She stood for a time on the veranda, looking at the empty rides, the deserted game booths and food tents, and she thought of Tony's boy. She wondered if after she was gone—the last of the Vassallos—if the rancor would end, the curse lifted, or if they would all continue paying for broken stone, even in death.

After the Mass held in honor of Saint Sebastian, Nella stood at the top of the church steps and watched the faithful pour down the street—a deluge of some three hundred men, women, and children. She caught a glimpse of her husband among them, pumping the air with his fists full of flowers. For a moment, she thought she saw Salvatore beside him, the hair gray and receding from his widow's peak, the nose large and aquiline, and the tight, fierce line of his jaw. It was the profile of a hardheaded man, a man who treasured away in his heart the hardened lessons of his youth. The kind of man who held his fist on high, a violent gesture but for the bouquet choking in his grip.

The runners flooded the front of the church, chanting and crying for their saint. When the bearers carried the statue out, the Nuri cheered and followed the procession around the block. The church bells pealed. The parking lot came alive as the festival began. Music blared from carnival rides and game booths. The air smelled of smoky grilled sausages and fried sugared dough.

She let the crowds carry her. They moved down the stairs, past the Tilt-A-Whirl and bumper cars, the Ferris wheel and carousel. Squeals of delight from children drowned out the music from the calliope as it played. She'd ridden the carousel once with David—after he'd eaten cotton candy and candied apples—and he'd thrown up on her shoes. She'd sat on the curb with him, rubbed his back while he drank club soda to calm his stomach. And then he'd begged her to let him ride one more time.

A lump caught in her throat like she'd swallowed a stone. She turned away. Heavy clouds moved in from the north, but they held their rain. She shook off the multitude and walked alone. She left the festival by the side of the main stage, coming out along the block of Pearl Street closed to traffic. It was not yet time for the auction.

At the corner stood an elm on the rectory lawn, where she stopped and listened to the old men gathered on the veranda telling stories to their grandchildren. She recognized them—all the faces of the families from Melilli she had known. Cardella. Santangelo. Morello. The other bearers of the statue. Even after all these years, just the sight of Rocco Morello made the scars on her arm ache. His grandson—Tony's boy— sat at his feet, picking white paint chips from the floorboard with his thumbnail.

The men talked over one another in loud, graveled voices. They didn't see her behind the tree, listening.

"The Magnano boy was the first from Melilli to settle in Middletown," Constantino Cardella said. "He ran off with pirates—"

"No, he stowed away on a freighter," Rocco said. "Everyone knows that." He lit a cigarette and extinguished the match with a wave of his crooked-fingered hand. "A fireman's family took the boy in," he said. "They raised him up and he became a fireman. But when he started to think of the pain he had caused his parents by running away, after all they'd done for him, a roof over his head and food on the table, he felt ashamed. He went to the priest, confessed his sins, and asked for God's mercy and forgiveness, and you know what the priest said? The priest said, 'Write your parents, tell them what you told me, and then save your wages and bring them here.' So Magnano worked hard and saved.

He brought his parents over. They came and brought their cousins over, and that's how all of us got here."

"Tell us about the statue," Tony's boy said.

"Yeah," the pear-shaped Santangelo boy agreed. He wiped his pizza mouth with his T-shirt. "Tell us that one."

And so Rocco told the children the story of how the statue came to Melilli and how, at the end of the Second World War, bandits broke into the church and blew the statue to pieces with dynamite. Behind the tree, Nella twisted the picot edge of her shawl. She felt a long-cooled fire rising in her throat.

"Were you there? Did you see it?" Tony's boy asked. He rocked back on his knees, looking up at his grandfather.

Rocco nodded his head yes. "I saw it," he said. He took a drag from his cigarette and exhaled a ribbon of curling smoke at the porch ceiling. "I saw the criminals, too, running away into the mountains." He watched the smoke through squinted eyes. "I will never forget the dirty faces of those two men."

"Why'd they do it?" Tony's boy asked.

"Boh," Rocco said. "Why? Who knows why?"

Nella moved without thinking. She stepped into the open, pressing her back into the bark of the elm. "You know that's not true," she said.

Everyone turned to stare at her. The old men, their fat faces quivering into frowns, made the mano di cornuto—the horned hand gesture of protection against the malocchio. The children, their mouths hanging open, sat gorgonized by her presence among them.

She pushed the shawl and sleeve of her sweater down. The flesh of her upper arm wobbled, the skin knotted and gnarled with red scar tissue. She fixed her gaze on Rocco.

He stubbed out his cigarette in the yellow glass of the standing ashtray. The smoky veil curled around his bent fingers. He cleared phlegm from his throat and hid his disfigured hands in the pockets of his suit jacket.

"That's enough," Don Salafia said. He stood behind the screen door in his black priest's frock and asked Rocco to fetch more folding chairs from the basement. Then he shooed the old men away, saying, "You gossip like women in your old age." And they rose from their seats like a flush of birds from shrubbery, collected their grandchildren, and shuffled into the festival crowd, chastened by age and the weight of secrets.

Tony's boy—wide-eyed and curious—approached Nella. He looked at the old burn marks on her arm. "Does it hurt?" he asked.

"Sometimes," Nella said. Then she knelt in the grass so she was his size, looking up at him slightly. His hard face made her think of Sicily. All the boys in Melilli had such grim faces when she was a little girl. But this boy, he had been born here, like his father. He should look more American, she thought. He should grow tall and handsome. He should go to college, find a good-paying job and a nice girl to marry. He should settle down, make a good life. "Why do you keep coming to my brother's house?" she asked him. "What do you want?"

"Will you tell me the real story?"

"And if I told you," she said, "no more sneaking around the house, breaking windows?"

"That was an accident," he said. "Please don't tell my dad."

She pushed herself up to standing and covered her arm with her sweater and shawl. "If I tell you all my secrets," she said, "you have to tell someone yours. It should be your papà, no?" Then she held out her hand for him, and he took it. His hand, warm and small in hers, reminded her of David's. David had asked her for the same thing—the real story—and she had given him only a dusty shoebox of secrets. But maybe it was time, and maybe there was finally a chance, for a new Melilli here.

Together, Nella and Tony's boy walked to Vincenzo's café and sat down at one of the umbrellaed tables. Vincenzo had the new overhead doors open, and Nella saw him through the sheer curtain pulled over the length of the opening. He was busy, tending to a rush of customers. She patted the boy's arm. Aspetta. Then she slipped inside, steamed milk for hot cocoa, and returned with two steaming cups and a plate of almond cookies. She took a seat. Clouds hung low in sun-hazed furrows. The curtain billowed in a damp breeze. The boy hunched at the table with his chin on his hands and watched Nella. She held the cup. It warmed her. "I had three brothers," she began.

AUTHOR'S NOTE

This novel is a work of fiction inspired by the stories my father told me as a child—unrelated until this book wove an imagined version of them together. Where I altered facts and geography to suit the needs of the fiction, I did so with the utmost respect and admiration for the people of Melilli and their experiences.

During the Allied invasion of Sicily in the Second World War, my father hid with his siblings and parents and neighbors in the many caves on the outskirts of their village. Surviving that difficult time is one of the many miracles they ascribe to their patron saint, Sebastian. My father often spoke of how the statue of Saint Sebastian came to Melilli, how it was borne—and has always been borne—by all the people of the village. The four families who live at the heart of that myth in this novel do not exist in the real myth of the statue. Similarly, the identity of the conspirator who broke into the church after the war and destroyed the statue remains unknown except in my version of events. Finally, among the many stories my father told me, the one of his cousins who perished while playing with an unexploded shell has never left me. Their story is sacrosanct and is not portrayed in this work.

ACKNOWLEDGMENTS

For her unwavering faith, love, and support, I am indebted to Camellia Phillips, who read every draft of this novel and never stopped believing in it or me. She showed me the way out of labyrinths of my own making. Without her wisdom and insight, I would be forever lost, this book unfinished.

For the exceptional teachers and mentors in my life who helped me find my way through the earliest versions of this novel, I am forever thankful to Alexander Chee, Frederic Tuten, Stephen Wright, David Gates, Dani Shapiro, Helen Schulman, Dale Peck, Laura Ress, and Susan Letzler Cole.

For their astute readings and insights, I thank Randall Lotowycz, Kathy Pories, Porochista Khakpour, Reinhardt Suarez, Darla Bruno, John Reed, Nancy Hightower, Leah Umansky, Scott Larner, Lee Matthew Goldberg, Dani Grammerstorf French, Elizabeth Castoria, Nicole Audrey Spector, Yew Leong Lee, Jason Napoli Brooks, Jim Freed, Scott Geiger, Gary Ford, Greg Sanders, Nick Burd, Christine Condon, Meredith Franco Meyers, Connor Coyne, Amanda Miller, Angela Starita, Stéphanie Abou, Laura Tisdel, Andrea Boudin, Josephine Ishmon, Elizabeth Wine, and John Bennett.

I am humbled and grateful for the friendship and support I've received over the years from Victoria Redel, Brando Skyhorse, Luis Jaramillo, Sam J. Miller, Christopher Phillips, Daydre Phillips,

Stephen Tolkin, Dan Videtto, Jeff Romano, Shay Hamilton, Michael Arafeh, Eric Sanders, Frank Giordano, Francis Shanoff, Brian Targonsky, James Schafer, Michael Patnaude, Nick Villarama, Graham Thompson, Edward Pichulo, David Marshall, Matthew Martin, Jennifer Martin, Jennifer Tobits, Anthony LaPila, Todd Pierce, Clint Paseos, Chris Flood, David Flood, Emily Marye, Giuseppe Salvitti, Ellen Sleight, Ronna Wineburg, Danielle Ofri, Joel Allegretti, Julia Phillips, Melissa Rivero, Sara Faring, Gina Marie Guadagnino, and the many wonderful authors who have read at the Guerrilla Lit Reading Series and shared their words and wisdom.

Thank you to Hafizah Geter, my brilliant editor, and everyone at Little A, and to Mark Gottlieb, my agent, of Trident Media Group.

Thank you to my parents, my brother and sister, my grandparents, and to my many aunts, uncles, and cousins.

Special thanks to George Trakas for the use of his home in Amherst, where I wrote parts of this novel, and for the tremendous dinners—clams and oysters—he prepared there and here in New York City. Also to Jason Everman and David Parke, for their military expertise and friendship.

I am also grateful to Brian Fender and Barbara Temos—your words of encouragement in support of me and this novel during graduate school and beyond kept me going. I miss you both very much.

And for their fellowship, I thank Jameson Proctor, Michael Heilemann, Susie Lim, David Natter, Nada O'Neal, Andy Farrell, James Skinner, Kimber VanRy, Michael Davey, and Michael Demko.

Finally, my eternal gratitude to Professor Gaetano Cipolla for his generous assistance and for all he does to promote and preserve Sicilian language and culture. Thanks also to the Scuola Italiana del Greenwich Village, and to the faculty and students of The New School's MFA program.

ABOUT THE AUTHOR

Marco Rafalà is a first-generation Sicilian American, novelist, musician, and writer for award-winning tabletop role-playing games. He earned his MFA in fiction from The New School and is a cocurator of the Guerrilla Lit Reading Series in New York City. Born in Middletown, Connecticut, he now lives in Brooklyn, New York. *How Fires End* is his debut novel. For more information, visit www.marcorafala.com.